## Praise for the Novels of Gail Fraser

### *Lumby on the Air*

"You'll find yourself and a sizable portion of your own whacky relatives attending this hysterical family reunion filled with food, fun, and familiar truths. Pull up a chair, turn up the volume on your radio, hike to the monastery, or haul yourself over to the county fair. Every which way you turn, you'll find a Lumby laugh and a sideways quirky glance at you and yours."

—Charlene Ann Baumbich, author of the Dearest Dorothy series, *Stray Affections* and *Divine Appointments*

"Carries the reader through a rich venue of interwoven story lines and memorable characters set against the backdrop of small-town life. . . . Grab a hot cup of cocoa, snuggle under a favorite quilt, and enjoy!"

—Katherine Valentine, award-winning author of the Dorsetville series and *The Haunted Rectory*

"Gail Fraser has created an enchanting landscape that I know readers will want to visit again and again. If we all could live in Lumby, the world would be a much happier place. I was utterly charmed."

—Donna Ball, author of *At Home on Ladybug Farm*

"What a wonderful pick-me-up to read about, what a wonderful place to live. There are so many joys, so many pains, so many helpful friends, new and old, to help along the way."

—Sister Cecelia, Prioress of New Skete Monastery

"What an agreeable world she's created!"

—Philip Gulley, author of the Harmony series

"Gail Fraser's Mitford-esque settings and engaging characters will charm readers of all ages. *Lumby on the Air* continues the fun as family reunions and eccentric relatives make life interesting for Mark and Pam. Pack this thoroughly enjoyable novel in your beach bag this summer—you won't want to miss this amusing adventure!"

—Christian Book Previews

"A trip to any part of Gail Fraser's cozy but edgy little universe is, simply put, 'Lumby-licious!' These characters walk right off the page and find a warm place in your heart."

—Robert Dalby, author of the Piggly Wiggly series

*continued . . .*

## *The Promise of Lumby*

"Readers who have traveled to Mitford with Jan Karon will find the trip to Lumby at least as pleasant and marked with a lot more laughter. If the world of cozy fiction has a capital, it's Lumby. Although I hesitate using the overused word 'charming,' it most definitely applies to *The Promise of Lumby* and its three predecessors. Gail Fraser tells wonderful stories that have kindness at their core—and are a gentle reminder of the goodness in people's hearts." —Cozy Library

## *Lumby's Bounty*

"A visit to the charming, whimsical town of Lumby is a refreshing change from our fast-paced lives. Challenged to host a hot-air balloon festival, its residents rise to the occasion: Lives change; love blossoms; a wild and irrepressible young man matures. A delightful read." —Joan Medlicott, author of the Ladies of Covington series

"Drop in on the sweetest small town since Mayberry, where the worst people are still nicer than the best people you know, and life's problems are solved by a backhoe, an industrial sewing machine, or monks wearing light-up tennis shoes. Your own troubles will melt away." —Bob Tarte, author of *Fowl Weather* and *Enslaved by Ducks*

## *Stealing Lumby*

"In the tradition of Jan Karon's Mitford series, this engaging inside look at small-town life will draw a bevy of fans to its old-fashioned story combining a bit of romance, a bit of mystery, and a multitude of quirky and endearing characters." —*Booklist*

"There's a . . . quality to the writing that lends an unrushed, meandering feel to the narrative as evildoers are dispatched and equilibrium is restored. Fraser's story is . . . as small-town cozy as they come." —*Publishers Weekly*

"*Stealing Lumby* is a classic cozy read, with good-hearted characters that face life's problems head-on. Readers can be certain that, despite heartache and loss, good will prevail, and evildoers will get what they deserve." —Cozy Library

"*Stealing Lumby,* second in the Lumby series, is as delightful as the first . . . . Where else will you find a moose wandering around a village with a folding deck chair enmeshed in his rack? . . . It's fun to become a part of the village and listen in to their solutions—some of which make one laugh out loud, while others are wise and knowing, and some are just plain crazy."
—BookLoons

***The Lumby Lines***

"*The Lumby Lines* goes straight to the heart. The simplicity, humor, and downright friendliness of the book make reading it a pleasure. . . . Readers will close this book with a sigh of contentment and a desire to visit Lumby again. The author has faithfully carved out a slice of small-town living and topped it off with a large helping of humor. This reviewer can't wait for her next visit to Lumby!"
—Christian Book Previews

"At a time when we seem to be taking ourselves all too seriously, Gail Fraser pulls a rabbit out of the hat that charms while it helps us relax. *The Lumby Lines* strikes just the right balance of playfulness, satire, and drama. A thoroughly enjoyable read!"
—Brother Christopher, the Monks of New Skete

"Unique. . . . You will be amazed by the great imagination of the author. . . . The reader is in for a treat. This book is a delight to read and one that you will thoroughly enjoy." —Bestsellersworld.com

"Gail Fraser has assembled a wonderful cast of characters and plunked them down in the middle of a beautiful town that rivals Jan Karon's Mitford for pure fun. Of course, there are obstacles to overcome, mysteries to solve, even some romance and reconciliation along the way to a very satisfying conclusion. Altogether a wonderful story, highly recommended."
—Cozy Library

"A setting reminiscent of Jan Karon's fictional village. . . . *The Lumby Lines* is a feel-good novel with lots of heart and angst. I was sorry to leave my new friends but have brightened since I learned that a sequel, *Stealing Lumby,* is coming soon."
—BookLoons

Books in the Lumby Series
by Gail Fraser

*The Lumby Lines*
*Stealing Lumby*
*Lumby's Bounty*
*The Promise of Lumby*

# LUMBY ON THE AIR

GAIL FRASER

NEW AMERICAN LIBRARY

New American Library
Published by New American Library, a division of
Penguin Group (USA) Inc., 375 Hudson Street,
New York, New York 10014, USA
Penguin Group (Canada), 90 Eglinton Avenue East, Suite 700, Toronto,
Ontario M4P 2Y3, Canada (a division of Pearson Penguin Canada Inc.)
Penguin Books Ltd., 80 Strand, London WC2R 0RL, England
Penguin Ireland, 25 St. Stephen's Green, Dublin 2,
Ireland (a division of Penguin Books Ltd.)
Penguin Group (Australia), 250 Camberwell Road, Camberwell, Victoria 3124,
Australia (a division of Pearson Australia Group Pty. Ltd.)
Penguin Books India Pvt. Ltd., 11 Community Centre, Panchsheel Park,
New Delhi - 110 017, India
Penguin Group (NZ), 67 Apollo Drive, Rosedale, North Shore 0632,
New Zealand (a division of Pearson New Zealand Ltd.)
Penguin Books (South Africa) (Pty.) Ltd., 24 Sturdee Avenue,
Rosebank, Johannesburg 2196, South Africa

Penguin Books Ltd., Registered Offices:
80 Strand, London WC2R 0RL, England

First published by New American Library,
a division of Penguin Group (USA) Inc.

First Printing, July 2010
10 9 8 7 6 5 4 3 2 1

LIBRARY OF CONGRESS CATALOGING-IN-PUBLICATION DATA:
Fraser, Gail.
Lumby on the air/Gail Fraser.
p. cm.
ISBN 978-0-451-23004-1
1. City and town life—Fiction.2. Villages—Fiction. 3. Eccentrics and eccentricities—Fiction. 4. Hotelkeepers—Fiction. 5. Radio talk shows—Fiction. 6. Real estate development—Fiction. 7. Northwest, Pacific—Fiction. 8. Domestic fiction. I. Title.
PS3606.R4229L863 2010
813'.6—dc22 2010009807

Printed in the United States of America



PUBLISHER'S NOTE
This is a work of fiction. Names, characters, places, and incidents either are the product of the author's imagination or are used fictitiously, and any resemblance to actual persons, living or dead, business establishments, events, or locales is entirely coincidental.

The recipes contained in this book are to be followed exactly as written. The publisher is not responsible for your specific health or allergy needs that may require medical supervision. The publisher is not responsible for any adverse reactions to the recipes contained in this book.

The publisher does not have any control over and does not assume any responsibility for author or third-party Web sites or their content.

To Chuck Bryson, who will never leave his beloved Bitterroots.
Thank you for enriching our lives so very much for so many years.
We miss you.

## Acknowledgments

My deepest appreciation goes to my editor at Penguin NAL, Ellen Edwards, who patiently worked through a very rough draft of *Air* to offer invaluable feedback that strongly influenced the final timbre of this novel. Thank you for keeping me headed north on Farm to Market Road.

And once again, all my gratitude goes to my agent, Nancy Coffey, for her unwavering loyalty to the series and her composure under fire when bombarded with the craziest of my ideas. Because you do what you do so well, I can do what I try to do that much better.

As always, love and thanks go to my husband, Art, who can see and feel Lumby more clearly than I can on some days. His never-ending support of my writing and steadfast belief in our world at Lazy Goose make it all possible.

Finally, I'd like to thank all those fans who have returned to Lumby again and again, bringing more family and friends along for the ride. Without you, these words would not have been written.

The towns, characters, and events depicted in this novel are entirely fictitious. While there may be a town called Lumby in this or another country, its location and depiction are different from the town I describe within this and other Lumby novels. Any resemblance to actual people, events, or places is entirely coincidental.

# LUMBY ON THE AIR

4-H
CLUB
HOUSE
HOTDOGS
HAMBURGERS
KETTLE KORN

OPEN
Tickets
CARNIVAL RIDES
Today's
EVENTS
TRACTOR PULLS
MAKING
AMERICA
GREAT
Pig Race
BACON BARN
KLUM

Lumby
Cold Water Pond
Red Moose Mill
Montis Abbey
Barns of Lumby
Goose Creek
Fork River
To Trout Lake
Farm-to-Market Road
Woodrow Lake
To Wheatley

ONE

# Invitation

**Wednesday night**

*Pam and Fark Walker*
*cordially invite you to*
*a family reunion*
*at Montis Inn*
*July 14–July 22*

*A celebration of 25 years of marriage*
*and a renewal of wedding vows*
*will be held on July 21 at 7 p.m.*
*Black tie optional*

Pam Walker rolled the ecru-colored card between her slender fingers as she sauntered from the bedroom into the kitchen at their home at Montis Inn. It was shortly before midnight, and all lights in their house were off except for the wrought-iron fixture above the large oak kitchen table where her husband, Mark, sat reading the newspaper. The old casement windows were open, and a gentle summer breeze wafted through the large room.

She placed the invitation on the table, continuing to study it as she tightened the belt around her robe. "You don't think the typo is a bad omen?" she asked, sitting down next to Mark. Not getting any response from him, she leaned over and petted Cutter, one of two black Labrador retrievers that were fast asleep by his feet. "You don't like it either, do you, boy?" she asked the dog.

"Honey," Mark said, without looking up, "it was my name they messed up, and I really don't mind."

Pam tucked her short ash-blond hair behind her ears. "It's still unbelievable that they were actually mailed out with that typo."

Mark softly laughed, seeing more humor in the mistake than his wife did. "I'm sure we're not the first couple who each thought the other had proofread the draft before giving the store the okay to address and send out the envelopes."

Pam continued to stare at the card as she thought about the coming week. "I still don't think it's a good idea that we're closing down the inn for nine days during our busiest season."

Mark shrugged. "It's a little late to worry about that. Like it or not, those invitations were mailed out a month ago, and everyone will be arriving in three days. Don't worry, we'll get through it," he said absently, turning to page four of the weekly newspaper.

The Lumby Lines

# What's News Around Town

BY SCOTT STEVENS July 11

A busy prefair week in our sleepy town of Lumby.

Main Street is abuzz with preparations for hosting this year's Chatham County Fair, which will open with great fanfare in exactly five days. Jimmy D will announce the start of the activities by detonating the town's 1892 cannon, the very one that misfired last winter, leveling the park's gazebo. Late yesterday afternoon, the cannon lost a wheel on North Farm to Market Road, so the scheduled dry run has been postponed until tomorrow at 10:00 a.m.

And good news for all swine owners and spectators alike: for the first time since the unfortunate tragedy when Mr. Olson's pig found its way into the farm combine exhibition during the Rocky Mount fair two years ago, the pig races are being reinstated. This year, they will be held Wednesday in Tent 6, directly across the path from the Bacon Barn.

The Parks Department has purchased eight new Porta Potties for the grand event. To their disappointment, though, the Porta Potties arrived two days ago with missing parts. The Parks Department has been notified that, due to weight restrictions, the Porta Potties were disassembled prior to shipment from the Atlanta airport, and the commodes never made it on the flight. Talk about lost luggage.

Finally, the good men and women of the Highway Department have done it once again: in an effort to make Fairground Road one way, two crews (each obviously unaware of the other) posted DO NOT ENTER signs at both ends of the street, thereby allowing no access to the fairgrounds. Sheriff Dixon has rescinded all motor vehicle tickets issued in the last forty-eight hours in violation of the signs.

Mark's laugh, as he finished the article, was halted abruptly when Pam said, "Fark!"

Clipper, the Walkers' other Lab, was startled out of a light sleep and barked in reply.

Mark grinned. "I'm actually starting to like my new name—it sounds like Hungarian nobility."

Pam shook her head in loving disbelief. "Honey, I guarantee that's not what it sounds like. If anything, I think it's a bad omen." She pulled the soft cotton collar up around her neck as if to ward off her concerns, then leaned back, closed her eyes and did what she did best: considered the best- and worst-case scenarios. She continued as if talking to herself. "I see it coming. The front page of *The Lumby Lines* will read 'Family Reunion Implodes at Montis Inn.'"

Mark leaned over and kissed Pam on the cheek. "That's ludicrous. Dennis Beezer would write a far wittier caption—something like 'Montis Murders Mortify Municipality.'"

She squinted at him out of the corners of her eyes. "You've been thinking about that for days, haven't you?"

"Weeks," he admitted with a sheepish grin. Laying the paper down, he turned in his chair. "I really don't understand why you're so concerned. I can't wait to see my family again."

"Including Lynn?"

"I'm sure she won't come," Mark replied quickly, not willing to consider any other possibility. He paused, trying to count the years since he'd last seen his brother and two sisters. "It's different for you—you talk to your mother every couple of weeks. But as close as my family was while we were all growing up, we lost touch when we went our separate ways. And then after a few strained holiday gatherings—"

"I remember."

"And then the civil trial. Not getting together came easier than making an effort to mend the rifts and smooth out the hard feelings. And ever since coming to Lumby, I haven't reached out to any of them. I think it's sad that we touch base only once a year with a Christmas card."

Pam pulled her knees into her chest and wrapped her arms around her legs. "In some ways, I've done the same with my mom. Although I've invited her here several times, I never really insisted that she come." She looked at her husband. "Do you think we've been selfish in not wanting to share Montis with anyone?"

Mark didn't reply immediately. "Not intentionally, but maybe," he finally said. "What we have here is so great, and we've built so many good relationships in Lumby, maybe some of our more casual friends from the past just got a little more distant. But this is good; inviting our families to join us as we celebrate our anniversary might be the fresh start that we need to bring them back into our lives."

"But having them *all* here, together, for an entire week?"

Mark took his wife's hand in his and held it tightly. "I think you're obsessing just a little."

Pam frowned and gently pulled free of his grasp. "Obsessing, am I? May I remind you that you haven't seen one of your sisters since you sued her husband, who stole a quarter of a million dollars from you?"

"Okay, seeing Lynn after all this time would be a little awkward. But I'm sure she won't have the nerve to show up."

"Even though she RSVP'd that she is planning on coming?"

"In writing—she couldn't even bring herself to call," Mark reminded her. "Lynn is only concerned with appearances; she always does what she thinks is socially correct. I'm sure we'll get a carefully worded and tremendously shallow letter from her tomorrow, regretfully canceling her plans to join us."

"You're probably right about that," Pam said, sighing deeply. "She would never have the audacity to come to our home. But what about Carter? Your brother-in-law is one of the most disliked national radio talk show shock jocks around, and he'll soon be walking down Main Street in Lumby, acting the ultracompetitive, confrontational jerk that he is, just to get fodder for his show."

Mark shook his head. "Nope, that's not going to happen. Carter promised that the reunion is off limits. He said he'll be broadcasting reruns during the entire week."

Pam raised a brow. "And you actually believe him?"

Mark picked up the newspaper in an attempt to escape any further discussion about the reunion. Although he would never admit as much, he was almost as apprehensive as his wife about his relatives descending on the small town of Lumby and causing mayhem at Montis Inn and in the life that he and Pam had so caringly and lovingly built together over the last several years. But he also knew that time was passing quickly, and that there would be few opportunities to rebuild the ties he once had with his brother, Patrick, and at least one of his sisters.

"Fark?" Pam said, still waiting for his response.

"Okay, Pam," he said, folding the newspaper. "Yes, I admit we may have a few small family issues, but when you really think about it, who doesn't?" Before letting his wife reply, Mark pushed the paper in front of her. "This," he said as he tapped his finger on a front-page article. "This will take care of everything."

Pam put on her glasses and began to read. "A pie-eating contest?" she asked in confusion.

"Yep," he said confidently, ignoring her skepticism. "Well, I mean, no, not that specifically, but the county fair—the entire thing, the whole enchilada."

Pam leaned back in her chair and crossed her arms. "What about the fair?"

Mark lifted his hands as if the answer was obvious. "It's opening on Tuesday, and it's the perfect distraction. Everyone can go to—"

"Their separate corners," she said glibly.

"No, to the fairgrounds. We'll all be too busy to argue. I've signed Montis up for a bunch of competitions."

Pam glared at her husband. "You're not serious."

Mark flipped over the newspaper so Pam could see the fair schedule. "Some of these events are going to be *so* cool," he said with mounting enthusiasm.

She continued to look skeptically at the man who had proven, on so many occasions, that he was adept at conjuring up harebrained schemes. "Don't tell me you're going to be chasing after a greased pig."

Mark looked insulted. "Of course not—that's for kids. But maybe we'll try the tractor pull and the demolition derby."

She panicked when she heard those words. "With our Jeep?"

"I haven't figured that one out yet," he replied. "And there's bull wrangling."

"*Bull wrangling*?" she repeated slowly.

Mark nodded and then said in his deepest voice, "With horns. Very dangerous. A real manly-man competition."

Pam covered her mouth as she laughed. "Oh, this train wreck is coming right at us a mile a minute."

Just thinking about the fair excited Mark to no end, and all of his unspoken worries about the reunion faded away. He shot out of his chair, kissed his wife on the head and poured himself another cup of coffee. "It's going to be great. And we can take little Jessica on all the rides."

Pam coughed. "How old do you think little Jessica is?"

Mark looked up in thought. "Well, when we last saw her, she was about four, and that was about four years ago, so she's around eight—the perfect age for going to the fair."

"I don't want to burst your county fair balloon, but we saw your niece eight years ago, and she was eight at the time, so that would make little Jessica sixteen and probably not all that interested in going on the carousel with you."

"No, that can't be," Mark said, waving his hand at her. "Your math is all wrong. She isn't that old."

"Train wreck," Pam repeated.

"Honey, you worry too much," he assured her. "And Kay will be here to calm everyone down."

Pam smiled at the thought of seeing her mother again. "She is a rudder, isn't she? Always so steady and levelheaded."

"Just like her daughter—very predictable."

Pam groaned. "That really means boring, doesn't it?"

"I guarantee that's one thing you're not," Mark said.

"Did I tell you she called the other day to ask if she could bring a friend?"

"Oh, that's great. Who is she bringing?"

"We talked so briefly, I forgot to ask, but I'm sure it's Noreen Buckman. Ever since Dad passed away, she's been Mom's closest friend—a wonderful companion for playing bridge and going to an early matinee. And I'm sure Mom doesn't want to travel alone." Pam thought for a moment. "I'll give them the two adjoining suites in the guest annex."

"Whatever you want," Mark said, taking his wife's arm and leading her into the bedroom. But instead of going to bed, he pulled two chairs in front of Pam's desk. "Let's go online and see what else we can do at the fair."

"It's late, honey. We've got to get some sleep."

"But this is *the* county fair," he said, turning on her computer. "It only comes to Lumby once every four years. This is the highlight of most folks' lives around here."

"And that alone doesn't concern you just a bit?" Pam watched over his shoulder as he booted up the computer and found the fair's webpage. "Click on Fair Sponsors," she said. "We should be mentioned."

As soon as the webpage refreshed itself, the Montis Inn name and logo popped up at the top of the page, separated from and far bigger than any of the other sponsors that were listed.

"Wow," Pam said, resting her hand on Mark's shoulder as she leaned closer to the terminal. "How did we get such great billing?"

"I gave them a little more than the normal donation," he said quickly.

"How much more?"

"Don't ask," he replied as he navigated his way through the site.

"Wait, what's that red notice?" Pam asked, pointing to the bottom of the page. She read aloud: "'July 14 Update: The Lumby Fire Department concession stand known for refried, chocolate-covered doughnuts will not be open until Wednesday due to damages sustained during a grease fire earlier this morning.'"

"That's too bad," Mark moaned. "I just love their deep-fried Twinkies."

"So the options for death at the county fair would be either heart attack from clogged arteries or being gored by a bull?" she asked.

He pretended not to have heard the comment and continued to scroll down to the events listing. "Here it is," he said.

They silently read the long list of activities: Fiddling Competition, Livestock Auction, Grange Judging.

"How about that?" he asked, pointing to the barrel races.

"Peanuts is our only horse, and she would have a nervous breakdown if you put a saddle on her back and asked her to trot between two barrels."

Mark nodded in agreement. "Okay, how about this?"

"Ox yoking?" Pam laughed. "That would be a challenge—we have neither ox nor yoke."

"All right," he said, "let me find Jimmy D's Web site. I hear he's listed the best competitions on his From the Mayor webpage."

Mark began to scan the results of his search but then abruptly stopped.

"What is it?" Pam asked.

"Huh. It seems someone's been blogging about Lumby on MySpace," he answered as he clicked on a Web site link.

Suddenly, they were looking at an attractive teenager with short strawberry-blond hair who was holding a can of Bolt, the highly caffeinated drink that had recently become an overnight fad with high school and college students. She wore a scoop-necked magenta tank top that fit tightly over her well-developed chest and, layered over that, a sheer black blouse that hung loosely off her shoulders. The cut of her hair, with long bangs, complemented her face, and although she was a few pounds overweight, anyone would consider her very cute on first impression. Wearing ample makeup and stylish jewelry, she looked as if she were in her early twenties.

"*Jessica?*" Mark stuttered.

Pam groped for words. "Seems your niece isn't so little anymore."

He blinked several times, trying to make sense of the MySpace page. He scanned Jessica's profile and then took another minute to skim his niece's daily blog entries from the prior week.

"Jessica is writing about coming to Lumby," he explained.

"Is that good?" Pam asked, sinking into the chair next to her husband.

"I don't think it's necessarily bad. She's calling it 'A Trip to Lumby Land.'"

Pam pulled her chair closer to the desk and tilted the screen for a better view. It took both of them several minutes to carefully read everything on Jessica's page, including the blog entries that related to their family reunion.

Pam gasped. "She calls Montis Inn a musty old monastery!"

"Remember, she's just a kid," Mark said, coming to his niece's defense. "And, honey, she's not that far off the mark: Montis is, in fact, a hundred-year-old abbey."

"But *musty*?" Pam cringed.

"That's just an assumption by a teenager who has never set foot in anything older than a new pair of jeans. I'm sure she didn't write that intentionally."

"Intentional or not," Pam said, running her hands through her hair, "this could be read and believed by *anyone*. To write about our inn and our town like that is just irresponsible."

"But honey, it's just the Internet." Mark shrugged. "Everyone knows that whatever they read should be—"

"Trashed," Pam interjected.

"No, just checked out thoroughly," Mark corrected as he continued to study his niece's webpage. "Oh, look, she also has a video."

Mark clicked on the button and a second later, pop rock music blared out of the computer speakers. An image of Jessica filled the screen.

"Hey, everyone," the teenager said. "Like, I'm being dragged out of my room tomorrow for a lame reunion in Nowhere, USA. My cam is on, so stay tuned. I'll be uploading Lumby Land streams every night."

And then the computer went silent.

"Well, that seems harmless enough," Mark said.

Pam sat motionless. "A stream?"

"A video," he answered as he quickly typed in another web address. "Let's see if she's on Facebook."

Pam glanced suspiciously at her husband. "How do you know about all these networking Web sites?"

Mark smirked. "I'm hip. I know what all the young kids are doing."

Pam patted her husband's shoulder. "Then you'll know exactly how to stop Jessica's blogging the second she walks in the door. The last thing we need is a rebellious teenager broadcasting our every move over the next week."

Mark raised his fist in solidarity. "I'm with ya, bro," he said in his best, albeit painfully unsuccessful jive.

# TWO
# *Bailing*

**Thursday**

Well before sunrise, at an expansive, ramshackle farm off of Killdrop Road just outside of Lumby, Mike McNear rubbed his gnarled hands, trying to smooth the ache that came from a lifetime of hard manual labor. Leaning back in his worn chair, he looked around the kitchen.

Bess, his wife of forty-four years, was standing in front of the stove preparing a pot of stew for dinner. The scene appeared to convey a pleasant snapshot of the American dream, as long as no one looked too closely or thought too long about what life was like on a struggling farm. But Mike had been doing just that: thinking.

Over the years, time had taken its toll on both the farm and its owner. Mike fell asleep each night fighting the gnawing aches deep in his muscles, and woke each morning to joints so stiff he could barely move. In his mid-sixties, he felt and looked like he was eighty. The ruggedness that many had found attractive when Mike was younger had long since hardened, leaving behind weathered skin on a broken body. His ill-cut hair and unkempt beard were white, and he wore thick bifocals.

The years had been kinder to Bess, though. She was fortunate not to have had any major injuries, and had taken care of herself the best she could. Her dark green eyes still sparkled when she smiled, and her long silver-white hair was always meticulously combed, frequently woven in a braid trailing down her back. Other than a few extra pounds on her short frame, she had no ills or torments to act as constant reminders of her hard life—except, of course, for her husband.

Sitting in the kitchen, Mike looked up at the ceiling. Born in the master bedroom on the second floor directly above him, he had assumed he would also die between those same head- and footboards, just as his father had, and his father's father before him. The years between birth and death were the same from one generation to the next: from sunrise to well after sunset, they would do whatever was necessary, first for the animals and then for the farm. Any time and energy remaining, of which there was little, would be spent on more personal matters, such as marriage and children.

Early morning light peeked through the windows, revealing a thin layer of dust on every exposed surface. The hearth still needed to be cleaned from the winter before, and the screens had not yet been put on the windows, so flies had found their way into the house.

"You need to keep up with your chores," Mike said to his wife.

Bess, who had grown used to unjustified criticism during their many long years together, gave a wary smirk. "I'd be delighted to, just as soon as you hire a farmhand to replace me mucking out the stalls and milking the cows. When I'm out there with you, I'm not in here cleaning or cooking our meals or washing our laundry."

Mike cleared his throat as he did whenever he was about to make a declaration. "Well, I've had it," he said.

Bess glanced over and noticed his untouched breakfast. "Not hungry this morning?"

Mike pushed the plate away. "Suppose not," he replied in a cold, gruff voice that perfectly matched his character. Theirs was a relationship of few words and fewer gestures of love.

"The cows are making a racket," Bess mentioned as she picked up his plate. It was unlike him not to tend to the cows when they began to make a ruckus.

"They can wait a while longer for me. I certainly have waited enough times for them."

Bess knew better than to respond or question when Mike was in a sour mood, which had become more frequent over the last year. To her surprise, that morning Mike continued to sit at the table, his arm stretched out, resting on the weathered oak table.

The cows continued to bellow, calling for their morning feed.

Bess brought the coffeepot to the table. "Would you like some more?"

"Suppose," he replied, pushing his mug toward her.

For the second time that morning, Bess noticed a change in her husband; Mike always had two, not four, cups of coffee before heading out for morning chores.

He looked down into the mug after taking a large gulp.

"I'm selling the place." His voice was slow and steady as he made the pronouncement.

Bess recoiled, instinctively turning her back to him so he couldn't see her reaction. She caught her breath. "Our farm?"

"The farm, the land, the animals—everything goes. I've had it."

Her head was spinning. "But what about the boys?" she asked.

"Three sons, and not one has stepped foot on the farm in ten years. They don't want it and as far as I'm concerned, none of them deserves it," he said bitterly.

"Where would we go?" she asked softly. "Lumby is the only home we've ever known. We couldn't leave here."

"Just watch me."

The chill in her husband's voice rendered Bess speechless.

"My ancestors founded this town," he continued, "and I'm the largest landowner in the county. You'd think I'd get more respect."

Bess was painfully aware that her husband had frequently been at odds with most of the townsfolk, and long ago she had accepted their isolation because of that discord.

"But Mike," she said, "we need to talk about this."

Mike continued to rub his hands together, trying to ease the arthritis in his fingers. "You can't tell me you're surprised, Bess. Every year it costs more and more to run this farm, and the herd keeps on getting smaller," he said. "And I'm going to be sixty-five years old next year."

"*We're* going to be sixty-five," she said, subtly reminding him that their birthdays were only two weeks apart.

He shrugged. "If I don't do it now, I'll take this farm to my grave."

Bess looked out the window above the kitchen sink. In the distance, on the north-facing knoll, was the family burial plot. She had never given the tombstones or the small cemetery much thought until that very moment. "I suppose we've never really talked about retirement," she said. "That's something we can look forward to over the next year or two. It's something to work toward."

Mike shook his head. "I'm selling the place. I'm cashing in."

"So you've said." Bess pressed her lips together, not wanting to say anything more until the idea of retirement settled over her. She opened a bag of new potatoes and began to methodically clean and halve one after another, dropping each into the simmering stew.

She would be the first to admit that for the last five years, work on the farm had taken a toll on both of them. Although they were land rich, owning more than four thousand mountainside acres, they were cash poor and unable to hire the help needed to maintain both the property and livestock. So Mike and Bess made do the best they could.

Thinking about their hardships, Bess found the idea of retirement more appealing.

Mike pushed his chair away from the table and stood before taking a final gulp of coffee. "Now . . ."

Bess expected that Mike would be heading down to the barn. "I'll help you with the hay bales this afternoon," she said.

"No, not that," Mike corrected her. "I mean I'm selling the place . . . now."

Bess looked over at him, puzzled. "This year?"

"This week, if possible," he said as he pulled a torn piece of paper from his pants pocket, picked up the telephone and dialed the number he had written down earlier that morning.

Bess listened intently.

"Joan? Mike McNear here," he said, and then paused. "Good. I've decided to sell the place and want you to put it on the market."

"Is that Joan Stokes?" Bess whispered.

Mike put his finger up to his lips. "Shhh," he said, hushing his wife as he frequently did. "Yes," he said to Joan. "The sooner, the better. You can come by this afternoon."

Bess's eyes opened in alarm. "No!" She stifled a yell. "Not today!"

"Hold a minute," Mike said, and covered the mouthpiece. "We're doing this, Bess."

"It sounds like *you're* doing this," she practically hissed. "I need at least a week to clean up before Joan comes by."

"Joan, seems Bess needs a little time. Let's make it Saturday afternoon at two o'clock. . . . And pull some ads together—we'll want you to give them to the Chatham Press as soon as you leave here . . . Fine. See you then."

When he hung up, a deafening silence fell over the room.

Trembling, Bess turned away from her husband, her face flushed with anger.

"Well," he finally said, "seems we have some getting ready to do."

When his wife didn't reply, Mike walked out the back door.

THREE

# *Missions*

**Friday**

Standing on the small porch in front of the Walkers' private residence at Montis Inn, Brooke Turner glanced at her watch: 6:08 a.m. She tugged on her husband's shirttail.

"I still think it's too early to be here," she whispered.

"Mark said to be here by six," Joshua replied. "We're actually ten minutes late."

Brooke leaned over, trying to peer into the kitchen window. "But the lights aren't even on."

Joshua tapped gently on the door. When there was no answer, he knocked a little harder.

Just as Brooke was about step off the porch, a car drove up and parked in the small lot next to the inn's main building. A man in his mid-thirties stepped out of the two-seater and grabbed three brown bags from the passenger seat. Even from afar, anyone could see he had a distinct European flair about him; his short, thin frame was immaculately dressed in well-pressed black pants and an intense azure-blue long-sleeved shirt. A black scarf hung loosely around his neck. A visitor would assume he was one of the many affluent guests who regularly stayed at Montis Inn.

Walking up to Brooke and Joshua, the man narrowed his eyes. "You two look like you're about to break in and rob the place."

Brooke smiled and gave André Levesque a warm kiss on the cheek. "You are far too dashing to be a chef."

"You haven't been to our dining room for months," André replied.

"Well, if my husband ever took me out to dinner," she said, tenderly slapping Joshua's arm, "we'd see you more often." She peeked inside the grocery bags. "Tonight's dinner?"

"Your choice will be Daube d'Avignon—Avignon lamb stew—or Canard à Toutes les Herbes."

"Herbed duck?" Brooke asked.

André nodded in approval. "Very good, your French is improving."

"They both sound delicious," she said.

"Not to interrupt," Joshua said, "but do you know if Mark and Pam were expecting us this early? Mark said we had a morning mission."

André laughed. "That sounds dangerous." He stepped onto the porch and pounded on the door, hollering out, "Mark! Joshua and Brooke are here!"

"Well, that's one way of getting his attention," Brooke laughed.

Within seconds, the front door flew open and Clipper and Cutter bolted out. The large dogs ignored the visitors, whom they saw all the time, and took off at full gallop toward the orchard to begin another day of wild abandon and mischievous adventure.

"Hi, guys," Mark said, rubbing the sleep from his eyes with one hand and trying to button his shirt with the other. He still wore the bottoms of his pajamas, which were bright yellow with small red fire engines. On his feet, he wore slippers imprinted with the face of a grizzly bear.

"Always the classy dresser," André commented.

Mark looked down. "Pam gave me the pj's as a joke, but I really like them. And the slippers were all my idea."

"What a surprise," André said.

Mark raised his hands as if they were bear claws. "Grrr," he growled with a menacing look. He opened the door wider. "Come in. I'll be ready in a second."

"I'm off to work," André said as he stepped off the porch. "Would you ask Pam to come by so we can finalize tonight's menu?"

"Will do," Mark said. After watching André walk away, he turned to Brooke and Joshua. "That man was a godsend. Best chef in the Northwest, and he turned out to be a really nice guy too." Yawning, he added, "I'm really sorry I overslept. Make yourself some coffee, and I'll be back in a minute."

"Take your time," Brooke said as she sat down at the kitchen table.

Since she'd come to Montis four years ago, after being asked by the Walkers to lend her architectural expertise to what had seemed the insurmountable task of turning a ruined monastery into an inn, she had grown to cherish the old place. Most especially, she loved the small building that Pam and Mark had chosen for their private residence.

Taproot, as they called it, was the smallest guesthouse of the original Montis Abbey compound, which had been home to an order of monks for roughly ninety years beginning in the early nineteen hundreds. When the number of monks had fallen too low to sustain the monastery, the few remaining brothers had moved an hour away to St. Cross Abbey. Thereafter, Montis was bought and sold several times over the decade until it finally became Pam and Mark's home, their dream, and the start of the second phase of their lives.

After the Walkers bought the fire-ravaged abbey, Taproot was the first building that they restored, with plans to live there only during the renovation of the abbey's grand main building. But they came to love the privacy and warmth that Taproot offered, and over the years they'd made it their home.

"I still love this place," Brooke said as Joshua handed her a mug. "I have such great memories of helping Pam and Mark restore it."

"Good morning, early birds," Pam said as she walked into the room.

Joshua raised his hands in innocence. "Blame that crazy husband of yours."

"You look like you need some breakfast," she said as she put a hand on Brooke's shoulder.

Brooke looked up at her closest friend with half-closed eyes. "I'm not quite sure why Joshua dragged me along. I'd still be in bed," she admitted.

"I'm glad you're here," Pam said as she poured herself some coffee. "I could use a bit of sanity around this place."

"Don't tell me Mark has some far-fetched ideas about the reunion," Joshua said.

"No, not the reunion. Right now he's totally absorbed in the fair, although I have no clue about the details. He's claiming that everything is 'top secret,'" she said, making quotation marks with her fingers. "But since he'll be so busy entertaining his relatives, the fair's competitions might pass us by without a trip to the emergency room."

"I heard that," Mark yelled from the bedroom.

Everyone laughed.

"When will your family start to arrive?" Brooke asked.

"If all goes according to schedule, everyone should be pulling in tomorrow," she replied, "so I need your opinion about a few ideas I have."

Mark rushed into the kitchen. "You ready?" he asked Joshua, pushing against his close friend with his shoulder.

For a moment, the wives looked at their husbands standing next to each other. Although they were closer than most brothers, the men shared few physical similarities. Mark was leaner and several inches taller than Joshua, and had brown eyes with thick dark brown hair that was becoming heavily speckled with gray. Joshua had a stockier body, longer sandy-auburn hair and intense dark blue eyes. But they shared easy, honest smiles and a readiness to laugh.

Joshua looked at his full coffee cup. "You haven't told me what we're doing," he said.

"Not in mixed company," Mark said, pointing to his wife, whom he kissed on the cheek. "We'll be back later, honey."

"Don't forget to go to the abbey for the tables!" she called out.

In a flurry they were gone. The last thing the wives heard was Mark saying, "So here's the plan . . ."

"Are you worried?" Brooke asked.

Pam grimaced. "About Mark or the reunion?"

"Both."

"Yes and yes," she said, grabbing a folder from the coffee table before sitting down next to Brooke. "Mark is out of control, but I'm hoping I can mange eight guests for a week without major damage."

"Eight?"

"We're sure Mark's sister Lynn will bail at the last minute," Pam explained as she spread loose papers across the table. "And Mom is bringing one of her girlfriends."

Brooke picked up the invitation. "Thanks again for inviting us," she said.

Pam looked surprised. "Of course we would—you're our dearest friends. Other than Mark, there is no one closer to me than you," Pam said, pushing Brooke's long, dark brunette hair off her friend's shoulder. "I've known you for a long time. . . . We've been through everything together."

Brooke remained silent, feeling the distant pain of being an only child who had lost her parents at a relatively young age. She had often wished that she had a family, and privately wondered why Mark and Pam seemed fairly distant from their own.

Pam continued to talk as she shuffled through her notes. "I'd like your opinion on what we have planned for the ceremony. Mark and

I would like the two of you to stand next to us when we renew our vows."

Brooke's soft brown eyes widened and started filling with tears. "Really?"

"Of course. We wouldn't have it any other way," Pam said, putting her arm around her dear friend.

## FOUR
# Berry

On a steep hill overlooking the monastic grounds of St. Cross Abbey, three nuns struggled to relocate a boulder only slightly smaller than the dozer being used to push it to the edge of the clearing. During the preceding week, after the loggers had left with most of the cut timber, the women had single-handedly cleared an additional eleven acres of the eighty they had purchased the year before.

Following directly on their heels was a team of eight sisters responsible for transforming the rough land into fields that could be cultivated by removing the remaining tree roots, picking out the smaller stones and leveling the topsoil. Very slowly, acre by acre, the vines that once grew the grapes of St. Armand wine in Oregon were being transplanted to the monastery in the small town of Franklin.

"Impossible," Sister Kristina yelled in order to be heard over the roar of the tractor's engine. "I don't have enough traction."

"How about moving it from the other side?" Sister Megan called out, wiping her forehead with her gloved hand.

"The boulder just may be too big," Sister Robin, a novitiate, thought out loud.

Kristina jumped off the tractor and stood next to Sister Megan.

The two made a startling contrast. Megan was fifteen years Kristina's junior and stood six inches above her. She had a lean, athletic frame, and her straight blond hair was cut just below her shoulders. Her blue eyes were arresting to any observer. Kristina, on the other hand, had a short, stout frame that was well accustomed to hard work. She wore heavy glasses and kept her dark brown hair cut quite short.

"I think it could start rolling," Kristina said, looking downhill where, a quarter mile away, their new annex stood.

Sister Megan studied the boulder and considered its worst-case trajectory. "A million to one odds that it would hit anything if it rolled downhill," she said. "Go for it."

Kristina pulled herself back into the cab of the tractor and dropped down into the seat. Grabbing the throttle, she revved the engine. Within seconds, she expertly maneuvered the dozer above and around the granite, placing the six-foot-wide steel blade up against the rock.

When she gently applied pressure to the gas pedal, nothing happened. The more power she demanded from the dozer, the more its wheels spun. She turned to Megan and shrugged.

Megan, who was leading the excavation efforts, glanced around the hillside. If they were going to run straight trellis lines from east to west, the rock had to be moved.

"Hit it with full force," Sister Megan yelled.

Kristina nodded and immediately backed the dozer twenty feet from the boulder. The woman, already on the upside of the rock, took several steps back.

When Kristina gassed the engine, the dozer's tires gripped the ground and thrust forward, quickly picking up substantial speed and tremendous force. Within seconds, the blade hit the boulder and sent it sliding across the hill. After five yards, it came to an abrupt stop.

Megan raised her arm and gave Kristina a thumbs-up. "That was good. Try it again," she yelled.

Kristina, who had already reversed away from the rock, let loose with the dozer and rammed the boulder going fifteen miles an hour. Unfortunately, immediately before the two collided, the wheels jumped to the left, causing the blade to catch the uphill corner of the rock. Instead of pushing it forward, the dozer sent the rock hurtling down the hill.

Robin gasped, "Oh, my gosh!"

"Look out!" Megan yelled to those downhill.

The rock was already halfway to the annex, rolling steadily down toward the parking lot. The sisters began running downhill, stumbling over loose stones.

Kristina flailed her arms. "Watch out!" she hollered.

Trying to keep her eyes on the boulder, Megan stepped into a deep divot, lost her footing and rolled several yards before regaining a foothold. A few seconds later, the boulder slammed into the side of a van that was parked next to the service entrance of the annex's kitchen. The sisters continued running at full speed down the hillside, with Robin, the youngest and most agile, first to arrive at the scene of the accident.

"Is anyone hurt?" Kristina called out.

Robin looked inside the windows. "I don't think so. The van is empty."

When Megan reached the van, she fell against the back door, totally out of breath. Sliding down onto the fender, she stared up to where they had been working. "A million to one," she said, exhaling. "Go figure."

"Whose van is it?" Robin asked.

"The monks'," Kristina answered as she joined the others.

Just then, several people—Sister Claire and Brother Matthew among them—came running out of the annex. Matthew's mouth opened wide when he saw the boulder bored into the right side of the vehicle. "What on earth?"

"I'm really sorry," Kristina blurted out. "We were clearing the field up there." She pointed to where the dozer sat. Everyone noticed her finger was trembling. "And—"

"Brother Matthew, it's my fault," Megan said. "I told Kristina to move the boulder." She tried to look away from the crumpled metal. "I'm very, very sorry."

Matthew lifted his hand to stop her apologies. "It was an accident. I'm assuming no one was hurt?"

"No, we're fine," Megan said.

"Was this the last of your clearing?" Sister Claire, the prioress, asked.

"I think we've done enough damage for the day," Megan said in an attempt at lightness, her voice cracking ever so slightly. She turned to Kristina and Robin. "Should we call it quits?"

Kristina looked up at the thickening clouds in the sky. "I think so, but let's just take a look at that last parcel we need to clear. We can get an idea of how much work is in store for us tomorrow."

"Again, we're very sorry," Megan offered. "Of course we'll support your insurance claim in any way we can."

"Just be careful," Matthew advised, unable to pull his gaze off the wreckage.

After the three women hiked back up the hill, they crossed the cleared field and headed to the tree line. They expected to find more virgin forest similar to what they had been clearing, but when they trekked twenty yards into the woods, they instead came upon a field of several acres covered with thick, tangled bramble bushes.

The shrubs looked similar to blackberry or raspberry bushes, with long arching stems that reached six feet in height. Those branches that had cascaded down trailed another three of four yards along the ground. The plants had compound leaves and three leaflets, and tiny, sharply curved thorns covered each limb. The fruit, though still young, was the size of an immature blackberry with the smooth exterior of a blueberry, pale gray-blue in color. Flowers were still numerous, indicating that it was a type of ever-bloomer, continuing to produce fruit throughout the season.

Megan tilted her head. "Huh."

Kristina leaned against the tree and gazed out over the field of shrubs. "How odd."

"Isn't it too early for berries?" Robin asked.

Megan replied, "That would have been my guess."

"This will be easy to clear," Kristina said. "No more than two hours."

Robin approached the nearest shrub. "What kind of berries are they?"

"I don't know. Possibly poisonous, given the bright red veins in the leaves," Megan surmised.

"Look at the birds," Robin said, pointing.

Small birds, the size of swallows, were flying among the thorny branches, spearing the berries with their long, thin beaks. They then climbed to about thirty feet, dropped the berry to the ground, circled and picked it up, and finally tossed it into their mouths in flight.

"How odd," Kristina said.

Robin picked a berry and popped it in her mouth.

"Aaa!" she screamed out, wincing in pain. She fell to her knees, convulsively spitting out the berry. She then clawed at her mouth with her fingers, trying to scrape her tongue clean.

"Robin!" Megan cried, running to her side. "It's poisonous! Get it out of your mouth!"

The young novitiate's mouth filled with saliva, which she kept spitting out so fast that she could barely catch her breath. "Ouch!" she screamed as she rolled on her side, trying to slap her forearm.

Megan and Kristina watched in fright.

"Get them off me!" Robin yelled.

Suddenly, Megan saw the small ants crawling up Robin's hand. She started slapping them off with her gloved hands.

"Take off your shirt!" Kristina said.

This was no time for modesty. Robin ripped off her blouse and threw it as far away as she could. Megan immediately started to brush off the ants that were now crawling up Robin's back. Kristina shook out the discarded shirt, and once she was certain that no ants remained, she used it to brush the rest of the ants off Robin.

"Turn around," Megan instructed.

"They're all gone," Kristina said, handing Robin her blouse. "Are you all right?"

"That really hurt," the young novitiate said with an obvious slur.

"Robin," Megan said. "Open your mouth."

"My tongue is numb," the young woman said, her lisped words running together, "but I think I'm okay. It's not getting any worse." She opened her mouth for Megan.

"Your tongue looks a little swollen."

"Those little monsters are nasty," Robin tried to say.

"It wasn't the berry?" Megan asked.

"I don't think so. As soon as I put the berry in my mouth, I felt a sting." Robin paused as she moved her jaw up and down. "But I think the berry tasted pretty good."

Megan cautiously approached a bush and studied its leaves. Bright red ants were scurrying up and down the thorny limbs, carrying berry pulp and pollen to and fro. She looked up at the sky and again studied the birds' odd behavior. "The birds are dropping the berries to knock the ants off," she concluded. "How clever."

Robin smiled faintly. "They're certainly smarter than I am."

Megan pulled her gloves as high as possible and quickly reached between the vines to pick a berry, then immediately threw it on the ground behind her. When she was sure there were no ants on it, she picked it up, blew off the dirt and took a small bite.

"Well?" Kristina asked.

Megan smiled. "Delicious. I've never tasted anything like it. It's a cross between a blackberry and a strawberry, and incredibly sweet . . . almost honey-sweet."

"Let's take a branch back to show the others," Kristina suggested.

"Be my guest," Robin said, touching her numb tongue with a fingertip.

Using a large tree branch to knock the ants off, Kristina was able to break off a long limb that offered a good sample of fruit.

"I'm sure Brother Matthew will know exactly what kind of berry this is," Megan said as they walked back to the dozer for a ride down the mountain.

"And hopefully he'll suggest how to get rid of the ants," Kristina added. "Maybe we should just burn those acres before I bring in the excavator. I would hate to be on the tractor and have a million angry ants put up a roadblock."

FIVE

# *Bull*

Sitting next to Mark in the Jeep, Joshua rolled down the window and rested his arm on the door. "This secret assignment—should I assume it's just running errands with you all morning?"

Mark was aghast. "Errands?! This is a classified *mission*, a clandestine operation in preparation for the county fair."

Joshua laughed. "And it's so undercover that you couldn't tell Pam about it?"

"Oh, no, she'd kill me. I was only able to get out of the house this morning by promising to swing by St. Cross Abbey and pick up some additional tables and chairs we need for the anniversary party."

Joshua was surprised—relieved, but surprised. "That's it? We're really going to St. Cross Abbey?"

"Of course not. That was just my excuse for hitching up the trailer." Mark pulled a neatly folded napkin out of his shirt pocket and handed it to Joshua. "Be careful, it's a little flimsy."

"In so many ways," Joshua teased as he began to read the list aloud. "'Sam's Feed Store—Chainsaw.' Mark, you already have two in the barn."

"They're not the type I need," Mark explained.

Joshua looked confused. "I thought chainsaws only came in one *type*."

"I've got to have one that's ultralightweight."

"An ultra-light chainsaw?" He sounded skeptical.

"Yeah. For the chainsaw art competition on Thursday."

Joshua burst out laughing. "You can't be serious! The guys who enter that event are professional artists who have been carving for years!"

"I know I don't have a chance in the world."

"So, why?"

He glanced over at Joshua. "A secret just between you and me?" Mark's voice was as soft as a whisper.

"Of course. I used to be a monk, remember?"

"Last week, I ran into Jeremiah at Brad's Hardware. He pulled me aside and asked if I would help him during the competition this year."

Joshua tilted his head forward as if looking for an explanation. "But he's taken the blue ribbon the last four years in a row. How on earth could you help him?"

"I think his sight is almost gone, and he needs someone to position the log and position him in front of it. And since only competitors are allowed into the ring . . ."

"He needs two good eyes to get him started."

"Exactly," Mark said. "Once he gets going, I'm sure he'll beat the pants off of me. You know, he's been doing it since he was ten years old." A look of sad compassion came over his face. "Although he didn't say as much, I'm sure this will be his last year to participate, and I just want to help him have one final memory at a fair that he's been going to longer than either of us has been alive."

"That's very nice of you," Joshua said, "but you know that means you'll have to sculpt something yourself."

Mark pointed his finger upward. "And that's why I need a featherlight chainsaw. Seriously, though, how difficult can it be to saw a bear out of a log?"

"You do know it's a timed competition?" Joshua paused, thinking back to the demonstration he had seen the year before. "Those guys can chisel the *Mona Lisa* out of an oak tree in six minutes flat. Everything goes a mile a minute—they swing the chainsaws around like cake knives. Wood chips fly everywhere."

"What I'm going to end up with might not look like much, but it will be worth a little humiliation to help out a friend, won't it?"

Joshua looked over at Mark and, in that moment, felt tremendously honored to be his closest friend. "More than you know," he said.

"Okay, what's next on the list?" Mark asked.

Joshua held up the napkin and continued reading. "Brad's Hardware for two dozen rolls of duct tape."

"That's where you come in. The duct tape engineering contest will be lots of fun. Without going into all the boring regulations right now, bottom line is that we need to build a movable or functioning object that is made of at least eighty-five percent duct tape."

"Sounds ridiculous but safe," Joshua said. He glanced down at the rest of the items written on the napkin and could guess where Mark was heading, figuratively and literally. "There's one thing I don't understand," he said. "Why the trailer if it's not really to haul the tables?"

"We really do need to go by St. Cross," Mark answered, "but our first mission today is to pick up Old Jesse and relocate him to our small barn."

Joshua was shocked. "The bull that almost impaled you last year?"

"He's much mellower now." Mark was trying to convince himself as much as Joshua. "And he's the only bull I could rent by the week."

"This may be a stupid question, but why do you need a bull regardless of his rental options?"

"We're signed up for the bull obstacle course. It's like a humane bullfight without swords and blood or any gross stuff like that."

Mark saw that Joshua wasn't quite following his explanation. "It's not rocket science; all we need to do is get a loose, unhaltered bull through an obstacle course using gentle coercion."

"*We?*"

Mark blinked in surprise at his friend's question. "Of course! I signed us up as a team—I knew you'd want to participate. See, we have this bull, Ol' Jesse, and we'll need to persuade him to walk between a few traffic cones."

"By gentle coercion?"

"Right!" Mark nodded. "Since we can't use a halter or a lead rope, and since you're not really allowed to touch the animal—a little like the Moo Doo Iditarod—you'll need to be in front calling him and I'll be in back, persuading him to—"

"Gore me?"

"No, to chase you."

Joshua threw the napkin in the air. "This is nuts!" he said. "This is a train wreck waiting to happen."

"Wow," Mark said, "those are the exact words Pam used to describe our family reunion."

"Unbelievable. Shouldn't you take on just one tempest at a time?" Joshua asked.

Mark was surprised by Joshua's suggestion. "Well, I'm certainly not going to give up the fair just because our relatives are here."

"How very unfamilial of you." Joshua chuckled. "When are they arriving?"

Mark's tone, and mood, changed in an instant. "Supposedly my sister Lynn will be arriving tomorrow at noon, but we're expecting her to bail at the last minute," he said seriously.

"You sound more excited to be manhandling the bull."

"It's complicated." Mark's voice had dropped an octave.

"How long has it been since you've seen her?"

"Let's see. Her husband stole two hundred fifty thousand dollars from my company seven years ago, so it's been just about seven years and one day." Mark's answer was laced with bitterness. He took in a breath. “The last time I saw her, she was in the courtroom at the trial to get my company’s money back. She was sitting like a little dull mouse behind her husband, Dan, while his attorney tore me to shreds. She knew exactly what Dan had done but said nothing.”

“I’m not totally following.”

“He had invested some money in my business, and when there was an unexpected windfall and I had a six-week surplus of cash, he pulled out his initial investment plus quite a bit more. Unfortunately, that was before all the projects were finished, so when the outstanding bills came due, there was no money left to pay anyone and my company went under. It was one of the worst times of my life.”

“So you went after your money?”

“I tried, but I had the most incompetent lawyer in Virginia and the judge ultimately ruled in Dan’s favor.” Mark shook his head, still in disbelief at the blatant injustice of it all. “And then Lynn immediately wrote a twelve-page letter to every member of our family, vindicating her lying husband and herself. No doubt,” Mark added in disdain, “she went to confession that very night—she was always great at using the church for her own absolution and righteousness.” He sighed deeply. “A few years later, Dan finally showed Lynn what kind of bottom-dwelling liar he really was by having an affair right under her nose. When she found out about it and confronted him, she assumed the affair would end and that she would blindly go on with life the way she always had. But Dan continued cheating on her, and even went so far as to suggest that Lynn divorce him, which she finally did.” He paused for a long moment. “She never, ever apologized to me—for defending her husband, for writing that letter that crucified me and for tearing the family apart by forcing everyone to take sides. And then she had the audacity to say she was coming to our family reunion at Montis—unbelievable.”

“But you invited her, didn’t you?”

“Yeah, but only as a formality. I’m sure she’ll bail at the last minute.”

Joshua stared at Mark, sensing the anger behind the strain in his friend's voice. "And here I was, thinking the worst that might happen this week is that you'd be gored by a two-thousand-pound bull."

But Joshua's concerns proved unwarranted, at least that morning. Within the hour, Old Jesse was eating grain in a freshly bedded stall at Montis Inn without any blood being shed and without Pam being any the wiser.

SIX

# *Buzz*

Mark and Joshua's next stop was the Lumby Feed Store.

"This is great!" Mark said, swinging a power tool over his head like a samurai sword. "It's the lightest chainsaw I've ever felt."

Sam, the owner and a good friend, watched the blade cut through the air. "Because it has just enough power to cut a toothpick."

Mark let the tiny chainsaw drop to the side. "But I'm going to be sculpting a bear," he said, and then added, "From a huge, huge log. Grrr."

"Well, that little electric saw won't even make a dent." Sam picked up the largest of the chainsaws on display. "This is what you need. It'll go through oak like butter."

Mark grabbed it with one hand, but as soon as Brad let go, the weight of the saw bent his wrist. "Ow!" he yelped, catching the saw with his other hand before it hit the ground. He lifted it chest high and then tried to bring it over his head, but it was too heavy. "Wow. This is really serious."

"It's what all the woodchucks use," Sam assured him.

"The *woodchucks*," Mark said mysteriously. "Well, I'm going to be a *woodchuck* this year, so I'll take it."

Joshua frowned. "Don't you think that's a bit too much for you to handle?"

"Like butter," Mark reminded Joshua. "One cut and—"

"Don't say it," Joshua warned.

Sam raised his brow in warning. "Be careful with that—you can cut a man in half in about two seconds."

"Good to know if my brother-in-law gets out of hand," Mark joked. "Put it on my tab, Sam."

"Where to next?" Joshua asked as they left the store.

"McNear's farm. He called and told me that he wants to sell some of his livestock, so we'll go over and pick up a couple of sheep."

Joshua looked baffled. "You have difficulty containing the few you already have. Why do you want more?"

"I'm just using the new ones as practice for the sheep-shearing contest."

"We tried shearing one of your sheep last spring and it was a disaster, or don't you remember?"

"But that's exactly why I signed up. We can learn a ton from the guys who show up at the event."

"Wouldn't it be better if you were a spectator?"

"I want to get close up—ask a few questions, work side by side with the professionals."

"And what are you going to do with the sheep after they're scalped? I thought Pam put a moratorium on buying any more livestock."

Mark looked at Joshua as if he were speaking Greek. "Do with them . . ." he said slowly, buying time to think of a logical reply. "Well, that's a mighty good question that has a simple answer." But before Mark gave any of the details of his plan, he escaped by changing the subject. "And then I want to swing by the fairgrounds."

An hour later, with two thick-coated sheep in tow, Mark and Joshua pulled into the Lumby fairground's parking lot. Numerous trucks, vans, RVs and trailers were parked across the grounds for easy access to concession stands and rides.

Lumby Landfill
Lumberyard
Mineral Street
Jimmy D's
S & T's Soda Shoppe
Brad's Hardware
Wools
Goose Creek
Feed Store
Hunts Mill Road
Lumby Elementary
Holy Trinity Church
South Grant Avenue
Loggers Road

Fairground Road
North Deer Run Loop
North Grant Avenue
Trade Store
Bank
Dickensons
Main Street
SR 541
The Green Chile
Chatham Press
Lumby Police
Lumby Episcopal
Cherry Street
The Bindery
Farm to Market Road
Funeral Home
South Deer Run Loop
To Deer Trail
Town of Lumby
Est. 1862
Lumby Presbyterian
To Wheatley

The band of carnival vendors and operators who traveled from one fair to the next during the summer months allowed themselves three days to set up, so the fairground was bustling with activity in preparation for Tuesday's official opening. By then, the service trucks would be gone, leaving straight rows of booths and rides between wide-open walking paths.

When Mark and Joshua stepped out of the Jeep, they noticed that many of the concession stands had been erected and that several were already serving a limited menu of hamburgers and sodas to those who were working the fair. Two young men were struggling to set up an arcade game that had fallen off the ramp of a heavily rusted van.

Although many of the carnival rides would be arriving the next day, the huge Ferris wheel, aptly named The Air, had already been assembled. The operating crew of three was just beginning to go through the long engineering checklist before they ran their first test. One of the operators had climbed up the frame of the ride and was swinging from a roped harness, trying to replace burned-out lightbulbs among those that outlined the massive wheel.

From all appearances, the worker was engaged in a serious conversation with Hank, the town's mascot, a plastic pink flamingo who was perched in the highest basket of the Ferris wheel, eating popcorn and sipping from a glass of freshly squeezed lemonade. Enjoying the unobstructed views of Mill Valley, Hank had taken up residence there just after The Air was assembled. Although his acrophobia had been acting up in recent months, the well-padded seats and security bar allowed for a good night's sleep. Hank, who thought himself more an eagle than some dim-witted wading bird, had seen many fairs come and go. This one certainly looked most promising. If nothing else, he would have penthouse accommodations for the week.

Mark walked over to the base of the Ferris wheel and looked straight up. "This thing is huge! I wonder if you can see Wheatley from the top."

"And farther," Jimmy D said, walking up and slapping Mark on the back.

Joshua shook Jimmy's hand. "If it isn't our honorable mayor."

"Oh, are you still mayor?" Mark joked. "I thought Hank won the last election."

"He stuffed the ballot box," Jimmy said tersely. "And a good thing we found out. I'd leave town if I was ever outvoted by a plastic flamingo with a fish phobia."

Hank would have protested had he heard Jimmy's slight.

Just then, Jimmy caught sight of someone across the way. "Dennis!" he called out.

Dennis Beezer, standing on the other side of the Ferris wheel, looked up from the fair catalogue that he had been reviewing and waved. As owner of the Chatham Press, he was making one final walk-through of the fairgrounds, confirming ride and vendor locations before printing the official county fair map.

"He's just the man I need to talk to," Mark said as Dennis approached.

"What drags you two over here?" Dennis asked, rolling up the pamphlet in his hand.

"That," Mark said, pointing to the catalogue. "I need to finalize my entries."

"Don't ask," Joshua warned the others. "But I can tell you that he just bought the only eighteen-pound chainsaw over at Sam's."

Dennis referred to his map. "The first-aid tent will be right over there," he told Joshua, pointing at the northwest corner of the grounds.

Everyone laughed, knowing how frequently Mark's carefully laid plans went wildly awry.

Mark raised his hand in protest. "Okay, maybe a few of my past projects have gone a little off course," he admitted, "but this time will be totally different."

This got the other men laughing even harder.

"I'm going to be a *woodchuck*," Mark said with conviction. "And we're doing the bull obstacle and sheep shearing. Maybe even some other events."

Jimmy held his belly, he was laughing so hard. "We consider ourselves warned."

"Does Pam know about your plans?" Dennis asked.

Suddenly, a man yelled from overhead, "Watch out!"

Joshua looked up just in time to push Mark out of the way. A giant metal letter *A* crashed to the ground from forty feet high, landing just inches away from where Mark had been standing.

Mark's eyes opened like saucers. "That could have killed me!"

"All you all right?" the worker yelled down.

Jimmy waved his arm. "Yeah, we're fine."

"You should step away while we're working on the sign," the man yelled back.

Hank nodded in agreement.

"Wow, that came really close," Mark said, looking up and seeing the worker suspended directly below the four-foot-high letters that now read: THE IR.

"Like you're not going to be killed next week by the bull anyway," Jimmy jested. "You bought yourself another seven days." He looked across the parking lot and saw the Montis Inn trailer. "You have the bull in there now?"

"No," Joshua answered. "We just picked up two sheep at McNear's farm."

Mark tried to move the *A* with his foot. "This thing is really heavy. It definitely would've killed me," he said, ignoring the conversation around him.

Dennis stepped toward Joshua. "Did you see anything unusual going on out at McNear's farm?"

"Yeah, it looked like some of his dairy herd was being loaded up for transport." Joshua thought for a moment. "And two of his tractor sheds were empty."

Mark finally pulled his focus off the instrument of death, as he would later call it. "Bess McNear pulled me aside when Joshua was loading the sheep and told me that Mike's selling the farm."

"He's the biggest landowner in Lumby," Jimmy said. "What he does with his land could impact all of us."

Joshua dismissed the idea with a wave of his hand. "That farm has been in his family for generations. He's feeling burned out, but I don't think he'd ever sell it. And if he did, he'd certainly never break up that property into smaller parcels. I'm sure it will continue to be a dairy farm for another hundred years."

Dennis disagreed. "I wouldn't be so sure about that, Joshua. He's brought Joan Stokes in to handle the listing, and she's running a few ads in our paper. One targets major real estate developers."

"Developers?" Jimmy looked surprised. "What do you mean?"

"Just that," Dennis said. "The ad suggests the possibility of a major subdivision for commercial use."

"But he can't do that," Mark jumped in. "Can he?"

"Actually, he can," Dennis replied. "When Joan came into my office to place the ads, she told me that the size of his parcel, along with some grandfather clause the town council voted in a few years ago, give Mike all the freedom in the world to sell to whomever he wants for whatever purpose they intend." He turned to Jimmy. "Do you agree?"

Jimmy nodded. "I vaguely recall that his farm was grandfathered a while ago. But . . ." His voice trailed off.

Mark turned to Joshua. "No way would he sell to a developer."

Joshua shrugged his shoulders. "I could be wrong—maybe he would."

"It wouldn't surprise me at all," Dennis said. "He's been griping for years, and he's angry at the townspeople. If he could cash in by selling to a real estate developer, regardless of what it would do to our town, I think he would take the money and run."

SEVEN

# *Cohabits*

The Lumby Lines

## Classified Ads

July 12

For Sale, Rent, Barter or Giveaway

---

They're everywhere—I need help. More free rabbits for pet or pot. Take as many as you want. They're breeding like rabbits. Call Cindy Watford. 695-0491

---

Cow manure. See Mike McNear @ the farm

---

Eight used Porta Potty doors—last year's model. Call John at the Parks Department, 925-0855. $50 each or $400 for all of them.

---

For Rent: Two fishing poles and tackle box. $2.00 a day. Call Timmy at 925-4040.

---

Sofa: brown leather, 5 years old. Seats six comfortably. Great condition until cigarette fire. Best offer. 925-8137.

---

Babysitting services. Seeking well-mannered, conversant children of any age 10-12. Please telephone 925-9263.

---

Return to nature. For rent: one-room rustic cabin. Some electricity if you bring your own extension cord. Fully operational outhouse. Available July 18-24 when I will be down in Florida. Call Phil 925-3928

---

Still in search of: Female soul mate to come with me to Florida July 18-24. Call Phil 925-3928

---

Eggs. Chicken eggs, guinea eggs, duck eggs. $2.00 a dozen. In cooler at end of driveway. Leave money in shoebox. 8 Cherry Street

---

Parachute. Never been opened. Used once. Slightly stained. $350 OBO. Lumby Sporting Goods.

---

Mannequin. Slightly used. Missing left arm and right foot. $30.00 Lumby Sporting Goods.

---

Mixing bowl set ideal for wife with round bottom for dough beating. $18 925-4735.

---

Two person hot tub with water. Call Phil 925-3928

---

1922 Miss America tiara and baton. $50. Call Sara 924-3361.

Two hours after having dropped off the sheep at the Montis barn, Mark and Joshua were turning into the driveway at St. Cross Abbey.

"Impressive progress," Joshua said, looking out the car window.

Twelve months before, the sisters of St. Armand Monastery in Troutdale, Oregon, had approached the monks of St. Cross with the idea of buying the land directly behind their monastery. The sisters' order and vineyard had grown too large for the property they owned on the west coast, and they were looking for a new home in which to expand their community and grapevines.

The changes at St. Cross since Mark and Joshua's last visit were noticeable; the final wing of the sisters' new annex had been roofed and painted, and much of the hillside behind the building had been cleared. Straight wire trellises attached to heavy stakes ran east to west along the slopes, and many of the transplanted vines were green with new foliage.

"The sisters certainly have accomplished a lot in a short time," Joshua commented.

"It looks like it's really coming along," Mark agreed.

Joshua smiled fondly. "They're an impressive group of women."

Joshua had firsthand knowledge of their work ethic; after finishing his doctoral work in agricultural genetic engineering the year before, he had been hired by Christian Copeland, a vintner and the largest private investor in the sisters' winery, to work with the sisters in researching and developing a more disease- and cold-resistant strain of grape. Since that time, Joshua had come to know the sisters quite well, having worked side by side with them as they relocated their vineyard to Franklin.

"You like working with them, don't you?" Mark said as they drove up to the monastery's main building.

"Very much," Joshua replied. "They know so much more about grapes than I do, but they're always open to my questions and ideas."

Just as Mark was parking the Jeep behind the main chapel, Brother Matthew walked past, his hands sunk deep in his pockets. Several yards behind the prior, four monks were pushing a van whose side was entirely crushed in.

Upon seeing his friends, Brother Matthew raised his hand to stop any questions. "You would never believe it," he said, glancing back at the vehicle. "I'll meet you in the kitchen in a few minutes."

"Perfect," Mark whispered to Joshua. "That will give us time to try out their new rum sauce that Pam's been talking about."

By the time Matthew rejoined them, Mark was licking the final drops of liquid off the spoon. "Delicious!" he exclaimed. "Each new rum sauce is better than the last," he told Brother John.

St. Cross Rum Sauce, the brothers' cornerstone business that Pam had helped them structure and launch four years earlier, had won international accolades in culinary circles and, in turn, had quickly become a household name. That business had already generated enough revenue to allow the monks to fund their own philanthropic foundation, which now reached the most impoverished corners of the world.

Brother John stood next to Mark, smiling proudly. "Vanilla Mango," he said. "We should have it in the stores by the end of the year."

"And how is it over ice cream?" Mark asked, glancing at the freezer.

John gave a robust laugh as he pulled out a gallon of Häagen-Dazs. "How is it you eat like a horse and you're still in perfect shape?"

"All in the genes—it runs in the family," Mark replied. "Speaking of which, I hope all of you are coming over to Montis next Saturday night for our anniversary party. Brother Matthew is presiding over a renewal of our wedding vows."

"Pam's really going to sign up for another twenty-five years?" the monk teased his friend.

"Yeah, isn't she great?" Mark said. "After the ceremony, we're going to party all night."

"Hopefully, that idea won't tempt too many of the brothers," Brother Matthew said as he took a seat next to Joshua. "Good seeing you again, Mark. We've missed you at vespers."

Mark looked sheepish. "I don't want to get on the bad side of your boss."

Matthew looked confused. "God?"

"You shouldn't go there," Joshua warned Matthew. "Mark has an interesting slant on religion, but it would take all afternoon for him to explain it."

Mark looked at his watch. "And we need to get back to Lumby before Pam notices we've been gone all day."

Just then, the double doors to the kitchen swung open and Sisters Megan and Kristina walked in. Megan was holding several long branches filled with berries.

"A peace offering?" Matthew asked.

"Sort of. I heard that you were unable to start the van," Megan said guiltily. "We really are so sorry."

"I've done far worse," Matthew said kindly, trying to alleviate the sisters' discomfort. "As long as all of you are all right."

"We were until the ant attack," Kristina said.

"Ants?" Matthew and Joshua asked simultaneously.

Megan handed Matthew a limb that she had taken off the berry shrub. "Directly behind the upper slope, we came across a couple of acres of thicket filled with this berry. The fruit, as well as the plants, are infested with what looks like fire ants. They stung Robin several times, but she's all right now."

Mark pulled a berry off the branch and popped it in his mouth.

"Mark!" Joshua gasped. "They could be poisonous."

"No, no, it's fine," Megan assured him.

"They're better than fine," Mark said, plucking another berry off the stem.

Both Joshua and Matthew accepted samples of the sweet berry before Mark took the branch from Matthew and stripped it clean. By the time he was done, his lips were blue.

Joshua looked at Matthew. "Do you know what kind of berry this is?" he asked. "I'm guessing it's indigenous, but I don't have a clue."

Matthew shook his head. "I've never seen it before. What's more odd," he added, "is that we've never seen any kind of fire ants around here."

Joshua looked at the berryless branch that Mark was still holding. Turning to Megan, he asked, "Would you show me where the bushes are? I'd like to take a sample to the university in Wheatley."

"Take all you want because we're either burning them all or dozing the field to the ground tomorrow," Kristina advised.

"You shouldn't do that until you know what you're destroying," Joshua said with some alarm. "Do me a favor—can you wait a few days until wc know what genus it is? The last thing you want is some unknown, noxious, invasive plant that keeps regenerating itself in the middle of your vineyard. It could totally destroy your fields."

"But we have no time to spare," Megan replied. "More vines will be arriving from Oregon next week, and they'll need to go in the ground as soon as possible."

"I think you should err on the side of caution," Joshua advised. "I don't know what this is, and I would hate to see all of your hard work destroyed by some unexpected fluke of nature. Over the next day or two, I'll try to get enough information about the bush as well as the ants to allow you to make an informed decision."

"And we'll certainly pray that, in the meantime, the ants find better accommodations elsewhere," Kristina added.

# EIGHT
# *Kay*

**Saturday**

When the alarm clock in the Walker bedroom went off at five thirty a.m., Mark was already dressed and making a pot of coffee. Pam dragged herself into the shower where she stood motionless under the hot stream of water for five minutes before washing her hair.

"I've got to go, honey," Mark called into the bedroom once he heard Pam turn off the faucet.

"No, wait," she called back. "I'll be out in a minute."

Mark slumped into an upholstered chair, accepting the fact that he wouldn't be slipping out of the house any time soon.

A few minutes later, Pam entered the kitchen, drying her hair with a towel. "Before you bolt out of here, can we go over today's plan?" she asked.

"I wasn't *bolting,*" Mark protested, all the while thinking that the word "escape" would have been far more appropriate.

"It's not even six in the morning," Pam said as she began to make breakfast. "I assure you, *if* Lynn comes—and you know she won't—it will be noon before we see her."

"I just can't believe she's really going to be here at Montis." Mark groaned. "Maybe she just forgot to mail her regrets or she got tied up and couldn't call yesterday."

"Mark, you need to accept the possibility that she could be arriving today."

He shook his head. "For all the harm she's caused, she wouldn't dare."

"You can tell her that when you see her."

"Which won't be any time soon."

"Right," Pam said dryly. "So there's no other reason why you're hurrying off at sunrise." She poured cereal into a bowl. "You know, Mark, if she does come, you won't be able to avoid her for seven days."

"She shouldn't be coming," he said bitterly.

"She's family, and this is a reunion. You'll need to be here when *all* of your relatives arrive."

"Well, I have a ton of errands to run and then I'm off to the Rocky Mount airport to pick up your mother," he said, looking around for his to-do list.

"Please give some thought about Lynn. It's going to be a miserable week if she joins us and you two don't come to terms with what happened."

Mark remained silent, slouching further down in the sofa.

"And remember to carry my mom's luggage. I'm sure she's gotten a lot older since we last saw her five years ago."

"I don't know about that," Mark said, taking a muffin from the plate Pam had placed on the table. "Kay sounded pretty spry when I spoke to her on the phone last week."

"*Spry?* My mother?" Pam laughed. "She's a seventy-five-year-old widow and as unexciting as I'll be at that age. I'm sure she and Noreen will play cards during the day and go to bed by eight every night."

"Spry or not, she'll find me at the gate waiting for her when she steps off the plane. If her flight is on time, we should be back around two." Mark set his cup in the sink and kissed his wife. "I need to get going."

"If Lynn is coming, she won't be here for hours," Pam reminded him.

"I've got to get down to the barn," Mark said, pulling excuses out of the air.

Pam grabbed her husband's shirtsleeve. "Speaking of the barn, I went down there last night to get a garden hose. Can I ask a really silly question?"

"Fire away," he said jovially.

"Why is there a huge bull in the horse stall?"

Mark's gaze faltered. "Well," he said slowly, stalling for time, "that's an easy one to explain." And then he froze as he frequently did when caught red-handed.

Pam crossed her arms. "Still waiting."

"I got it for the kids," Mark said. "That's it—for my niece and nephew while they're visiting."

"A petting zoo, of sorts?"

"Exactly!"

"Your niece is sixteen, and your nephew just turned twenty-one. I guarantee they're not interested in Old McDonald's Farm. And a bull with horns longer than your arm doesn't quite fall into the cute-and-cuddly category," Pam contended. "What's he really for?"

Mark stepped around the table. "Honey, there are some things you just don't want to know about, and I assure you this is one of them."

"But Mark—"

Before she could finish, he was out the door. "I'll be back this afternoon with Kay," he called over his shoulder.

Pam looked around the empty kitchen. "I hope so," she said to herself.

The Lumby Lines

# Sheriff's Complaints

BY SHERIFF SIMON DIXON July 14

**4:12 a.m.** Mini Cooper vs. moose on MM15 by Priests Pass. No competition—moose won.

**5:42 a.m.** Ford vs. moose on MM16 west of Priests Pass. No injuries to either.

**6:03 a.m.** Moose nails side of pickup with antlers on MM16. Pickup towed to Dakin's Garage.

**6:13 a.m.** Call from Presbyterian Church. Raccoon cornered in choir balcony. LFD dispatched.

**7:16 a.m.** Town resident reports that all men's socks hanging on clotheslines from the night before have disappeared.

**8:19 a.m.** Resident at 44 Hunts Mill Road reports Sophia Meyers has been waving toilet paper from her upstairs window for 10 minutes. Appears to be trapped in bathroom. LFD dispatched.

**8:22 a.m.** Dennis Beezer reported smashed windshield from trout dropped by eagle overhead.

**3:59 p.m.** Lumby Sporting Goods called with complaint that a man is groping their mannequin for sale.

**4:26 p.m.** Debbie Herbert requested that a parking ticket be written for tractor that someone left in her driveway.

**5:47 p.m.** Hannah Daniels submitted complaint that all Jimmy D's socks were taken from clothesline.

**6:06 p.m.** Call from little Matt Sipperley. Saint Bernard swallowed mom's cell phone. Dr. Candor contacted.

**11:01 p.m.** Cindy Watford requested immediate assistance evicting two bats from her house.

A soft tap sounded on the door.

"The coast is clear, honey. Lynn's still not here," she said, expecting to see her husband.

Instead, André Levesque poked his head in. "Am I supposed to be avoiding someone named Lynn?" he asked.

Pam grinned. "No, that's Mark's job for the day. That, and manhandling a bull that's down in our barn."

André laughed. "If it's not here to be slaughtered and cooked, then I'm staying out of it."

"Very wise of you. So what are you doing here so early?"

"I'd like to go over the schedule for the week," André said. "You can tell me what meals need to be prepared and for how many."

"Thank you!" Pam said, kissing him on the cheek. "It's so nice that someone is taking this reunion seriously. But I haven't thought through all the meals yet."

"Then let's just talk about tonight's dinner and tomorrow's barbecue, and we can hold off any decisions about the other meals for a few days."

Pam exhaled. "That's how we'll have to take it, one step at a time."

ᔕ

Pulling into the airport parking lot at Rocky Mount, Mark continued to scribble notes on an old gas receipt. Littering the backseat were other torn bits of paper that also contained important to-do's for the week. Even Mark would have to admit that the chores for both the reunion and the fair were mounting up faster than they were getting done.

Remembering yet another to-do Pam had assigned him that morning, he turned off the car. "Food Shop," he wrote on the back of the metered parking ticket. He felt around in his pocket for the food list she had given him and, not finding it, began scavenging among the other notes. Coming up empty-handed, he decided to start his own list: "Beer, Ice Cream."

A plane flying overhead approached the runway, reminding Mark where he was and why he was there. Looking at his watch, he was shocked to realize that Kay's plane was scheduled to have landed ten minutes earlier. He abandoned all lists and dashed out of the car and through the revolving doors of the terminal. He sprinted down the long concourse, slowing next to each terminal gate to read the departure and arrival information.

Mark reached Gate 7 just as passengers from LaGuardia were beginning to disembark. Mark, taller than most of those waiting for friends and family, stood behind the growing crowd.

When he saw Kay Eastman's familiar face, he waved and called, "Kay! Over here!" He ran up and took his mother-in-law in his arms, lifting her off the ground. "We're so glad you're here. You look fantastic!"

Anyone would agree; an older version of Pam, Kay was a striking woman in her mid-seventies who could turn more heads than most women in their forties. She had large, gray-blue eyes that were set off by short, thick silver hair, cut beautifully to frame her face. She wore rose-framed glasses, and her dress was, as always, impeccably styled.

"Fantastic," Mark repeated, noticing the twinkle in the woman's eyes. "I hope Pam is as gorgeous when she's your age."

"It's all in the genes," she said, stepping away from Mark. She tilted her head, getting a good look at him. "And you're as handsome as ever—a few years older, a few more wrinkles around the eyes, but very handsome, indeed. So how's my favorite son-in-law?"

Mark kissed her cheek and whispered, "I'm your *only* son-in-law."

"But still my favorite," she replied with a wink.

"Let's go get your luggage," he said, taking her by the arm. "Pam can't wait to see you." But Kay resisted Mark's lead. "Is something wrong?" he asked.

She pointed toward the gate. "One minute," she said.

"Oh, right," Mark said, realizing that they had to wait for Kay's friend Noreen. He raised his brows and grinned. "Maybe you and Noreen met some tall dark stranger on the plane?" he teased.

Before Kay could answer, an older gentleman who was carrying several small bags walked up to Kay and handed her a purse. He was just as attractive and as immaculately dressed as she was.

"Nice pickup," Mark whispered in his mother-in-law's ear.

"I had to wait for the plane to clear to pull our bags together," the man said in a soft baritone voice that had a hint of a New England accent.

"Do you have Pam's gift?"

The man rearranged his packages so as to free one hand, which he placed lightly on Kay's shoulder. "Stop fussing," he said with a familiarity that surprised Mark.

"You two met on the plane?" Mark asked.

"Mark, I'm so sorry—how rude of me," Kay said, blushing with embarrassment. "This is Robert Day. Robert, this is my son-in-law, Mark Walker."

Robert smiled broadly and extended his hand. "It's such a pleasure to finally meet you. From everything Kay has told me, I feel I already know you and Pam."

"It must have been a long flight," Mark said, knowing how Kay could talk up a storm when she was in the mood or had more than two glasses of wine. "Nice meeting you too," he said, shaking the stranger's hand before turning back to Kay. "Was Noreen seated in one of the last rows?"

"Noreen Buckman?" Kay said in surprise. "Why would you think she's on the plane?"

Mark was baffled but simply assumed that he had misunderstood what his wife had said about Noreen. "No reason. Are you ready to go?"

Kay nodded once. "Ready, captain." She giggled.

Mark felt awkward walking away from the man to whom he had just been introduced, so he said, "Have a nice day," as he escorted Kay off to the luggage claim area.

But Robert Day didn't allow himself to be left behind and walked next to Kay on her other side.

Persistent, Mark thought. He obviously wants her phone number. *I'd* want her number if I were his age. In fact, I'd want *his* number if I were her.

"What color is your bag?" Mark asked.

Kay took hold of Mark's hand. "Robert can take care of that. You and I need to get caught up."

Without being asked, Robert joined the travelers who were huddled around the one small luggage carousel. Mark was about to suggest that Kay give the poor fellow her phone number and send him on his way when an alarm went off and the metal conveyor belt began to move.

"How is Pam?" Kay asked.

"She's great," Mark answered, keeping a watchful eye on Robert, which wasn't hard given the man's height. "She's a little nervous about the reunion, but she's doing well."

Robert's head disappeared in the crowd. A second later, he lifted two bags off the conveyor and rejoined them. "I think we have everything," he said.

"You're a dear," Kay replied. She turned to Mark. "The test of a relationship is to travel together."

"Relationship?" Mark asked hesitantly.

Kay leaned back with a start. "Oh, my!" she exclaimed. "You thought I just met Robert on the plane?"

Mark was at a loss. "Didn't you?"

"No, no," she corrected him. "Robert is my . . . friend."

"Your *friend*," Mark repeated. "As in the friend you're bringing to the reunion? That friend?"

"With benefits," Robert added with a playful wink.

Kay lovingly jabbed his side. "Mark, close your mouth," she said. "Your jaw is on the ground."

"You two . . . ?" Mark stammered.

"We two," Robert said, taking Kay's hand.

Pam is not going to like this, Mark thought. "For how long?"

They looked at each other and smiled. "One blissful year," Kay said.

Mark was thinking as quickly as he could. "You also live in Connecticut?"

"Yes," Robert said slowly, giving Mark time to connect the dots. "At the very same address," he finally added.

Kay beamed like a teenager in love. "I so want him to meet everyone."

"Oh," Mark said, and then thought about how Pam might react to the surprise. "Oh," he repeated in a more menacing tone. "Pam doesn't know about this, does she?"

"I could never find the right time to tell her," Kay admitted.

"*In a whole year?*" Mark asked.

"Time flies, doesn't it?" she said apologetically. If she wasn't so cute, Mark might have gotten angry. "You know how Pam hates surprises. And she hates change more than that. And you waited until our anniversary to tell her about Robert? Thanks, Kay," he said sarcastically.

"Oh, she'll be fine. Robert will win her over in no time," Kay said, squeezing her boyfriend's hand.

"At least that's the plan," Robert added.

Oh, Pam is going to be *so* not happy about this, Mark thought while trying to force a smile. "All right then, this will be great." He picked up their two bags and led the way to the parking lot. What a train wreck.

## NINE
# *Lynn*

Shortly before noon, a nondescript rental car crept past Montis and continued a quarter mile north toward Lumby before pulling off the road and stopping. Although no one had noticed, it was the fourth time that morning that the car had driven in front of the inn, and the fourth time it had stopped and waited a short distance away.

After several cars passed by, the driver made a wide U-turn and, upon reaching the stone building at Montis Inn, pulled slowly off Farm to Market Road and parked in a visitor's spot.

Pam, who was stirring batter at the kitchen counter, pushed the curtain aside when she heard the crunch of gravel. Even from a distance, she recognized the woman seated in the car who was obviously engaged in a lengthy conversation with herself. She remained there for several minutes, her mouth opening and closing and her arms moving in animated gestures.

"Lynn," Pam whispered.

After several more minutes, the woman finally stepped out of the car and walked directly to the passenger side. Pam squinted, trying to get a better look at her sister-in-law. The fifty-eight-year-old woman was what Pam would describe as inoffensively plain—

neither physically attractive nor unattractive. She had changed very little since the last time Pam had seen her in the courthouse seven years before; she still had short mousy-brown hair, large brown eyes and a long thin nose that matched a sharp chin. She had few, if any, physical similarities to any of her siblings.

"Huh," Pam murmured.

Lynn, whose back was turned to Pam, opened the passenger-side door, unlatched the seat belt and pulled something or someone into her arms. Even from across the courtyard, Pam could hear Lynn talking in a high, animated voice. "It's all right, sweetheart. We're here."

A child? Pam wondered. When Lynn turned around, Pam dropped her spoon. In Lynn's arms, cradled as carefully as a baby, was an enormous cat.

"A *cat*?" Pam said, stifling a laugh. "She's been talking to a cat?"

"Look, Coco!" Lynn said, pointing across the road. "Look at the apple trees."

Suddenly, Clipper and Cutter bounded around the corner of the annex and headed directly toward Lynn, barking all the way. Lynn screamed. Coco, reacting more to the scream than to the canines barreling down on her, extended her claws into Lynn's arms and jumped onto the top of the car. Lynn screamed again, either in pain or in fear, and began swinging her arms wildly, trying to beat the Labradors away. Clipper and Cutter, being the kindest and most fun-loving of dogs, thought Lynn was teaching them a new game and showed their appreciation by jumping up and trying to lick every part of her face.

Through all the commotion, the dogs never saw the cat on the car roof. Even if they had, they would have been much more interested in the crazy woman playing with them.

"Aggg!" Lynn yelled again as she fell to the ground from the weight of the dog's pushing against her.

Both Labradors assumed this was another part of the fun and welcomed the invitation by jumping on Lynn's shoulders and roughhousing as they did frequently with Mark.

Pam ran out the door at full speed. “Cutter! Clipper!” she called from the porch. “Dinner! Come here!”

“Dinner” was their reason for existence and the only word the dogs ever heard when they were excited. They turned in midair and bolted toward Pam. As they sprinted into the kitchen, she slammed the door behind them and ran over to help Lynn.

“I’m so sorry, Lynn,” she said. “They’re a little excitable but totally harmless.”

Lynn pulled herself off the ground and reached frantically for her cat, which was still on the car roof, paralyzed with fear.

“Coco, honey, come down,” Lynn pleaded, tapping gently on the car. When the animal got close enough, Lynn grabbed her and pulled the cat into her breast.

Lynn didn’t even acknowledge Pam’s presence.

“Okay,” Pam said, “let’s pretend this never happened and start over.” She put on a huge smile and opened her arms. “Lynn!” she said with vibrancy. “How wonderful to see you again. Welcome to our home.”

Lynn’s gaze darted around the compound. “Are the dogs locked up?”

“Yes, they’re in our house,” Pam said as she hugged her sister-in-law.

Lynn’s face was flushed. “Those monsters should be on a leash.”

“It’s so nice to have you here,” Pam said.

Lynn pulled the cat’s face close to hers. “Poor Coco,” she cooed. “Mean dogs, good Coco.” Lynn looked around again. “And Mark, is he here?”

“Don’t worry. I don’t think he’d give you the same greeting that our dogs did,” Pam said, trying to make light of the situation.

Lynn glared at Pam, finding no humor in her comment.

“No,” Pam answered more seriously. “He went to the airport to pick up my mother. Your luggage is in the car?”

“In the trunk. Also bring Coco’s bed and food,” Lynn directed.

Pam took a deep breath. “We have a suite ready for you in the annex.”

Before Pam finished her sentence, Lynn was already walking down the path. "And Coco will need her toys," she said over her shoulder.

"Unbelievable," Pam said under her breath as she unpacked the trunk of the car. After grabbing the cat's necessities and a small suitcase, she caught up with her sister-in-law. "We thought this would be more convenient than a long flight of stairs in the main building."

"Beautiful hydrangeas," Lynn said prissily as they walked down the flower-lined path. "Although blue may have been more complementary with the stone wall, it's still very nice."

A backhanded compliment is better than no compliment at all, Pam thought. "Thank you," she said, struggling with the luggage.

"And these purple bitterroots are very nice. Aren't they your state flower?"

Pam couldn't conceal her surprise. "I'm surprised you know that."

"I've been working for the American Horticultural Society since my . . ." Lynn swallowed on the word "divorce." "For the last four years," she continued. "And one of my projects dealt with native Northwest flora."

"I didn't know you were working," Pam said as she struggled to open the guest annex door without dropping any of Lynn's bags.

"In Washington, D.C.," Lynn retorted.

"I'd love to hear more about it. Maybe you can give me some advice for our courtyard plantings," she said, leading Lynn down the hall. "Your room is the first on the left."

Once inside the suite, Lynn laid Coco gently on the bed. Coco was, indeed, a gorgeous cat with brilliant blue eyes and an off-white body with a much darker face, legs and tail.

"He's huge!" Pam blurted out.

"*She* is a show-winning champion Seal Point Birman, and *she* is pregnant by the top-rated Seal Point Birman stud in the country."

"Ah, a Birman stud," Pam repeated solemnly. "Sounds like something I'd like to have."

Lynn didn't laugh. "Perhaps you are unaware, but it's a serious business, and she's quite rare."

"She looks like a big Siamese," Pam commented.

"Hmph," Lynn groaned as she leaned over and kissed her cat. "Siamese are so . . . common."

Pam raised the peace flag. "Well, Coco is certainly beautiful. When is she due?"

"My veterinarian thinks it will be around July thirtieth."

Pam went over to pet the cat, who was sprawled out on the bed, gently clawing into the bedspread. "And travel is safe for her?"

"I would never have come if it wasn't," Lynn replied as she filled Coco's food and water bowls. She then fluffed Coco's cat bed and scattered toys around the room. After she had seen to the needs of her pet, she began to unpack her small travel case.

Carefully, she removed and unwrapped one candle after another, and placed them around the room. After setting a dozen candles of varying heights on the dresser and nightstands, she brought a handful more into the bathroom.

"Do you light all of those at night?" Pam asked as she looked up at the smoke alarm and wondered if Mark had replaced the batteries as she had requested.

"Usually," Lynn said. "Candles have such a calming effect—they're a comfort."

"There was a tremendous fire here," Pam said, hoping that part of the monastery's history would gently encourage Lynn to be very careful with so many candles. When Lynn didn't respond, Pam added, "Something we would hate to have repeated."

Lynn ignored the insinuation. "We should let Coco sleep now—she's exhausted," she said, shooing Pam from the room.

Once outside in the courtyard, Pam took a deep breath. "Lynn, I feel your visit has gotten off to a rocky start. Why don't you come in and have some lunch? I'm about to make myself a sandwich."

"I thought you had a chef," Lynn said in a tone that was more of an accusation than a question.

Pam nodded. "We do, for the inn's restaurant," she explained. "But Mark and I make most of our own meals."

Just then, a van pulled off Farm to Market Road and parked next to Lynn's car. A man wearing a long, black-hooded robe stepped out from behind the wheel.

Seeing a friendly face, Pam felt her disposition change instantly. "Matthew!" she said, engulfing her close friend in a warm embrace. "I really can't tell you how glad I am you dropped by."

Matthew wasn't used to being greeted with such adoration and regarded her with curiosity. "I'm glad to see you, too, Pam."

She stepped aside to introduce her guest. "Brother Matthew, this is Lynn Sutton, Mark's sister."

"Lynn Walker," she said, correcting Pam.

Matthew smiled benevolently and bowed slightly. "It's a pleasure to meet you." He turned back to Pam. "I'm assuming your reunion has begun?"

"Off to a great start just a few minutes ago," Pam said, forcing a smile. "Lynn met Clipper and Cutter firsthand."

Matthew laughed heartily. "And you survived to tell about it? Very good." To Pam, he said, "I was just returning from Wheatley and was hoping to find Joshua."

"He and Mark were together this morning, but he left when Mark took off to Rocky Mount airport to pick up my mother."

"I see," Matthew said.

Pam saw concern on her friend's face. "Is everything all right?"

"Sister Claire and the others have asked me to speak to Joshua about his recommendation that they stop clearing one of their fields."

"Is this about the mystery shrubs that Mark told me about last night?"

Lynn's ears seemed to perk up, but she held back from asking any questions.

"Precisely," Matthew said. "The sisters are deeply concerned that any delay in preparing the land will jeopardize their efforts to successfully transplant the vines from Troutdale."

"Perhaps Joshua is at home. Do you want to use our phone to call him?" Pam offered.

"Not necessary—I'm heading into town anyway," Matthew replied before turning to Lynn. "A pleasure to meet you. I'm sure we'll see each other again on Saturday if not before."

When Matthew drove away, Lynn asked, "Saturday?"

"Our anniversary celebration." Pam was disappointed that she had to remind Lynn why they were having the family gathering. "Matthew will be presiding over a renewal of our marriage vows."

"So the monks really *are* friends of yours?" Lynn asked.

"You sound surprised."

"A little," she admitted. "Mark was never one to jump at the opportunity to go to church."

"There are different ways to show belief, aren't there?" Pam said. "The monks are very good friends. They stood behind us when we first bought Montis, and that was the beginning of some of the closest relationships that Mark and I have. They're family."

"*Family?*" Lynn asked, sounding insulted.

"Yes, they are most definitely part of our family," Pam said with conviction. Changing the subject, she continued. "Why don't you come in for a bite to eat?"

"When will Mark be back?"

"That depends on when the plane lands, but soon," Pam said.

"Well, I'm certainly not ready to see him," Lynn said. "I'll drive up and look around your little town of Ludley."

"Lumby," Pam corrected her.

"And please check on Coco in an hour."

"Why?" Pam asked

Lynn looked at Pam as if she had asked a stupid question. "To make sure she's comfortable, of course."

Pam's smile was strained. "Of course."

After Lynn drove away, Pam returned to Lynn's suite with additional clothes hangers that Lynn might need. Smelling a faint whiff of Coco, she opened the window enough to take care of any cat odors she feared might linger for weeks. "Be good," she said, petting the cat's head as she walked out.

After a quick lunch, Pam finished preparing two more guest rooms with fresh linens and towels. Walking down the hall of the annex, she decided to do as Lynn had requested: check on Coco.

She cracked open the door to her sister-in-law's suite and whispered the cat's name, not wanting to startle her if she was sleeping. Peering inside, she was stunned to see a flurry of down feathers blowing softly around the room. In addition to those in the air, feathers had settled on every piece of furniture in the suite. Scrutinizing the bed, Pam quickly noticed a shredded pillow that was, no doubt, the target of Coco's claws. But there was no sign of the attacker.

"Coco!" Pam barked out as she made her way through the floating down. The bathroom was empty except for the shredded remnants of her new terry-cloth towels. "Coco!" she called out again.

The suite was empty. Pam's gaze went to the open window. "Coco!" she called.

A meow came from the woods behind the annex. Just past the edge of the mowed lawn, about twenty yards from where she was standing, Pam spotted Coco crouching at the base of a large oak tree. Resting on Coco's back was a large, brown and gray . . . cat? Pam squinted to get a better look.

When Coco stepped forward, the animal came into full view.

"Coco!" Pam screeched. "Get away from that raccoon!"

The raccoon, which appeared to be trying to mount Coco, was startled. Coco seemed to be enjoying the attention she was getting and ignored Pam's squeal altogether.

"Coco!" Pam yelled again, running toward the animals. "Get off her!" she yelled at the raccoon, flailing her arms wildly. The raccoon looked up, and its amorous mood seemed to change in a heartbeat. It bolted from the scene.

Pam scooped the cat up into her arms. "Coco, are you all right?" she asked, examining the purebred feline, which seemed no worse for wear.

What to do now? Pam asked herself, not wanting to return the cat to the bedroom for fear of having both the upholstered chair and bedspread destroyed by Lynn's darling angel.

Coco snuggled against Pam's chest. "You are not forgiven," Pam whispered to her. Back in Lynn's suite, she stuffed the oldest of the unshredded towels into a laundry basket and then gently laid down Coco, who seemed totally unflustered by everything that had happened. The cat scratched at the towel, circled once and settled down, purring loudly. Pam noticed her huge belly undulating from the movement of her unborn kittens.

Guilt swept over Pam for not taking better care of her charge. Then again, she thought, the cat seemed agreeable to just about anything, including having a quick fling with a local varmint.

After thinking through her options, Pam brought Coco down to the one place that seemed at all reasonable given the situation: the barn. But as soon as she approached the stalls, she remembered that Old Jesse was a houseguest. The way he was throwing his head about suggested that he was becoming more ornery the longer he stayed penned up. The bull snorted and banged his long horns against the metal bars of the stall door.

As quietly as possible, Pam slid into the empty stall next to Old Jesse and gently placed the basket, and Coco, in the far corner. She then brought in fresh hay and a shallow water dish.

"I'll be down with your food in a minute," she whispered.

If Pam had looked back as she left the barn, she would have seen Coco get up and begin to explore her new home.

TEN

# *Symbiotic*

On the second floor of the Lumby Library, Joshua sat alone at a large cherry table by the window. With several books already open in front of him, he reached for a magazine from a tall stack of research journals he had gathered that morning. He picked up the branch of the berry shrub that he had brought with him and held it up to the light, turning it slowing between his fingers.

Chuck Bryson—a very tall, lean man in his late sixties, with thick gray hair that hung below his ears and an easy, timeworn smile—walked up behind Joshua and put a hand on his friend's shoulder. "An olive branch?"

Joshua immediately recognized his voice and smiled. "Not olive, but that's about all I know," he said, turning in his chair. "I haven't seen you in weeks."

"I've been at Berkeley working on a new physics curriculum," Chuck replied.

Joshua looked surprised. "I thought you were going to retire at the end of spring term."

"That was my intent, but the university had different plans. So we compromised: one class and four doctoral students, but the syllabus was atrocious." Chuck glanced at all the books on the table. "Doing some research?"

"I am. It's a puzzle and somewhat of an embarrassment, actually. Maybe you can help me," Joshua said, pulling the closest available chair next to his. "Do you have a minute?"

"I always have time for a good mystery," Chuck said.

Joshua handed Chuck the branch he had taken from the monastery's property. "Sisters Megan and Kristina were clearing the upper field where they intend to plant grapevines. Well hidden behind a thick grove of evergreens, they found a field of berry shrubs that have dense arching and biennial stems, or canes, similar to blackberries. The branches root from the node tip when they reach the ground." He handed Chuck the branch. "Mark and I just happened to be at the monastery yesterday, so I went up and cut several samples. Unfortunately Mark ate most of the fruit on the way home."

Chucked laughed. "That's no surprise." He touched one of the few remaining berries. "They're edible? Because with Mark, you can never be sure."

"That's so true, but yes. In fact, they're delicious." While Chuck sampled the fruit, Joshua continued his story. "I went to the botany lab at the university in Wheatley last night and looked at the cuttings under the microscope, but I saw nothing out of the ordinary. I sent limb and fruit samples to three agencies this morning and hope to hear back by Tuesday or Wednesday." Joshua opened a folder that had been hidden under a large textbook and handed Chuck a color photograph of the microscope's image.

"It looks to me like a bunch of cells," Chuck said apologetically, "but I'm not a biologist."

"However, you've lived here for so long and it's one of your hobbies, so you know indigenous plants better than anyone in the state."

Chuck scrutinized the fruit. "I don't have a clue. Could it be a mutated hybrid of a blackberry? Or an accidental grafting of a blueberry?"

Joshua looked baffled. "In truth, I don't even know what genus it is; my guess would be *Rubus*, making it similar to a blackberry or loganberry."

"Or *Vaccinium*," Chuck said, thinking it might be a variant of the blueberry.

Joshua slid one of the textbooks in front of Chuck. "This is the closest plant I've found so far," he said, pointing to an artist's rendition done in colorful pastels, "but that plant hasn't been seen around here, or anywhere for that matter, since the end of the gold rush in the later part of the eighteen hundreds."

"Very possiblc," Chuck commented.

"What is?"

"The sisters may have uncovered a plant variant that was assumed to be extinct." Chuck then popped another berry in this mouth and tasted its sweetness. "You're right—delicious. Sweeter than any blackberry with a hint of strawberry."

Joshua ate another as well before continuing. "What's equally fascinating is that the bush seems to have a symbiotic relationship with a type of fire ant that I've never seen in the area. The shrubs are infested with them, so much so that it's impossible to pick any of the fruit without being attacked." He then described how the birds dropped the fruit while in flight in order to knock the ants off the berries.

"Did you see any pollinators—any honeybees?"

Joshua thought for a moment and then shook his head. "None. I know this sounds crazy, but I think the ants were pollinating the flowers. I'm pretty sure I saw what looked like pollen sacs on their legs."

Chuck's eyebrows shot up in surprise. "Really?"

"I'm not sure, but it would seem virtually impossible for another insect to get to the fruit without being stung."

Chuck took a closer look at the branch. "Fascinating," he whispered. "Did you get any samples of the ants?"

"No, I thought it was the berries that were of interest."

Chuck smiled. "You would, being an agriculturalist. I'll be attending Sunday liturgy at the monastery tomorrow morning and will ask Sister Claire to show me the berry patch after the service."

Joshua laughed. "It's a little bigger than a patch, Chuck. These plants cover several acres."

Chuck continued to study the branch. "I have always found it fascinating how, more often than not, world-altering discoveries are discovered by accident."

"World-altering?" Joshua asked with some skepticism. "The berries?"

"No, young Joshua," Chuck replied. "The ants . . . definitely, the ants."

Knowing full well that Lynn, who was as determined to stay away from Mark as Mark was to stay away from her, would not be returning to Montis anytime soon, Pam had ample time to improve upon Coco's new living quarters. With three cans of tuna, an old quilt and several pillows in hand, she returned to the barn. During her walk down Farm to Market to the barn's driveway, she practiced her apology for opening the window while strengthening her argument as to why Lynn's champion Birman cat was, and would continue to be, relegated to an old horse stall.

"The most important thing," Pam rehearsed, "is that your Coco is no worse for wear, and it's fortunate that, despite the raccoon's dismay, I caught the teenagers before anything too serious could happen." She smirked when she thought of another retort: Lynn, your cat is a hormone-raging floozy who was looking for a one-night stand with a sexy, masked bandit that mistook her pregnancy scent for that of a female raccoon in heat.

Pam pulled the stall door open. "Where are you, Coco?" she cooed.

The stall was empty.

"Coco?" she called out.

Pam held her breath, trying to hear the faintest of responses.

When there was none, she darted out of the stall and began to look frantically around the barn. She climbed the ladder to the hayloft even though she knew that it would have been impossible for Coco to have found her way up there, but the loft would give Pam an aerial view of the inside of the barn. But all she saw was Old Jesse standing quietly by the corner of the middle stall.

Back on the ground floor, she called again, "Coco!"

Suddenly, there was a soft, high-pitched meow coming from behind her.

Pam twirled around and came face-to-face with the bull.

*Meow.*

"Coco?"

Pam inched forward and peeked inside Jesse's stall. Curled up in a bed of clean, dry wood shavings was Coco, as content as a very pregnant cat could be.

"Oh, my—"

The bull snorted and shook its horns. Pam leaped back just as Jesse threw his head in the air again, though he made no attempt to break down the door. That could happen at any second, Pam thought wearily.

"Coco, come!" Pam whispered, as if she were calling a young puppy that was just starting to learn its commands.

*Meow,* Coco responded and began purring.

The bull circled its massive body around in the stall and lowered its snout against the cat. Its nose was so close to the cat's head that when it exhaled, Coco's ears blew back.

"No!" Pam screamed, thinking that the bull was about to kill Coco.

Instead, Jesse kept his enormous head hung low to the ground, allowing Coco to rub her face against his muzzle.

"Okay, Coco, the fun is over. Come here, kitty."

But Coco wasn't the least bit interested in leaving.

When Pam shook the stall door to get Coco's attention, the bull looked at Pam and tossed his head in the air, snorting wildly. The beast moved sideways so it was standing directly between Pam and the cat.

Pam threw up her arms. "Fine, you win. If you love that cat so much, then you can keep an eye on her. I don't have time for this," she said as she turned and walked away.

Suddenly, the cat screamed out in the most bloodcurdling sound Pam had ever heard. Thinking that the bull had just stepped on the poor animal, Pam ran back to the stall.

Another scream from Coco. But the bull was on the opposite side of the stall.

Pam looked through the bars and saw Coco restlessly circling in the bed she had formed with the shavings. Coco bore down as another contraction waved through her body.

"Oh, no," Pam said. "Not here . . . not now."

Before Pam could think of what to do, Coco laid down and delivered the first kitten, then immediately licked the sac from its face. The bull approached Coco's bed and sniffed hard enough to send shavings into the air. He then backed away and stood quietly in the far corner.

Just then, the school bell rang out across the Montis compound, clanging three times. It was the bell that Pam used to call Mark when he was working in the barn. She looked at her watch and guessed that he had returned from the airport and was now looking for her.

Coco screamed out again, but with less intensity than before. Pam watched as another kitten was born.

The bell clanged.

There was nothing Pam could do right then to help Coco. "I'll be back," she told the cat as she hurried out of the barn.

ELEVEN

# *Years*

When Pam reached the crest of the orchard, she caught sight of Mark standing on the porch with the bell rope still in his hand, looking down Farm to Market Road, no doubt expecting that she would be driving up in one of their utility vehicles. Although she was breathing heavily from sprinting up the hill, she continued to jog toward the inn.

The bell rang out another three times.

"Mark!" she called out, waving to him. "I'm here!"

When Mark spotted her, he jumped off the porch and ran across the road. "Hey, honey, Kay's here," he said. For some reason, he seemed to be trying to block her view of her mother.

"How is she?" Pam asked through short breaths. "How does she look?"

"She looks great . . . really great," Mark said, running alongside her, "but we need to talk."

"We can talk later," she said as she crossed Farm to Market Road.

"But Pam," Mark said, grabbing her arm, "there's something you need to know."

In her excitement, she broke free and ran up the stairs and into the lobby of the inn.

"Mom?" Pam called out.

"In here," Kay sung out.

Mark was on Pam's heels as she dashed into the living room. "I need to tell you something, honey," he said, trying to catch up with her.

"It can wait," she said over her shoulder. When Pam saw her mother standing by the window, she cried out, "You're finally here!" They hugged each other so tightly it was obvious neither wanted to let go. After a long embrace, Pam studied Kay from head to toe. "You look wonderful."

Kay touched Pam's cheek. "I've missed you so much."

Mark cleared his throat, hoping to get Pam's attention.

Pam took her mother's hand. "How was the trip? Tell me everything."

Mark coughed.

"What is it, Mark?" Pam asked, turning on her heels.

Across the room, a stranger was standing next to her husband.

"Excuse me," Pam said, blushing. Thinking the man was a vacationer who wanted to make a reservation, she asked, "May we help you?"

At first, no one spoke.

Pam looked at the man, who was looking at her mother, who was staring at Mark. Her glance came full circle. "What's going on?" she asked.

"This is what I wanted to tell you, honey," Mark said. "Kay brought a friend."

"I know. Where's Noreen?" she asked, looking around the room again.

"Noreen's not the friend she brought," he said, tilting his head several times toward the stranger.

Pam furrowed her brows. "I don't understand."

Kay strolled over to the man and put her arm through his. "This is Robert Day. Robert, this is my daughter, Pam."

The older gentleman grinned. "So I guessed," he said with a twinkle in his eyes. "It's very nice to finally meet you. Kay has told me so much about you."

Pam was speechless.

"You can close your mouth, dear," Kay said to her daughter as she used her index finger to push Pam's jaw up.

"Kay invited Robert to our reunion, honey," Mark said as delicately as possible. "Isn't that nice?"

Pam tried to clear her head, but it was filled with a hundred questions. "Oh" was all she could say.

Mark decided to push forward. "Let's show you to your rooms," he said.

Kay flipped a delicate finger in the air. "One room will be just fine, Mark."

Pam was shocked. "Mother!"

"Oh, Pam, we're not teenagers," she retorted.

Mark put his hand on Robert's back to escort him out of the war zone. "Why don't we go out and get the luggage," he suggested.

"Good idea," Robert agreed.

Once the men were out of the room, Pam spun around and stared at her mother. "*Who in the world is Robert?*" she demanded, swallowing each word.

"A close friend of mine, dear."

Pam strained to see the meaning behind her words. "How close, Mother?"

Kay sauntered around the large living room, looking at the paintings on the wall. "We've been dating for about a year."

Pam felt as if someone had pushed the air out of her chest. "*A year?* But you never told me."

Kay's smile became a wince. "The time never seemed right."

"We talk almost every week!" Pam argued.

"Well, darling, I knew how you would respond."

Pam's felt her defenses go up. "And how would that be?"

Kay raised her arms and flung her hands loosely at the wrist. "Need I say more?"

"But why would you bring him *here*? You can't be *that* close."

"That's not really true. We're *together*, if you know what I mean," Kay said, with a wink.

"No," Pam said slowly. "I don't know what you mean." She resisted shooting a sarcastic wink back at her mother.

"Oh, Pam," Kay said very lightheartedly. "For goodness' sake, we have a sexual relationship."

Her eyes opened wide. "Mother!"

"Well, I'm so glad you're happy for me, dear," Kay said, kissing her daughter on the cheek. "Now, let's go help the men unpack."

Before Pam could reply, Kay was out the door.

After showing Kay and Robert to their room, Mark left them alone to rest and returned to the kitchen, where he found Pam pacing the floor. The minute he closed the door behind him, he was assaulted by a barrage of questions.

"Do you think she has dementia? Maybe she's lost her senses and doesn't know what she's doing," Pam said, talking a mile a minute.

"I think—" Mark started to say.

"She shouldn't be behaving like this."

"Kay's not—"

"An affair is *so* unbecoming."

Mark raised a finger. "I don't think it's an—"

"I'm sure he's taking advantage of her. He's probably broke," she ranted on.

"Robert doesn't appear—"

"And she should have told me!" Pam yelled.

"She probably wanted—"

"It's been going on for a *year*!"

It was obvious to Mark that Pam was an emotional wreck, spiraling out of control. Tears welled up in her eyes. "They—"

"For a year!" she repeated.

Mark reached out to her. "She seems quite—"

"Well, she certainly doesn't have my approval," Pam said.

"That's good because she doesn't seem to be asking for it," Mark slipped in, stunned that he was finally able to finish a sentence. But his comment wasn't well received.

Pam glared at him. "Whose side are you on?"

"Honey, this isn't a battle—there are no sides," Mark said, trying to calm her down. "But I've never seen your mother happier. And Robert seems like a really nice guy. I think both of them are incredibly lucky to have found each other."

A tear rolled down Pam's cheek. "But why didn't she let me know? I'm her only family."

"Maybe she wanted to tell you in person—give you a chance to know Robert before you came to any conclusions."

Pam grimaced. "A little too late for that, don't you think?"

"She also knows that you don't like change," Mark added tentatively.

Pam had no response because she knew just how true that statement was.

"Why don't you go talk with her?" Mark suggested. "You two love each other so much. Don't let Robert get in the way of enjoying the little time you have together."

The Windsor clock chimed, catching Mark's attention. "Has Lynn called to cancel yet?" he asked.

"No," Pam said, running her fingers through her hair. "She arrived a few hours ago."

"*What!?* She's here?"

Pam shook her head, thinking more about her mother than Lynn. "No."

"So she didn't come?" Mark asked in relief.

"Yes, she did,"

"*Pam, you're driving me nuts!*" he said, taking hold of her arms to grab her attention. "Is she or is she not here?"

"I'm sorry," she said, finally hearing the alarm in Mark's voice. "She arrived a few hours ago, and after moving her cat in, she drove to town. She should be back shortly."

"I can't believe she had the nerve to show up like that," he said.

"Who? Kay or Lynn?"

"Lynn, of course," Mark said, jumping up from the chair. "I have some errands to run in Wheatley." He grabbed his car keys that were lying on the table. "I'll be back later."

"Given Coco's mishap, I guarantee that you'll be the least of her concerns when she returns," Pam said.

Had Mark heard Pam's comment, he might have paused to ask who Coco was, but he was so intent on escaping before his sister returned that any explanation would have made little difference in his resolve.

An hour later, Pam knocked on the door to her mother's suite. "Yes," Kay said in a light voice. Seeing her daughter's face peek in, she smiled. "This room is charming, Pam. You and Mark must be so proud of everything you've done here."

Pam stood in the doorway, feeling awkward. "Thank you," she replied.

Robert continued to unpack a suitcase that lay open on the bed. Pam watched in disbelief as he carefully folded Kay's bras and underwear before putting them in the dresser. Her heart ached as she remembered how her father used to do the same so many years ago.

"Kay told me that the monastery was all but ruined by fire and neglect when you bought it five years ago," he said, as he hung one of Kay's blouses in the closet. "You've accomplished an amazing transformation."

Pam inhaled deeply. "Thank you, Robert. Would you mind if Mom and I have a minute alone?"

"Not at all. In fact, think that's a wonderful idea," he said with a warm smile. "Do you know where I can find a strong cup of coffee?"

"There's a fresh pot in the dining room," Pam said, and explained briefly how to get there.

Before leaving, Robert said to Kay, "Don't lift any of the heavy suitcases. I'll help you finish unpacking when I get back."

"You're a dear," she replied.

After Robert closed the door behind him, Pam started pacing. Kay picked up her small toiletry case and disappeared into the bathroom. When she returned, Pam was still pacing.

"Pamela, you're wearing out the carpet. What are you so nervous about?" Kay asked.

Pam took her mother's arms and sat her down on the edge of the bed. "We need to talk, Mom," she said.

"About Robert, I assume? I promise you, I don't need the birds-and-the-bees lecture."

"Of course, about Robert," Pam said. "You have to admit, he's quite a shock."

"Only when you see him in his swim trunks." She laughed. When she saw that Pam wasn't smiling, she became more serious. "All right, I admit our relationship took me totally by surprise as well." She paused. "I suppose that's why I didn't tell you, or anyone, when we started dating. It was so foreign to me. Can you imagine, *me* having a boyfriend at *my* age?"

"It's no surprise—you're a beautiful woman," Pam said, gently pushing back her mother's bangs.

"But it had been so long since I was with someone," Kay confided. "I wanted to tell you, darling, but I didn't even know how I felt, and I was so unsure where the relationship was going. And then one small step led to another, and we gradually became more serious." She looked into her daughter's eyes. "I should have told you, I should have shared all of this with you, but it wasn't because I was trying to hide something. I just couldn't quite believe that I was so lucky to have found a man like Robert, and I thought it might not last."

"But now you seem so casual about your relationship with him."

"I guarantee, Pam, casual is one thing I'm not," Kay said. "I treasure him, and our relationship, more than anything in my life."

The words stung Pam. "You make it sound like you *love* him."

Kay was surprised. "Well, of course I do!" she proclaimed. "He's the most caring man I've ever met."

Pam winced. "More than Dad?"

"That was a lifetime ago." Kay looked down at her hands. "I don't want to compare the two—it's not fair to either of them."

Pam took a deep breath and sifted through all the questions she had, trying to decide which one to ask first. "How did you meet?"

Kay smiled at the memory. "At the opera. We both love the theater."

"Has he ever been married? Does he have children?" Pam's questioning began to sound more like a rapid-fire interrogation.

"His wife passed away eight years ago," Kay answered. "And he has two boys who are both married with children of their own."

"Have you met them?"

"We have dinner with them every couple of weeks," she said.

The thought that her mother had another life separate from hers tore at Pam's heart.

"You would like them," Kay added.

"No doubt," she said, her words dripping in sarcasm. "Where does he live?"

The question took Kay by surprise. "As of four weeks ago, with me."

"*In our house?*"

"In *my* house, yes," Kay said, her tone becoming more parental.

Pam's thoughts turned suspicious. "Is he living off you?"

Kay laughed. "Are you really asking me if he's a gigolo? He's wealthier than I am, for heaven's sake. In fact, he pays for just about everything."

"But why do you have to live together?"

"We're better together—life is more exciting," Kay explained. "It's as simple as that." She paused, giving Pam time to consider what she'd said. "You're making it into something much bigger than it is. I found a man whom I love and who loves me. With any luck, we'll be together for many more years." She took Pam's hand in her own. "Someday, you'll be my age, Pam, and I will be long gone. If God is willing, I hope Mark is beside you, sharing those final years. But if not, if fate doesn't follow what you have so carefully planned out, I wouldn't want you to be alone if there was a man as kind as Robert who offered his heart and soul to you."

Pam started crying. "I do want you to be happy," she whispered.

Kay fought back her own tears as she brushed them off her daughter's cheek. "I know you do, darling," she said tenderly. "And I know you'll fall in love with Robert as much as I have."

"I'm sure I will."

"Now," Kay said, changing her tone, "we're looking forward to a marvelous week. Could Robert and I borrow your car tomorrow morning?"

"Sure," Pam said, catching her breath. "But if there is somewhere you want to go, Mark can take you."

Kay returned to the chore of unpacking and pulled from their suitcase two pairs of sneakers, a camera, water bottles, and an empty backpack. "It looks like you're getting ready to climb Everest," Pam teased. "Did you bring those for Mark and me?"

"No," Kay replied. "Robert and I plan on doing a little canoeing and white-water rafting while we're here."

"*You can't be serious!* River rafting around here is very dangerous."

"And that's exactly why we're getting a good guide," she said. "We hear those class-four rapids can be really tricky."

"Mother!"

"Well, darling, this is such a beautiful part of the country. We certainly want to take full advantage of all the outdoor activities that are offered."

"Since when do you like outdoor activities, Mother?"

"I always have. And while we're here, we want a little adventure."

"No, you don't," Pam corrected her. "No one's taking full advantage of anything. This isn't a park in Greenwich, Connecticut, Mom. These are the Rockies, and there's a lot of dangerous wilderness out there. You and Robert should just relax around the inn, and then Mark and I will take you to the fair when it opens."

Kay withdrew a heavy pair of hiking boots from her suitcase. "I think we may have a different idea of what fun is, darling."

The Lumby Lines

# Lumby Forum

**An open bulletin board for our town residents**

July 14

---

Come to Dakin's Garage for a free tune-up with any major engine job. Try us once and you'll never go anywhere again.

---

Seniors for Lumby kayaking class 10:00 a.m. Tuesday at Woodrow Lake dock. Must supply own life vest, sunscreen. Defibrillator provided.

---

Monday Pray and Fasting at the Episcopal Church beginning at 9:00. $18.00 per person. Cost includes meals.

---

The Lumby Checker Club (formerly known as the Lumby Scrabble Club, formerly known as the Lumby Chess Club) has been renamed the Lumby Monopoly Club. Donations of board games, money and Get Out of Jail cards would be appreciated. Join us 7:30 Wednesday nights, 2nd floor library.

---

Monthly meeting of the Young Mothers club for those who want to become mothers will meet this Thursday morning with the Minister in the Presbyterian Church parlor.

---

Ed's Plumbing. The best place to take a leak. 925-5462.

---

Join us. Episcopal Church Sunday sermon: Jesus walks on water. Bible study Sunday night: Searching for Jesus.

---

Ice Cream Social at the Lumby Feed Store Tuesday 5:00. Women who are giving milk should arrive thirty minutes early.

---

Mrs. Wilbur sincerely thanks all those who sent flowers, condolence cards and contributions on the death of her husband.

TWELVE

# *Chicken*

After a successful open house for one of her listings on the north end of town, Joan Stokes stopped by her office to gather the paperwork she needed for her next appointment. She wasn't a bit curious about Mike McNear's earlier phone call. Over the years, he had called her on several occasions with grand plans for selling his property, but when it came time for ink to be put on the contract, he always balked. Joan was sure this time would be no different.

Although Joan had lived in and been the primary Realtor around Lumby for most of her adult life, she had seldom gone down Killdrop Road. In fact, as she turned her Audi onto the poorly maintained dirt road, she tried to remember when she was there last. Perhaps four or five years ago, she thought, as her tire hit a deep pothole.

Killdrop Road was one of the first horse-and-buggy roads that was formed in the newly founded town of Lumby during the eighteen hundreds. Heading west through town, West Main Street came to an abrupt end shortly after crossing over Goose Creek. To the right was a trail that residents referred to as Milldrop since it was only used as a logging path to the evergreen-covered mountains above. No doubt all of the wagons that had traversed the trail's narrow and at times treacherous slopes, with its fatal drop-offs, had been making their way to or from the lumber mill in town.

When the U.S. Division of Forestry decided to reduce its ownership of Northwest woodlands in the 1890s, Augustus McNear, Mike McNear's grandfather, acted quickly and purchased three thousand acres due west of Goose Creek. However, local habits were hard to break, and many residents continued using Milldrop Road, and the property around it for their personal four-season recreation—it did, after all, have some of the best trout streams and hunting fields in the area.

Being able to tolerate the trespassers for only so long, Augustus finally took matters into his own hands and claimed what was rightfully his by posting a large sign immediately after the bridge at Goose Creek: KILLDROP ROAD IS NOW PRIVATE. ALL TRESPASSERS WILL BE SHOT.

No one quite knew if Augustus was simply a poor speller or if renaming the road was his attempt to threaten anyone thinking about venturing onto his land, but eventually, the new name settled in and became legal on the town's books.

Over the next century, the McNear assets increased by another one thousand acres as a result of shrewd business dealings made by McNear's father and then Mike McNear himself. And none of them ever spent a penny more than was necessary on making the road passable.

Joan tightened her hands on the steering wheel as the Audi's front shocks gave way when she hit a water-runoff trench halfway to Mike's farm. "Impossible," she said loudly, and accelerated even faster, thinking that she might be able to skim over the ruts.

As Hank jumped back from the speeding car, the compass around his neck flew into the air. He pushed his white construction hat off his eyes and shook his head. With cars boomeranging in and out of the massive divots, it was a dangerous location for anyone to be working. Although he wore a bright fluorescent vest, he felt it provided little protection in such an adverse environment.

For the better part of two days, Hank had kept one wing on the tripod and his beak to the transit, surveying the front acreage of McNear's farm, beginning with the corner pin closest to West Main Street. Under his other wing, he held a copy of the plat map that had been drawn twenty years before. He blinked quickly as he watched Joan Stokes across his triangulated sight line.

Speed only made the driving worse. Slowing the car to a crawl, Joan tried to more carefully navigate the road hazards, but it was virtually impossible to miss all the ditches, furrows and holes. This road was reason enough not to list his house, she thought. Thank goodness he only called her every five years—one more trip out here, and her car would need new suspension.

As the road curved to the left, Mike McNear's farm came into full view. Joan stopped the car to assess that critical first impression, that thumbs-up or thumbs-down emotional reaction her customers would have upon first seeing the property.

"What a dump," she whispered, recalling a word that she had deliberately erased from her vocabulary when she became a Realtor so long ago. "A gem in the rough," she corrected herself, and immediately began thinking of other buzzwords for the ad she was running in the local paper. "Unlimited possibilities" might also work.

The farmhouse was old and neglected, as were the four cattle barns, chicken houses and assorted outbuildings. Although there had been no rain for at least a week, everything looked like mud.

Joan rolled down her window and inhaled, then immediately turned up her nose; everything smelled of manure—cow, goat or pig, it didn't matter. Manure was manure to Joan Stokes, and its only useful purpose was for her flower garden.

"Oh, my," she said aloud, and quickly rolled up the window.

As Joan turned onto a tractor path that led to the farmhouse, her car bounced out of control. Just as she passed the broken gate, about a hundred feet from the front door, a chicken that had been resting in the furrow woke too late to get out of the way. Joan gasped as the car ran over the bird. A second later, she looked in her rearview mirror—the chicken was as flat as a pancake.

For a moment, she wondered why the chicken didn't cross the street.

Just as Joan put the car in park, two huge, slobbering dogs ran out from behind a broken screen door. One started biting at her car's front tire, and the other lunged at the driver-side door. Startled, Joan slammed her hand on the horn and kept it there, hoping that the dogs would back off.

"Get outta here!" Mike McNear yelled as he stepped through the front door onto the dilapidated porch. He picked up a dog bone and threw it at the dog that still had his incisors sunk into the tire. "Drop it, Bo!" he said.

Mike's dogs did what his dogs always did: ignored him.

Mike reached inside the front door of the house and pulled out a shotgun, aimed it in the air and fired. That was just enough to grab the dogs' attention and stop their assault on the Audi. Mike shot the gun once more.

"Get to the barn, now!" he yelled as he walked stiff-legged out to meet his guest. "Sorry about that, Joan. They don't like strangers," he explained as he opened her car door.

"Well, that's certainly understandable," she said, taking his hand and stepping out into several inches of mud.

"Should have worn boots," he advised.

Standing next to each other, the two offered a startling contrast: Mike, a haggard man tired of life whose farm clothes had seen better days years before, and Joan, a vibrant woman also in her sixties with bright eyes, glistening silver hair and a petite frame that was always impeccably dressed in bold, coordinating prints.

"I'll keep that in mind," she said, suppressing a smile. "I hate to tell you, Mike, but I ran over one of your chickens back there," she said, pointing toward the dead poultry.

Mike lifted his gun, aimed and shot at the already-flattened chicken. Pieces of its body went flying into the air, but there was no blood. In fact, there were no feathers, and the head exploded as if it were a plastic tennis ball.

Joan looked quizzically at Mike.

"That's just a rubber chicken I wallop every now and again—keeps the other chickens in line, if you know what I mean."

Joan continued to stare in disbelief. "I do," she said, although she didn't at all.

"Let's take a walk," he said. "Want to show you the improvements I've made."

Mike's stride was three times that of Joan's so he was yards ahead of her after taking just a few steps. "New fan in the chicken coop—cost me eight hundred bucks," he said, pointing to one of the large outbuildings. "And I'm throwing in all the crap in the shed—well-kept equipment in there. You want to see that now?"

Joan raised her hand. "Later," she assured him. "But that's good to know."

"Had a fair spring—another eight calves."

"And that's good to know as well," Joan said, jogging to keep up with him.

He led her between two milking barns, adding, "New pumps and stanchions."

"Ah," she said.

When they were past the outbuildings, halfway back to the farmhouse, Joan paused, slowly turned 360 degrees, and then focused her eyes on the mountain. That was the part of the deal that was truly worth something. "How many acres do you have, Mike?"

"Four thousand, three hundred, twenty-two, with options for another eight hundred further up the north slope."

She continued to look past her immediate surroundings, past the stacked straw bales and manure mounds. A gem in the rough. "How many of the forty-three hundred acres are cleared for farm use?"

"A little over four hundred."

She didn't take her eyes off the mountain. "Why don't we go inside and talk?" she suggested.

Although Mike was surprised that Joan wasn't interested in finishing his tour, he welcomed the idea of getting down to business and to seeing some numbers written in a contract.

"Good," he said. "Bess made us a cobbler just for the occasion." He looked down at Joan's feet—her shoes and ankles were covered with muck. "Should have worn boots," he repeated as he headed into the house.

Once inside, Joan saw that nothing had changed since her last visit, although she was sure Bess had been working her fingers raw cleaning since Mike had called the day before.

"Bess, how delightful to see you again," Joan said, giving the woman a hug.

Although Joan was several years older than Bess, she looked at least fifteen years younger. Bess blushed. "I'm sorry we aren't quite ready for you."

"Your home is as lovely as ever," Joan said, trying to put her at ease.

"The cobbler, Bess," Mike said sternly. To Joan, his reminder sounded more like a serious reprimand for not having the dessert already on the table.

"Coming, coming," Bess said, shuffling into the kitchen. A minute later she returned holding a hot Pyrex pie plate between two potholders.

"Ice cream," Mike said.

Bess rolled her eyes and then winked at Joan. "Yes, I know, Mike. Believe it or not, I've served cobbler a thousand times without your help. I think I can do it just once more without destroying the universe as we know it."

"Humph," Mike grunted, and took his seat at the head of the table. Then, without pretense or forewarning, Mike blurted out, "What number do you have in mind?"

Bess sat across from him, and Joan positioned her chair halfway between them. "That all depends on how quickly you want to sell it," she answered.

"Tomorrow," he said adamantly.

"What?!" Bess exclaimed.

"You heard me, Mother," he said, using her nickname as he did when he knew she was angry at him.

"We agreed last night that we would wait until the fall," she said.

"This morning I decided I've milked one too many cows." He turned to Joan. "I want out—now."

Joan intentionally fumbled with some papers in her briefcase to slow down the conversation. She opened her notepad and began to scribble some words and numbers, buying time for Bess's and Mike's emotions to calm. Finally she looked up.

"I think three million would be a possible starting place."

Mike jumped out of his chair. "Three million? My place is worth twice that! That's less than a thousand an acre."

"But a lot of it is mountain—it's not tillable or buildable because of the vertical drop," Joan explained.

Bess placed her hands squarely in front of her, spreading her fingers as wide as she could. "Are there similar farms on the market?" she asked.

"There are," Joan said, handing Bess a six-page printout of farm listings. "These are comparables—current listings of properties similar to yours—that I printed out from the multilisting service. All are within an hour of here. Some have more acreage with no buildings, some a little less land with newer houses. But in general, you can get a good sense of where your farm would fall into the mix."

Bess looked through the sheets, asking various questions as she studied the details of each listing. "What is this line, 'Comm'?"

"It indicates whether the land is commercial," Joan explained.

Bess continued to look at the listings. "The price per acre seems much higher for commercial property."

"It is," Joan said. "Although the size of your property could give the buyer commercial options, I assumed you wanted to sell it as a residential property . . . as a farm."

"Tear down the buildings for all I care," Mike said. "If you can get more from a developer who wants to bulldoze the place, that's fine by me."

"Mike!" Bess exclaimed. "You can't be serious!"

"Watch me," he said. "Once we're out of here, they can do whatever they want."

"But you know that a developer with this amount of land could change Lumby forever. He would control everything."

"Just the way I've controlled everything for fifty years? Ha! Don't make me laugh," Mike said bitterly. "My family founded this town and I'm the single largest landowner in Chatham County, but I've never gotten the respect I've deserved." His cheeks were flushed with anger. "You find me the biggest real estate developer you can, and I'll sell the land in a blink of an eye just to teach this town a lesson it should have learned a long time ago."

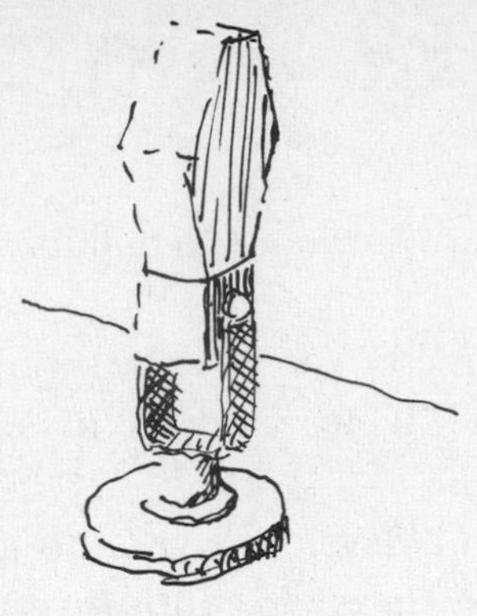

# THIRTEEN
# *Protecting*

When Lynn returned to Montis later that afternoon, she looked around for Mark and, seeing that the coast was clear, slipped into the guest annex unnoticed. Quietly opening her bedroom door so as not to disturb Coco if she were asleep, Lynn tiptoed in. She was startled to find the room covered with white goose feathers. What was more disturbing was that Coco, as well as all of her pet's belongings, was nowhere in sight. She assumed she was in the wrong room until she saw the sweater she had draped over the back of the chair before leaving earlier in the day.

"Coco?" she whispered, looking around the room before checking the bathroom and then the closet. "Coco?" she called out, her voice becoming more anxious.

After scouring every inch of the suite and finding no evidence that her cat had ever been there, Lynn panicked. She ran out of the guesthouse and across the courtyard and banged on Pam and Mark's door. Although Mark was the last person she wanted to see, Coco's well-being took precedence.

"Pam? Are you there?" she called out.

When no one answered, Lynn ran through the dining room and

found Pam in the kitchen talking to the inn's chef. Lynn charged into the room. "Where is she?" she cried.

Focused on the evening's menu, Pam asked, "Who?"

Lynn's face was beet red. "Coco! Where's Coco?" she shrieked.

"Oh, Coco," Pam said, collecting her thoughts while preparing for an onslaught. She forced a casual, lighthearted tone. "The funniest thing . . ."

"Where is she, Pam?" Lynn demanded.

André, who apparently wanted nothing more than to get out of the line of fire, stood up and retreated to the stove.

"Lynn, calm down," Pam said, arranging papers on the table. "Coco is just fine. In fact, more than fine. . . . You have more than Coco now."

Lynn narrowed her eyes. "What are you talking about? Where is she?"

"Well, it's a funny story," Pam said, taking Lynn by the arm and escorting her outside. "First, there were feathers everywhere. It seems Coco went to town with a few of the down pillows on the bed. And then she went out for some fresh air, and that's where she was approached by the raccoon."

"What do you mean *approached*?"

"Well, lustfully targeted might be a more accurate way of saying it, if you know what I mean." Pam winked at her.

Lynn took a second to process what Pam was saying. "*A raccoon tried to have sex with my little Coco?*"

Pam kept marching Lynn toward Farm to Market Road. "That would be one way of putting it. But I stopped the shenanigans, even though Coco seemed quite interested in his advances." As soon as she said it, Pam wished she could take back the words. "If you know what I mean. When I approached those crazy kids, the raccoon headed for the hills, and poor, dear, sweet Coco was left with a broken heart."

Lynn was speechless with horror.

Pam charged forward with the story. "As there was a lot more bedding and furniture that Coco could have damaged, I thought it best that she be given a suite of her own. So I brought her down to the barn and made her as comfortable as possible."

Lynn felt dizzy. "My priceless cat is in a *barn*?"

"And just loving it. Maybe a little too much," Pam said. "I went back to retrieve her bed and all of her toys, but when I returned, Coco had moved into another stall that was a little . . . inaccessible."

"Why was it inaccessible?"

"Well . . . there's a bull in it," Pam said mildly.

When Lynn stumbled, Pam tightened her grip on Lynn's arm so she wouldn't fall.

"And then the funniest thing," Pam said brightly. "Coco went into labor! I called our veterinarian, Tom Candor, and gave him all the details. He assured me that she was doing just fine."

"So who's with her now?"

Pam hesitated, searching for an answer. "Old Jesse."

"Is that one of your employees?"

"Not exactly," Pam said, and picked up her pace toward the barn. "Jesse is the bull."

Upon hearing that, Lynn broke into a full sprint toward the barn. By the time she dashed into the center aisle, she was completely out of breath. In a panic she looked in the first stall and saw Coco's bed and her toys scattered in the sawdust. She turned to Pam, who had caught up with her, and began to open her mouth, but before she could ask, Pam pointed at the next stall.

The sleeping bull woke up with a start. Jesse snorted to clear his lungs and then tried to poke his head through the bars on the upper half of the door. Lynn gasped when she came eye to eye with the enormous animal. She jumped back, which startled the bull all the more.

*Meow.*

That familiar call was followed by a chorus of tiny, high-pitched squeals. In the far corner, Lynn spotted Coco with a large litter of kittens squirming around her belly. Old Jesse turned and approached the nursing mother. He lowered his massive head and opened his mouth.

Lynn gasped. "They'll be killed!"

She was about to charge in to rescue her cherished pet when Pam grabbed her arm. "I think it's okay," she said. "Coco's been in there all day, and he's had every opportunity to hurt her if he wanted. The way he's staying so close to her, I think he would probably kill you before he'd harm Coco or those kittens."

Lynn pulled her arm from Pam's grasp. "Well, that's certainly reassuring," she said sarcastically.

The bull started to lick Coco, whose purring could easily be heard by the women.

"Just leave them be," Pam suggested.

"This is ridiculous," Lynn protested. "I'm not going to leave her in a *barn*."

"I think you should," Pam said, staring at the bull. "For whatever reason, Old Jesse seems to be protecting Coco, so I doubt you could get to them even if you wanted."

Lynn crept into the adjacent stall and bent down, trying to peer through the spaces between the wooden planks. She stared at the kittens in awe. "Eleven," she whispered. "No, twelve."

Pam stood directly behind her, studying the newborns. Even from a distance, the color differences between the mother and the kittens were noticeable. "Boy, given that they're purebreds, I'm surprised they all look so different from Coco," she commented.

In her panic, Lynn hadn't notice the obvious: the kittens looked radically dissimilar from each other as well as from their mother. She rubbed her eyes and looked again at her show-winning champion Birman, which had been bred to the highest-ranked Birman stud in the country. Lynn's gaze turned puzzled. Wanting a closer view, she lowered herself on her hands and knees and pressed her face against the largest crack in the stall boards.

Although she had never seen such a young litter of kittens before, Lynn was certain that Birman kittens, as with other colorpoint cats, were born white; only at a week old did the darker "point" colors on their heads and legs begin to show.

The kittens in Coco's litter were every imaginable color combination: four were calicos with pronounced patches of tan, black and white; several were various shades of gray with darker tiger stripes; and a few were orange tigers. One appeared to be solid black except for its two front paws, which were white. The smallest of the litter had a dark tortoiseshell coat with a caramel-colored tip at the end of its tail.

Lynn stared at the mongrels in disbelief. How could those mixed-breed kittens have come from that pedigree? she asked herself again and again.

"I love the little calico trying to nurse Coco's tail," Pam said, pointing at the kittens. "And the tortoise-colored one is precious."

"This is all wrong," Lynn muttered, incredulous.

"I know it's not ideal, Lynn, but I really think Coco and her kittens are safe in there. Nature has a funny way of working itself out when left alone."

"No. It's the kittens—they're wrong," Lynn moaned. "They should be pure white."

Pam looked over at the wild assortment of colors. "Seems Coco may have had some fun with the neighborhood tomcat," she teased.

Lynn jumped up and stared down her nose at her sister-in-law. "All of this may be a huge joke to you, Pam, but it means a lot to me!" she barked. "As pathetic as it sounds, Coco is really important in my life, and I've spent a fortune breeding her." Her eyes began to fill with tears. "And you stand there, making light of my efforts." Her face was flushed and her voice had escalated to the point of yelling. "Well, I'd like to see how you would cope if you had to live my life these last few years. And you've been judging me since the second I arrived."

Pam was shocked by Lynn's attack but also felt rightfully embarrassed by her own behavior, and she gave Lynn credit for calling her on it. "You're right," Pam said. "I'm sorry. Maybe I haven't taken this whole Coco thing seriously. But you arrive totally unexpectedly—"

"*How can you say that?*" Lynn spat. "I sent you a note saying that I would be here."

Pam cringed. "You did, but we never thought you would actually show up. Why would we? You've made no attempt to contact Mark since the trial. We didn't think you would want to ruin a family reunion by—" Pam bit her tongue.

"Showing up?" Tears ran down Lynn's face. "Is that what you think? Well, maybe I realized that this might be the last chance I have to reconcile with my brother."

"Then you have to stop avoiding Mark and focus on apologizing to him instead of on the fact that your cat was moved to the barn," Pam said with little sympathy.

Lynn dropped down to her knees in the corner of the stall. "Just leave me alone."

Pam knew it was best to take her sister-in-law's advice and withdrew to the calm of the inn.

~

When Carter Reed drove past the turnoff to the barn in his Lincoln Navigator, neither he nor his wife noticed Pam walking on the dirt drive toward Farm to Market Road. Instead, their gazes were glued on a century-old stone building, the beautifully restored Montis Inn located just ahead.

Carter's wife, Nancy, leaned forward, her hands on the dashboard. "It's much larger than I thought it would be."

"As long as there's enough room for the equipment," Carter responded.

"Maybe you should have told them when they asked why we weren't taking the private plane," she said hesitantly. "I don't think Pam likes surprises, and since Mark specifically asked you not to—"

"Let's not go there again, Nancy." His naturally loud voice boomed in the car. "My staff and all the electronics for my sound studio are in the van right behind us. We're all here. I had no choice."

"If you say so," she demurred.

The national press had called Carter a "round" man; he had a short, round body but also, more recognizable, a deep, clear round voice that was heard each weekday morning on more than four hundred affiliate radio stations with a listening audience of roughly nine million.

Had Carter not been lodged behind the steering wheel, he would have turned around to smack his son's leg. He adjusted the rearview mirror so he could see Corey in the backseat. "We're here. Turn off your iPod."

Corey didn't respond to his father other than to do as he was told, stuffing the headphones into his backpack.

"Get a grip, Corey. You've been acting like a delinquent since we left home," Carter said, glancing at him again in the mirror.

"I just don't see why I had to come," Corey replied, repeating what he had said several times during the eight-hour drive from Seattle.

"Two words: family reunion. And you're part of my family. So suck it up and be polite."

Nancy kept her eyes on the inn. "Your cousin, Jessica, is coming," she reminded her son.

"Great," he said sarcastically. "She's in high school."

"She's sixteen, and you're barely twenty-one. Not much difference," Carter said, although he knew that was an insult to the young man.

Carter turned slowly into the parking lot and pulled up next to a blue rental car. The van that had followed the Reed's car for the four hundred and fifty mile trip parked next to them.

The van's driver, a young man with Asian features and a placid expression, was the first to jump out. He inhaled deeply and stretched out his arms that were stiff from the long drive.

"This place is great," Kano Lee said, slapping his hands together. He opened the back of the van where a sound engineer had been rewiring microphones since leaving Seattle. "Worm, you're up."

"I'm ready to rock and roll," the young man said, hopping out of the van and uncurling his long, thin body. "That seat is murder on my back, but both mics are primed and ready to go." He brought his left knee up to his chest, held it there for several seconds and then did the same with his right knee. At twenty-seven, Worm—or Warren Smith as he was known until high school—had the energy and resilience of a fifteen-year-old, the long hair of a rocker and the technical experience of a man twice his age.

"Where do you want us, boss?" Kano called out.

Carter swung his legs out of the car, grabbed the top of the door and pulled himself out. "Just relax for a minute," he said, gesturing with his hands to hold down the volume.

Nancy, who was also quite heavy, got out of the car and straightened her skirt before walking up to the front porch. She knocked on the massive, deeply carved wood door. "Hello?" she called out. When no one answered, she turned to Carter. "I don't think anyone is—"

The door swung open.

"Nancy!" Mark greeted her, wrapping his arms around his sister. He tried to lift her off the ground as he always had but only brought her to her toes. "I've missed you!" he said, giving her big kisses on both cheeks. He was surprised by how much weight she had gained since the last time they'd seen each other, but he kept that to himself.

"How's my little brother doing?" she asked, getting a good look at him. "Eight years older, but more handsome than ever."

"And you look great," Mark replied.

"Maybe a pound or two heavier," she admitted, "but nothing that a little dieting can't take care of."

"Well, not this week," Mark said. "Pam's lined up some great menus."

Carter stepped onto the porch and barked, "Marko!"

Mark rolled his eyes. He hated the nickname that Carter had used ever since they'd first met. "Carter," Mark said, extending his hand.

"Fine place you have," Carter said in a tone layered with condescension and surprise. "How much did this set you back?"

"Enough," Mark said, dodging the question.

Mark gave Nancy another hug. "It's great to have you guys here. Where's Corey?"

"In the car pulling his things together," Nancy said.

"Corey, get over here," his father bellowed.

The back door opened, and the tall, long-limbed college kid stepped out. Mark's jaw dropped. "That's Corey?"

The boy leaned against the car and waved. "Hey, Uncle Mark."

"Wow, time flies. Grab your stuff, Corey—I have your name attached to a few projects." Mark looked over at the two men standing by the van. "Why don't you go inside, and I'll join you in a minute." He turned back to Carter. "It seems we have some unexpected visitors."

"Actually, they're with me," Carter said.

Mark was confused. "More family?" he guessed.

"Employees," Carter corrected him. "There's been a change of plans, Marko. We'll be broadcasting live from Montis Inn this week."

Mark stared at his brother-in-law in disbelief. "No, you're not, Carter. We talked about that. You said you would run repeats."

"I can't disappoint my fans like that. They've been hearing me talk about coming to Lumby for weeks now. The ratings have skyrocketed."

Mark looked to Nancy for support, but she didn't offer any. "No, Carter," he said. "You can't go back on your word. This is our family reunion."

"Well, it's a done deal, Marko, so suck it up and adjust your thinking. Where do we set up?" he asked. "We need the largest room you have."

"It's not going to happen," Mark said.

Carter didn't wait for Mark to lead the way; he just barged into the lobby of the inn and continued straight into the living room, which he quickly assessed as being large enough to easily accommodate his production. Returning to the porch, he waved to his men.

"In here, boys. Do what you have to," he instructed as they began to remove equipment from the van. Mark's face was still glazed with shock. Carter looked at his watch. "We go live in thirty-nine hours."

## FOURTEEN
# *Transgressions*

By the time Pam returned from the barn, the transformation of Montis Inn into a broadcast studio had begun even though Mark had done his best to halt Carter's invasion. Several large pieces of equipment had been transferred from the van and were being prepped on the front porch before being brought inside. Carter was directing his employees, which apparently included Nancy and Corey, on how to set everything up.

Mark, who had been keeping a watchful eye out for his wife, saw Pam before she noticed any of the commotion, thanks to a tall hedge that ran along the front walkway.

Running down the steps, Mark reached Pam and took her in his arms. "Hey, honey. Where are you going?" he asked cheerfully, trying to block her way. Knowing that Carter's new plans to broadcast from the inn would put additional stress on his wife during the coming week, he wanted to soften the blow as much as possible.

"Mark, I just fought with Lynn—I'm in no mood for games," she said. "And André was expecting me in the dining room twenty minutes ago."

"Just push it through the door," a man yelled out.

"Who was that?" Pam asked, trying to look around her husband.

"Okay, Pam, there's been a slight change. But I don't want you to get mad—I had nothing to do with it. In fact, it might be fun for all of us."

"Then just take that ancient door off its hinges!" the same man called out.

"Is that Carter's voice? What is going on?" Pam demanded.

"Guess what, honey?" Mark said with exaggerated animation. "Carter arrived with Nancy and Corey, who's now a mile tall."

Suddenly, there was a crash, and what looked like a commercial-sized copier came to rest flipped upside down on the sidewalk, just yards behind Mark.

Pam pushed past him, turned the corner and froze when she saw all the equipment on the porch.

"You folks all right?" a young man asked as he leaped off the porch and ran up to Pam.

She looked at his face, a familiar face that had changed markedly. "Corey?"

"Hey, Aunt Pam," he said, smiling.

Then she peered over his shoulder at the paraphernalia being moved inside. "Is all that equipment *yours*?"

"Oh, no, not mine. We're setting up for Monday's broadcast."

Mark jumped in to explain. "That's the surprise, honey. Carter is broadcasting his talk show live from Montis all this coming week. He's calling the segment Lumby on the Air. Is that cool or what?"

"What," Pam answered tartly.

She watched in silence as men she didn't know removed the hundred-year-old door from its iron hinges and set it aside like it was a piece of old trash. "Don't worry about the molding—just be careful with the equipment," a deep, familiar voice said from inside.

"Carter," she whispered.

"Yeah," Corey said. "Dad's stoked to be going on the air during the reunion. New material, as he puts it."

Just then, André walked up the path, stepping around pieces of the broken copier in order to join Pam and Mark. Gawking at the wreckage, he said, "I'm guessing this isn't a good time to talk."

"I'm so sorry," Pam apologized. "I got tied up at the barn . . . and then this happened." Her voice trailed off in helplessness.

"That's understandable." André handed Pam a stack of papers. "Here's what I've pulled together for the first part of the week. Why don't you take a look at it when you have a minute and we can discuss it later this afternoon."

Pam stuffed the pages under her arm without taking her eyes off Carter's workers. "Thanks very much. I'll introduce you to everyone tonight," she said. "Oh, and we hope your daughter will come as well."

André smiled cordially. "Anaïs is looking forward to it."

When Pam and Mark were alone, she looked at her husband for an explanation. "Why is Carter doing this?" she whispered as softly as she could, considering how angry she was. "He promised he would take the week off."

Mark turned his back so his voice wouldn't be heard by anyone except his wife. "Carter said something about the ratings going through the roof when he started talking about going to a family reunion out in the boonies."

"Great," she said. "Ten million folks have been told that Lumby is *the boonies.*"

"Well, honey," Mark said cautiously, "it's really not far from the truth. We do have more cows than people here."

"But they're not hick, podunk cows," Pam sneered. "They're Lumby cows," she added, and then immediately realized how stupid that sounded. "Have you shown them to their rooms yet?"

"No, Carter wanted to unpack the equipment first."

"This means we won't have a living room for the entire week?"

"It seems that way," he said. "Carter didn't give me time to suggest any other location, and before I knew it, he had pushed all the furniture against the walls."

"Unbelievable," Pam said, running a hand through her hair. She took a deep breath and tried to collect her emotions. "I'll take care of getting them settled in. Before you do anything else, you've got to go down and get that bull out of the small barn."

Mark was curious why Pam had become fixated on the bull's well-being, but given her mood, he wasn't about to ask.

It wasn't until Mark was halfway down Farm to Market Road that Pam realized she had forgotten to mention one small thing: Lynn was also in the barn.

Huddled in the adjacent stall, close to Coco's makeshift bed, Lynn recognized Mark's whistling long before he entered. Panicked at the thought of running into him so unexpectedly, she scrambled to the stall's front corner so as not to be seen. Mark would have to slide open the door, come all the way in and then look left to spot her.

"So what did you do to upset Pam so much?" Mark asked Old Jesse as he walked down the center aisle, grabbing an empty bucket that he proceeded to fill with sweet oats.

The sound and smell of the feed quickly caught the bull's attention. With an empty stomach, Jesse was, for the moment, more interested in the oats than in his young feline charges, and he turned on his haunches, pushing his head against the stall door. Had Coco been there, and not out looking for mice as she was, Jesse would have certainly stayed by the cat's side even if it meant missing a meal.

"You just love your grain, don't you, boy?" Mark chatted as he unlatched the door and opened it a few inches. He had learned that with a feed bucket in one hand, he could easily maneuver the large animal just about anywhere he wanted. Much like Mark, when it came to food, Jesse stayed relatively focused.

When the bull put its huge muzzle into the bucket and began eating, Mark latched a rope to his halter to lead him out of the stall.

*Meow.*

Mark stopped in his tracks and tilted his head, listening all the harder.

*Meow.*

Realizing that the noise was coming from behind him, Mark

gently nudged Jesse over so he had full view of the sawdust-covered floor. When he spotted the litter, he involuntarily jerked, pulling the feed away from Jesse. The bull snorted and tossed his head in objection.

Trying to rush as calmly as possible, Mark opened the door to the adjacent stall, led the bull in, and then slid the door closed behind him. The bull, which was not happy about being separated from both the feed bucket and his new family, slammed his horns against the door's metal railing. He stomped back several steps, snorted and threw his head against the wall.

Suddenly, a female scream came from inside the same stall. Lynn jumped up and tried to grab onto the bars of the door so that she could pull herself over the top metal railing.

The bull, even more startled than Lynn was, backed into the corner as if preparing to charge.

Acting instinctively, Mark opened the stall entrance just enough to grab Lynn's arm. As he pulled her out, she lost her footing halfway through the door and fell to the ground. Jesse flared his nostrils in warning.

"Help me!" Lynn screamed.

Mark reached under her arms and dragged her to safety, sliding the door closed as soon as her feet had cleared the opening. He was shaking so badly, he had a difficult time securing the latch. When the iron bolt finally slid down and the door was secure, he collapsed on the ground next to his sister.

Jesse slammed his horns into the wall, and both of them covered their heads, expecting wood to go flying. But the planks took the blow with no major damage or breech.

"*What were you doing in there?!*" Mark yelled at the woman, the question fueled by adrenaline.

Lynn pushed herself up so that she was sitting on her side, trying to catch her breath.

She lifted her head so that Mark could finally see who it was. He stared at her. "Lynn?" he asked in disbelief.

When she raised a hand to her mouth, Mark noticed her fingers were trembling. Pulling himself to his feet, he extended a hand to help her up. Suddenly, his sister, whom he had not seen in seven years, was inches from him, looking into his eyes. She was white in terror—either from her close call with the bull or from being so close to her brother.

She pulled her gaze from his. "I'm fine," she said briskly.

He continued staring at her. She looked much older than he remembered. Her hair, which was once auburn and softly curled, was now straight and heavily peppered with gray. And the warmth he had always seen in her eyes was gone. Her gaze was cold and guarded.

Mark stepped away, wanting to escape the fight that would surely ensue. He waited for her tangled lies that would dredge up the worst days of his life. He waited to hear the same excuses she had told their family while defending her thieving husband. He waited to be reminded that the judge had ruled in *their* favor. Mark braced himself for all of it.

But she just continued to stand there, her head down.

Finally, Mark broke the silence. "I'm sorry about the bull. It wasn't intentional," he said. "I didn't know you were there."

"I know that," she said, without looking up.

Before turning and walking away, he added, "I really didn't think you would come to our reunion. It's probably best that we keep our distance during the week." He shoved his hands deep in his pockets and walked out of the barn.

He was well down the driveway when Lynn called out, "Mark!"

He didn't stop. He still felt too much anger to listen to whatever she had to say, to whatever deceit and falsehoods she would surely tell.

"Wait!" she said. "Please." It sounded like a plea, a dire request.

Mark turned and looked at her, standing by the barn door. Suddenly, all the anger he had suppressed for so many years exploded. "*There is nothing for us to talk about!*" he yelled. "*Your husband destroyed my company!* He stole hundreds of thousands of dollars from me, and you had the audacity to defend him! And then you had to send a letter to our family being holier than thou because some inane, incompetent judge ruled in his favor." Mark was shaking with anger. "Your husband is a liar and a thief."

"I know!" she screamed out.

Those were the last words Mark was expecting to hear.

"I know," she repeated, this time more softly.

They were still twenty yards apart, but neither took a step toward the other.

"But I didn't know then," she swore.

"That's a lie," Mark spat out.

Lynn's eyes filled with tears. "I didn't want to know what he had done. I didn't want to be married to a man who could have stolen from my own brother. So I ignored the truth." Words poured out of her as she desperately tried to explain. "A year after the lawsuit, he admitted that he had pulled that money out of your company knowing full well that you would be left holding the bag."

"*Why didn't you tell me?*" Mark demanded. "Why didn't you tell the family?"

She took the first tentative step and then continued walking toward him ever so slowly. When she stopped, she was close enough for Mark to see the tears running down her cheeks.

"That was the first time I ever knew that he had taken the money from you and deliberately lied in court," she said.

"And you just kept up the appearance, never telling the family the truth?" Mark asked bitterly.

"I didn't know what to say," Lynn cried out. "Our marriage was in shambles, and he was having an affair. I thought if I told anyone, he would leave me."

"If he was having an affair, why didn't *you* leave *him*?" Mark had no sympathy for her.

She wiped her face with her hands but continued to cry. "He was all I had. I had no job, and the house was in his name. I had no life for thirty years except as his wife."

Mark was torn between anger and sympathy for his sister. "How could you have become so dependent on him?"

"All along, I believed what he told me," she said between sobs. "I now think everything he said was a lie since the very first day we met."

Two hours later, Mark and Lynn were sitting outside the barn with their backs against the red siding. During that time, there had been a monumental change: an estranged brother and sister had asked every last question and said every last word they had wanted to share over the last seven years.

Although Lynn never directly apologized for her *own* actions during or after the trial, and although she had never even thought about speaking the words "I'm sorry," she did openly admit to Dan's wrongdoing, so Mark was finally able to accept what had happened. He let go of his anger at her husband's corruption and the lawsuit and put the pain behind him so that he could once again share the love he had for his sister, no matter how deeply it had been buried. And Lynn was finally able to share with her brother all of Dan's deceptions. She believed that through her confessions, her blameless involvement would be forgiven or forgotten enough to allow the beginning of a new relationship with her brother.

After all was said, they then worked side by side and returned Old Jesse to where he belonged: standing watch over Coco.

## FIFTEEN
# *Shaver*

By late afternoon, Montis Inn had been transformed; the living room had become a live-broadcast studio, and Carter's family and crew had taken over the second and third floors of the main inn, although Pam had previously prepared suites in the guest annex for them. The backyard, behind the formal dining room, was set up for a large barbecue with four long tables positioned end to end. Red-and-white tablecloths flapped loosely in the afternoon breeze.

On the patio, André stood poised in front of the hearth of the outdoor barbecue island, where he had arranged hickory wood in the open pit. He looked at his watch and then glanced over at Pam. When he caught her attention, she too checked the time.

"Why don't you go ahead and start," she called over to him.

André lit a match to the paper he had stuffed under the kindling, and soon the pit was ablaze. Anaïs sat close to him on the stone wall, watching the smoke drift toward the deep azure sky. They had been casually talking about Anaïs entering her junior year of college that coming September.

Brooke and Joshua sat at the farthest table and appeared to be in a lengthy debate with Carter, whose voice boomed out across the backyard every few minutes. Nancy, who had long since become accustomed to watching her husband take center stage, sat quietly next to him.

After hours of tedious electrical work, Kano and Worm were unwinding with a game of badminton against Kay and Robert and losing pitifully to the older couple. They had agreed to play by Worm's golden rule: everyone had to continue holding their respective margarita glasses upright during play, and whoever lost a point had to take a sip. After twenty minutes of volleys, Kano and Worm were well into their second pitcher.

Corey had found a quiet corner away from the growing commotion, watching the koi swim lazily in the pond. Every so often, he threw in a few Cheerios that André had set out on the bench for that purpose. When his father's voice broke out over the soft chatter, he looked up. But mostly he kept his head down, as he did throughout most of his life.

"These are called dog rocks," Pam said, kicking the immense stone on which Corey sat.

The idea intrigued him. "You name your rocks?"

Pam laughed as she took a seat next to him. "No, the monks did a long time ago. I unearthed them when we were excavating for the pond and I was sure they were part of a huge religious monolith. Turns out they were the stones that the monks sat on when cooking hot dogs outside."

Corey laughed softly. "Who'd have thought?"

"Yeah," Pam said, shrugging her shoulders. "Who'd have thought?" She paused, looking around the groups of adults. "I get the feeling you were brought here against your will."

Corey tossed some more Cheerios to the fish. "'Kidnapped across state borders' would be the legal term."

"Hopefully your visit won't be as painful as you might be expecting."

Corey broke a soft smile. "It's really great to see you and Uncle

Mark again. It's just hard to be in such close proximity to Dad, twenty-four seven."

"I'm sure he can be a little insufferable at times," she agreed.

Corey had always liked Pam's forthrightness. "He can indeed," he concurred. "By the way, I got a call from Jessica a while ago—they'll be here in about an hour."

"Do you guys stay in touch?"

"We used to, but she changed a lot this last year, and along the way we lost contact. I think she dumped me for some cooler kids. I always liked her sense of individuality—she was okay with not being perfect—but then overnight, she started to jump through hoops to be part of the 'in' crowd at her high school."

"Thirty years later, and I still remember all the cheerleaders in their tight clique at my school."

Corey looked at Pam in surprise. "You weren't a cheerleader?"

Pam shook he head. "Never wanted to be."

"Well, it seems Jessica has gotten some attention from this group of kids because of what she's doing online, and now she's determined to be one of them. She's really into Internet networking, personal blogging, uploading video streams, posting to YouTube, that sort of thing. But what she says online she says just to gain popularity."

Carter's voice boomed out across the backyard. "Of course we would air it!"

Corey looked up and watched his father for a minute. "If you didn't know any better, you would guess that Jessica was my sister—she's a lot like Dad." He paused, thinking about the two, but keeping all other thoughts to himself.

"And you?" Pam asked. "How are you doing at college?"

Corey's demeanor picked up immediately. "Great," he said, sitting taller. "Georgetown is fantastic. The professors are just so involved and committed."

"Do you know what your major is?"

"Definitely pre-law," he said emphatically.

Pam raised her brows. “Well, that’s a surprise. You want to be a courtroom lawyer?”

Corey brushed off the idea. “No, I think that’s the nasty end of the business. I want to be either a mediator or a judge. I’d like to find the common ground between two opposing positions, using what the Constitution and law say.”

Pam smiled. “That makes perfect sense,” she said, patting him on the leg. “Good for you.”

He looked up at his father. “I wish my dad thought as much.”

“He doesn’t approve of your choice?”

Carter was gesturing wildly with his arms. “Thc law is somcthing my dad tries to avoid, other than touting the right of free speech when the FCC gets on his case or when someone tries to sue his radio syndication.”

“Well, you stay the course, Corey. I think you would make an outstanding judge. Perhaps someday we’ll see you sitting on the Supreme Court.”

Corey blushed. “Can you image how cool that would be?”

“Very cool,” Pam agreed. “And I’m quite sure you’re smart enough to get there.”

Just then, two large rams ran around the corner of the building, tugging Mark behind them. Lead ropes were knotted around his waist and wrapped around his left forearm.

“Look what the sheep dragged in,” Carter joked. His thunderous voice startled both rams, and they bolted sideways in unison, pulling Mark to the ground.

Pam watched in alarm. “Oh, this isn’t good at all,” she muttered.

Corey laughed. “Is Uncle Mark really as crazy as he appears?”

“More so,” she replied, without taking her eyes off her husband.

Mark sat up, dug his heels into the ground and began to reel in the animals. “No need to help—I got them!” he called out, although no one had gestured to lend him a hand. “Well, that doesn’t mean *you,*” he said to Joshua.

Joshua passed Brooke his drink before calmly approaching the sheep, speaking to them in a low, even voice. Just as he was about to take hold of one of the animals' halters, Carter yelled out again, "Barbecued mutton!"

The alarmed rams leaped sideways, knocking Joshua off his feet. As he hit the ground, he had enough sense to grab and hold on tight to one of the lead ropes that had become untied. Although both men were lying prone, the animals weren't going anywhere.

"Not to worry, folks, everything is under control," Mark said, raising his arm and waving. He scrambled to his feet and offered Joshua a hand up.

"Why did you bring McNear's sheep up here?" Joshua asked.

"Well, I'm not going to practice on my own sheep," Mark replied, sounding as if the explanation should have been obvious. "And I thought it would be fun to try before dinner."

Hearing what Mark had said, Pam hurried to his side. "What are you talking about, honey?"

The foursome had stopped playing badminton and was now standing next to Nancy and Carter, forming a loose circle around the sheep.

"Shearing. I think I might need some practice before the fair's competition. If anything, I can get my feet wet enough to ask the professionals some questions when we're waiting to go into the ring." Mark rolled up his sleeves. "And I didn't want to look like a total beginner."

"Which you are," Pam added.

"Last year, the winner sheared his sheep in two minutes, twenty-four seconds," Joshua reminded him.

"You're not helping a lot with that kind of attitude," Mark teased.

"But you can't even get the sheep to stand next to you," Pam contended.

"Well," Mark said, giving Joshua the rope that he had been holding, "that's why I need this practice. I'm sure there's more than one way to shear a sheep."

"Actually, there probably is only *one* way," Joshua corrected him.

"O ye of little faith," Mark contended. With great drama, he pulled a Remington electric shaver from his back pocket.

Pam laughed. "You're not serious?"

Kay clapped her hands. "Good thing that wasn't on when you fell over. You might have shaved off your pe—"

"Mother!"

Everyone broke out laughing.

Joshua looked at the small razor. "What are you planning to do with that? Shave their eyebrows?"

Pam blinked. "Is that the razor I gave you for Christmas last year?"

"Honey, hair is hair," Mark explained. "I don't think it makes much difference to the shaver."

Joshua countered, "Other than it taking you two hours instead of two minutes to shear that ram."

Kay raised her fist in solidarity. "Go for it, Mark!"

"Don't encourage him, Mom," Pam said.

"Okay, Marko. Only wimps do this type of thing for fun. I've got my timer right here," Carter said, removing a heavy gold watch from his thick wrist. "A hundred bucks says you can't shave him in four minutes."

"Don't be a jerk, Carter," Mark replied. "All of this *is* just for fun—it's just a county fair."

"And we don't have a hundred bucks to toss away," Pam added.

Carter ignored what they said and looked down at his watch. "Tell me when you're ready."

Mark rolled his eyes. "Okay, you can time me, but no betting. Let me get ready." After tugging up his pants and loosening his collar, he grabbed the halter of the smaller of the two rams, pulled it next to his leg and held up his shaver with great fanfare. "I'm ready."

Carter looked at his watch. "Three, two, one, go!"

Everyone was expecting fur to fly, but unlike a real shearing competition that went a mile a minute, Mark seemed to begin—and stay—in slow motion. While holding on to the rope, he stepped over the sheep so that he was facing the animal's backside, and secured the sheep between his legs.

"Ten seconds," Carter called out.

Mark turned on the shaver and placed it at the top of the sheep's butt. "Easy as pie," he said, as he shaved a one-inch-wide and very wavy strip along the sheep's back, going from tail to head.

Since the razor was moving so slowly, the vibration tickled the sheep, which began to struggle against Mark's legs. The more the sheep squirmed, the more inconsistent the shearing became and the wavier the lines grew. Mark tried to shave another strip next to the first, but found it impossible to keep it straight.

"Thirty seconds."

Mark glanced up at Carter. "What happened to twenty seconds?"

"Gone ten seconds ago, Marko," Carter quipped.

A soft gust of wind crossed the backyard, lifting and carrying the loose wool everywhere. Small clumps floated in the air and landed gently on the surface of the pond, which started a feeding frenzy among the koi below. Other small clumps of fiber found their way into people's drinks.

Mark had just finished shaving the second row along the sheep's side, looping down to its belly, when Carter announced, "One minute."

"Okay, let me try something different," Mark said. Instead of working back to front, he placed the shaver at the bottom of the sheep's stomach and brought the razor up and over to the other side, shaving a circle around the animal's girth.

One large clump of wool lifted into the air, drifted ten yards and landed on the open fire pit, where it immediately burst into flames. No one noticed since all eyes were focused on Mark. Another gust of wind blew the flaming wool off the pit and into the kindling box, the contents of which immediately combusted. It wasn't until the small box was engulfed in flames that Robert yelled, "Fire!"

Brooke was standing closest to the hearth and did what most anyone would do—she doused it with her frozen margarita. Unfortunately, the alcohol just spread the fire that much faster. In all the commotion, one sheep took off toward the woods. Not wanting to be left alone, the other sheep struggled against Mark's hold.

Pam grabbed the ice bucket, filled it with pond water and splashed it on the kindling box. The fire spat out, and smoke ballooned into the air.

"Is it out?" Mark called over to Pam.

Carter had not taken his eyes off his watch. "Three minutes."

Mark was now on the ground, directly underneath the sheep, with the animal's legs straddling his own. "You can stop the clock," he told Carter, trying to stand up. "This shaver isn't working very well."

"You think?" Joshua asked sarcastically. "Professional shearers have blades four times larger."

Mark handed Joshua the lead rope so he could step away and take a good look at his handiwork. The pathetic-looking animal had shaved lines going in all directions around its body.

"Not a bad first attempt, if I do say so myself," Mark said, plucking wool from his hair.

"You can pay me later," Carter said, slapping Mark on the back.

"It's not about winning or losing, and it's definitely not about the money," Mark said.

"You're wrong there, Marko. The *only* time it's not about winning and losing is when it's about the money, and that's most of the time," Carter pronounced loudly. "And I bet there'll be a dozen opportunities to prove that to you over the next week."

## SIXTEEN
# *Rare*

After Mark and Joshua had corralled the renegade rams and brought both back to the barn, André began cooking the steaks. Carter stood over his shoulder, telling the chef what to do. As Pam refilled everyone's margarita glasses, she prayed that André would still be working at Montis when the family reunion was over. Kano and Worm had challenged Robert and Kay to a game of bocce ball, and the older couple had already taken a healthy lead.

"Not too much," Brooke said as Pam refilled her margarita glass. "If I get drunk, I'll be a total embarrassment."

Pam looked over at her mother and Robert, who were kissing in between throws. "You wouldn't be the only one."

Brooke studied her friend. "I don't get you sometimes. Your mother is a vibrant woman. In fact, she reminds me a lot of Charlotte Ross, just fifteen years younger. What's wrong with finding love at her age?"

"I suppose I'm happy Mom found a companion."

"Suppose?"

Pam immediately corrected herself. "No, I really am happy. I just wish she had told me about their relationship. It came as such a surprise." Pam continued to observe the couple. "And I think they egg each other on to do things that are far too dangerous for people their age. They're actually going white-water rafting and rappelling off cliffs, and I've got a problem with that."

"I think you're right to be concerned, but I don't think that's Robert's fault—he doesn't seem to be twisting Kay's arm. In fact, your mom asked me about hiking in the mountains west of town. She said Robert's knee might hold him back, but she has every intention of taking a rock-climbing class while she's here."

Pam groaned. "Why can't she just act her age?"

"She's obviously in love," Brooke commented. "And where would you prefer her? In some safe nursing home?"

"Better that than dying in a tragic accident," Pam retorted. "When Mom was married, she acted normal, but now . . ." Pam watched her mother high-five Robert after tossing her ball. "Now, she's out of control."

"Out of whose control? Yours?" Brooke asked cautiously.

Given Pam's glare, Brooke thought she may have crossed that invisible line beyond friendship and honesty. When Carter's voice boomed across the backyard, Brooke found an easy way to change the topic. "So how is everyone else getting along?"

"It's nice to see Nancy again," Pam said, glancing over at the picnic table. "She and Mark are just a year apart in age, so they were the closest growing up."

Brooke nodded. "She didn't say a word when we were talking with them."

"No one can get a word in when Carter is around," Pam said. "Nancy is surprisingly normal given the circumstances. I think she has to constantly shield herself from Carter's bombastic character. And they have a great son, Corey, who's a sophomore at Georgetown."

"The other side of the country," Brooke commented.

"And on a different floor of the inn. I'm sure that staying clear of his father is deliberate on his part. They're total opposites—Corey's very levelheaded and a real peacemaker."

Brooke took another sip of her drink. "I know you're going to hate me for saying this, but I think it's pretty cool that you have such a famous celebrity standing right here in your backyard."

Pam winced, and Brooke knew that, again, she might have said the wrong thing.

"Carter will be broadcasting his radio talk show from our living room this week," Pam revealed.

Brooke leaned closer to her. "I've only listened to him a few times," she whispered. "It's not my idea of entertainment, but he obviously appeals to the masses—he has a huge, loyal following."

"Nine million—I know," Pam said wryly. "I think if he stood for something or passionately believed in something, I'd give him more credit. But he's not a Republican or a Democratic—he's politically apolitical. His show is nothing more than him stirring up strong differences of opinion. He feeds on people's prejudices, encourages zealots, and instigates conflict at every opportunity."

"Does he personally get into the fights?"

"Seldom if ever," Pam said. "He's the most competitive person I know—needs to win anything and everything—but he usually doesn't take sides on his show, unless of course he needs to play devil's advocate just to antagonize a caller. Most of the time, he just sits there and hands out the daggers."

"That's probably how he wins," Brooke surmised.

Pam looked at her in surprise. "How do you mean?"

"Well, if he sets up his callers so that there are two losers in the argument, and he's lambasting both regardless of their opinions, than Carter becomes the victor each and every time."

"Huh, I never thought of it like that."

"Does Lynn get along with him?" Brooke asked.

"Lynn gets along with her cat, Coco," Pam said sarcastically. "Mark and I were both so sure she wouldn't come. We're still in denial that she's here."

"Has she talked with Mark yet?"

Pam cringed. "Not that I know of. They haven't spoken a word for years, and I'm sure he'll do everything in his power to avoid her for the next seven days." She swirled the frozen slush round in the pitcher and then whispered, "I wasn't very kind to her today. I feel bad about it, but she makes it impossible to be empathetic because she's so . . ."

Brooke waited for Pam to continue. "So what?"

"So . . . Lynn," she said. "She's a perfectionist—"

Brooke chuckled at the pot calling the kettle black.

Pam slapped her friend's arm. "Insult received," she said. "But she has no substance about her." Pam took a long moment to think about her sister-in-law. "Whatever she does, she does for the sake of perception or to prove that, in one way or another, she's better than the rest of us. In a way, she built this illusion of a perfect marriage to a perfect husband living in a perfect house in an upper-class town, and then it all crumbled in front of her. So she's now a divorced, bitter fifty-eight-year-old facing the cold realities of a lonely life."

"Under all that pretense, there may be a very nice woman," Brooke said.

"It will take a better person than me to find out, I suppose," Pam confessed. "My patience wears thin when someone is that condescending."

"We're back," Mark chimed.

Pam and Brooke simultaneously froze; Mark and Lynn were walking toward them, arm in arm.

Brooke grabbed Pam's elbow and whispered, "I thought you said—"

"I did," Pam murmured back. "Hi, honey," she replied, making every effort to hide her surprise. "You two ready for dinner? I think André is about to take the steaks off the fire."

"Old Jesse gave us a hard time. He almost killed my sister," he said, squeezing Lynn's shoulder, "but she and I have everything under control now."

"And Coco?" Pam asked.

"Doing her best under the circumstances," Lynn said with surprising acceptance.

Before Lynn could describe Coco's condition in detail, a car horn blasted from the parking area. "Hello?" a man's voice called out. "Is anyone home?"

Pam pulled Brooke close to her. "Patrick, Mark's other brother. He's a high school teacher in Virginia, and his wife, Elaine, is a language tutor. Both are very nice—he's very much like Mark," she whispered.

"We're back here," Mark yelled as he took off toward the courtyard.

Pam watched her husband leap over a boxwood hedge, catch his left foot on a water hose and tumble to the ground.

Patrick ran up to give Mark a hand. "And everyone says I'm the goof!"

"You look great," Mark said, giving his big brother a bear hug.

"And you look *old*," Patrick said, laughing.

Elaine nudged her husband aside. "That's not true. You're as cute as ever," she said, kissing Mark on the cheek. "How I ended up with your brother and not you, I'll never know."

"It's great to have you here," Mark said, walking back to the car with them. "We're about to start dinner. I'll show you to your rooms and then you can come out and have a margarita."

"Or four," Patrick said, wrapping his arm around Mark's neck and pretending to wrestle with his brother. "It's so great to be here. Thanks for inviting us."

"It was a good time for all of us to get away," Elaine added.

When Mark opened the car door, he was surprised to see Jessica lying on the backseat with her eyes closed. "Is she all right?" he asked.

"She's in 'the zone,' as she calls it," Patrick answered.

From earbuds that attached to an iPod, music was blasting away.

"Jessica," Mark said, tapping the girl on her knee.

She slowly opened one eye and looked around in a haze. "Hey, Uncle Mark, what's happening?" she said.

"Who are you?" Mark teased.

When Jessica stepped out of the car, Mark was blown over to see how much she had grown—in every imaginable way. "You were just a kid a few years ago. How did you get to be so old?"

"That was ages ago, Uncle Mark," she said, slipping her iPod into the hip pocket of her jeans. Hating her own height, she rolled her shoulders.

"You're gorgeous," Mark said, hugging her.

As she shook her head, her short, strawberry-blond hair rose. "I'm too tall," she said.

"Tall is good. Guys love tall girls," Mark said.

"Not at my high school, they don't. They used to call me Giraffe."

"Well, you can talk to Pam about that—she was taller than you at your age, and she loved it. And then we've got a lot of catching up to do," Mark said. "Pam's prepared a nice room for you in the guest annex."

"Annex?" Jessica said. "It sounds like a prison."

Mark laughed. "Montis was built as a monastery about a hundred years ago."

Jessica circled in place, glancing at the various buildings. "Cool. You have cable, right?"

"Don't we wish," Mark said.

A look of panic washed over Jessica's face. "Well, I need to access the Internet," she said, looking at her mother.

"We have satellite," Mark explained. "Better than dial-up but not as fast as cable."

"But I can upload fifty-meg streams?"

Mark glanced between Patrick and Elaine, thinking they might be more technically attuned to what their daughter was asking about, but both shrugged their shoulders.

"Sure," Mark said, without having the faintest idea. "Anything is possible at Montis. We'll make it work."

Jessica sighed with relief. "Great. I brought all my equipment," she said, as she reached into the backseat and pulled out two laptops.

"Jessica stays online all night," Elaine explained.

"Been there, done that," Mark said with a wink. "But usually I end up doing something stupid at two in the morning that just gets me into trouble with Pam."

"Aunt Pam doesn't surf?" Jessica asked.

Mark chuckled. "The Internet? Only when she has to for business. Maybe you can show her a thing or two while you're here."

Jessica grinned. "This will be prime."

"Kay." Mark waved to his mother-in-law, who was just leaving the annex with two sweaters draped over her arm. "You remember Patrick and Elaine?"

"It's wonderful to see you again," Kay said, greeting them.

"And this, believe it or not, is Jessica," Mark added.

"My word," Kay said as she embraced the teenager. "I haven't seen you since you were knee-high. Do you remember all the fun we used to have together?"

Jessica blushed, not knowing how to answer without offending the woman.

"Not to worry," Kay said, putting her at ease. "Last time we were together, you asked me to be your honorary grandmother."

"Oh, that's right," Jessica said slowly as a smile came to her face. "I used to call you Grams, didn't I?"

"You did indeed," Kay said with a giggle. "And I loved it."

"Okay, Grams, then you can show me to the annex," Jessica said, sliding her arm through Kay's.

As the sun set, Mark and Corey lit lanterns that had been set up throughout the compound. They then repositioned the tables so that they formed two long rows—one for the food that was being served buffet style and the other for the guests to sit at. Brooke and Pam brought out numerous platters and bowls of side dishes, including steamed corn, Kay's zucchini casserole and the renowned Montis Inn Caesar salad. Joshua filled glasses with a Merlot André had purchased directly from Christian Copeland, the owner of Copeland Vineyards in Sonoma Valley, California.

After everyone had taken their seats, Mark stood and raised his glass. "Pam and I would like to thank all of you for traveling here today and for sharing in our wedding anniversary celebration. We've wanted to have a family reunion for the longest time, and we're so glad you're here. Also, the county fair is opening in a few days, so there will be plenty to do."

Some clapped, others tapped their forks against their glasses, and the younger adults hooted.

Mark continued, "I think—"

Carter would have jumped from his seat had his bulk allowed him to. Instead, he leaned forward and bellowed, "I think, Marko, you should let someone else get a word in edgewise."

Mark blinked at the man's rude interruption, but being the good host that he was, he conceded. "And Carter obviously has the floor," he said before sitting down.

"It's a good day when families make their way across our fine nation and come together, even in a place like this," Carter said.

Pam bit her lip.

"Over this coming week, we certainly won't have the cultural benefits that we would have had in Seattle, which I originally suggested as the setting for this gathering, but there may be some redeeming value to fresh air and mountain views. . . . Oh, wait, Seattle has those too," he joked, although no one laughed. He cleared his throat. "Great to see everyone again, and I expect each of you to tune to 80.4 AM at six o'clock local time, Monday morning, to hear the first broadcast of Lumby on the Air. I guarantee it will knock your socks off."

"I don't want my socks knocked off," Pam whispered to Brooke, who was seated next to her.

When it became obvious that Carter had said his piece, André placed large pewter plates in the center of the tables. Each plate was stacked high with thick sirloins, and each steak had a small flag in it. He explained, "Those with blue markers are rare, yellow for medium and red is well-done. Bon appétit."

Carter immediately helped himself to the largest, rarest steak on the pile and returned the platter to the table, without passing the dish to anyone else. He jumped into a conversation with Kano and Worm about the upcoming broadcast. “Let’s reserve four call-in lines. Hopefully we can get some local yokel caller who wants to go up against some of my New York City fans.”

“That’s all we have here,” Pam interjected.

Carter looked up from his steak. “What? Local yokels?”

“No—phone lines. We only have four phone lines coming into the inn,” she explained.

“Well, we’ll just use those and tie in some wireless,” he replied before turning to his associates. “Worm, take care of it.”

“But Carter,” Pam said with strained politeness, “we still have a business to run. We need to use our own phones.”

Carter pretended to be confused. “Pam, we’re only on the air for three hours each morning—eight to eleven Eastern time, which would make it six to nine local time.”

“Actually, that’s when most of our reservations are phoned in,” she said.

“Not this week, darling,” he pronounced. “I have a daily audience of nine million listeners.”

“Well, I suppose you’ll have a few less than nine million call-ins this week,” she said more firmly, kicking Mark under the table.

Mark came to her defense. “At the very least, Carter, we’ll need our main phone number kept open.”

“For what? One or two calls that *might* come in?” Carter asked, lathering a baked potato with butter. “If this is about wanting me to mention your little inn on the air, don’t worry, you’ll get plenty of plugs.”

Pam put up her hand. “Actually, we don’t want you to mention Montis on your show.”

“Carter, we really weren’t expecting you to broadcast this week,” Mark reminded his brother-in-law, “so you need to be a little more flexible.”

"Nine million listeners, Marko, and they'll all be tuning in Monday morning to hear *moi*. They want to know about Lumby, and I'll give them an earful."

"That might be a problem," Mark said. "This isn't the city where there's anonymity. We live here, and we know everyone in town—they're our friends. We really don't want you talking about Lumby or Montis."

Carter leaned back so that he looked larger and more rotund than ever. In a loud voice he chuckled. "Are you trying to censor me, Marko?"

The other conversations that had been going on—Lynn obsessing about Coco, and Kay talking about rafting—all stopped mid-sentence. A silence fell as everyone's eyes shifted between Mark and Carter.

Mark shook his head but didn't back down. "Not censoring—just requesting that you remember that Lumby is a small town. It's our town, and we don't want any of our friends hurt by thoughtless comments."

"You're starting to sound like Andy Griffith in Mayberry," Carter added.

"You're not too far off track there," Joshua said, coming to Mark's defense while trying to lighten the tension.

"All I'm saying," Mark said, loud enough for all to hear, "is that this is our community, and we care for the people who live here. We don't want you to make any derogatory comments about Lumby. This is a peaceful place, and besides, no one else really cares about what happens in our small town."

Pam squeezed his leg, letting him know how thankful and proud she was of him for saying that.

"Wrong, Marko. They care about what I tell them to care about," Carter huffed. "People are war ants. They thrive on confrontation. The adrenaline of fighting is a real high."

The only two people who were not dumbfounded by that comment were Nancy and Corey, who was sitting at the end of the table with the other young adults.

“Is your dad always such a jerk?” Jessica asked just loud enough for Corey and Anaïs to hear. Anaïs was startled by the bluntness of Jessica’s question.

Corey looked at his father for a long time, and carefully considered his reply. A sad, resigned look came over his face. “Yeah,” he replied slowly. “Most of the time he is.”

SEVENTEEN

# *Perils*

**Sunday**

On Sunday morning, alarm clocks throughout the Montis compound began ringing as early as five o'clock. Since many people hadn't gotten to bed until well after midnight the night before, and since some had been less than sober when they'd enthusiastically agreed to go to Sunday service at St. Cross Abbey, the wake-up calls were generally not well received.

As usual, Pam was already removing the first trays of scones from the oven before any lights came on in the guest rooms.

"Why did you wake me up so early?" Mark asked as he sat at the island with his eyes opened just enough to look at his coffee mug.

"I can't do all this alone—I need your help," she said as she set a large bowl in front of him. Mark watched as she measured out each ingredient for her homemade granola.

"More raisins," he requested. "And more cranberries."

When she was done, the bowl was half filled. "Here," she said, handing him a large wooden spoon. "Go ahead and mix it up."

"How about the—"

Pam placed a large bottle of honey on the island.

"Great," he said as he picked out some raisins and popped them in his mouth.

"You fell asleep before I got out of the shower last night," Pam said. "I never had a chance to ask you about Lynn."

"Wow, Lynn," he said, finally waking up. "Was that a shocker or what?"

"Certainly surprised me. What happened between you two?"

"I almost killed her."

"*What?*"

"Well, Old Jesse almost killed her when I put him in the same stall where she was hiding from me." He was speaking very quickly. "And then I saved her life, and then I walked away, but she called to me. And then we talked for a couple of hours. It was great."

"Did she apologize?"

Mark started picking out the cranberries and eating them. "Yeah, I guess so, but not in so many words. But she told me that Dan finally admitted that he had lied to my accountant and had taken my company's money knowing full well that I would have to declare bankruptcy a few months later. He also told her that he had lied several times on the stand because he had no intention of returning a penny to me."

Pam was stunned. "Why didn't she tell the family all that after she found out?"

"Because she didn't want to cause a strain in their marriage, even though it was already on the rocks."

"Then why didn't she say anything after her divorce?" Pam said.

"I asked her about that." Mark paused, trying to remember her answer. "She felt that her life was already in such shambles, and she was too embarrassed to admit that she had been conned by her husband for so many years."

"But her admission of her husband's guilt doesn't absolve her of her own wrongdoings," Pam said in a strained tone. "With the letter she wrote and phone calls she made to your relatives, she really turned the family against you the minute the judge ruled in their favor."

Mark squeezed honey onto the dry granola mixture. He didn't want to think about what his wife was saying; he didn't want to go back in time and stir up the same feelings. "I guess it just doesn't matter anymore. All I know is that we're talking again, and now we'll have a good time this week."

"But—"

"Hello," Kay called from the dining room. "Is anyone here?"

"Maybe they're not up yet," Robert said.

"But the lights arc on. Hello?" she called out a little louder.

Pam opened the swing door of the kitchen and peered out. "Mother?" she said in surprise. "What are you doing up so early?"

"We wanted to take a morning walk before we meet our pilot in a couple of hours."

Pam froze. "*What pilot?*" she asked, just as she noticed the pair of beat-up New Balance sneakers on her mother's feet. "And since when do you wear sneakers?"

Kay lifted her leg and pointed her toe. "These old things? They're very comfortable."

"Kay has it in mind that we should take our first gliding lesson today," Robert explained.

Pam looked bewildered. "Hang gliding?"

"No, in a two-seater plane," Robert replied.

"With no engine," Kay added. "You know—gliding." She lifted her arm and flew her hand through the air as if it were an airplane.

Mark kissed Kay on the cheek as he scooted through the kitchen doorway. "I'm out of here. Have a wonderful time and be safe."

Pam wrung the towel around her hands. "And that must be incredibly safe," she said with dripping sarcasm.

"Those were my thoughts exactly," Robert said, "but then I did some homework and found out that the gliders are actually more aerodynamic and safer than most planes with engines."

Pam immediately disregarded what he had said. "And you two are going up alone?"

"Heavens no, darling. We'd get ourselves killed," Kay said, straightening the bold red-and-white bandanna around her neck. "Our pilot will be taking each one of us up for an introductory flight. It will be great fun!" she exclaimed. "But we're supposed to bring our own lunch. Do you mind if I take some wine and cheese?"

"I absolutely do mind. I'll make you a lunch basket that won't get you hammered before you're airborne," Pam said, opening the kitchen door all the way. "Come in and have some breakfast."

"That's really not necessary," Robert said. "We're both light eaters in the morning."

"I insist," Pam said, taking two mugs from the shelf and filling them with coffee. "Here are some freshly baked blueberry scones."

As Kay and Robert looked over the brochure for the flight school, Pam went into high gear and finished pulling together the makings of a plentiful breakfast buffet, which she placed on the long table in the dining room for her other guests, who would be arriving shortly.

From the refrigerator, she produced leftover steaks from the night before, horseradish, mayonnaise and lettuce and assembled two thick sandwiches on ciabatta bread. Retrieving a wicker picnic basket that was stacked on the top self of the pantry, she began to fill it with plastic containers of various side dishes. Finally, she added several bottles of water.

Kay took one more sip of coffee. "No wine?" she asked, disappointed.

"No wine. I want you alive and well for dinner tonight," Pam said as she handed Robert the basket. "We're all heading over to the monastery for liturgy and should be back by about two."

"We'll be done well before then," Robert said. "Thanks so much for making us lunch."

"Off you go, kids," Pam tried to tease. "Be safe."

Once they were out the door, Pam collapsed in a chair. Gliding?

she asked herself. Why on earth would Mom want to do that at her age?

By eight in the morning, everyone had finished breakfast and was waiting on the front porch for Pam and Mark to coordinate rides to the abbey. Carter was inside, giving last-minute directions to Kano and Worm, who were staying behind to get the phone lines squared away.

Lynn, having spent much of the night in the barn watching over Coco, looked surprisingly relaxed and well rested. She had combed her hair differently that morning, and lighter-colored makeup noticeably softened and improved her appearance. Pam realized she was actually attractive.

Patrick and Elaine were seated on the stoop, quietly talking to each other. Carter clapped his hands as he walked outside, grabbing everyone's attention. "Marko, why don't you take Lynn and Pam? Patrick and Elaine can come with us."

Corey leaped down the stairs. "Dad, I'm going with Uncle Mark also." Before his father could object, Corey bolted toward the Walkers' Jeep.

Pam turned to Elaine. "Is Jessica coming?"

Elaine shrugged apologetically. "She said she was still tired from the trip and didn't sleep that well last night."

"Just as long as she was sleeping alone, that's what I say," Carter snickered.

Suddenly, Mark's bright yellow, World War II 1944 BMW R75 motorcycle drove past the inn, heading north on Farm to Market Road. Robert beeped the horn, and Kay waved from the sidecar.

Pam gasped. "Mother!"

"It's all right, honey," Mark said, swinging his arm around her waist to keep her from racing after her wayward parent. "I showed Robert how to drive it yesterday."

"To drive around our property, yes. But Mark, they're going to the airport in *Rocky Mount*."

"Well, that's nuts," Mark commented. "My motorcycle can't make it past Main Street without breaking down."

Pam scowled. "Did you tell them that?"

Mark grimaced. "I would have if they had asked me."

"Great," she mumbled. "Instead of dying in a glider, my mother and her boyfriend will be killed on a sixty-year-old motorcycle skidding out of control at Priests Pass."

After an hour's drive, Mark led their two-car caravan through the small town of Franklin and turned into the long driveway at St. Cross Abbey. Even Lynn, who was in the middle of one of her isn't-Coco-so-cute stories, became silent as they pulled up behind the main church.

Stepping out of the car, everyone could hear chanting coming from the chapel. "They're just finishing matins," Pam explained.

"As soon as they're done," Mark said to Pam, "why don't you take everyone inside. I need to swing by the kitchen for a minute."

"Not now, Mark. Please stay with us," Pam said, knowing full well that he wanted to see what new recipes the monks were concocting. "I'm sure John will give you samples during coffee hour."

"That's a good thing," Mark said, turning to Corey. "They have the *best* rum sauce you've ever had over ice cream."

"Given I've never had rum sauce, I'm sure it will knock my socks off, Uncle Mark." Corey grinned.

Mark smiled. "Well, you need to stick with me." He fondly swung his arm around the nephew's neck. "I want to show you everything."

"Wonderful," Carter cackled, watching Mark and his son. "The naive leading the naive."

Mark turned to Pam. "Should I resent that?"

"I never do," Corey said.

Although Pam hated Carter's condescending attitude, she couldn't help but laugh. "We still love you, honey," she said, kissing her husband.

"So let's get this show over with," Carter said, clapping his hands.

The sound echoed between the buildings and across the compound.

"Shh," Pam shushed him. "They're still in matins."

"Nothing like a good monk story to start the broadcast tomorrow," Carter said in a slightly softer voice. "I can always count on five thousand calls as soon as I bring up God. This will make great fodder."

Pam, who was about to lead the group across to the chapel's entrance, swung unexpectedly around and stared at Carter so coldly that he stopped in his tracks. "Not *one* word about the monks on your show, Carter," she said. "And not one word about St. Cross. Don't test us on that because if we even think you might mention them, you'll be ending your stay with us."

Carter looked to Mark for support.

"Believe her," Mark warned. "You're out of here if you say anything about the monks."

Carter was flabbergasted to be shot down so quickly, and for no good reason, and by Pam and Mark of all people. But he understood what he was up against. "Okay, you win," he said, raising his hands in surrender. "Nothing over the air about the monks. Promise."

Pam stared him down for several more seconds and then took a deep breath and exhaled loudly, as if to signal the end of the fight.

Lynn, who had separated from the group, paid no attention as she studied the climbing roses clinging to the chapel's stone wall.

The chanting faded and silence fell over the monastery.

"Matins has just ended. Is everyone ready to go in?" Pam asked, forcefully lightening her voice as she pulled the chapel doors open.

As the Walkers had promised, the monastery was as extraordinary on the inside as it was on the outside, aglow with hundreds of candles placed throughout the single-room chapel. Brothers and sisters were interspersed in the pews, sitting quietly in prayer. Since no one pew was completely empty, the Montis clan broke up and took whatever seats were available. Lynn walked halfway down the center aisle and slid into a pew on the left side. Sister Claire, who was wearing a long black robe, looked up at her and smiled. Nodding her head, she silently gestured for Lynn to sit down next to her.

Just as Lynn took her seat, an exceedingly tall man slipped into the same pew, taking the seat next to her. Lynn glanced at him quickly, first noticing his long hair and then his ruggedly attractive face. Although he was cramped for space, he casually stretched his long legs out under the pew in front of them.

"Excuse me," the sister next to Lynn whispered politely before leaning forward and reaching across her to tap the knee of the man on the far side. When he looked at the sister, a delightfully genuine smile filled his face.

"Do we have a date at the berry patch after the service, Chuck?" the sister asked.

"Yes, and Joshua may join us."

"Perfect. I like threesomes," she said, a devilish twinkle in her eye.

Lynn raised her brows. "Progressive order," she softly said to herself.

The man the sister had called Chuck overheard her comment and chuckled.

"What amazing candles," Lynn observed.

"Thank you," he whispered.

She looked at him in surprise. "Excuse me?"

"Thank you," he repeated with a smile.

"I was commenting on the candles. They're stunning," she explained.

He nodded. "Yes, thank you."

Suddenly, a light from the ceiling shone down on a Bible that lay on an intricately carved podium. The podium's natural redwood appeared to glow.

Lynn inhaled quickly, as if such beauty was almost startling. "That's extraordinary."

"Your compliments are a delight to hear," Chuck said.

Lynn laughed in disbelief, thinking the man next to her was possibly deranged. "*Who are you?*" she whispered.

He seemed to be about to introduce himself, but just then, the tower bells rang throughout the monastery, indicating the start of liturgy.

Brother Matthew approached the altar and lowered his head. "Let us pray."

As Mark's relatives would say later, it was one of the most delightful services they had ever attended. Everyone thought that the voices of the two communities—the brothers and the sisters—harmonized in such an extraordinary way that anyone attending the a cappella service couldn't help but be swept away.

When the final amen was sung, Chuck waited a moment, not wanting to seem too impatient to meet the woman seated next to him, although doing so had been on his mind during the entire service, and even before, when he'd first noticed her outside admiring the chapel's roses. Few women he knew would take the time to appreciate the flora of St. Cross Monastery, as she had done before liturgy. Chuck stood as soon as she did. Just as he cleared his voice to introduce himself, Pam, who had been sitting two rows behind him, touched his arm and gave him a warm embrace.

"We don't see you often enough," she complained to her good friend. "I wish you'd come to Montis more regularly." He looked around and saw the woman he wanted to meet following Claire out the other end of the pew. "Chuck?" Pam said, trying to get his attention.

"I'm sorry," he said, kissing her cheek. "Where's Mark?" he asked, using the chance to glance around the chapel. To his disappointment, the woman was gone.

"He went over to help set up for coffee hour."

"I'm sorry?" he asked.

Pam couldn't help but notice how distracted Chuck seemed. "Is everything all right?"

"Fine," he said, observing who was walking out the door. "Are you staying for a while?"

"Just for a cup of coffee."

"I'm heading over there myself," Chuck said, hoping that the woman he had sat next to might join them during the coffee hour, which the monks hosted after each Sunday service.

As Chuck and Pam headed for the door, Sister Claire came up from behind them and took hold of his sleeve. "Oh, no you don't," she said. "We have a date."

Pam smirked. "I shouldn't ask, should I?"

"You're invited as well," Claire said. "I'm taking Chuck up to the ridge to show him the berries firsthand."

"Joshua told us about those," Pam said. "Has anyone identified them?"

"Not yet, but I'm hoping he and Joshua will come up with some answers," she said. "Would you like to come along?"

"I'll have to pass. We have family visiting this week, and we need to head back to Montis. Speaking of which, Chuck, why don't you come by this afternoon for a Sunday barbecue? Very informal. We'd love for you to meet our relatives."

Chuck looked around the church one more time, hiding his disappointment. "That would be wonderful."

"Then we'll see you around two o'clock."

EIGHTEEN

# *Muleta*

At the McNear Farm, Mike folded the seven-page preliminary engineering report and slid it carefully back into the manila envelope in which it had been delivered the previous afternoon. He then peered down at the new plat map that clearly showed the results of the first and only survey that had ever been done on the McNear land, a survey that Mike had asked for the week before in preparation for putting his farm on the market.

As with most large parcels of land across the country that had been initially delineated in the 1800s, the McNear property borders were originally marked by stone walls that had long since fallen and hundred-year-old trees that had long since died. Although it was an expensive investment, having the survey done in advance removed one contingency that certainly would have been attached to any offer made on his farm: a legal confirmation of all boundary lines. The plat map, which at Mike's request included lines that reflected one possible way of subdividing the land, looked like a Scrabble board with one hundred forty-eight little cookie-cutter parcels. This laid out a viable subdivision option, making it a much more enticing purchase for anyone considering the land for future development.

"It's payday," Mike whispered to himself. His sense of imminent escape was almost palpable.

"Good morning," Bess said as she walked into the room. She was bright-eyed, having slept through Mike's incessant tossing and turning in bed.

"The coffee tastes stale," he complained.

"Then I'll make us a fresh pot," she replied as she did most every morning.

While Bess began breakfast, she studied her husband, who was deeply engrossed in the property map spread out before him. Although their years together had stunted most of her emotions and had tainted many of her memories, she could still remember why she had married Mike McNear forty years before; if nothing else, he was an honest, hardworking man. She tilted her head as she continued to think about the man he had become, which was easier than thinking about the woman she had become.

He was still as honest and as hardworking as on the day of their civil ceremony on the second floor of Wheatley's state building, but an invasive bitterness had crept in between the seams of his character. This animosity was the mortar that held together the different facets of his aging personality. And Bess was the first to realize that she was the collateral damage—the innocent victim in his fight against the world. But she had made that bed and taken those vows, and she would stay by his side until her last breath.

"Did you not sleep well?" she asked.

"Maybe a bit anxious thinking about the surveyor's proposed plat map. He dropped it off yesterday," Mike said.

Her interest piqued, Bess put down the bowl in which she had been scrambling eggs and wiped her hands on a towel. "May I see?"

Mike grabbed the paper and doubled it over. "No need to, Mother," he said. "Just an idea I'm talking about."

"Talking to whom?"

"Joan Stokes," he said before adding, "And Russell Harris."

Bess's eyes closed with suspicion. "Why are you talking to our lawyer?"

Mike sighed loudly to show his exasperation.

"Well?" she asked again.

"He knows the deed and any restrictions on the property. I don't want the town messing up a good deal."

She pursed her lips. "How could the town mess up the sale of our farm?"

"Because we might be selling to a real estate developer," he blurted out. "To a developer, not a farmer. To someone I care nothing about who will hack up this forsaken farm in a hundred different pieces. I'll be buried six feet under before I let the town mess up the deal of a lifetime."

Bess stood in the middle of the kitchen, speechless. Although she had watched their herd of dairy cows diminish in size over the years, and although she had heard Mike rant and rave about selling the farm more than once, she had never thought he would actually consider selling the land to someone other than another farmer.

"Well, don't just stand there," he rumbled, not wanting to hear a rebuttal. "Go make some breakfast."

The Lumby Lines

# Real Estate

July 15

---

Single car garage for nothing bigger than Mini Cooper. Must share. $8/month. Call now 925-0746

---

For Rent: Theater above Lumby Feed Store. Great for private parties or drama club. Guinea hens will be removed beforehand. $6 a day. See Sam.

---

For Rent: Three horse stalls in back of Lumby Feed Store. Great temporary housing for your spare livestock. Daily turnout in backyard. $35 a month. See Sam.

Charming one-room rustic cabin with Martha Stewart colors. No phone and limited electricity but that's what "rustic" means. July 18-24. Call Phil 925-3928

---

Office space available: Was Denny Anderson's before he passed. First and last month deposit. $220/month. Tenant will have to remove dentist chair if they don't want it.

---

Still available. 60x20 Barn. 4 stalls with hayloft. Priced reduced. Negotiable. North on Hunts Mill Rd. 925-4338

---

A gem in the rough. 40 acre abandoned trout farm off of Deer Trail Lane. Currently inaccessible but offering lots of privacy. Eagle habitat. Call Joan Stokes at Main Street Realty 925-9292 and let the best Realtor in town find your dream home!

---

For sale or long-term rent: One 8x14 burial at the local cemetery. Recently divorced and plans for eternal afterlife have changed. Price very negotiable. Call Mac Patterson 925-8033.

---

For sale: One lovely 8x14 burial lot under enormous oak tree with good views of lake. Recently divorced and won't be lying next to Mac after I pass. $250 for both. Call Ellen Patterson 925-6927.

---

Main Street Realty presents four-thousand acre dairy farm with unlimited commercial development opportunities. Exclusive listing with Joan Stokes.

Upon returning to Lumby from St. Cross Abbey, Mark led the caravan on a roundabout route through town toward the fairgrounds. From Main Street, everyone could see the Ferris wheel as it revolved slowly in the sky.

Mark turned left onto North Grant Avenue and headed north. "We need to keep a hawk's eye on everything that's going on at the fairgrounds," he said, looking at his nephew in the rearview mirror. "There are so many more events this year, and some of the competitions are going to get pretty serious."

"What have you signed up for?" Corey asked from the backseat.

"Bull wrangling," Mark said in a low, ominous voice.

"Wrangling?" Corey asked.

"Not exactly." Pam turned in her seat to face Corey and Lynn in the back. "Joshua and Mark think they can lead Old Jesse through an obstacle course."

Corey thought for a moment, looking perplexed. "What's so difficult about taking hold of a bull's halter and walking him around?"

"Oh, no," Pam said. "That would be too intelligent. These silly goofs are doing it without a halter, a lead rope, or a bucket of oats."

"No physical contact with the bull at all," Mark clarified.

Corey looked even more confused. "Then how do you get him to go where you want?"

"Joshua's going to be a living muleta running in front of the bull," Pam replied.

"What's a muleta?" Lynn asked.

"The red cape that matadors use," Corey answered.

Pam raised her brows. "I'm impressed."

The young man blushed. "Eighth-grade Spanish."

"But isn't that dangerous?" Lynn asked.

Mark sat taller in his seat. "Sure. It's a deadly serious competition."

Pam rolled her eyes. "Lynn, what Mark's not telling you is that most of the bulls are so old and arthritic, they can barely take two consecutive steps without wheezing up a storm. Except, of course, Old Jesse, who has a fire in his belly."

"If Joshua is in front, where are you going to be, Uncle Mark?" Corey asked.

"I'm the rover, circling the bull to make sure he stays on course. Okay, here we are," he said, turning into the fairgrounds parking lot.

Hank stood at the gate dressed as a clown. Although he had actually been looking forward to the carnival, now that he was dressed like Bozo, he was having serious doubts. But Jimmy D had personally requested that Hank stay positive and show his support by being a one-bird publicity team for the fair. Had Jimmy known that Hank had lingering issues with carnivals that began in his fledgling days, and had Jimmy also known that the noises of the fair brought endless nightmares that woke Hank up at all hours of the morning from his perch on the Ferris wheel, the town mayor would never have made such an appeal of the town mascot. But first and foremost, Hank was a loyal Lumby resident, and he would bend a wing in any direction just to support the town he so dearly loved.

"There's a plastic pink flamingo dressed like a clown," Lynn said.

Pam glanced over at Hank, who, out of total embarrassment, tried to hide his face under the bright orange Ronald McDonald wig. "I'm sure he hates every minute of it. He's probably just counting cars, but he'll be happier when he starts collecting tickets tomorrow."

Corey chuckled.

"And why is he dressed like a clown?" Lynn asked.

"Now, that's a good question," Pam said. "Everyone knows he's terrified of carnies."

Lynn was confused. "But—"

"They're goofing on you, Aunt Lynn," Corey said kindly.

"Actually, we're not," Pam said.

"Okay," Mark said as he parked the car. "Let's check it out." He jumped out of the Jeep and waved to Carter to park next to him.

"That Ferris wheel is so much bigger than the one they had in

Wheatley," Pam said, her head bent back as she gawked at the structure towering over the fairgrounds.

Carter heaved himself out of the car and looked up. "Is that what you've been talking about, Marko?" he asked, pointing to the Ferris wheel. "It looks like a kiddie ride."

Pam tried to ignore his patronizing tone. "It's four stories high," she said.

"Okay," Mark intervened, "there's a lot to explore. Let's plan to meet back here in an hour."

Carter and Nancy, followed by Patrick and Elaine, joined the others, who were already heading toward the main gate, where two men were hanging a freshly painted ADMISSIONS sign above the entrance.

"This little fair has got to be a joke, Marko," Carter said, slapping his brother-in-law on the back. "Great fodder for the show, though."

Mark and Pam glanced at each other in dismay.

"Maybe it's not to your standards," Pam said, "but we're proud of it."

"So my standards are too high now?" Carter asked, feigning innocence. "You could put every single ride inside one of the buildings at the Washington State Fair." He looked over at the 4-H building, where several teenagers were already washing down their livestock. "Piddly, but it's pretty good fodder. We'll have a great time with this on the show."

"This isn't what your listeners are interested in," Mark said. "And we agreed you'd lay off Lumby."

Carter shook his head. "I certainly don't remember saying that. And my fans are most definitely interested in Lumby because I'm here and I tell them what's important."

"It's just a quiet, peaceful, out-of-the-way town. All and all, very unexciting," Mark argued.

"That's where you're wrong, Marko. There is no real peace anywhere, just beds of festering conflict."

"Not in Lumby," Pam insisted.

"Give me one day, and I'll prove you wrong," Carter said. "I can get the best of friends to go after each other in two minutes flat."

"And just how useful is that?" his son asked.

"Ah, the fruit of my loins doth protest," Carter snickered. "Because, son, conflict gets the juices flowing and the synapses jumping. Life would be mighty boring without contention."

Corey shook his head in repugnance. "A fight for fight's sake is ludicrous," he said before turning on his heels and walking away from the group.

"Who would have ever guessed he's my son?" Carter snipped.

"Mark Walker!" an attractive older woman called out from behind them.

Mark turned and then smiled broadly. "I haven't seen you in forever," he said. "Don't tell me you're selling the fairgrounds?"

"That would never happen," she said.

Mark stepped back. "Joan, this is my brother-in-law, Carter Reed. Carter, this is a close friend of ours, Joan Stokes. She owns Main Street Realty and has given us invaluable advice and help over the years. In fact, she was our broker when we bought Montis."

Carter shook her hand. "Nice meeting you."

"Your reputation precedes you," she said sweetly. "I heard rumors that you were coming to Lumby. I'm sorry, I have to admit I've never listened to your show, but I hear it has quite a following."

Carter puffed out his chest. "Nine million strong."

"How nice," Joan said in a cool, polite tone. She turned to Mark and slid her arm through his. "May I ask a favor?"

"Name it," he said.

"I just listed a large property west of town—"

Mark glanced at her coyly. "Mike McNear's farm?"

"My, word travels fast," she said. "The price is three million, so I'm advertising to high-end buyers."

Mark whistled. "I was just out there yesterday. In truth, I'm a little shocked it's listing for that much—the place looked really unkempt," he whispered.

"The farm itself isn't really worth anything, but Mike has four thousand unrestricted acres that are protected on three sides by state and national forests. It's a gem for residential or even commercial development."

"So . . . you want me to write you a check?" Mark laughed.

"A little less painful than that. I was hoping to put a few flyers advertising the property in your lobby. You have clientele who just might be interested." She reached into her soft leather briefcase and withdrew a large envelope with his name on it. "There are about a dozen here. If you need more, just call and I'll swing by."

"I'll put them out when we get home, but we're closed this week for our family reunion and won't have any guests until next Monday."

"That's fine," Joan said, patting Mark's arm. "With any luck, it will be sold by then. I have a buyer flying in tomorrow to look at it."

Mark was impressed. "Flying in. Wow. Is it one of those farm conglomerate guys?"

"No, Mr. Shaw is a developer who may be interested in building a ski resort here," she said.

As soon as the name was mentioned, Carter raised his brows. "Vince Shaw?" he asked.

Joan immediately regretted mentioning her client's name. "Yes," she said, but offered no other information.

"Do you know him?" Mark asked his brother-in-law.

"Not personally. He's called into the show a few times, and I know about his development projects in Aspen and Telluride. He certainly knows how to build some successful asphalt jungles and ski resorts. Real controversial, though, and hated by most environmentalists. We always get great ratings when he goes on the air."

Before hearing any more, Joan said, "I need to scoot."

"We'll see you on Saturday?" Mark asked.

She winked. "I wouldn't miss your ceremony for the world. And thanks for putting out the brochures."

Strolling on the other side of the 4-H building, watching the teenagers groom their animals, Pam, Elaine and Patrick had fallen behind the others.

"This is charming," Elaine said, taking hold of Patrick's hand.

"What a great childhood they have," Patrick said, watching a young girl tend to her goat. "In our corner of Virginia, we're not as rural as you are here, but we're certainly closer to farms than to the city."

"But the kids still get a lot of urban influence," Elaine said.

"Our daughter certainly does," Patrick added.

"I'm sorry she didn't join us this morning," Pam said.

Patrick looked at Elaine. "I'm sure she's still sound asleep," he said.

"Getting her to join us for church on Sunday mornings was a battle we lost quite some time ago," Elaine added.

Patrick sighed deeply. "In truth, we've lost a lot of battles along the way with Jessica."

Elaine squeezed his hand. "You make it sound as if everything is a win-or-lose outcome with her."

"Frequently, it is," Patrick countered. "And we've given in on almost every occasion."

"She needs her own space," Elaine said.

"No, she needs us to correct her course when she can't see the road. She's become such a different person this last year, I don't even recognize her," Patrick admitted.

Elaine was clearly embarrassed to be disagreeing with her husband in front of Pam. "Sorry for washing our laundry in public," she said.

Pam shrugged. "I can't image how anyone raises a kid in these times," she said sympathetically. "I know I would find it impossible, trying to buffer all the peer pressure kids feel today. And the technology that they have at their fingertips is unbelievable."

Patrick turned to Elaine. "Speaking of which, I thought we were going to have her turn off all of her electronics during the family reunion."

Elaine looked at the ground. "It would have ruined her week, but she promised not to blog or upload any videos, and only to text when absolutely necessary to keep in touch with her friends."

"I love you, dear," Patrick said, "but I think we're so out of touch with Jessica, we don't know what would ruin her week."

Elaine turned to Pam to explain. "Jessica was doing really well in her freshman year—she had a nice group of friends and was making great grades—and then, almost overnight, she became obsessed about being part of this tight 'in' clique. She dropped her other friends, and she's no longer interested in any of her classes. It's almost as if she's sabotaging herself and intentionally pulling in lower grades. And she's become obsessed with her appearance."

"She says she's too tall one day and then too heavy the next—it's always something," Patrick added. "She threw away most of her clothes and is only wearing what her new friends wear."

"But she seems as sweet as she always was," Pam said.

Patrick shook his head. "She's always had good manners, and on the surface the changes seem fine. But I think she's pretty frustrated right now. She's trying too hard to get noticed and accepted by this specific group of kids, and she's forgotten who she really is and what she values."

"You two must see a lot of that in school," Pam said.

Elaine was the first to reply. "Since all of my tutoring is one-on-one, I don't see any of the kids in a group."

"And I only see them at a distance," Patrick replied. "I teach mostly seniors who have already landed."

"Landed?" Pam asked.

"Kids who have already established their circles of friends," Patrick said.

"Jessica is just fine," Elaine said protectively. "She's just trying to find her place."

Patrick shook his head in disagreement. "She's jumping through hoops of fire, and she has no idea how burned she can get."

## NINETEEN
# *Schmucks*

Contrary to her parents' assumption, while the others were strolling around Lumby's fairgrounds, Jessica was not only awake but up and hovering precariously over Old Jesse's stall. In fact, most of her activities since arriving at Montis had escaped her parents' notice or scrutiny.

The evening before, Jessica had rearranged the furniture in her room by pushing together two nightstands to form a desk for her electronic equipment, which included two cell phones, an iPod, two laptops, an assortment of web cameras, several zip drives, and one portable keyboard. After a few hours of restless sleep and well before the procession left Montis for St. Cross, she was online again, scanning her friends' blogs and replying when appropriate. In vain, she tried to contact a few of her new friends by jumping into trendy chat rooms. She only slid back into bed and feigned sleep for a few minutes when her parents quietly checked in on her after breakfast.

Before choosing the final location for her remote camera, Jessica had secretly explored most of the Montis compound, including Pam and Mark's private residence. But it was the size and smells of the small barn that most appealed to her, although she would never have admitted it to either her family or friends—in her circle, barns were considered dull if not totally hick.

She was enjoying a few minutes of private pleasure sitting in the hayloft watching the animals below her: a badly sheared sheep walked down the center aisle and disappeared around the corner, and the bull called Old Jesse obsessed over every move made by her aunt Lynn's cat. When Coco left the stall to go hunting for fresh food, Old Jesse kept one watchful eye on the kittens and another on the hole Coco used for access, impatiently waiting for her return. When Coco finally did reappear, the bull was more excited than her brood and licked her body until she was soaked.

"This could be pretty good," Jessica whispered as she thought about how she could edit a relatively innocuous barn scene into a hilarious video that she would post on her blog. And, for a good laugh, there was always Aunt Lynn talking to her cat. With any luck, most of her friends would see it. With great luck, her video would go viral and be seen by hundreds of thousands. One viral video on YouTube would surely guarantee a permanent place in the clique.

Jessica began to inch her way from the floor of the loft onto a foot-wide crossbeam that ran between the rafters in the ceiling, well above the stall. Old Jesse looked up and, not liking the commotion overhead, carefully stepped over Coco and her litter to protect them from debris falling from the beam. Jessica looked down and, not liking the long horns that were pointed up at her, decided not to press her luck by crawling out any farther.

She expertly attached the micro video camera, no larger than a deck of cards, to the side of the beam and angled the lens so that Jesse's stall was in full view. After making one final adjustment to the equipment, Jessica slid back to the loft.

"Perfect," she whispered.

Once downstairs, she used various grooming brooms to conceal a wireless receiver and amplifier on the shelf closest to the barn door. This was needed to boost the video signal up to her room in the guest annex, where she would subsequently download it into her computer, edit it, overlay a sound track, and then upload the stream to the Internet for all to see.

Leaving the barn, she accidentally kicked one of the oat buckets, knocking off the lid. The animals responded in kind: Old Jesse ran his horns against the iron grates of the stall door, and Peanuts, the draft horse, neighed loudly from the pasture.

Peering out the barn to ensure no one was watching, Jessica grabbed a small can of oats, opened the gate to where Peanuts was grazing, and calmly walked up to the horse. With an extended palm full of feed, she spoke softly to the animal.

"Would you like some oats?" she asked.

The horse whinnied and licked the feed, mouthing Jessica's fingers with its soft lips to ensure it had gotten every last grain. Jessica stroked the neck of the beautiful animal, which responded by pushing its head into her chest.

"You can't tell a soul I was out here with you—this is *so* not cool," she confided as she scratched the horse's forehead. Glancing around the serene, verdant pasture, she exhaled in envy. "You must have it pretty easy here. Plenty of grass and a couple of sheep to keep you company." She began combing the mare's mane with her fingers. "No pressure to be anything other than a kind, lazy old horse." The horse whinnied as Jessica rested her head on its withers. "You like that, don't you?" she asked, gently scratching its coat with her nails. "And you don't care how tall or fat I am, just as long as I keep stroking your neck, don't you? Well, just between you and me, horse, I wish I could stay here forever."

A car driving down Farm to Market Road caught Jessica's attention, and she hid behind the horse's body. "Okay, that's it, I've got to go," she said, giving the horse one final handful of sweet feed.

Back in her bedroom, Jessica booted up her computer. While she was waiting, she took out a can of Red Mad Dog she had hidden deep in her suitcase. Although her parents had banned the drink in their home, and although she not only disliked its taste but also hated how the caffeine sped up her heart, Jessica ensured that she had an ample supply because it was what everyone else was drinking. She hoped that, in time, she would come to enjoy not only the flavor but also the artificial high—the buzz, as her peers called it—that Red Mad Dog delivered.

She sat at her desk, breathed deeply, and began typing for her blog.

day 2 in lumby land in the middle of nowhere surrounded by lameness. totally boring so i just set up a web cam down in the barn. so totally lame it's funny: this out of control bull is protecting a bunch of barn cats that my aunt lynn thinks are purebreds. the cat walks right, the bull follows. the cat circles the barn, the bull follows. and aunt lynn is going totally nuts trying to get her little darlings out of there--she's so emo. i'll hang there for a few days and then move the camera over to the inn where my uncle carter is broadcasting his radio show. we'll see exactly what happens when he goes off the air. should be tight--I'm amped. how cool will that be? g2g.

After loading her entry and posting it on her webpage, Jessica looked at the time. It would be another twenty or thirty minutes before the others returned, long enough to jump into an online chat room and see if there was anyone in the area that she could hang with for the next week.

She first searched for a forum to join—a chat room that was geographically targeted to the area. Within a few minutes, Jessica found RaveInNW.com. Perfect, she thought, and immediately registered under her usual pseudonym, abt2party. When she entered the chat room, there were forty people already online carrying on several different conversations.

flyman1964: hey abt2party. flyman1964 here from denver

Several others had taken note of the new username and welcomed her. Jessica got right down to the point as she always did.

abt2party: hey fly. imprisoned in lumby for a week. anything happening nearby?

cronk19: where in the world is lumby?

abt2party: lol. i keep asking that myself

amhikt: youre about 2o mls wst of rocky mount

roacher: we have a rave tonight at 11pm--3 hrs drive north of u

abt2party: can't do--no wheels. something closer?

marley3823: blowout wheatley this thur

abt2party: like your username—after bob marley? how cool is that. i love his music

marley3823: 17 west city road

abt2party: possible

flyman1964: where u from?

abt2party: middleburg va. on family vaca. u?

flyman1964: butte

nightcrawler: salt lake surrounded by crazy mormans

postpunk: spokane

42BiteMe: calgary

nightcrawler: oh canada 2cool

2bshades: was up in vancouver for dark wave in may

42BiteMe: cult-cult jam?

2bshades: omg it was sweet

abt2party: saw them in dc. nothing else going on around here?

marley3823: more cows than people in this area and cows don't drink

abt2party: ok—thurs night. will hitch to wheatley but then need directions to rave.

marley3823: raves are a little different up here

abt2party: right now, i'll take any blowout party there is

Just then, Jessica heard cars pull into the drive.

abt2party: parents just landed

marley3823: you old enough to drink?

Jessica was surprised by the question. Who cares? she thought.

abt2party: old enough to know how to have fun

She quickly turned off her computer and put her iPod headset on as she jumped on her bed.

ꟹ

Carter squeezed himself out of the car and beat his chest several times with open palms. "Nothing like bringing home the juice the day before we air."

Mark closed the door of the Jeep. "The juice? What's that?" he asked.

"Good old-fashioned yuk-yuk, Marko," Carter said, stretching out his arms. "The can't-believe-it-if-you-didn't-see-it-for-yourself stories that nine million people tune in to listen to."

"Remember, Carter," Mark said, "the family and Lumby are off limits."

"No, no, no," Carter said, shaking his head. "I only agreed that the monks were sacredly unmentionable. Everything else is fair game."

Lynn, who was standing next to Mark, took a few steps back. "Well, take me off your target list," she warned Carter. "I don't want to be the butt of any of your jokes."

"Of course, not you, Lynn," Carter said innocently. "Just your cat."

If Lynn's eyes could have launched daggers, Carter would have been feeling his wounds.

"I mean, really," Carter continued, his voice booming across the courtyard. "A prize-winning purebred feline is set up with an aristocratic equivalent and then squirts out a bunch of worthless mongrels. What a proverbial kick in the—"

"Carter!" Lynn exclaimed.

"You don't want to go there, Carter," Mark said, coming to his sister's defense.

"You folks are just a bunch of pansy as—"

"Okay!" Pam exclaimed, raising her arms. "Let's take a break. We're having ribs and chicken on the barbecue, and André has cold beer on tap. Why don't we all go and change into something more comfortable and then make our way to the backyard?"

"Sounds like a great plan," Patrick said.

"We're off to see Jessica," Elaine said. "We'll be out shortly."

Pam glanced over at Lynn, who hadn't moved a step since her rapid-fire exchange with Carter. "Lynn, why don't we go down to check on Coco?"

Lynn didn't take her eyes off Carter as she replied, "That's a good idea. I think I'm ready to face another bull."

And then Pam did something that surprised even her; she put her arm around Lynn's shoulders and walked her away from the group. "I'll go with you," she said. "Mark, hold down the fort."

Nancy pulled Carter toward the main building. "We'll be back down in a while."

Carter looked over his shoulder. "And will you please find something tougher than a badminton game, Marko," he said. "It's time we go man-to-man."

"Yeah, whatever," Mark said under his breath.

"That's what I say most of the time," Corey said.

Mark jumped, startled to hear the boy behind him. He stood face-to-face with Corey, who was leaning against the car only a few feet away.

"Crap," Mark said, embarrassed to have been overheard. "That didn't sound quite right."

"It sounded honest," Corey replied.

"Look," Mark said, "I shouldn't have said that. Your dad's a good guy—"

"Whose actions speak louder than words, which are deafening."

Mark thought for a minute, trying to understand what Corey meant. "He's Carter Reed. You can't expect anything more from him."

"Actually, he's my father, and I expect a *lot* more from him."

Mark was taken aback by the astuteness of his nephew's comment. "When did you get so insightful?"

"When you're left alone in the water," Corey said, watching his parents walk up the porch steps, "you learn how to swim pretty fast."

Mark kicked a stone next to his foot, searching for the right words to say. "First and foremost, he's your father."

"Not true, Uncle Mark," Corey said with no bitterness in his tone. "First and foremost, he's Carter Reed. You have to give him credit for all that he's accomplished. I might think he's a little misguided, but there's an entire country out there that thinks otherwise."

On the walk to the Montis barn, Lynn had to step more quickly to keep in stride with Pam, who was significantly taller. To avoid tripping, she kept her eyes on the rough ground.

"I'm sorry Carter made fun of Coco," Pam finally said. "You didn't deserve *that*."

"You make it sound like I deserved something," Lynn said.

Pam slowed her pace and considered Lynn's reply. Pam knew Lynn was right—that's exactly what she'd meant. "Well, Lynn," she said cautiously, "sometimes it's not easy to talk with you."

Lynn stopped dead in her tracks. "What do you want from me?" Her voice flamed with anger.

"You could start by apologizing to Mark," Pam blurted out, and then looked as shocked for saying it as Lynn did hearing it.

Lynn's cheeks flushed. "Apologize for what?" she exclaimed.

"You can't be serious!" Pam said in disbelief. "You need to apologize for what you did after the trial."

Lynn glared at Pam. "*Dan* was the one who stole from Mark, not me!" she yelled.

"But that doesn't mean you were innocent, Lynn. You pitted Nancy and Patrick against Mark."

"Because the judge ruled in Dan's favor! How many times do I have to say that?"

"But you know Dan stole the money and lied about it!"

"I didn't know that until later."

"And that's when you should have said something to everyone." Pam took a quick breath. "You should say something now."

"I will not!" Lynn slammed her fist against her leg. "There's nothing to say."

"I give up," Pam said, lifting her arms in the air and then letting them drop.

"You just wait to see how you react when you're betrayed," Lynn spat.

Pam blinked, startled by the comment. "Mark would never break our vows."

"That's exactly what I thought."

"But you had some clue that Dan was a dishonest schmuck the day you married him," Pam said.

Lynn stepped back as if she had been hit. Pam drew her brows together. "Didn't you?" she asked, to which there was no reply. "What were you thinking all those years when he acted like such a jerk?"

"Dan acted no more a jerk than Carter does," Lynn said.

"How can you stand there and defend Dan in any way?" Pam asked. "There's a huge difference between Dan and Carter. Carter is an idiot with some major misconceptions who might one day wake up and get it. But Dan doesn't even have a moral compass. People know exactly where Carter stands—right smack in the middle—but everything that Dan did was under the covers." Pam bit her lip at her choice of words.

Lynn had heard enough. She turned on her heels and headed for the barn, her hands pushed deep in her pockets.

Pam remained where she was. "You've got to make things right for Mark," she called to Lynn's back.

"I already have. The whole thing was Dan's fault—not mine," Lynn said, without turning around. The crack in her voice was a sure giveaway that she was crying.

## TWENTY
# *Harnessed*

In the backyard of Montis Inn, Robert was kneeling behind Kay, trying to tighten a yellow nylon strap on the harness that was wrapped under and around her torso. Piled high on the picnic table next to them was climbing equipment they had rented that afternoon in preparation for their outing the next day.

Kay picked up a small metal loop that was hinged on one side. "What did he call this, dear?"

Robert tipped his head. "I forget. Something like a cabinert?" he said. "I think we may have a problem with this harness—your waist is simply too small."

"You don't seem to have any complaints about my waist any other time," she whispered.

Robert chuckled as he stood up behind her. Wrapping both arms around Kay, he kissed her on her neck. "Nor will I ever," he murmured back. "But this contraption is too loose on you. I've pulled the straps as far as they go, and it's just not snug enough."

He grabbed hold of the shoulder pads and shook the harness. Kay was so light that Robert lifted her off her feet, her body bouncing around like a puppet. She burst into laughter.

"I love when you laugh," he said. Robert picked Kay up again, and she wrapped herself around him, giggling like a young girl.

"This is going to be fun, isn't it?" she said into his ear.

"Like everything we do," he replied.

Just then, André came around the corner of the dining room carrying a tray to the barbecue grill. He cleared his throat so the couple would know they were not alone.

"Hi, André," Robert said, lowering Kay to her feet.

"Good afternoon to both of you," he said. "Very nice attire, Kay. Is that a new AARP designer top?"

"This old thing?" Kay joked, pulling at the straps of the harness.

"We're going hiking tomorrow," Robert explained.

"*Rappelling*," Kay corrected him.

"Whatever you say, dear."

"Hey, André," Mark called out from a dining room window, "do you want the pan of ribs in the refrigerator?"

"That's Mark's way of saying I should hurry up because he's hungry," André said in a low voice to Kay and Robert. "That man can eat three times his weight and never gain a pound."

Mark's voice rang out again. "You want the ribs?"

Everyone laughed.

"You can bring out the bruschetta," André called back. "And why don't you throw away that leftover barbecue chicken on the top shelf?" André winked at the others.

"Yeah, good idea." Mark headed for the kitchen.

Several minutes later, Mark walked into the backyard licking sauce off his fingers.

André glanced over at him and asked, "The bruschetta?"

Mark looked as if he had been caught red-handed and bolted back to the kitchen without saying a word. When he returned, he noticed Kay's harness still strapped around her body. "Is that for this afternoon's activities?" he asked as he placed a tray of appetizers on the table closest to André.

Kay beamed. "It's for our lesson tomorrow."

Mark looked confused. “You’re going parachuting?”

“No, but that’s a pretty good suggestion,” Kay said, nudging Robert with her elbow.

Mark looked alarmed. “I’m not suggesting that at all.”

“We’re going rappelling up in the mountains,” Robert said.

“*Rappelling,*” Kay repeated.

Mark was befuddled. “Rock climbing?”

Kay stretched her body to test the feel of the harness. “I think rock climbing involves going up and rappelling is when you go down,” she said, “but I suppose we need to get to the top of the cliff somehow so there’s probably a little hiking involved.”

Mark shook his head. “This isn’t good.”

“Why do you say that?” Kay asked. “It’s a perfect way to spend a beautiful afternoon.”

“If you’re twenty, maybe,” Mark said before thinking.

Kay rolled her eyes. “Don’t tell me you think we should be in a nursing home too?”

“Kay, we need to talk,” Mark said, taking hold of her thin hand. “This idea of yours will drive Pam nuts. She was up half the night worrying about you.”

“Worried about what?” Kay asked, truly oblivious to the perils that her daughter saw so clearly.

“That you’ll get hurt,” Mark replied, and then added, “Or worse.”

“We’re all going to die sometime,” Kay retorted. “During the few healthy years we have remaining, we’re not going to live so scared that we don’t go outside.”

“But *rappelling*?” Mark asked.

“It’s relatively safe,” Robert offered. “We met the instructor on our way back from Rocky Mount. By the way—great motorcycle.”

Mark was relieved. “So it didn’t break down or anything?”

“Ran like a charm,” Robert. “I appreciate the opportunity to drive it.”

Kay grinned with a twinkle in her eye. “And the gliding was tremendous," she said. "A tow plane pulled us up to eight thousand feet. The views were spectacular!"

"That was the bumpy part," Robert added, "but as soon as the pilot released the towline, it instantly became quiet and still."

"For a moment, it felt like we were hovering, and then the glider gently floated forward." Kay looked at Robert and beamed. "It's a once-in-a-lifetime sensation that I've never had before, and I'll certainly never forget it."

"I think you found more lift than we did on our flight," Robert said to Kay.

"It was just amazing, Mark," she continued, her eyes dancing with excitement. "In the plane, we watched for eagles who were gaining lift, and when we spotted one, we glided over to the same thermal. The pilot banked the plane in a tight circle, and we started to climb and gain altitude. And then the thermal would weaken, and we'd begin to glide around looking for another eagle and another thermal. It was one of the most extraordinary things I've ever done."

"I'm glad you two had such a good time, but rock climbing is very different," Mark said.

"We're going with a good group," Robert explained as he handed Mark a brochure of the climbing school.

Mark skimmed the sales pitch and began reading aloud. "'It's a unique and extraordinary opportunity for adventurous souls to experience the exhilaration of exploring the jagged cliffs of the Northwest. It is an initiation into the unexpected, an opportunity to achieve thrills beyond your wildest dreams. You'll reach deep within yourselves and discover strengths of body and spirit you never knew you possessed. You will conquer the dangers of nature in the raw.'" He looked up and caught both Kay's and Robert's eyes. "Like gravity," he quipped. "Did you notice some of these words: 'jagged cliffs,' 'natural dangers'? Need I say more? Now, let's get you out of that thing before Pam—"

"Mother? What on earth are you doing?" Pam asked, hurrying over from the courtyard.

"Catches on?" Kay whispered to Mark. "Hello, darling," she said sweetly, raising her voice and watching Pam jog toward them. "Wonderful weather for your barbecue."

Pam frowned. "Why are you wearing a harness?"

"To see if it would fit, of course," Kay replied.

"They're going rappelling tomorrow," Mark blurted out.

Seeing Pam's horrified reaction, Kay immediately backtracked. "More like a country stroll," she said.

Pam picked up a handful of the mountain climbing equipment that was lying on the table. "Since when do you need carabiners for a stroll?"

"That's it!" Kay said, elbowing Robert. "A car-a-*bi*-ner," she said, pronouncing each syllable slowly. "We need to remember that—it's called a carabiner."

"No, you don't need to remember that." Pam looked exasperated. "And how about this?" she asked, still wanting an explanation from her mother.

"Pam, for goodness' sake, we're taking an experienced guide with us," Kay said.

"You're going to kill yourself."

"Not unless the rope breaks," Kay quipped.

Pam's look of alarm deepened. "I didn't even think about that possibility."

"It won't happen—Kay's too lightweight," Robert said, picking her up by the harness straps.

Kay giggled. "Stop doing that."

Pam began to untie the nylon straps. "We'll talk about this later."

"Yes, when we tell you all about it tomorrow evening," Kay said in a stern voice.

André approached the group. "Finally, a man of reason," Pam said, glancing up as she loosened the fastenings from around Kay's legs. "André, would you not agree that rock climbing at my mother's age is preposterous?"

André thought for a moment. "Actually, not at all. Activity of all kinds keeps the heart young."

Pam glared at her chef. "Traitor."

Just as the harness dropped from around Kay's body, Chuck Bryson rounded the corner. "Good afternoon, one and all," he said.

"Chuck, have you met my daredevil mother, Kay?" Pam asked.

"An honor," Chuck said, shaking her hand as she stepped out of the harness.

"And Robert Day, this is our good friend Chuck Bryson," Mark added.

Chuck eyed the gear on the table. "Another competition for the county fair?" he asked Mark.

"No," Mark replied, "but before you leave, you need to go down to the barn and see Jesse. He's our entry for the obstacle course, and he's enormous."

Chuck laughed. "I'll do that—I haven't seen that old bull in years. But why the rock climbing equipment?'

"My mother and Robert are going rappelling tomorrow," Pam told Chuck with evident disapproval.

Chuck's eyes lit up. "Outstanding! Last month I went up to the vertical drop near Bearclaw Pass with a local climbing club from Lumby. I was holding on for dear life, but it was absolutely exhilarating."

Pam glowered. "You're fifteen years younger and in much better shape," she argued.

"Never too old, that's my motto," Chuck said.

"I give up." Pam began stuffing the carabiners into her pockets just to get them out of sight.

"Is there anything I can do?" Chuck asked.

"I think you've done quite enough," Pam retorted.

"Great," Mark said, grabbing Chuck's arm. "I'm taking Chuck down to see Old Jesse. We'll be back in a minute."

"No, you don't," Pam said. "We need to start getting ready for dinner, and I need some help around here. Would you please get rid of all this climbing tackle?"

"Sure, honey," he said, hoping that out of sight, out of mind would prove true for his wife. Mark looked at Chuck and shrugged. "Go on down," he suggested. "I'll join you in a few minutes."

As Chuck walked off, Pam called out, "And would you make sure Coco has plenty to eat?"

Chuck waved his hand, wondering who exactly Coco was.

TWENTY-ONE

# *Skirt*

"Do you think she's sleeping?" Elaine asked in a low voice as she and Patrick walked down the hall to their daughter's room.

"If she is, she shouldn't be," Patrick responded. "It's not good that she's up until all hours of the morning and then sleeps all day."

Elaine shrugged. "Some kids don't respond well to a regimented schedule."

"But Jess isn't one of them—she needs more structure."

Elaine dropped her shoulders in resignation. The rules she had so carefully laid out for raising their only child had changed dramatically over the prior twelve months—inclusion gave way to exclusion, control gave way to freedom, conversation gave way to detachment, and grades just gave way. Although Elaine never said as much—and although each parental decision she made, she made for Jessica's happiness—she had come to the uncomfortable conclusion that her daughter was an innocent victim of her own shortcomings as a mother.

"She'll grow out of it. She'll mature," Elaine said, once again avoiding the reality of changes she had seen in Jessica.

“Not without limits and definitely not without direction,” Patrick said.

Elaine’s defenses rose. “We’re her parents—of course we give her direction.”

“No, Elaine, we enable her. We both hate conflict, so we give her a free pass to do whatever she wants,” he said, summing up the problem.

Elaine stopped in midstep. “So your answer is to hover over her and police everything she does?”

Having had this exact conversation more times than he could remember in the last few months, Patrick sighed in frustration. “Obviously not. But she’s making bad decisions now, and I think it’s because of her new friends.”

“I’m not even sure you could call Missy and Emily friends,” Elaine said.

“It doesn’t matter. She’s certainly doing everything possible just to fit in,” Patrick commented. “I barely recognize her anymore.”

“It could be a lot worse,” Elaine said, abruptly ending the discussion. She tapped gently on the bedroom door. “Jessica? Are you in there?” She was going to peek in the room but discovered the door was locked. “Jessica?” she said sweetly. “It’s dinnertime.”

Patrick wasn’t as patient, and knocked loudly. “Jess, it’s us.”

A few seconds later, Jessica opened the door. Music was blasting from the earbuds hanging around her neck. She wore a low-cut navy shell with a light blue blouse over it and a very short blue skirt. She had on eye makeup, blush and lip gloss, and several silver earrings dangled from each earlobe.

Not waiting for an invitation, Patrick stepped into her room.

“Can we come in?” Elaine asked before crossing the threshold.

Jessica watched her father walk toward her makeshift desk. “Doesn’t seem to be my decision, so sure, come on in,” she said, plunking herself down on the bed.

“You missed a wonderful service at the monastery,” Elaine said cheerfully.

"I was tired."

Patrick was staring at one of the two computer screens that appeared to be relaying a live video of a bull following a cat around a stall. A woman's voice was heard: "Coco, how's my sweetie doing?"

Jessica tried to hold in her laughter.

"That's Lynn's voice!" Patrick glanced over at his daughter and pointed at the computer. "What is this?"

Jessica shrugged. "Just a stream."

"In English, please."

Jessica looked at her mother. "Mom," she whined.

For once, Elaine didn't jump to her daughter's defense. She remained silent, staring at the screen as well.

"Jessica?" her father said.

Jessica rolled her eyes. "It's a live cam feed from the barn."

Patrick took several seconds to think through Jessica's explanation. "You put a camera down in Pam and Mark's barn?" he asked in reproach, trying to control his rising anger.

"Yeah," Jessica said, grabbing a pillow and pushing it into her lap. "Aunt Pam said to make myself at home."

Patrick slapped his hand down on the desk. "You know darn well this wasn't what she meant."

"Well, she didn't tell me not to," Jessica shot back.

"Jessica!" Patrick yelled. "When are you going to grow up and start respecting other people . . . including your mother and me?"

Jessica punched the down pillow. "It's no big deal."

"Wrong," Patrick said. "It is a big deal in addition to being a huge invasion of privacy."

Elaine finally spoke. "Jessica, did you do this to watch the kittens?"

"Oh, be real," Patrick said to his wife. "So why, Jessica?"

Jessica sighed dramatically and dropped her face into the pillow.

"Jess! Answer me."

She looked sheepishly at her father. "Aunt Lynn was acting so lame about her stupid cat, I thought it would be funny to put it up on my webpage."

Patrick flushed with anger. "And have you been laughing all morning?"

"Well, yeah," she said in a perfect valley-girl accent. "I got a lot of hits as soon as Aunt Lynn went into the barn."

"Hits?" Elaine asked.

"Kids who come to my page," she said. "All my friends and maybe a couple hundred more."

"Jessica . . ." Elaine began softly.

"Turn it off NOW!" Patrick yelled, grabbing his daughter by the arm and sitting her in front of the computer. "Do it now."

"No, Dad," she said, crossing her arms in defiance. "Everyone does this. All my friends stream."

"I don't care," Patrick said sternly. "You're not going to make your aunt a laughingstock."

"What's the harm in it? She would never know," Jessica fought back.

Patrick stared at his daughter. "How can you be so insensitive?"

Tears poured out. "But this is why they like me. This is why I'm getting popular."

"It isn't, darling," her mother said. "It just seems that way right now."

Patrick added, "If this is all that matters to your friends, you're better off without them."

"You know nothing about them!" Jessica stormed. "*Everyone* in school wants to be their friends."

"Well, it's not going to happen *this* way. Unplug it now," her father demanded.

Jessica knew when the battle was lost. She brushed off her tears with the backs of her hands and began typing on the keypad, her fingers flying to every correct key. Within seconds, the video stopped and the screen displayed her normal desktop.

"It's off," Jessica groaned.

Patrick exhaled. "Thank you," he said. "Next, you'll apologize to

Pam and Mark and Lynn, and then after dinner, you and I will go down to the barn to remove that camera."

Jessica refused to look at her father. "I can do it myself," she huffed.

"I'm quite sure you can," Patrick said, "but we're doing it together. I intend to become more involved in what you should and shouldn't be doing."

Jessica turned in her chair and looked innocently at her mother. "Mom," she bleated.

Patrick saw the pain in his wife's eyes. The fact that Jessica was obviously trying to manipulate her angered him all the more. "Don't go there, Jessica," Patrick warned. "You've been playing us against each other for far too long."

Elaine changed the subject, as she always did when a serious argument seemed inevitable. "Why don't you get cleaned up so we can go to the barbecue together?"

"I'm dressed," Jessica said belligerently.

"Not appropriately," her father countered.

"But Missy has the same skirt, and her parents let her wear it to school!"

Patrick shrugged. "I don't care about Missy. I care about you."

Jessica threw herself on the bed. "Now you're going to tell me what to wear?"

"No, just what *not* to wear, and that skirt is not acceptable," Patrick said.

"But Mom bought it for me." Again she tried to play one parent against the other.

Patrick was stunned. "Elaine?"

Elaine caught her husband's glare. "I gave Jessica my credit card when she and her friends went to the mall. She said she needed to buy some new clothes."

"Obviously she doesn't have the good judgment needed to shop on her own. Jessica, put on a pair of pants. We'll be waiting outside."

Jessica dug in her heels. “I don’t want to go to your lame party.”

“It will be fun, sweetheart,” Elaine said.

Patrick intervened. “Actually, it probably won’t be a ton of laughs for you,” he said bluntly, “but you’re a member of this family and sometimes we have to do things that we’d prefer not to, but we do them for the people we love.”

Jessica laughed. “Like you really love your relatives,” she said sarcastically.

“What are you talking about?” Patrick demanded.

“Carter Reed for one,” she said. “He’s a pompous, arrogant bully. Both of you are hypocrites for pretending to like him and sucking up to him because he’s some famous shock jock. You won’t even admit he’s a bottom dweller. Even his own son thinks he’s a total jerk.”

At that very moment, Corey was standing in the hall about to knock on Jessica’s door. He heard every word she had bitterly spewed.

## TWENTY-TWO
# *Requests*

In the backyard, Pam shook out a green-and-white gingham cloth and let it drop gently over one of the picnic tables. Preparations of that evening's dinner were going as smoothly as could be expected.

"Corey will be here in a few minutes to help out," Nancy said as she joined Pam. "He went over to the annex to see if Jessica is coming. And Carter is still working on some problems with the sound engineers." She began folding napkins lying on a nearby chair. "Is there any way I can help?"

Pam glanced around, thinking about what still needed to be done. She spotted her husband standing precariously on a ladder, struggling to untangle a string of tiny lanterns he intended to drape among several trees.

"How about lending Mark a hand?" she asked.

"Will do," Nancy said happily, heading off in her brother's direction.

From the kitchen, Kay arrived carrying several serving bowls, which she placed on the table. "This potato salad looks scrumtious—lots of dill, just the way I like it," she said as she helped Robert with the tray of condiments he was juggling. "Do you want all of these here, or should I spread them among the tables?"

"There is just fine, Mom," Pam said. "Robert, would you see if André needs any help? He should be in the kitchen."

Robert winked at Kay. "My pleasure."

When Robert was out of earshot, Pam moved closer to her mother. "I just don't understand you," she said. "Why would you want to do something so risky as rappel down a mountainside?"

Kay answered as she had several times before, although she suspected her words would once again fall on deaf ears. "Just enjoying life, darling."

"But if something goes wrong . . ."

"Pamela," Kay interrupted, "at any moment in our lives, something could go wrong. You, my dear, have been a worrier since you were two years old."

"And just like Dad, it's served me well."

"It put your father in an early grave," Kay said sadly. "He was always so cautious—he was never able to let go."

"But he was happy," Pam said, looking for confirmation.

Kay lifted one shoulder. "To some degree, I suppose. But could he have been happier? There's no doubt in my mind."

"But rappelling and rafting do not equate to happiness," Pam argued.

Kay sat down at the end of the picnic table. "To some, they do. To me, at this stage in my life, rappelling is great medicine."

"But *why*?"

"Because it means I'm alive and still young enough to be excited . . . and exciting," she explained. "And Robert and I find such joy in each other's enthusiasm."

Pam frowned. "You're not doing all of this because of Robert, are you?"

"Oh, no." Kay chuckled. "If anything, he's the more levelheaded one." She paused and gave Pam a devilish grin. "Do you like him?"

The abrupt change of topic threw Pam off. "I suppose so."

Kay took hold of her daughter's hand. "Pam, do you *like* him?"

Pam winced. "You didn't tell me about him for a year, so I'm assuming it really doesn't matter if I like him or not."

Kay looked away, stung by Pam's words. Tears began to well up in her eyes. "I'm sorry. I should have told you about Robert," she whispered. "I don't want you to hold that against him."

Seeing her mother's sadness broke Pam's heart. She wrapped her arms around her and held her. "I'm so sorry I said that. I love you so much," Pam said, holding on as tight as she could. All of the emotions that had been building within her for days suddenly poured out. "I don't what anything bad to happen to you. I don't want anything to take you away from me."

Kay tightened her arms around the daughter she deeply loved. "I'll never leave you," she whispered. "I will always be part of you."

"Like Dad," she sighed.

"Like Dad," Kay said.

Pam pulled away and wiped her mother's eyes before wiping her own. She then looked at Kay as if she were seeing her for the first time. In front of her was a strikingly attractive older woman with beautiful gray-blue eyes. Pam lovingly pulled her mother's silver hair back behind her ears. She was still crying when she finally said, "Yes, I like Robert very, very much. Just promise me one thing."

"What's that?" Kay said, brushing her cheeks dry.

"That you'll be very careful—that you'll *both* be very careful."

Kay pulled her daughter close and kissed her on the cheek. "We will."

~

"We really haven't had a chance to talk much, have we?" Nancy asked as she continued to hold the ladder for Mark. Together, they had successfully hung two lines of lights and were working on a third.

"It's been a little nuts around here," he admitted.

"So how's my favorite brother doing?"

"Patrick is your favorite brother," Mark teased.

Nancy slapped his calf. “That’s just what I tell him when you’re not around.”

Mark grabbed the end of the string of lights that Nancy held up for him and then wrapped the wire around a limb. “I’ve been meaning to tell you how impressed I am with Corey. You’ve raised a bright, pleasant young man.”

Nancy beamed. “He’s turned out well, hasn’t he?”

Mark draped the wire over another branch. “He’s so much more mature than I was at that age.”

Nancy laughed. “He’s more mature than you are now.”

“I resent that, even though it’s totally true.” Mark laughed. “You just wait to see how Corey reverts back to being a kid when I drag him to the fair.”

Nancy glanced around the backyard, appreciating the beautiful gardens and the koi pond. “I’m sorry our folks aren’t alive to be here,” she said wistfully. “Dad would have loved this place, and Mom would have been delighted to see all of us together.”

Mark looked over at Pam and Kay, who were sitting close together. “I envy Pam for still having her mother.”

“If our mom were here, I would have to keep her separated from Carter.” She thought for a moment. “Actually, neither of our folks really liked him that much.”

“I wouldn’t say they disliked him,” Mark said, coming down from the ladder. “We were just surprised that he’s the one you chose.”

“There was little choice in the matter, remember?” Nancy said. “I wasn’t planning to get pregnant until after we had been married for a few years. And when Corey got started early, Carter insisted we marry.”

“It seems Carter insists on a lot of things,” Mark said under his breath.

“You take him too seriously.”

“Carter Reed wouldn’t have it any other way,” he said, as he carried the ladder to the next tree while Nancy unraveled another strand of lights. "Do you know what he's planning to say on the air tomorrow?"

Nancy shook her head. "He never talks to me about his show."

"Really?" Mark asked in surprise. "That just amazes me. You two seem so close."

"Not really," she replied. "I'm close to him, and he's close to himself."

It was the first time Mark had ever heard his sister say anything derogatory about her husband. "Wow, I thought you were his number-one groupie. What do they call them? The Loyal Ideos?"

"Yeah, ideo because of their different ideologies. His critics call his fans Carter's Farters, for obvious reasons. But I would say that I'm his number-one wife, not groupie," she replied. "He's given me a wonderful lifestyle to which I've become accustomed, so I feel the least I can do is support him a hundred percent."

"Isn't that kind of like buying your love and loyalty?"

She laughed at her brother's naïveté. "He buys a lot of things."

Mark jumped down from the middle rung of the ladder. "Is there any way you can reel him in so he doesn't talk about the reunion or about Lumby?"

She passed him the string of lights. "I would never try, because I know that if I did, he'd just ignore me and do whatever he wanted."

Mark looked down at his sister. "But he'll listen to you."

She shrugged her shoulders. "No, actually he only listens to himself. Sorry, Mark, but my hands are tied."

Mark's sigh of resignation was loud enough for Nancy to hear. "Well then, is it worth me trying to talk to him again?" he asked in desperation.

"Unless you have something better to do," she answered as she grabbed on to the ladder while Mark made his way up to reach a high limb. "Just keep in mind that the reason Carter is so famous is because he's done it his way and his way appeals to nine million people. The one thing he has is great instinct about his audience—knowing what they want to hear."

Back on the ground, Mark folded the ladder while Nancy collected the empty party-supply boxes. “But doesn’t he see that his exposure to so many people comes with some kind of social responsibility?”

“When his feet are put to the coals, he claims his show is nothing more than total entertainment. That’s the main reason he doesn’t side with any one political party or ideology. He can claim neutrality and hide behind it while he brings the far right and far left into the boxing ring.”

“To beat each other up,” Mark added.

“To the death, as Carter says. And he’s the ultimate umpire and marketer.”

“What a delightful purpose in life,” Mark said sarcastically. “It seems he’s handing samurai swords to two enemies and then telling them to go at it until there’s only one person standing.”

“Actually, Carter would prefer it if neither were standing at the end,” Nancy retorted. “But Mark, if anyone is at fault, it’s the nine million people who tune in each morning to listen to him. If they didn’t want to hear those verbal bloodbaths, Carter would be selling used cars in Seattle.”

Mark leaned over and kissed his sister. “You’re right,” he said. “But if you could just say one word to him about not including any personal family stuff in his show, I would really appreciate it.”

## TWENTY-THREE

# *Target*

On his way to the barn to see Old Jesse, Chuck detoured through the fields to check on the beehives, which he had been hired to tend during the many years that the monks had lived at Montis Abbey. He easily navigated his way through a labyrinth of narrow, almost hidden paths within the woods that connected the orchard and the apiary.

He was thankful to see that the hives were as healthy now as the last time he had visited; dramatic bee colony reductions, which had left so many hives empty across the country, had not yet affected the Montis bees.

Chuck's next stop was the large barn that he, along with many other friends and tradesmen, had helped build the year before. Several sheep grazed just outside the barn's entrance, and close to them, a half dozen chickens pecked at the ground. Peanuts, the draft horse, stood inside eating hay. Looking around the vast space, Chuck once again marveled at how Mark kept his barns immaculately clean and well organized despite his apparent lack of organization in other aspects of his life.

Strolling into the small older barn, Chuck first noticed two long horns sticking through the metals bars of the upper half of the center stall's sliding door.

"Old Jesse," he said softly, so as not to startle the animal. Slowly, he approached the stall and peered in, and came eye to eye with the bull. Jesse snorted and threw his head up, his horns scraping against the bars and rattling the door.

"I see your disposition hasn't changed much," Chuck said. "Let's get you some hay and save Mark a trip down tonight."

Chuck lifted a full bale of hay from on top of a dozen other bales neatly stacked by the ladder that led to the loft. Knowing better than to open the stall door, he studied its walls to see how much lift he'd need to toss the bale over the top. Not being as strong and spry as he once was, he swung both the bale and his weight back and forth several times to gain momentum. On the final forward thrust, he let the hay go with as much force as he could muster. Unfortunately, Chuck had miscalculated both the direction and the height of the bale; it flew over the door, over the corner of the stall and into the adjacent stall.

"Ow!" a woman cried out.

Chuck was startled to hear a voice, and even more shocked when the woman who had attracted his attention that morning at St. Cross Abbey walked out of the stall covered with hay.

"What is it with me and this barn?" she asked as she brushed off her blouse.

"It's you," he said.

"It's me?"

"I saw you at the monastery."

"You're the odd man who sat next to me."

Chuck looked hurt. "Odd? No, I'm Chuck Bryson."

"You kept saying thank you," Lynn reminded him.

"You kept complimenting my work," Chuck countered. "You're not Coco, are you?"

"*What?*"

"Pam asked me to ensure Coco was fed."

"No. I'm Lynn, but I'm getting hungry."

"Well then, can I take you to dinner?" he teased, grinning.

Her smile in reply delighted Chuck. "Thank you." She started to pull hay out of her hair. "I'm sorry about this," she said, pointing to more straw on her shoulders.

"It was intended for Jesse," he explained.

"So I gathered."

"Are you all right?"

"This is a dangerous place. Every time I come down here, I get clobbered."

"Are you staying at the inn?"

"For the family reunion." At his puzzled looked, she explained, "I'm Lynn, Mark's sister."

Chuck's smile widened. "Oh, very good."

She studied him for a moment. "So why did you keep on saying 'thank you' in the chapel?"

"You commented on the candles, which I made from beeswax collected from Pam and Mark's beehives."

"Ah," she said, nodding. "And the altar?"

"Jonathan Tucker, a woodworker in town, and I carved it many, many years ago."

"So you're not odd, just a talented man of few words."

"Thank you," he said, bowing slightly. "So who's Coco?"

Lynn pointed into the stall. Chuck peeked through a large gap between the stall planks and, in the corner of the stall, saw a gray cat with a dozen kittens curled up on her stomach. Old Jesse was standing guard, his hooves just inches from the cat's body.

"That's something you don't see every day," Chuck said.

"I came down to move Coco and the litter out of the bull's stall," Lynn confessed.

"And I'm guessing you could use some help?"

She nodded shyly. "I could."

"Well then, let's get Coco and her family out of there," Chuck suggested as he looked around for a container. "Here," he said, handing Lynn a large cardboard box. "I'll pass the kittens out to you first."

Sliding the stall door open, Chuck entered the stall holding a full feed bucket well in front of him. When Old Jesse realized that there was food to be had, most of his aggression toward Chuck faded away. As soon as Jesse began eating, Chuck snuck to the back corner and began moving out the litter. Picking up two kittens, a calico and an orange tiger, he smiled in delight.

"What a marvelous example of genetic diversity," he said softly as he passed them through the bars to Lynn, who placed them gently in the box.

"That was totally unplanned, I assure you," she said in a low voice.

"The litter?" Chuck asked in a whisper so as not to alert Jesse.

Lynn rolled her eyes. "No, the *genetic diversity*. I paid a fortune to breed Coco to another champion Seal Point Birman, and the last thing I expected were mongrels."

Chuck gave her another handful of squirming kittens. "But they're no less valuable just because they're not purebreds."

"The litter would have been worth more than five thousand dollars if the kittens were Birmans. Now they're worthless."

"Worthless? Have you really looked at them?" Chuck asked, holding up a precious gray tiger with piercing blue eyes. "How can you say that about this little guy?" He snuggled it against his chest. "Or this one?" he said, handing Lynn a tricolored tabby that had one black ear, one white ear and a brown nose.

Lynn wished she could take back her words. "I didn't mean worthless, just . . . less valuable."

"To whom?" Chuck asked as he continued relocating the litter. "Another breeder?"

"You sound like you disapprove."

"I think too many animals in our country are euthanized because they don't have homes, and purebreds just add to the overpopulation." His comment was very matter-of-fact and nonjudgmental. "I think I understand why breeders do what they do, but nature needs genetic diversity to remain strong."

Lynn carefully cupped the smallest of the kittens—a tiny tortoiseshell with soft brown eyes—in her palms and held it close to her neck, thinking about what Chuck had said.

"Coco is all—" She stopped herself from saying "I have."

Chuck chuckled as he removed the final kitten, which immediately began to suckle his pinkie. "You'll have great fun with them."

When the litter was safe in the box, Chuck picked up Coco and was about to slip out of the stall. But within seconds, it became obvious to both him and Lynn that Jesse had no intention of letting his primary charge out of his sight. The bull backed up from the feed bucket, took two steps sideways and immediately had Chuck pinned into the corner with a horn on either side of Chuck's rib cage.

"Chuck!"

"Don't panic," he breathed.

"Now what?" Lynn whispered.

When Coco meowed, Old Jesse pushed forward, digging the tips of his horns deeper into the stall wood. When he snorted, Chuck felt hot air on his chest.

"Put her down," Lynn suggested.

"But you want her out of here."

"Not this badly. Go ahead, drop her," Lynn said.

Since Chuck was trapped on all sides, the only thing he could do was let go of Coco from waist height. As soon as the cat hit the ground, she ran out of the stall, presumably looking for her kittens. Jesse yanked back his head, pulling the tips of his horns out of the wood. He turned his massive body, and once clear of the stall door, he loped after the cat as she skirted down the center aisle of the barn.

Chuck crumbled down to the ground and sat on his haunches, trying to catch his breath.

"Are you all right?" Lynn asked, joining him in the stall.

"I think so," he said. "Where did they go?"

"That way," Lynn said, offering him a hand up.

Once outside the barn, they both froze. Not more than twenty yards away, Old Jesse was standing in the open field. His head hung low to the ground, just inches away from where Coco sat cleaning herself.

"We can't leave Jesse out here," Chuck said. "He really is a danger if he's on the loose."

Lynn looked back at the barn. "I have an idea," she said before disappearing inside.

Suddenly, a loud choir of kitten squeals could be heard coming from the barn. Coco's ears perked forward, and an instant later, she was running at full speed back to her brood. Old Jesse was no more than two feet behind her, keeping pace with the sprinting feline.

Coco ran into the stall and began nuzzling her kittens, all of whom Lynn had returned to the sawdust bed. When Jesse followed her in, Lynn slid the stall door closed and slung the heavy latch shut.

"Very smart," Chuck said.

"Love knows no bounds, does it?" she asked, brushing her hands together.

He tilted his head and smiled, gazing warmly at Lynn's beaming face. "No, it doesn't."

ᔕ

Sitting next to each other on a bench close to the koi pond, Jessica and Anaïs were as different in appearance as they were in character, which they were quickly discovering for themselves. Jessica wore a stylish top and designer pants while Anaïs had on a simple pair of white cotton shorts with a pastel-green button-down shirt. Their makeup and hairstyles were additional indicators of how dissimilar the young adults were; Jessica had a couture cut from a famous Virginia salon while Anaïs had long dark hair pulled back and tied with a white ribbon.

Anaïs filled her glass from a pitcher of lemonade on the bench next to her.

"Want some more?" she asked Jessica.

"No way," she said, immediately covering her glass with her hand. "Don't want to dilute the vodka too much."

Anaïs looked over at Jessica's parents, who were talking with Pam. "Your folks let you drink?"

"Are you nuts? They'd kill me if they knew."

"Where did you get it?" Anaïs asked.

Jessica looked around to ensure no one could overhear her. "I stumbled on the liquor cabinet in the dining room this morning."

Anaïs looked confused. "I thought all of you went to the monastery."

"That was only for dweebs," Jessica said, talking a long, slow sip of her drink, "so I helped myself."

"But that's stealing," Anaïs whispered.

"No, it's not. Aunt Pam said that we should help ourselves to anything we want."

Anaïs looked at Jessica's glass. "I don't think she meant *that*."

"Whatever," Jessica said, blowing her off. "Look over there—I think Corey is checking you out."

Anaïs glanced across the yard and caught Corey's stare. He nodded and smiled at her.

"He seems like a nice guy," Anaïs said.

Jessica shrugged. "If you go for that type."

"What type?"

"The straight arrow," she answered. "He's a do-gooder geek type." She took another sip of her drink. "Do you ever go to Wheatley?"

Anaïs was surprised by the unexpected question. "I live there with my mom."

"What's it like?"

"Mostly really nice, but it has one bad section that we stay away from. Why?"

"I want to look around," Jessica said. "Can you give me a ride there after the party tonight?"

"Sorry. I'm staying here with my father for the next couple of days."

"Your dad lives at Montis?" Jessica asked. "What a drag that must be."

"Actually, it's pretty cool. He has his own place over there," Anaïs said, pointing to the woods in the far corner of the property. "I may be going down to see Mom on Thursday, and you can come down with us then, but you wouldn't have a way to get back."

"I can thumb it," Jessica said, sticking out her hitchhiking finger.

"That's so not safe," Anaïs warned.

"But I hear Lumby is perfect," Jessica said sarcastically.

"It's stupid to hitchhike anywhere," Anaïs replied.

Corey approached the two young women. "Hey," he said to Anaïs.

"You can settle an argument, Corey," Jessica said. "Anaïs says that hitchhiking is dangerous."

"She's right," Corey said, without having to give it any thought.

Anaïs looked up at Corey and mouthed "Thank you."

"You two are such wimps," Jessica said.

"Anaïs?" André called out from the barbecue hearth. "Can you give me some help?"

Anaïs stood and handed Corey her drink. "Save my place," she said.

Corey watched Anaïs join her father.

"You're disgusting," Jessica said. "You just want to get her in the sack."

Corey sat down next to his cousin. "You really don't know me at all," he said. "She seems incredibly nice, and right now, all I'd like to do is talk with her."

Jessica rolled her eyes. "Yeah, right. You guys are all the same."

"You shouldn't make sweeping generalizations about people—about me, about Anaïs, or about my father." He paused. "I heard what you told your folks a while ago."

Jessica downed the rest of her drink. "Isn't eavesdropping a little below you?"

"I was coming over to get you for dinner," Corey explained.

She refused to be embarrassed. "Well, you're the one who called him a jerk."

"I know, and I shouldn't have," he said softly.

"It's forgotten. Just chill about it." Jessica said. "Are you doing anything tonight?"

Corey looked around. "Just the barbecue."

"Come by my room about midnight," she said. "I've got some cool webs up on my screens that you might like. We can do some surfing."

Corey was surprised by her invitation and couldn't help wondering about her real motivation. "Other than school work, I'm not a big Internet user," he admitted.

"Well, we'll change that tonight," she said. "Midnight—my room."

TWENTY-FOUR

# *Hammered*

"I have arrived. Let the games begin!" Carter trumpeted as he walked into the backyard. He clapped his hands and rubbed them together in anticipation of something more exciting than rewiring an amplifier. "Marko?" he called out.

Mark had just finished using a ladder and was leaning it against the back wall of the guest annex. He forced a smile. "Over here."

As Carter strolled toward his brother-in-law, he greeted everyone he passed as if he were the host. "Good seeing you again," he said to Robert, shaking his hand. "Great day for a party, isn't it?" he asked Elaine. He tried to put his arms around Pam, but he was too rotund to bring her close. "What would we do without you?" he bellowed so all would hear. "And where's Corey?"

Corey was still sitting next to Jessica. "Here, Dad," he called out.

"Well, get over here, son," Carter said, waving his arm. "We're going toe-to-toe with Pam and Mark."

Pam glanced at her husband, assuming he knew what Carter was talking about. "You've lost us, Carter," Mark said, moving beside his wife. Corey also joined the group.

"Time we go nose-to-nose," Carter said, smacking the young man on the back.

"Is that different from toe-to-toe?" Pam quipped.

"We need some raw competition, some Montis Olympics," Carter said.

Pam subtly grabbed Mark's hand and squeezed it tightly, letting him know that this was not the time or the place for Carter to force them into a serious competition.

"We're going to be eating pretty soon," Mark said. "Why not plan something for tomorrow afternoon?"

Carter wouldn't hear of it. "Nothing like the present. It's now or never, do or die."

Pam squeezed harder.

"Unless, that is, the Walkers are total wimps," Carter added, egging them on.

Pam dropped Mark's hand and rose to her feet. "Name your game," she said belligerently.

Mark was startled to see his wife take the bait so quickly. "Honey, André is about to put on the ribs," he reminded her.

She hated to be called a wimp, especially by a man like Carter Reed. Fire burned in her eyes. "That can wait," she said. "What do you have in mind? Some badminton?"

Carter laughed so hard his belly shook. "You so underestimate me, Pam." He surveyed the backyard as he considered his options. Then, something caught his eye; lying on the ground next to the stake used for the volleyball net was a long-handled sledgehammer.

"Urr ye up fur some real gams, aye?" Carter asked with a heavy Scottish accent.

Mark held back a smile. He would never admit as much, but Carter's Highland drawl sounded amazingly authentic. "Reed isn't a Scottish name," he quipped.

"Mostly English, but there's a bit of Irish and Scot in there," Carter said, walking over to the volleyball court. "One of our most famous ancestors is Philip Reed, a U.S. senator from Maryland, elected in 1806. He claimed to be Irish Scottish English. Good man."

Corey laughed. "Except for the fact that he attested to having cut off the head of an American deserter during the Revolutionary War so that it could be displayed to the troops as a deterrent."

"They learned a lesson," Carter huffed, defending his many-times-great-grandfather.

When Carter got to the volleyball court, Pam smiled, knowing that the competition was over before it began; both she and Mark were very quick and agile and had been playing two-man volleyball since spring.

But unexpectedly, Carter bent over and, with some difficulty, grabbed the yellow handle of the sledgehammer. "An auld-fashioned hammer flin," he said.

Pam's smile melted away. Although she knew nothing about throwing such an object, she did realize that in this case Carter's body mass would work to his advantage.

Carter picked up a board at the end of the bocce ball alley and dropped it close to the center of the backyard. "Longest throw takes all," he said.

Pam immediately saw the disadvantage of that rule: there was a good chance Carter would have the single longest toss, so if it was an individual effort, and not a combined team score, he would surely win. That raised her hackles. "Let's make it more of a team effort," she suggested. "We'll add up the total distances of all team members."

"Whatever," Carter said, not taking time to seriously consider Pam's recommendation. "Let's go," he said impatiently, swinging the hammer to and fro. "You can't step past the board until the hammer has landed, and we'll measure from the center of the board out to the closest part of the hammer's head."

"We need a measuring tape," Patrick said.

"It's in the top drawer to the right of the sink," Mark said to Pam, who was already running to their house. On the way, she passed Kano and Worm headed toward the backyard.

"Are we late?" Kano asked.

"Not at all, the fireworks are just about to start," Pam replied. "Go help yourself to a beer."

"Team up!" Carter trumpeted. "Corey, Elaine, and, let's see . . . Jessica, over here." He motioned for them to move to his side. "Patrick and Nancy, you're with Pam and Mark." Carter eyed the members of each team. When he was satisfied, he raised the hammer. "Let's have at it."

"How about us?" Kay asked, taking hold of Robert's hand and raising them both in the air.

Carter scoffed. "Can you even lift this?" Although the words "old lady" didn't end his sentence, they were certainly implied.

Mark shook his head. He was so glad Pam hadn't heard that.

"I heard that!" Pam said, jogging back to the group with a tape measure in her hand. "They're in better shape than you are, Carter. We want them on our team."

"Fine," Carter said. "We'll take Worm and Kano."

"That's ridiculous," Mark said.

Pam scrutinized the team members, who were now standing in two groups. "Robert, would you mind going over to Carter's team?"

Robert kissed Kay before defecting. "Sorry, dear."

Pam continued. "Worm, why don't you join us, and Kano, you can help Carter out. André and Anaïs, would you like to join us?"

Both quickly shook their heads. André put his arm around his daughter in solidarity. "We'll be your impartial judges. Bribes are not only accepted but encouraged. And we accept all major credit cards."

"I'll go first," Carter said, to no one's surprise.

With great bravado, he stepped behind the plank. He swung the sledgehammer backward and then, with as much force as possible, flung it forward, releasing it as it reached its zenith.

Everyone gaped as the hammer flew straight up in the air, hung for a second and then dropped with tremendous speed. It landed not far from Carter.

André extended the tape measure. "Four feet, two inches," he called out to Anaïs, who began recording the distances.

Carter spread his arms to keep anyone from walking into the throwing area. "That was just to test the hammer," he said gruffly. "That didn't count."

"We're only given one throw each, Carter. No mulligans," Pam said, with others voicing a similar opinion.

"All right, fine," he said angrily. "Have it your way."

"Mom, why don't you give it a shot?" Pam said, leading Kay to where Carter had stood. Pam lifted the hammer and put the handle in her mother's thin, seemingly fragile hands. "You have it?" she asked, before letting go.

Kay tightened her grip around the hammer's handle. "Okay," she said, "I'm ready."

"Let her rip," Mark said, clapping his hands in support.

Kay lifted the hammer a few inches from the ground, swung it several times between her spread legs and then released it. To everyone's surprise, it landed well in front of her.

"Way to go, Grams!" Jessica said, giving Kay a high five.

André knelt down. "Five feet, nine inches."

"Fine effort, Kay," Mark called out.

The next several throws were uneventful; Robert, Elaine, and Jessica each added less than six feet to their respective team's score, and Worm and Corey were disqualified for stepping over the board after their throws. Nancy submitted impressive numbers, followed by Patrick's disqualification. Although Pam heaved her best, she was considerably outdistanced by Kano, whose throw went three times further than anyone else's.

"What's the score?" Carter yelled out.

André looked at the pad Anaïs was holding and quickly added the numbers. "Your team is ahead by ten feet, seven inches."

"We stand undefeated!" Carter bellowed.

"Wait a minute," Pam said. "Mark hasn't had his turn."

"No need," Carter said. "Not a chance in the world he can throw that far."

"Maybe I can," Mark said.

"Okay," Carter replied as he pulled out his wallet from his pants pocket, "I'll put a hundred bucks on you not going the distance."

"That's ridiculous," Mark said.

"Dad, he's right—it really isn't necessary," Corey said under his breath.

"Then make it two hundred." Carter withdrew four fifty-dollar bills and stuffed them into his shirt pocket. "Marko, you're up!"

Mark had been studying the different throwing techniques used by the others and knew exactly what he was going to do. He rolled his shoulders and stretched his arms before picking up the hammer.

"Everyone stand back. I need a lot of room," he said as he gripped the very end of the handle with both hands. Mark picked up the sledgehammer using both hands, and to everyone's surprise, he started turning in a circle with the hammer swinging out in front of him. The faster he spun in place, the higher the sledgehammer rose.

After six complete rotations, Mark had built up tremendous momentum. He closed his eyes and let go.

When the hammer took to the sky, Mark's twirling body completed a final revolution before crashing into Carter, who was standing several yards behind him. Carter had such mass, though, that Mark bounced off him and landed in a heap on the ground.

The hammer continued to sail through the air, turning end over end in an elliptical rotation. As people would later say, it reminded everyone of the bone thrown at the beginning of *2001: A Space Odyssey*.

Seconds later, the hammer crashed down in the center of an empty picnic table.

"Tough luck, Marko," Carter said, without helping him to his feet.

"What a great throw, honey!" Pam exclaimed. "André, what's the distance?"

Carter rushed over to the table and tried to take the tape measure from André. "Wait a minute!" he bellowed. "That throw is disqualified."

Mark stumbled to his feet, his head still spinning. "Why?"

"Obviously, it's out of bounds," Carter answered.

"You never said anything about boundaries," Pam protested.

"That's true, Dad," Corey said. "The throw should be counted."

Carter glared. "Remember which side you're on, son."

"All those who think Mark's throw should count," Pam said.

Everyone except Carter raised their hands. "This isn't a majority vote," he objected. "We'll leave it up to the judge."

He turned to André and, with his back facing the others, pulled the fifty-dollar bills far enough out of his shirt pocket for André to see them.

André stared at Carter for several seconds before measuring the distance Mark had thrown. "The winning team by four inches is . . . Carter's," André announced.

"Nice try, everyone," Pam said jovially as she kissed her husband. "I think we all deserve ice-cold beers. Dinner will be ready in ten minutes."

As André made his way back to the barbecue hearth, Carter moseyed up next to him and pushed something into his hand. When André opened his palm, he saw several neatly folded fifty-dollar bills.

"You can't be serious," André scoffed.

"A deal is a deal," Carter said.

André was incensed. "Do you actually think I lied?" he asked, stuffing the money back into Carter's pocket.

Carter leaned closer to André. "If that's the way you want to play it," he said with a large wink, "it will be our secret."

André stepped back. "There's no secret. It was a game, Carter, and you won fair and square by a few inches."

Carter winked again. "You bet. Give me the word if I can do something for you. Just name it."

André bit his tongue. "You've done quite enough."

As the others were winding down from the competition, Chuck and Lynn strolled through the courtyard on their way to the backyard. They stopped every few feet to examine a different plant in the flower bed that ran along the side of the path.

"The coreopsis is stunning. And this is one of my favorites: Evening Primrose," Lynn said as she touched a delicate petal. "And I think this is a Rocky Mountain Penstemon. Is that right?"

"It is," Chuck said. "I can't tell you what a delight it is to talk to a horticulturalist who knows so much about our local flora."

Lynn laughed. "I've never been called that before—a horticulturalist. It sounds so formal. Even after taking a Master Gardeners course, I still think of myself as just a weed-puller."

"Who just happens to work for the Horticultural Society," he added. "You identified every plant in the courtyard."

"Because they're all very common. I still have so much to learn," she said, leaning over to examine another species. "I suppose that's why I love my job—it's never boring, even when I do nothing more than cataloging all day."

"You must have a lovely garden at home."

Lynn straightened and looked up at the passing clouds. "Actually, I don't, but I'm hoping to someday." She crunched her nose, disliking the truth she was about to share. "Until a few months ago, I was living in a small apartment."

"From the little I know of you, that surprises me."

"I suppose you could say I'm trying to rebuild my life. I was divorced a few years ago, and the apartment was all I could afford after Dan and I first separated," she explained. "Everything was so hard. After thirty years of following someone else, I had to make all the decisions by myself, and a little apartment seemed safe." She paused for a long moment. "It's taken a few years to get my feet on the ground, to settle into a job—I never thought I would have to earn a living. Funny how things work out." She laughed. "In April, I finally bought a small house which I'm just beginning to make my own. And there's plenty of space for a garden as soon as I can find the time."

"It sounds like you're just starting a wonderful adventure."

"I suppose so, but it certainly doesn't feel that way," Lynn admitted. "In fact, sometimes I still feel like I'm living someone else's life."

Chuck raised his brows. "But is it a good life?"

Lynn was taken aback by the question. "What?"

"The life you're living, is it a happy one?" he asked with genuine interest.

Lynn stared at Chuck as if he had spoken in a foreign language. No one had asked her that question for many years. "Is my life happy?" she repeated. He gave her time to consider her answer. She looked up at the sky again. "I have Coco," she finally said.

His smile was warm. "Animals are wonderful companions."

She had been expecting ridicule, and instead, this man standing next to her seemed to understand something no one else did. "They are," she said, feeling a relaxation flow through her body that she hadn't experienced in a long time.

## TWENTY-FIVE
# *Ribs*

Just as André was removing the ribs off the fire, Chuck and Lynn joined the others who were already seated at the picnic tables. "Good evening," Chuck said to everyone, sliding in next to Lynn once she had sat down.

"Did you see Old Jesse?" Mark asked excitedly.

"We did a little more than that," Chuck said, patting Lynn's hand on the table. "He certainly gave us a challenge."

Pam, who was sitting on the other side of the table, saw their exchanged wink. "So I'm guessing you two had a chance to meet?"

Lynn nodded. "Down at the barn."

"And Coco?" Pam asked, passing Chuck a bowl of salad. "Did you get her moved to another stall?"

"That's where we hit a snag," Lynn said.

Chuck laughed. "An understatement. That cat certainly seems to attract a lot of suitors. I've never seen anything like it."

"What with the raccoon and the bull, I get the feeling that Coco has a better sex life than I do," Lynn quipped.

Chuck burst into laughter. "Coco probably has it up on all of us."

Pam couldn't help but notice the energy between them. "Chuck is our town's resident . . ." She paused, searching for the right word.

Chuck raised his brow in anticipation. "I can't wait to hear this."

Pam tilted her head, considering her close friend. "What would we call you, exactly?"

"Hopefully nothing that my students call me," Chuck said.

Pam laughed. "Our resident shepherd?"

He grunted in dismay. "That makes me sound like a dog."

"How about our two-legged luminary?" Pam offered.

He smiled in approval. "Much better."

Lynn slanted a look at Chuck. "You didn't mention you're a teacher. I should have talked less and asked more about you."

"I enjoyed talking about flowers so much more," he whispered. "But Pam is correct—I teach at UC Berkeley."

"Don't let his modesty mislead you," Pam said. "He's a tenured professor of physics."

"Wow," Lynn said.

"Do I hear a who-would-have-thought somewhere in there?" Chuck asked.

"I suppose I'm a little surprised just because I assumed you lived here," Lynn replied.

"I do, just outside of Wheatley up in the mountains," Chuck said. "My doctoral students actually teach the classes, and I fly there every few weeks."

"Chuck?" Kay asked from the other end of the table. "Would you like to come rappelling with Robert and me tomorrow? We're leaving at the crack of dawn."

He glanced at Lynn and raised his brow. "Would you be interested in a hike tomorrow?" he asked.

Lynn shook her head. "Oh, no," she answered. "Coco may need me."

Chuck didn't agree. "Animals have an amazing ability to fend for themselves. And even if Coco can't, it appears there's one bull that will ensure no harm comes her way."

"But she really knows nothing about living outside," Lynn retorted.

"Given the freshly killed mouse I saw in the stall, she's probably more self-sufficient and capable than you give her credit for."

Lynn's eyes opened in alarm. "She killed a mouse? But there's plenty of Ocean Fiesta in her feeder."

Chuck grinned. "I assure you that mouse tartare is much more delectable than any dry food you can provide."

Lynn frowned. "I noticed the food level wasn't going down. I just assumed she wasn't hungry."

Chuck coughed lightly. "With a dozen kittens to milk?"

She rolled her eyes. "Pretty stupid of me, huh?"

"Not at all," he said kindly. "I think when we see an animal, or a person for that matter, in only one context, then that's the framework we tend to limit them to." He paused to take a sip of beer. "I think you'd be amazed by how quickly and happily Coco could adapt to her new life in the barn."

"But I want her back in my room with me," Lynn said in soft disappointment.

"That's different than *Coco needing* to be back in your room," he replied casually. "Would you like to go hiking tomorrow?"

Don't get involved, Lynn told herself. She dropped her head. "I don't think so."

"Smart move—rappelling is too dangerous" Pam said under her breath.

Kay elbowed her daughter. "I thought we resolved all that."

Pam leaned over and kissed her mother on the cheek. "I'm sorry—we did."

Robert, seated on Kay's far side, leaned forward. "Pam, why don't you join us? It would give you a chance to see just how vigilant Kay and I really are."

Pam shrugged her shoulders. "I just have too much to do around here. Maybe on Tuesday," she said.

Chuck looked across the table. "I'd also like to take a rain check.

I should really spend some time working on the beehives tomorrow."

Lynn's interest picked up. "Are you collecting wax?" she asked. "Will you be making candles?"

"Affirmative on both counts," he answered. "Would you like to join me?"

Her reply was hesitant. "Maybe. I so love candles, and I've always wanted to see how they're made."

Chuck smiled broadly. "Then it's a date."

She recoiled at the word, fearing that one thing would lead to the next and would ultimately lead to her being hurt once again.

"More of a tutorial," she corrected him.

Pam grinned. "Ribs?" she said, offering the platter to Chuck and Lynn.

"That's preposterous!" Carter boomed from the other end of the table. The party hushed as everyone stared in his direction. "Why is everyone looking at me?" he demanded. "Mark just made a ludicrous comment." He hit his brother-in-law in the arm. "Go ahead, Marko, tell them what you said."

Mark frowned. "We were talking about how the town is reacting to the news about Mike McNear selling his place."

"I didn't know that was common knowledge," Pam said.

"It is now. Joan posted a flyer in her window and has run ads in several local papers. Anyway, my point was that the residents of Lumby shouldn't just roll over and play dead to some developer who wants to buy McNear's farm and use it to make a ton of money."

Carter put out his hand. "See what I mean?" he asked the others.

"I agree with Mark," Pam said.

"Hear, hear," Chuck added.

Carter raised his hand to stop any further comments. "But something like that would put your little nothing of a town on the map."

Mark scowled. "Should we resent that?" he asked Pam.

"Look, all I'm saying is that this McNear fellow should sell his land to whoever's willing to pay the highest price," Carter said.

Pam leaned forward. "Without regard to the town's well-being?"

Carter shrugged. "It's not the town's business."

Pam's voice went up an octave. "But don't you think we have a responsibility to each other?"

"Would that be a financial, moral or social responsibility?" Carter said sarcastically.

"All of the above!" she argued. "Our town is defined by how we treat each other. And it's that sense of responsibility that lies at the heart of our community."

"Rubbish. When all else fails, we're responsible only to ourselves," Carter countered.

"And our family," Nancy inserted.

"So all we are is a country of three hundred million autonomous souls with no accountability to each other?" Pam asked.

"Just about," Carter huffed.

"I find that idea totally heartrending," she said.

Mark intervened. "What would happen if someone came into your neighborhood and wanted to change it in a way you didn't like?"

"Carter would just buy him off," Nancy said, tapping her husband proudly on the arm.

"None of you get it," Carter said. "It's not just the real estate developer who would get rich—the money would flow down to all the residents . . . from the store owners to the schmucks flipping hamburgers, even to you two here at Montis. You would have more business than you would know what to do with."

"We already do," Pam said flatly.

"The fact is, Carter, all of us like our town the way it is," Mark said. "More tourism and more money aren't going to make anyone any happier. Lumby is a quiet place to live, and everyone wants it to stay that way. Surely you can understand that."

"A couple hundred bucks says you're wrong, Marko," Carter bantered as he reached for his wallet. He pulled out two hundred-dollar bills and threw them on the table. "I'll ask that question on the radio tomorrow, and I know that ninety-nine percent of my listeners will cave in and admit that money talks louder than anything else in our lives."

"Don't bother," Mark said. "I won't be listening."

Patrick was staring at the money. "You carry that kind of cash around with you all the time?"

"Chump change," Carter said.

"What do you do with all that money?" Elaine asked.

"He buys airplanes and real estate," Nancy answered.

"What do you mean by real estate?" Mark asked.

"Well, Marko, hate to break the bad news, but I'm one of those nasty developers you hate so much."

Mark cringed. "You never told me that."

"You never asked," he said. "And the projects are just numbers on a spreadsheet to me. I have a couple guys who manage my portfolio so I don't have to get involved in any of the details."

"Easy way to keep your hands clean," Pam said.

Carter stood up. "You guys might think I'm the devil, but I guarantee you should be praying for someone like me to buy that McNear farm. At least I wouldn't cut down every tree and turn it into an asphalt jungle with some huge megamall."

"What would you do with it?" Patrick asked.

"No idea. Maybe low-end vacation villas. Who knows?" he replied, dismissing the question. "Then we could see each other all the time. Wouldn't you love that, Marko?" He locked his arm around Mark's neck and rubbed his knuckles into Mark's head.

TWENTY-SIX

# Confessions

Shortly before nine o'clock, and well after everyone had finished coffee and dessert, Carter was the first to retire to bed.

"I'm not on vacation like the rest of you—I've got to get rolling first thing," he announced from the head of the table. He tossed a napkin at his sound engineer, who was several places away. "Kano, Worm, call it a night. You both need to be on your best game tomorrow morning at five."

Mark, who had worked his way over to his wife shortly after dinner, spoke softly in her ear. "I don't know how anyone could work for a guy like that."

"Nancy, you too," Carter said. "Let's go."

"Or be married to one," Pam replied in a low voice.

Mark thought back to his conversation with his sister earlier that evening. He whispered, "She didn't feel she had much of a choice way back then." He paused as he watched Nancy do as she was instructed. "And now she's just too used to it all."

Pam kept her voice down so only Mark could hear. "You sound as though you're defending her."

"Not really." He continued speaking softly. "I think most people envy them because they have a bazillion dollars, but I actually feel pretty sorry for Nancy. And when Carter's not being a total moron, I feel a little sorry for him too."

Pam raised her brows. "Wow. Given the beatings that he's always dishing out, that's mighty magnanimous of you."

"I just think about where he's going to be in ten years—he might be rich, but I'm absolutely sure he'll be very much alone."

Pam watched Carter escort the others toward the main building. "Thank you for dinner and have a good evening," she whispered sarcastically under her breath.

Mark put his arm around his wife and pulled her close. "It was an outstanding meal, honey," he whispered. "They might not have said it, but I'm sure they appreciated everything about it."

"Thank you." She kissed him tenderly. "I shouldn't have said that. I suppose I'm just tired. But they could have at least said good night to all of us."

Mark knew how Pam took such rudeness to heart—it was as if their silence was a personal affront to her. "Why don't you relax, and we'll take care of cleaning everything up," he said.

"We?" Pam asked.

"The men," he answered. "Come on, guys," he called to the others as he jumped out of his seat. "I need some help bringing all this stuff into the kitchen."

Within seconds, André, Patrick, Robert and Mark were heading toward the kitchen with arms full of plates, silverware and bowls.

"He really is a gem," Kay said to Pam as she kept her eyes on the men until they disappeared around the corner.

"Robert?" Pam asked.

"I was talking about Mark, though Robert is definitely made from the same mold."

"They do have their similarities. Now, if you would excuse me for a few minutes," she said to her guests, "I'm going to lend them a hand."

When Pam entered the kitchen, Robert was alone and had already begun loading the commercial dishwasher. "I just passed the other guys. Are they bailing on you?" she asked.

"No," he said as he slipped another plate into the rack. "They went out to finish clearing the table."

"Here, Robert, let me do that," she said, offering to take his place in front of the washer.

"That's quite all right. I do the dishes every night at home."

The comment struck Pam by surprise. It was the words that were missing: he did the dishes *for Mom* every night in *their* home. "But you're a guest here," she said.

"I was hoping you would think of me more as family than a visitor."

Pam stuffed a dry towel under her belt as she always did before working in the kitchen. "I'm sorry. I'm finding all of this a bit difficult. We barely know you," she admitted. "But it's obvious you make my mother very happy. She seems like a different person now." Pam went to the sink and began washing the serving bowls.

"She's the one who saved me," Robert said.

Pam looked over at him. "Why do you say that?"

He sighed heavily before answering. "My wife was sick for many years, and I was her caretaker. By choice," he added emphatically. "I wanted to be there for her, but it was hard, especially toward the end when she was incapable of even sitting up on her own. My sons tried to help—they're really good boys—but they had their own families to care for." He paused before loading several more dishes. "After she passed away, I retreated from life. And then I met Kay. Somehow, she found a way to open that door I had shut, and she gave me the strength and courage to walk through it. It was like coming out the other end of a long, dark tunnel." He looked at Pam. "In a lot of ways, I owe her everything. She shared her passion with me and gave me a desire to live again. She put excitement and thrill . . . and love into this old heart and body of mine, and I'll always feel blessed for having her in my life."

By the time he finished speaking, Pam's eyes had filled with tears. "I didn't know," she said.

"Not many people do. I'm a private person and never felt comfortable sharing that part of my life. It was years ago, and Kay has taught me to keep my eyes on today and tomorrow."

Pam laughed. "That certainly sounds like her."

Robert leaned against the center island. "I know that I'm with Kay today, and I want to make sure we are with each other tomorrow."

Pam winced. "Given your plans to go rappelling, I'm quite certain you will be."

"No, Pam," Robert said in a more serious tone. "I mean tomorrow in the broader sense. I want to be by her side for whatever years we have left."

Pam was unclear as to what, exactly, Robert was saying. "And I'm sure you will be, if that's what my mother wants."

"She does, but she's worried about you."

Pam tensed. "Why would she worry about me?"

"Your relationship with Kay is so important to her. She would never want anything or anyone to come between you two."

"Ah, I see," Pam said, finally catching on. "She wants my approval of your relationship."

"Not quite," he said. "I want your blessing to ask your mother to marry me."

The bowl that Pam had been holding dropped into the sink and sank slowly under the water.

ᔓ

At eleven thirty, Corey walked across the courtyard on his way to Jessica's room. The party was over in the backyard, and only Chuck and Lynn remained, sitting across from each other at one of the cleared tables.

Hank, who felt snubbed for not having been invited to Sunday dinner at Montis, stood close to the koi pond. Just in case the opportunity presented itself for him to mingle, which it hadn't that evening, he was appropriately attired in his best casual party attire. Although he had not yet been introduced to any of the

Walker relatives—an embarrassing oversight and social faux pas that he was sure would be corrected the following day—he found himself quite interested in Chuck Bryson's new friend. He had heard she had a cat that would knock his socks off, had he been wearing any.

Corey waved to the couple before disappearing into the guest annex. He gently knocked on Jessica's door. "Enter," she said from inside.

He cracked open the door and looked in. Jessica was seated in front of one long desk that she had fashioned using the nightstands. On it sat at least two different computer screens, each with its own keyboard. Electrical cords and data cables ran everywhere on, in and around her makeshift work space.

"This looks like a PC repair store," Corey said, stepping into the room.

"Grab a seat and bring it over," she said, nodding toward a chair she had crammed in a corner of the room. "It's flyin' tonight."

"What's flying?" Corey said.

Her fingers raced over the keyboard, typing faster than Corey could keep up with. "YouTube feeds and MySpace postings. Everyone's on tonight."

"Who is everyone?"

"Everyone that matters—all my friends. And then there's probably a couple thousand who will be hitting my site after midnight." Jessica continued to type as she spoke. "They're all expecting another posting on my blog."

> the end of day 2 in lumby land. helicopter parents found out about video feed from barn and pulled the plug. crap. reunion continues 2b huge drag but good food and an open liquor cabinet. my uncle is shock jock carter reed--has taken over everything. he goes live tomorrow 8am est on 80.6 am. corey, my cousin, just crashed the room. g2g.

He read as she typed. "I *crashed* the room?"

"You gotta make it bite, make it interesting," she explained. "That's why they keep on coming back."

"You sound just like my father," Corey said.

Jessica shrugged. "Yeah, maybe. But I don't get millions of dollars for doing this."

"What *do* you get out of it?"

Jessica answered without a moment's hesitation. "Missy and the others think what I do is real cool."

Corey watched her interact with her laptop. "That's what *they* get out of it. What's in it for you?"

"More friends, of course," she said, as if the answer was self-evident. Her BlackBerry on the desk vibrated. "Is this cool or what?" She picked up the small device. "My mom bought it for me as a bribe to behave this week." Jessica typed in a text message using her thumbs and then put the BlackBerry down again. "Where's your page?" she asked, signing into MySpace.

"I don't have one. I only use the private network at college."

"Well, we need to change that right now." She pulled up the registration screen. "What do you want your username to be?"

Corey shook his head. "I don't know."

She looked up in the air, thinking for a moment. "Okay, let's do COREYR. It's boring but easy to remember. When we think of a better one this week, we'll change it." She typed COREYR into the top box. "What's your password? No, don't tell me," she said, handing him the wireless keyboard. "Go ahead and type in a password at least eight characters long with one or two numbers in it.

Corey did as he was told and handed the keyboard back to Jessica.

"Want a beer?" she asked as she took a Heineken out of a cardboard box under the table.

"Where did you get that?"

"The refrigerator in the kitchen, where else?" Jessica could see by Corey's expression that he didn't approve. "Lighten up, C-man.

We're going to have a good time tonight." She gave Corey her beer and opened another for herself. "Cheers," she said, tapping the bottles together.

"Okay, now, let's fill in your MySpace profile," she said, typing quickly.

Jessica began to bombard Corey with questions at a dizzying rate: What's your favorite music? Television? Books? Heroes? Seattle's your hometown? Right? Where did you go to school? And so on. Between each question, they both took gulps of beer. The pattern of questions and beer went on for close to a half hour. By the time Jessica had entered all thc answers, Corey, who seldom drank, was beginning to feel the effects of the alcohol.

"Okay, now the fun starts," she said, picking up her BlackBerry. "I need to take a photo of you. Go over there and sit on the bed."

Everything seemed a little out of kilter as he crossed the room. He sat down, tried to straighten his shirt and smiled. "Look okay?" His words were starting to run together.

"Way too stiff. It looks like a mug shot. Everyone is much more cool than that," she explained. "Try taking off your shirt."

Corey was feeling too loose to object and unbuttoned his shirt. To Jessica's surprise, he had a nicely sculpted chest.

"Very hot for a geek," Jessica said. "Do you work out?"

"Some," he said, flexing his muscles.

She held up her BlackBerry and began snapping photographs of him. "We'll pick the one that looks best," she assured him. "Now, let's do a video."

"Why?" Corey asked, still drinking beer and beginning to slur his words.

"So everyone can get to know you. Just say what you want, and then we'll overlay some graphics and music."

"What should I talk about?"

Jessica thought for a moment. "We want something gripping, provocative, controversial." She paused. "Why don't you tell me about your father?"

Corey laughed, thinking back to that very evening when, after dinner, his father had walked away with his employees and Corey's mother without saying a word to him. His head was spinning from all the beer.

"Let me tell you about Carter Reed . . ."

Thus began Corey's unscripted and unedited oration filled with some angst, some frustration and so much sadness that, at one point, Jessica fought back tears. His emotions were wrapped up in, and his words were laced with, a profound regret that he had never connected with his father. Had Corey not fallen into a beer-induced slumber on Jessica's bed, his soliloquy would have carried on for much longer than the seven minutes he spoke.

While Corey slept, Jessica uploaded the photos to his new webpage and planted the video on YouTube for any and all to see. She then jumped over to RaveInNW.com and began typing.

abt2party: hey everyone

flyman1964: look whos back. youre becoming a regular

abt2party: the room seems buzzing 2nite

marley3823: ton of traffic

postpunk: hey abt2party

flyman1964: you still in our area?

abt2party: still stuck in lumby. okay to link a youtube?

flyman1964: sure

abt2party: www.youtube.com/m17282/coreyreed

nightcrawler: im going there now

2bshades: me2

abt2party: its carter reeds son

flyman1964: the shock jock?

abt2party: 1 and only

flyman1964: cool. will blast it out to a couple thousand in a few min

abt2party: tnx

marley3823: party still on for thur in wheatley. you coming?

abt2party: absolutely--have to hitch down but i'll be there no matter what

TWENTY-SEVEN

# *Proof*

**Monday**

*"Good morning, America! Welcome to* The Carter Reed Show*—the only on-air forum that impartially pits ideology against ideology, idiocy against idiocy. Today is July sixteenth, and as promised, we are broadcasting live from Lumby in a special edition of the show that we're calling Lumby on the Air.*

*"To prove to all of you ideo naysayers who were convinced I would never set foot in a small town that I'm really here, let me read from this morning's twelve-page paper,* The Lumby Lines. *I'm holding it my hands, and I can guarantee you it's not quite* The New York Times. *Twelve pages in all, and the last page has the weather, obituaries, the school lunch menu and a list of specials at Wools, whatever or whoever Wools is.*

*"Wait a minute. Kano just told me that Wools is a small country clothing store on Main Street. Well, for what it's worth, if any of you are actually interested, they seem to have a great deal on yellow snow parkas. It's eighty-two and sunny—get real, folks, who needs a snow parka in July?*

*"So there we have it: the* New York Times *of Lumby, which, I've been told, is the end all and be all of journalistic excellence in the Northwest. I am told that, for the first time in its history, the newspaper will be publishing a daily supplement on the county fair all week. Knock your socks off, folks. All right, moving right along to the front page of* The Lumby Lines, *here's the breaking news:*

The Lumby Lines

# What's News Around Town

BY SCOTT STEVENS July 16

An unusual week in our extraordinary town of Lumby as we prepare to host the Chatham County Fair.

The raccoon that recently baptized itself with holy water by falling into the Presbyterian church's baptismal font has apparently changed his address to Concession Stand #4 on Fairground Road. After receiving two frantic calls from the stand's owner last night, members of the Lumby Fire Department rescued the raccoon from the bowels of Erma's cotton candy vat, where he had gorged on cotton candy for several hours. Dr. Candor examined the animal, which was covered in pink and blue candy fibers, and said he was no worse for wear, although he would be on a sugar high for the next two days.

Along those lines, a small black bear that was obviously attracted to the sounds and smells of the fair came out the woods due north of town and made a midnight visit to the Orvis fly-fishing exhibition, where he caught and ate all seven adult sockeye salmon that were swimming in their display pond.

With one day remaining until the fair's grand open-

> ing, the Parks Department is looking for an immediate solution to their toiletless Porta Potties. The toilets, which were misplaced during the shipment of the outhouse stalls, have been located and were supposed to have been flown into Rocky Mount yesterday. However, United Airlines has informed our mayor that they are still sitting on the tarmac at the Atlanta airport awaiting transport.

Without missing a beat, Carter pointed to the headset covering his ears—no sound was coming through. Worm turned a knob on the control panel, and a moment later, Carter nodded and gave a thumbs-up. He then leaned forward, his chest resting on the table, and put the microphone close to his mouth. This increased the vibrato, giving his on-air voice a personal urgency.

*"Continuing with this fantasy they call real news, the next section reads:*

> In unrelated news, Steve Wilbur's car, which has been illegally parked in front of Chatham Press since his untimely demise two weeks ago, continues to be ticketed by the Police Department. Lumby Funeral Home has informed the police that, while they prepare Wilbur for his final resting place, they will retrieve the keys that were in his pants pocket the night of his bizarre accident. A collection has been taken up to cover all parking fines. Donations can be made at Chatham Bank on Main Street.
>
> Those driving on Farm to Market Road yesterday were privileged to witness a twenty-first-century jousting match between two goliaths of the field: an adjustable hay baler hit the header of a combine harvester. Both machines sustained serious damage. It was a steel-against-steel, New Holland–vs.–Caterpillar moment if ever there was one.

*"Yes, loyal ideos, I have arrived. I have met the enemy and it is . . . country hicks who drive their tractors at a snail's pace so that it takes forever to get here from Seattle. We should have taken my private plane, just like Nancy, my personal ball and chain, reminded me every ten minutes. Just between us, though, the tractors drove me absolutely nuts! To hell with corn—just get them off the road.*

*"Which brings us to our first question: Who should be banned from the road? Let's open the phone lines and get into it before I start running at the mouth about where I am and what I'm doing in the middle of nowhere. On line one, we have John from Newark, New Jersey. John, ideo at will."*

*"John, here. I think everyone over the age of sixty should get the* *bleep* *off the road."*

*"Keep the language clean, John."*

*"Sorry 'bout that, but it's a hot spot for me. I haul on the Jersey Pike six days a week, and those old, wrinkled-skinned geezers get into the left lane and crawl slower than they have sex. They're a* *bleep* *nuisance."*

*"Shoot 'em all. Is that it, John? A little harmless euthanasia for every senior?"*

*"Yeah, I suppose so. It'd certainly make my life a bunch easier."*

*"Okay, on line two, we have Marybeth in the Windy City. Marybeth, ideo at will."*

*"The federal government should take control of licensing drivers because the states are totally inept at doing anything. There should be annual tests for everyone, everywhere, no exceptions."*

*"So, Marybeth, you'd be all right with standing in line for six hours at some motor vehicle office every June first?"*

*"Well, no, not me. I haven't driven for eighteen years. There's no need to in Chicago."*

*"Okay then, line five, we have Madison from Madison. Is that right, or is Worm just pulling my leg? Madison, if you're there, ideo at will."*

"It's the real deal, Carter, direct from Wisconsin. Sitting here eatin' a block of cheese waitin' for the ice to freeze to do some fishin'. I think anyone under the age of twenty-one should get off the road. Some idiot teenager who's not even old enough to vote slammed into my pickup a few months ago. The kid had no insurance, and his dad's pleading innocent. So, what? I'm stuck with a two-thousand-dollar repair bill, and the kid's now driving around in his mother's car. So I say, get all the teenagers out from behind the wheel where they can do real damage."

"I'm sure we're going to get some calls on that. On line three, Andy from New York City. Andy, ideo at will."

"The *bleep* who said the federal government should take control is insane. They can't even fart in the dark without spending a billion dollars. They'd tax the crap out of us just to consider the idea. *Bleep* like that should keep their mouths shut."

"You need to drop the personal attacks, Andy, but we get your point. On line one, we have Ariel from Denver. Ariel, ideo at will."

"I'd like to respond to John in Newark. My parents are in their eighties, and both are outstanding drivers. They also own hybrids and have a zero-carbon footprint, which is more than you can say about your gas-guzzling tandem trailers. If everyone knew what kind of emissions those trucks put out, you're the one who would be banned from the road."

"Thanks for the comment, Ariel. Line two, Jackson from the Bayou."

"Just outside Leesville, Louisiana."

"Nothing better than Cajun crawfish over dirty rice."

"Nothing better this side of heaven. My daddy cooked it up every Sunday after church till the day we put him six feet under, but he was still smiling."

"All right, Jackson, ideo at will."

"My daddy always said, 'Fool me once, shame on you; fool me twice, shame on me.' I think we should have a one-strike rule. One ticket or one accident, and that's it."

"For your entire life? I seldom take a position, but coming from *someone who gets a ticket every couple of months, I find that a little extreme."*

*"Then it's folks like you that we need to get off the road. But keep doing your show—love listening to you every morning."*

Within an hour, Kano's computer logged more than three thousand attempted call-ins with only a few dozen getting through. The call-in volume would have been tenfold in Seattle, but the limited telecommunication lines coming into Montis resulted in a busy signal being heard by nine out of ten ideos who tried reaching Carter Reed that morning.

The broadcasted dialogue continued at a dizzying, relentless pace for the callers, the listeners, and Carter. Every six minutes, there was a one-minute commercial break, which gave Kano time to redial any prior callers who were highly offensive or emotionally wounded. If they wanted to continue their onslaught, they would jump to the front of the call queue.

Only when the debate got extremely heated did Carter allow two people on the air at once. That morning, he chose Ariel and John: an elder-respecting flower child against a middle-aged, beer-drinking trucker. Perfect, Carter thought.

*"Line three, John from Newark is back and asked to cut in. John, re-ideo at will."*

*"No offense to anyone out there, but from Denver is full of* *bleep*."*

*"John, we're bleeping you out most of the time. You gotta clean it up."*

*"Sorry, but who the* *bleep* *cares about a carbon footprint if some old geezer is driving a ridiculous hybrid that can't go any faster than forty in a seventy zone?"*

Within one minute, Ariel was back on the air, vigorously countering the attacks. The more virulent and obscene John's comments, the angrier Ariel's defense of her parents and the planet became. The sparks flew between them for another eight minutes, with no commercial break.

Unfortunately, John was bleeped out for his vulgar language a lot of the time, so listeners mostly got Ariel's point of view, which was so laden with environmental pretentiousness that callers were begging to get on the air and give her a dose of reality.

When verbal brawls took over the show, Carter would lean back and smile. These offered the easiest, sweetest parts of his broadcast.

During the Ariel bashing, as it was quickly becoming, Pam peeked around the corner carrying a tray with fresh coffee and pastries.

"Come on in," Carter said. "We're free for a few seconds." Although the volume was turned down, the shouting voices of the two callers could still be heard in the background.

"You go, girl," Worm said right after Ariel threw some global-warming statistics at the truck driver.

Pam looked around the room—it was filthy. Partially filled paper coffee cups were scattered everywhere, and crumbled napkins had been thrown on the carpet. For some unknown reason, the cushions had been removed from the sofa and heaped in a loose pile behind the control panel that Worm was constantly working. He was partially reclined with his feet resting on an antique side table.

*"And that death threat ends the first hour of* The Carter Reed Show. *We'll be back with Lumby on the Air after this news update."*

"You're off," Kano said as he hit a switch that began a live news feed from the radio station in Seattle.

"Great, fresh coffee," Carter said, holding his cup out for Pam to fill, although she had already placed the pot on the table within his reach.

"Did you want something, Carter?" she asked.

"I'm running on empty. Fill her up, dear," he said. "So what do you think so far?"

"Sorry, Carter, I haven't been listening," she replied, pouring his coffee while reminding herself that he was only going to be there for another five days. "We don't have a radio in the kitchen, and I've been cleaning in there for about an hour. It looked like you guys were pretty determined to make yourselves some omelets this morning."

"Couldn't sleep," Carter said, "so I yanked the guys out of bed at three thirty."

"I see," she said, as she began collecting dirty plates.

"Just keep the coffee coming," Carter said. "When we wrap at nine, we'll be over for a nice meal."

Pam didn't try to hide her surprise. "You will?" she asked. "Unfortunately, André is off today and I'll be at the fair with Mark. But by all means, make yourself at home. Just please put everything away where you find it—that would save me a lot of time when we get back this evening."

"Another Montis feast for us tonight?" Kano asked.

"We're all meeting at The Green Chile in town at seven o'clock."

Carter raised his finger at his sound engineers. "You two are working tonight, so don't even think about it."

"Thirty seconds," Worm announced.

Carter began poking among the pastries. "How about some of those blueberry things?"

"I'm sorry?"

"Those scones," he said. "They're real good."

"I'll see what I can do," Pam said, using the promise as a polite excuse to leave.

"Well, feel free to stick around," he said as she walked out. "We're doing another segment on that ridiculous thing everyone calls a newspaper."

In the middle of the lobby, Pam stopped in her tracks and actually thought about staying for a while. Listening to Carter's show was like watching a car accident—it was hard to turn away.

"Maybe." She waved. After she walked around the corner and was well out of sight—but still within hearing distance of Carter's makeshift studio—she took a seat on the steps leading to the second floor of the inn. She pulled her knees into her chest, inhaled and waited for the assault.

"Three, two, one," Kano said, and after a beat, Carter began speaking.

*"Kano just passed me a note saying that some of you are asking about our Lumby experience thus far. That would narrow our discussion down to what we did yesterday, which I have to admit was better than expected. We went to St. Cross Monastery—one magnificent abbey tucked in the mountains about an hour from here. Those are the monks who make the famous St. Cross Rum Sauce, which I can now personally endorse after having had it over Häagen-Dazs last night for dessert. Perfectly sinful in every way.*

*"So, getting back to our trip to the monastery, I haven't set foot inside a church for darn near twenty years, but their chanting just about brought me to my knees. I was so swept away that I slipped them a check for ten grand. That should keep those celibate brothers praying for a while, don't you think?"*

Pam was stunned.

*"But I swore to some important people that the monks are off limits as far as this radio show is concerned, so that's as far as that discussion goes. But believe you me, there are a hundred other thorns that we'll look at during the next four days of broadcasting Lumby on the Air. Coming up next, another reading from the journalistic masterpiece* The Lumby Lines, *followed by our next topic: transsexuals in the workforce."*

TWENTY-EIGHT

# *Extinct*

Joshua smiled as he turned his car into the long driveway of St. Cross Abbey. He felt a sense of coming home, of belonging, whenever he drove through the monastic property. Although he had never lived there, he had spent many of his younger years with the monks when they resided at Montis Abbey. Thinking of that chapter in his life always brought back fond memories, and he took delight in any moment he spent with his old friends.

St. Cross looked inviting that day with its expansive front lawn and well-manicured gardens. The community members had already begun their daily chores after first attending matins and then eating breakfast. Several monks and sisters were out on the grounds tending to the shrubs, trees and garden beds.

Joshua recognized Sister Robin and Brother Marc working side by side, laying fresh mulch in a rose bed. He thought about how different the monastery was now that the Sisters of Saint Armand had joined the monks. For whatever reason, the abbey didn't appear so austere.

Brother Matthew was just leaving the small chapel when Joshua stepped out of his car. “You’re here quite early,” Matthew commented.

“I have a meeting with Sister Claire in a few minutes,” he explained.

Matthew nodded. “Yes, about the berries. She told me.”

“Will you be joining us?”

“If you could give me a minute, I need to see Brother Aaron first.”

“I’m sure we can wait.”

The new annex built by the nuns was stunning. Although the stone facade’s traditional appearance complemented the other buildings in the compound, the interior reflected a more contemporary style with an open floor plan. Abundant natural light flooded into the community room through south-facing windows, offering beautiful vistas of the newly planted vineyard.

Sister Claire was already seated at the table speaking softly to Sister Megan. Sister Kristina was filling a carafe with freshly brewed tea.

“Joshua, come join us,” Claire said. “Perhaps you can help us decide about the Merlot vines.”

“What’s the question?” he asked, taking a seat across from her.

“One of our transport crates was damaged on its way from Oregon, and the roots of two dozen plants were exposed. They’re are still alive, but we’re discussing the risk to the other vines if we plant them.”

Sister Megan continued. “If the roots were contaminated with a fungus or bacteria—”

“You could lose more than just those vines,” Joshua said.

“Exactly,” Claire confirmed.

Megan tapped a pencil on the table while she thought. “We could separate them from the rest of the vineyard if we planted them in Zone A.”

“What’s Zone A?” Joshua asked.

Sister Kristina laughed as she joined the others at the table. “That’s what we’ve named the berry field. A is for ants.”

Matthew knocked on the partly open door. "I hope I haven't held up the meeting."

"Not at all," Claire said. "We were just talking about using the berry field for some of our Merlot vines."

Joshua leaned forward. "That's what I'd like to talk with you about," he said. "I received a few calls this morning from three plant biologists on the East Coast—two who work in private labs and one at the Department of Agriculture. Independently, they confirmed that the berry plants, *your* berry plants, are a species that was thought to have vanished quite some time ago."

"Like fifty years ago?" Megan asked.

"No," Joshua answered. "More like five hundred years. Archaeologists found similar berries in the stomach and intestines of animal remains they dug up in the southwest corner of the state. But there was no question that, until now, it was assumed that that genus was extinct."

"And extinct they should stay," Kristina said, slapping her hand lightly on the table to kill another ant. "Every day, the ants' territory expands. They've made their way down to our abbey, as you can see." She pointed to another ant that was circling the base of her coffee mug. "And they're getting more aggressive."

That came as no surprise to Joshua. "They're simply reacting to the vibration in the ground from the bulldozers and fieldwork. The biologists think that this shrub was fairly common across this region until eight hundred years ago and that it slowly died out over a three-hundred-year period. In addition to the berries being forage food for deer, it's thought that indigenous Indians used them for both staining their hides and as a food source."

"Brother John has already used the berries in some of his recipes," Matthew commented. "Last night, he created a new berry rum sauce that, I must admit, was outstanding,"

"What's the berry's name?" Claire asked.

Joshua removed a small slip of paper from his shirt pocket. "I thought you might ask that," he said, and then wrote on the whiteboard: *Vaccinium fallosutum* of the Ericaceae family. "*Vaccinium* is the closest genus to what you have—a variant in the blueberry family—but if your berry is determined to be genetically unique, then I suppose you would have the opportunity to name it yourselves."

"If it ever comes to that, you can take care of it, Joshua. We're too busy growing grapes," Claire said.

"And the ants?" Kristina asked.

"Ow!" Megan yelped, slapping her ankle. "That's the second time I've been bit today."

"I'm sorry for the problems they're causing," Joshua said, glancing at Megan, "but the entomologists are extremely excited about what I showed them. These ants aren't unique except in the way they're pollinating the berry flowers. The general theory is that these ants could ultimately be used to fertilize crops. With the honeybee population dropping at an alarming rate, we're seeking a viable substitute, and the ants might fit the bill." He paused. "A lot of people are asking you to keep the plants where they are, at least until we can drum up a place where they can be successfully relocated."

Kristina spotted two ants on the table and leaned forward to examine them. Her nose was inches from the table. "This is *so* inappropriate," she said, continuing to watch the bugs. "Now it looks like they're having sex or something!"

"In a monastery of all places," Brother Matthew jested.

"Are they really?" Megan said, leaning over for a closer look.

"Sisters," Claire said to reclaim their attention. She turned to Joshua. "I would hate to disappoint anyone, but we need to clear that land. You're asking us to reduce the size of our vineyard by several acres, and that's just not possible. Another shipment of vines is due to arrive next week and scheduled to be planted on some of that ground. That soil is the richest we have."

"I understand your position," Joshua said, "but what happens if it really is an extinct vine? Disturbing any part of that ecosystem could have an irreversible effect on both plant and animal."

"But they're spreading," Megan said.

"When they find no food, I'm sure they'll go back to the vines," Joshua said.

Claire turned to Matthew. "Are any of the ants in your buildings?"

"Thankfully, not a trace," he answered.

"Yet," Kristina added as she squashed the pair. "And I actually feel badly for doing that."

Claire closed her notepad. "I suggest we wait just a few days to give everyone a chance to come up with a solution. But," she said, turning to Joshua, "that might be all the time we can afford."

Megan saw another ant crossing the table, heading in her direction.

*Smack.*

TWENTY-NINE

# *Shaw*

A stretch limousine from Rocky Mount Airport maneuvered down the hairpin curves of Priests Pass on its way to Lumby. Vince Shaw, a tall, lanky man in his early fifties, stretched out his legs in the backseat, taking no notice of the natural beauty that surrounded him.

He felt time was passing too quickly, and time was one asset his vast wealth could not buy. In the last year or so, his ink-black hair had started tuning gray, and now, he needed to keep a pair of reading glasses handy. His body was stiff from the long flight from New York City, although his private plane had offered more comfort than any commercial flight would have.

The chauffeur slowed the car to watch a moose graze by the side of the road. "Gorgeous country out here," he said with an appreciative smile.

Shaw ignored the comment and put a cell phone to his ear. The conversation lasted no more than sixty seconds, during which he spoke only four words: "Get it done, now."

After hanging up, Shaw reached over to the control panel and turned up the radio. Carter Reed was artfully juggling callers a mile a minute.

"Never listen to that man," the driver commented. "He's just another Genghis Khan."

Shaw considered the remark. "You give Carter Reed too much credit—Genghis Kahn was brilliant."

"Maybe. But Reed's too extreme for me."

"I find him totally anemic and innocuous, but I think his callers are absolutely fascinating."

"But he incites the fights," the driver contended.

"*He's* not the fighter, and that's the critical difference," Shaw said, as if making the closing statement at a trial.

The chauffeur nodded, although he didn't understand the point his passenger was making.

Shaw closed his eyes and listened to the argument on the radio, which had become personally vindictive. "Utterly fascinating," he said to himself, and then raised his voice so the driver could hear. "If nothing else, Carter Reed deserves credit for understanding human nature and benefiting from the very worst in us all. He certainly is a successful parasite."

Driving past the Wayside Tavern, Shaw glanced up at a freshly painted sign on the right-hand side of the road.

**WELCOME TO LUMBY**

**This Year's Host of the**

**Chatham County Fair**

**July 17–22**

A plastic pink flamingo wearing blue shorts and a blue-and-white striped rugby shirt sat at the base of the sign. His long, skinny legs were bent at the knee so that he could rest a drawing pad on his lap.

That very morning, Jimmy D had taken Hank off his job of manning the fairgrounds gate and asked him to act as the town's official fair ambassador, greeting people as they arrived in Lumby. Hank, though, had much more serious business at hand, or at wing, as it were: the duct tape competition. Between the quick hello waves to all who entered town along Main Street, he remained focused on the design of his entry.

Lying on the ground was a book he had checked out of the library that came highly recommended: *The Coral Reefs of the World*. He looked down at a two-page color spread of the Great Barrier Reef, studying the various structures of the coral, and then he began to draw a sketch from which he intended to duct tape his way to fame and fortune.

The driver glanced in his rearview mirror. "Are you here for the fair?"

Shaw couldn't help but chuckle at the preposterous idea. "No."

"Well, if you have time on your hands, it's a real treat."

"No doubt," Shaw said, proving he was a man of few words when he wanted a conversation to end.

"They say the Ferris wheel is the biggest in the state," the driver said, pointing through his front windshield at the ride, which towered over the town. "It's called The Air."

Shaw checked his watch and saw that he was ahead of schedule. "Drive me around the area for the next ten minutes."

"Where would you like to go?"

"I've never been here, so you decide," Shaw said impatiently.

The driver clicked on the blinker and turned right onto North Deer Run Loop. "Well then, we have to start at the fair."

Just as they were approaching the gated entrance, Shaw told the driver to pull into the parking lot. "Just drive up and down the aisles," he said.

"Are you looking for a place to park? Because with this limo—"

"No, just drive through the parking lot and continue on," Shaw instructed.

The driver shrugged his shoulders. "Not much of a view of the fair from here, though."

Shaw didn't reply. Instead, he studied the makes, models and years of the cars parked in the lot. Such simple expeditions always told him more about the local demographics than any statistics or research report ever could.

"I've seen enough," Shaw said. "We can leave now."

After driving thc length of Fairground Road, the driver turned left onto Hunts Mill and then, at Jimmy D's, took another left onto Main Street.

"This is downtown Lumby," he said proudly.

Shaw remained silent, staring out the window. At the traffic light, which randomly blinked different colors (Shaw wondered why the malfunctioning light hadn't been fixed), the driver turned onto Farm to Market Road. Within a minute, they were well out of town, traveling through a lush valley with mountains in full view to the west.

"Slow down," Shaw said abruptly as he lowered his window.

The landscape had been accurately described to him; although the mountains were considered the foothills to the Rockies, their elevation was substantial. "All right, drive on," Shaw finally directed.

He was still staring at the mountains when they passed in front of Montis Inn. At Fork River, the limousine turned around and returned to Lumby. "Where to now?" the driver asked.

"Main Street Realty," Shaw said. "Do you need an address?"

"Absolutely not. Everyone in the region knows where Joan's office is located."

A few minutes before his scheduled appointment, Shaw stepped out of the limo and, carrying a large briefcase, walked into the small home that, many years earlier, Joan had converted into her office. She was talking on the phone, so he stood in a small waiting room.

On the coffee table was the most recent copy of *Entrepreneur* magazine, with a large photograph of him on the cover.

As soon as Joan hung up, Shaw extended his hand and introduced himself. "I assumed," she said, smiling. "I'm Joan Stokes. It's a pleasure to meet you." She examined his face and then looked over at the magazine. "A very good likeness."

"Unfortunately, anonymity is impossible in my line of work."

Thinking back on the negative article she had read about him the night before, she said, "Your projects certainly have their critics."

"My only objection is that reporters never bother to interview those people who benefit, do they?" he quipped. "Their spin is sensationalistic."

"It would appear that way," Joan said, offering him a seat. "In truth, I'm surprised you wanted to come out to see the property so quickly."

From his briefcase, Shaw removed a pad of legal paper with a list of questions he had written down during the flight to Rocky Mount. "If the land is everything you said it is during our phone call yesterday, there should be several development companies knocking on your door within the next few days. I wanted to beat them to the punch."

"Yes, I've already received inquiries from two."

"For a Realtor who's listing a prime piece of land, you sound less than enthusiastic."

Joan opened a desk drawer. "I suppose I'm waiting for one or two farmers to show some interest."

Shaw chuckled. "At that price? It won't happen because it's not a viable financial model. Even with all the subsidies the government doles out, without a huge amount of cash up front—which you and I both know working farmers don't have—they'd be financially buried in no time."

"And that's what I think is unfortunate," she said.

"You're against commercial development of this farm?"

Joan sat up and looked him in the eyes. "Not at all. I'm neutral—I need to be." She paused. "I explained to you yesterday that I'm representing both you and the seller, so everything needs to be aboveboard."

"But what's your *personal* opinion about my kind of project?" he asked. Clearly, he was using her more as a sounding board of community opinion than he was curious about her individual attitude toward big business.

"As a Realtor or as a resident of Lumby?" she asked.

"Both."

Joan thought for a moment and then chose her words carefully. "I would say that as farmland, the property is significantly overpriced. But it's fairly valued if you're going to either subdivide or develop." She paused before continuing. "As a longtime resident of Lumby, I see advantages and disadvantages to either choice."

"A politically safe answer," Shaw said.

She looked out the front windows of her office and saw old Jeremiah walking his mare toward Wayside Tavern. She wished she could somehow extricate herself from the situation, from the deal, and from Vince Shaw.

Vince sensed exactly that. "Are you familiar with Bradley, Wyoming?" he asked.

"I've never been there, but yes, I know of it."

"Four years ago, it was a podunk, run-down town. Local unemployment was eighteen percent, and most of the small businesses were struggling. We went in and built one resort on a couple hundred acres—a beautifully designed vacation spot of eighty town houses, fifty chalets, and one main lodge with two hundred rooms. Within eight weeks, just eight short weeks, employment dropped to two percent, and within six months, personal property and school taxes fell by eighty-four percent. It now has the lowest tax mill rate in the state because of the money my resort is pouring into the town. The project even subsidized a new community college." He leaned forward in his chair. "It put Bradley, Wyoming, on the map."

“But what about the residents who didn’t want to be on your map?” she asked.

“They certainly didn’t complain about the new restaurants or the urgent care center we threw into the deal.”

“No, I suppose they wouldn’t,” Joan said, standing up. “Let me collect my things, and we’ll drive over there and take a look.”

When Joan stepped outside, she wasn’t at all surprised to see the black stretch limo parked in her driveway. “Perhaps it’s best if we take my car,” she suggested. “It’s a little more maneuverable.”

“We’ll take the limo,” Shaw said. “Most people know just how wealthy I am—no reason to hide it.”

## THIRTY

# *Waterfall*

The limo traveled along Main Street as Shaw looked out the window and Joan introduced him to the small town.

"Chatham Press publishes *The Lumby Lines* and owns the bookstore across the street," she said, pointing to the stone building at the corner of Main Street and Farm to Market Road. Her love of the town could be heard in her voice. "The Green Chile is well known for its margaritas. If you have no plans tonight, perhaps I could take you to dinner there?"

"That would be fine," he said.

"Across the street is our library. And the Feed Store, down there, is one of the oldest buildings in town and has an amazing history. Well worth taking a stroll through, even if you have nothing to buy. And, of course, there's Brad's Hardware."

"A good location for a Home Depot," he said.

Joan laughed. "Brad's is one of the most popular stores in town. No one would want to get rid of it. And we certainly don't have the population or the business volume to support a big store like Home Depot."

"Not today you don't," Shaw said dispassionately.

Just outside of town, they crossed Goose Creek and turned onto Killdrop Road, a dirt road canopied by large oak trees.

"The property begins just after that small cemetery," Joan said. "The road is a little over a mile long and is in need of some repair."

The limousine bounced as it hit several consecutive potholes. "Obviously," Shaw said.

"The owner insisted on being present when you look at the property, so you'll be meeting Mike McNear and his wife, Bess. Mike comes from one of the oldest families in the county—his grandfather was one of the founders of our town."

"Ah," Shaw said, clearly uninterested.

When the farm came into view, Joan asked the chauffeur to stop. "Let's look at the property before seeing the farm," she said, getting out of the car.

Stepping over a small stone wall that ran alongside the road, she led Shaw to a knoll that offered a panoramic view of McNear's land.

"Roughly, his four thousand acres begin at the base of that mountain," she said, pointing toward the north, "and continue to that ridge. It's a very clean rectangle with no irregular parcels or inaccessible acreage."

From his jacket pocket, Shaw withdrew a pair of compact binoculars that he put up to his eyes. He then spent several minutes studying the terrain.

"And he owns to the top of the mountain?"

"And beyond. The property line is actually on the other side of the crest."

Shaw continued to scan the property. "The waterfall—does that flow year-round?"

Joan looked in the same general direction but couldn't see any cascade. "We'll need to ask the owner," she said.

Shaw lowered his binoculars, but continued to examine the land as if it were a battlefield he had just conquered. "It looks fine, Joan," he said. "Assuming the sellers don't make a heyday out of it, let's plan to make an offer today."

Although Joan wasn't surprised by Shaw's decisiveness, she wanted to slow down the pace. She knew from experience that it was the fast deals that more often than not never came to closure. "Why don't we go look at the farm?" she suggested.

"The farm is irrelevant," Shaw replied, "except for the expense we'll have to incur to tear it down. What do you think of a million cash with a closing in three months?"

Joan bit her lip. "The listing price is three million. You don't want to annoy the seller so much that he digs in his heels."

Shaw headed abruptly back to the limo with Joan following. "Then make it one and a half million cash with ten percent down and no contingencies," he said over his shoulder.

Once back in the car, Joan said, "I know the owner is looking for a faster closing than three months."

"That's nonnegotiable. It will take that long to get a site plan done and have all the approvals in place."

"But if there is a snag in the zoning—"

"Then I'll pull out of the deal and lose the deposit. Better to risk a hundred and fifty thousand than a couple million."

"Let's go to the farmhouse and get your questions answered," Joan said, nodding at the driver to proceed.

Mike was already in the farmyard when the limo approached. He had been standing behind the shed watching Joan and her client ever since they'd walked up on the knoll.

When Shaw opened the door, Mike was there, jutting his hand toward the man's face. "Mike McNear," he said, a little too eagerly. "Let me show you around the place."

"I'm interested in seeing a scaled plat map," Shaw replied.

"In the house," Mike said. "The wife has some coffee and baked sweets in the oven."

Ushering Shaw to the front porch, Mike kicked aside an old screen door that had fallen off the summer before. "It's a great place," he said, entering the kitchen.

Joan immediately noticed changes to the home that indicated

Bess had been hard at work preparing for the showing. She felt a tinge of guilt, knowing that Bess's spotless kitchen wouldn't matter in the least. "It looks great," she whispered to Bess.

"Right over here," Mike said, bringing Shaw into the living room. On the wall hung a four-foot-square map of his property. "Just updated to show all the outbuildings."

Shaw stood in front of the map and studied it carefully. "You show no elevations," he commented.

"Well, it would cost a hundred thousand to get a topography of those mountains," Mike grumbled, looking to his wife for corroboration, but Bess remained silent, pursing her lips.

"Mike, let's not talk for the surveyor," Joan said in a disapproving voice. She really disliked showing a property with the owners present because, without fail, they would say something to their own disadvantage. Mike was worse than many.

"The adjacent land?" Shaw asked.

Joan answered before Mike could. "To the south and west is federal forest and to the north, state forest."

"Here's the deed," Mike said, pushing it into the man's chest. "You can see for yourself."

After skimming through the four pages, Shaw returned his focus to the map. "There are no commercial building restrictions, correct?" he asked.

"None," Mike confirmed.

"Why are you interested in the farm, Mr. Shaw?" Bess asked out of the blue.

"I'm not. I just want the land," he replied without looking up.

Bess frowned. "What would you do with it?"

Before glancing over at Bess, Shaw put his finger on the map so as not to lose his place. "I'd tear down the farm," he said, "and then build a resort, a ski resort."

Bess glanced at Joan with a dismayed expression.

"The plans are very premature," Joan explained. "Endless procedures and approvals need to be in place before Mr. Shaw can deem the project viable. Would you not agree?"

"Absolutely," Shaw agreed. "For every hundred pieces of land we look at, we might buy one. And then for every three pieces of land we go ahead and purchase, two will remain undeveloped because of unforeseen snags. Our last proposed project in Utah was canned because of a water issue."

"Plenty of water here," Mike said forcefully. "Our well produces thirty-two gallons a minute.

Shaw smirked. "We need a thousand times that, but that's just one hurdle that we'll consider in due time."

Bess tugged on Joan's sleeve. "Would you help me in the kitchen a moment?"

Once they were out of earshot, Bess took hold of Joan's arm and backed her against the refrigerator. "*Tear it down?* You can't let that happen."

"Bess, Mike told me to find a buyer," she said apologetically. "Mr. Shaw is a good candidate."

"But Mike doesn't know what he's talking about. I told him that I'd leave him before I'd turn the farm over to someone who would destroy our land."

"I guarantee this would not destroy your *land*. In fact, if it is anything like his project in Bradley, Wyoming, what he has in mind for this place could turn around the economy of Lumby. The store owners and restaurants would have more business than they would know what to do with." Suddenly, she stopped, realizing that she was sounding just like Shaw, defending the idea of exploiting a hidden paradise for money. "I need to get back," she said.

Just as Joan returned to the living room, Shaw was answering one of Mike's questions. ". . . have a Starbucks on Main Street and possibly change the name of the town—Lumby just doesn't have a high-end ring to it. They'll be beating a path to this hole-in-the-wall just like they did in Telluride."

"How about some coffee?" Mike said as he bolted from the room, dragging Joan with him. "Joan, you can help me. Bess, go keep Mr. Shaw company."

Joan found herself once again pushed up against the refrigerator door.

"We have him hooked!" Mike was so excited, he had to force himself to keep his voice down. "I knew it the minute I saw that fancy limousine. City folk always have lots of money. I want to raise the price to *four* million."

Joan looked at Mike in disbelief. "We can't do that, Mike. He's seen the listing—he knows the price. If this deal falls through, we can talk about adjusting the price then."

"You have to make this happen," Mike said in an intimidating tone.

"I'll do the best I can," she countered. "You're not at all concerned about the buyer being a real estate developer?"

"Bess might be, but she doesn't know what she's taking about. I told her I'd leave her before I held on to the farm a day more than necessary just so we could sell it to a dirty pair of overalls."

"I'm assuming by that you mean another farmer," Joan said.

"Just bring me an offer," he said before dashing back to Vince's side.

As Joan followed Mike back into the living room, Shaw caught her eye. "There's some paperwork in the car I need you to look at. Please join me."

At least it won't be against the refrigerator door, Joan thought. "We'll be back in a minute."

Once outside, Shaw took in a deep breath. "I suppose there is something to be said for country air." He scanned the peaks of the mountains. "McNear wants out more than I want in. Make the offer for one million flat with a hundred thousand deposit and a four-month close."

"I think that's too low," she advised, "but if that's your decision, we'll go back to my office and draw up an offer, which I'll present to the owners this afternoon. At least then we'll see exactly where they stand."

Joan just hoped that Mike wouldn't be holding a shotgun next time she came by.

## THIRTY-ONE
# *Viking*

Pam sat on the lobby stairs listening to the next segment of *The Carter Reed Show*. She was already incensed by his comment about slipping the monks some money, and her ire only grew upon hearing him pit one bigot against another.

When she had heard enough, she snuck out the front door, shaking with anger. The dirty plates she had collected rattled in her arms, in danger of falling. As she stepped off the porch, she saw Mark standing in the parking lot next to the Jeep. She was so focused that she never saw the huge duct tape contraption on the roof of the car.

"I hate your brother-in-law," she said, storming up to him.

"And good morning to you, honey," he joked.

"I'm sorry," she said, kissing him on the cheek, "but Carter just said he gave a ten-thousand-dollar check to St. Cross Abbey."

Mark waved it off. "He's just pulling your leg."

"Mark, he said that on the air to nine million people," she said. "He's definitely not bluffing."

"Wow," he said, as he stepped on the tailgate to hoist himself up on top of the car's roof.

"He made it sound flippant, like some kind of bribe or payoff," she continued.

"Would you hand me that rope please?"

Only after Pam had handed Mark the tie-down did she notice the object on the roof. It looked somewhat like a robot and was made entirely of shiny gray duct tape, measuring eight feet long, eight feet wide and five feet high. It was, in fact, almost as large as the car onto which it was strapped. An assortment of appendages, wings and extensions jutted out from all sides.

Pam tilted her head to the left and then to the right, thinking it was a prehistoric tarantula. She finally gave up. "What in the world is it?"

"It's our entry for the fair's duct tape engineering contest," Mark said proudly.

"I should have guessed."

"Joshua and I put it together earlier this morning before he left for St. Cross. He had to go talk to the monks about the whole berry-berry situation, but he said he'd be back in time for the judging."

"But what is it, *exactly*?"

"That all depends on what you mean by the word 'exactly,'" Mark teased. Pam frowned at her husband. "Okay, I would have to say that it's *exactly* the *Viking 2*—you know, the Mars lander, with its own spectrometer and electron microscope attached to the bottom."

Pam burst out laughing.

"No, really, honey, this thing is great," Mark insisted. "We used some of the spare windows in the basement so you can look inside. It even has retractable legs with footpads. And we taped a picture of the universe on top of the antenna so it feels just like you're reaching out for the Milky Way."

She grinned. "It feels just like that."

"Well, that's just for special effect," he said, rolling his eyes. "I could explain everything to you now, but I don't have time. Just know that this is brilliant."

"Brilliant," she repeated.

"First prize guaranteed," Mark said, tying down the lunar landing arms. "A replica of the *Galileo* space probe won last year, and I'm hoping it's the same judge this year—he's a real space buff."

Suddenly, with no apparent cause, one of the mechanical arms broke off and dropped onto the hood of the car.

"Honey, would you throw that in the backseat? I'll fix it when we get to the fair."

"So what are we going to do about the check Carter gave the monks?" Pam asked.

"Nothing," he answered. "That's between Carter and the guys, and it has nothing to do with us. But if you ask me, that's a pretty nice donation."

"Don't back Carter on this," Pam warned.

"I'm not," Mark said. When she didn't respond, he knew it was time to change the subject. "I was surprised to see Kay and Robert up so early. I think they'll have a great time today."

"I hope they'll be safe," she said. "When I was alone in the kitchen with Robert last night, he told me that he wants to marry Mom. I think he was looking for my permission."

"What?" Mark asked, distracted.

"That's more than what I said. I was speechless."

Mark continued securing down the duct tape entry. "But you did say yes, right?"

Pam kicked a stone with her toe. "Actually, no. I was too stunned. I walked out of the kitchen."

Mark stepped down from the roof of the car. "And you haven't talked to him since?"

Pam shook her head. "Just this morning to see them off, and I didn't say anything about it."

"The poor guy," he said.

"Don't make me feel more guilty that I already do," she appealed. "Anyway, what does my approval have to do with anything? They'll do whatever they want."

Mark took the mechanical arm that Pam was still holding.

"Obviously, it means a lot to him. Honey, it's only you and Kay in your family, and he wants you in on it. I think it's very chivalrous of him."

Just then, Patrick and Elaine walked out of the guest annex with Lynn close behind. When Patrick spotted Mark and Pam in the parking lot, he waved and headed in their direction.

"A scale model of the *Viking*," Patrick said, walking up to the Jeep and grabbing hold of one of the lander's footpads. "Out of duct tape no less. Very impressive."

Mark turned to Pam. "See, what did I tell you? It's really authentic looking."

Suddenly, the footpad that Patrick was holding fell off in his hands.

"See?" Pam said.

"We have separation, mission control." Patrick laughed. "Here, do something with this," he said, pushing the disc into Mark's chest.

"It's our entry for the duct tape engineering competition," Mark explained. "The winner gets, like, a hundred cases of the stuff."

"How many rolls are in a case?" Patrick asked.

"Something like fifty," Mark said. "That should last us for a while."

"No, really, Mark?"

Lynn peeked through the window. "It looks like it's about to cave in the roof of your Jeep."

Mark tied down another leg. "That's what Joshua said."

"How did you get it up there?" Lynn asked.

"I used the tractor, and Worm and Kano helped Joshua lower it in place."

Elaine looked over at the main building. "Carter is in there now broadcasting?"

Pam nodded. "He is."

"Are you guys coming to the fair with me?" Mark asked.

Patrick pulled on one of the extendable legs. "I thought the fair opened tomorrow."

"It does—Tuesday is the official opening," Mark explained. "But today is even better. They call it pre-day. That's when they judge the more—"

Pam interjected, "Ridiculous—"

"*—interesting* competitions," Mark said. "And the rides are half price because they're shaking out the bugs. They normally break down halfway through, and when they do, you get a free ticket that you can use during the week. Oh, and food is half price 'cause everyone's getting used to their grills."

"Meaning everything is burned?" Elaine asked.

"Yeah, but that black crispy stuff is great on barbecued chicken," Mark said.

Elaine turned to Pam. "I think we'll pass and go down to Woodrow Lake for a swim. Jessica is still sleeping. I heard her typing away on her computer at three this morning."

Pam was surprised. "Do you really let her stay up as late as she wants?"

Elaine nodded. "That's what all her friends do. She self-monitors—she knows her own body better than we do. If her internal clock runs behind ours, then we adjust to it," she explained almost clinically. "But if you could keep an eye on her, we'd appreciate it."

Lynn rolled her eyes. "The last time I asked Pam to do that, Coco was screwed by a raccoon." Everyone was startled by Lynn's language. "Why is everyone looking at me?" she asked defensively. "I'm not the one who nailed poor little Coco."

Mark burst out laughing, followed by everyone else.

"You're priceless," Patrick said, giving his sister a squeeze. "Do you want to join us for a swim?"

"No," Lynn said. "I need to head down to the barn."

"Well, have fun," he said, waving goodbye.

As Patrick and Elaine walked down the drive, Pam called out, "Remember that we're all meeting at The Green Chile in town. Reservations are for seven."

"See you then," Elaine called back.

As they were crossing the road, a hybrid car pulled up and parked behind the Jeep. Chuck Bryson stepped out.

"Everyone is certainly up early today. Good morning, Lynn," he said. Chuck studied the *Viking* for a minute. "Your entry for today's competition, no doubt?" he asked Mark.

"I have a good feeling about this one. It might even win first place," Mark said, trying to sound more confident than he actually was. "What are you doing here?"

Pam quickly answered, "I asked Chuck to do some work on the beehives." That was her best excuse to get Chuck to come to Montis so that he and Lynn could have more time together.

"But we just added some new frames and supers to the hive last week," Mark said.

"There are a few other things that need to be done," Pam told her husband.

"I don't think so, honey. I've taken care of everything up there."

Pam kicked him with the side of her foot. "Well, it's a good thing Chuck came by because Lynn might be interested in going up to the apiary with him."

Mark finally caught on to Pam's intentions. "Oh, I get it," he said. "Yeah, that's a good idea. That whole place needs to be cleaned up. It's a total mess up there. It really is a two-person job."

Pam rolled her eyes. "Very discreet, honey."

Chuck turned to Lynn. "It appears that we're wanted up in the fields. Would you like to join me?"

He extended his hand, but Lynn took a few steps back. In the light of day, she had decided she had more sense than to get involved with a stranger. "I don't think so," she said. "I need to check on Coco."

"I'm sure she's fine. But we can go by the barn on the way up to the beehives," Chuck offered. "I'd so enjoy continuing our conversation from last night."

"No," Lynn said, looking at Pam. "No, I'm going to stay here. Pam needs my help cleaning up before I go down to the barn."

Chuck was totally confused. The evening before, they had sat under the stars until well after midnight, talking as if they had known each other for years. Now, Lynn couldn't look him in the eyes.

Being a true gentleman, Chuck backed off. Although he didn't understand why Lynn was acting the way she was, he assumed she had good reason. "If that's what you want," he said, clearly disappointed. "But if you change your mind, I'll be up there for a while."

Chuck reached into the back of his SUV and withdrew his hive equipment, bowed and made a quick retreat. Crossing Farm to Market Road, he disappeared into the thick orchard.

Pam looked at Lynn in disbelief. "What was that about?"

"What do you mean?" she said.

"You had such a great time with Chuck last night. Why didn't you go with him?"

Lynn rubbed her eyes in frustration. "It's because I had a great time, all right?" she said angrily.

"I don't get it," Mark said.

"I'm just getting out of a relationship," Lynn said.

Mark leaned against the Jeep and crossed his arms. "But Lynn, you've been divorced for four—or has it been five?—years."

"That's not what it feels like to me," she said. "It feels like I was just lied to and cheated on. And it feels like my divorce was finalized yesterday."

"But it wasn't yesterday," Pam said. "You need to move on."

"You don't think I know that?" Lynn spat out.

"The only way to get unstuck is to say yes," Mark said.

Pam took her husband's hand and squeezed it gently, thanking him for saying that.

"And then have the exact same thing happen to me again?" Lynn said bitterly. "I'm not that big a fool."

"If there's anyone you can take a chance on, it's Chuck Bryson," Pam assured her.

Mark added, "We've known him for years. He's the greatest guy in the world. He even makes me look like a schmuck."

Lynn wiped her eyes.

“Why don’t you go up and join him?” Pam urged. “Don’t have any expectations and don’t worry about the future. Just be two people who have come together for a very short time, who enjoy each other’s company and can say goodbye in a few days with good memories.”

Lynn gazed up toward the fields.

“Go ahead,” Mark said, “It’s a chance that may not come this way again.”

THIRTY-TWO

# *Flushed*

Standing among the apples trees, Lynn studied a sketch that Mark had drawn of the property, highlighting the path to the apiary, then turned in a circle to take in her surroundings before continuing to walk deeper into the orchard. Approaching the far west side of the field, where the rows of apple trees ended abruptly, Lynn spotted the overgrown path to the beehives.

In the distance, she saw Chuck in the open field, standing next to a multicolored structure as tall as his waist. From his white hat hung a fine mesh that dropped to his shoulders, and over long sleeves, he wore a pair of yellow leather gloves that almost reached his elbows.

On the ground next to him lay an assortment of beekeeper's paraphernalia that included another hat and a second pair of gloves he had brought along in the hope that Lynn would find her way to him. While he worked, he spoke to the bees in a low, soothing voice just loud enough for Lynn to hear.

"There's no reason to be so bothered," he said as he held up a narrow frame covered with honeycomb and swarming with bees. "You can buzz your heads off, but we still have work to do."

When a bee became trapped under his veil, he laughed. "So small to be so silly," he said, lifting the webbing in order to shoo the bee away.

For quite some time, Lynn stood motionless in the underbrush, very much out of view. Every so often, a bee would circle around her and then disappear. She continued to watch Chuck as he worked at a slow, steady pace scraping off the frames and then placing them back into their colorful boxes. Occasionally, she heard him whistle. She was tempted to join him, but each time she was about to walk out of the forest and into the open, sun-drenched field, fear and logic told her to stay where she was. *Why expose myself?* she asked over and over again.

Just as she turned to leave, Chuck called out, "Wait!"

She froze, stunned that she had been seen.

"You're missing all the fun," he said.

She walked to the edge of the field. "How did you know I was here?"

"The bees told me—they've been visiting you for the last fifteen minutes," he said. "Would you like to see?"

Lynn nodded slowly. "Yes, I would."

"Give me one minute."

Chuck returned the frame he was holding to the box and, on top of that, replaced a lid and the cover that had been leaning against the hive. He picked up the veiled hat and the pair of gloves and walked over to her. "I'm so glad you decided to come up. Let's get this on you," he said, lowering the hat over her head and then pulling it down and securing the veil around her shoulders. He handed her the gloves. "Now you look the part—they'll never know."

"Who?"

"The bees," Chuck replied.

Lynn, of course, thought Chuck was teasing and laughed nervously.

He narrowed his eyes. "Are you all right?"

“I don’t want to get stung,” she said in an anxious voice.

“I can’t promise you that won’t happen,” he said, “but if it does, I guarantee that the pain will be nothing compared to what you’re anticipating.” He paused, tightening the veil’s drawstring. “That’s the funny thing about life; most of the time, what we fear never happens.”

That’s probably true, Lynn thought. “Yes, I think I’m ready.”

“Okay, then, let’s meet some bees.”

As they approached the hive, Lynn’s eyes opened, not in alarm but in delight at the sound that came from the hive.

“I call it singing,” he said. “The pitch will vary depending upon how excited they are or how hard they’re working.”

“Working?” Lynn asked.

“Always. They’re building comb, bringing in pollen, or just maintaining the correct temperature in the hive. In the dead of winter, when it’s five below zero out in this field, it’s ninety-three degrees in there. The vibrations of their wings heat the air.”

“That’s amazing.”

“They’re also their own air conditioners,” Chuck said, delighted to see Lynn’s interest in something he loved. He handed her a large tin can with an accordion side and a spout from which rose a soft gray plume of smoke.

“This is a smoker,” he explained. “Why don’t you squeeze it a few times?” When she did, the smoke immediately thickened. Chuck placed his hand on the lid of the hive. “When I crack open the cover, you need to put the nozzle into the hive and smoke the bees.”

“This will get them to leave?” she asked.

“Oh, no,” he said. “It just calms them down for a while.”

She squeezed the smoker and billows of smoke drifted into the hive. “Got it,” she said, nodding.

When Chuck lifted the lid, she inserted the nozzle into the crack and gently squeezed.

“Again,” Chuck said, removing the cover altogether. “Now you can smoke between the frames." As she did, the pitch of the buzzing dropped. "Do you hear?" he asked.

She nodded, never taking her eyes off the inside of the hive. Although bees were everywhere, she wasn't at all nervous—she was captivated.

Chuck worked calmly and quickly, pulling out a frame heavily laden with honeycomb from which honey dripped. She stared at the hexagonal wax cells of the comb. The design was perfectly symmetrical. After scraping the honeycomb into a bucket he had brought, Chuck picked up a small piece and allowed most of the honey to drip off. He handed it to Lynn, and she turned it over many times, examining it from different angles.

"The engineering is remarkable. Each cell is identical in shape and size," she said.

"I've always found it amazing that a colony of forty thousand bees has a collective knowledge and an inbred ability to build something that complex and exacting," he said.

"Amazing," she said. "How do they know to do that?"

"It's in their DNA," he said. "In scientific experiments, larva hatched and raised in isolation immediately began building the same comb pattern. When we're collecting honey, we pull the frames out and put them into a spinner—a centrifugal machine. The comb on the frame is basically left intact and can be returned to the hive where the bees will immediately begin filling the cells with more honey. When you rob them of the honeycomb, which is also where they lay their larvae, the process is slowed quite a bit because they have to remake the comb. A honeybee will consume more than nine pounds of honey in order to secrete just about one pound of wax, so it makes sense to keep the comb intact whenever possible."

"But you're taking it now," she said.

"We're taking just a small amount," he explained, although Lynn didn't fully understand. "Why don't you add a little more smoke, please?"

She put the spout close to the frames and squeezed. "That's what candles are made from?" she asked.

"Most candles sold today are made from paraffin, which is a sludge by-product of crude oil. But most quality, homemade candles are made with pure beeswax. They burn slower and longer, are soot free and dripless and actually emit a much brighter light from the flame."

For the next hour, Chuck and Lynn worked on the hives, collecting several buckets of honeycomb. Lynn became so proficient that on the last hive, she did everything herself while Chuck stood back and watched.

"You were great," he said as they walked through the orchard on the way back to Montis.

A broad smile spread across her face. "You're a good teacher," she replied.

"The next step: making candles." He thought for a moment. "I need to be at the fair tomorrow, but perhaps you would like to come over to my house the day after and lend me a hand."

This time, Lynn didn't hesitate. "Definitely."

ꟹ

At the Lumby fairgrounds, just as Mark was about to step up on the roof of the Jeep to untie *Viking 2*, Joshua's car pulled in. "Perfect timing," Mark said, as Joshua got out. "How are the guys at St. Cross?"

"Waiting for you to try a new rum sauce they just concocted out of berries that have been thought extinct for five hundred years," Joshua said with some amusement. "I have a jar for you that Brother John sent over."

Mark looked toward the concession stands, hoping to see an ice cream booth in order to sample the rum sauce in the best possible way: poured over a scoop of French vanilla.

"Not now," Joshua said, knowing full well what Mark was thinking. "The competition begins in thirty minutes." He reached into the backseat of his car and pulled out one of *Viking*'s duct-taped legs. "I found this on Farm to Market Road," he said, handing it to Mark.

"Good thing that didn't happen in space," he said seriously. "I wonder what else fell off."

"This," Joshua said, passing him a footpad.

"Not to worry," Mark said. "I brought another ten rolls of tape with me."

"Like we don't have enough already," Joshua quipped. "How are you planning on getting that down from there?"

Mark stepped up on the roof and tried to lift one corner.

"I don't think you should be walking around on the roof like that," Joshua warned.

"Oh, don't worry. These Jeeps are built like tanks."

Mark placed his feet in between the cobweb of appendages and legs jutting out of the *Viking*. Suddenly, they heard a metal crack.

"What was that?" Joshua asked.

Another crack followed.

"I think it's the *Viking*," Mark said.

"Mark, it's made of duct tape. How could it possibly crack?"

Just then, with a screech of bending metal, Mark and the *Viking* dropped down several inches.

"Did the Jeep's roof just cave in?" Mark asked, holding on to the lander's feeble antenna.

Joshua looked inside the car and saw that the roof was indeed dented. "That's affirmative, *Viking*."

"Okay, Pam's going to be really upset this time," Mark said, "so let's get this thing off as quickly as possible. We need to be really careful."

Joshua laughed. "If you dropped this from a ten-story building, I don't think it would look any less ridiculous."

"Try lifting your corner," Mark instructed.

Joshua heaved, but *Viking* didn't budge. "There's no way you and I can do this alone."

Standing as tall as possible on the car roof, Mark looked out across the fairgrounds and spotted Dennis and Jimmy by the announcer's stand. He whistled and waved his arms. "We need to move this," he yelled to Jimmy. "Get one of the tractors."

Twenty minutes later, *Viking 2* had been relocated to the judging area but had sustained serious structural damage during the move and was listing dangerously to one side.

Of the first nine entries, Mark would later say that only one was memorable: a twelve-foot-tall replica of the Statue of Liberty. It would have been a strong contender for first place had Lady Liberty not broken in half at the waist during transport.

"Walker," Sal Gentile, the judge, called out.

"Here!" Mark said, raising his arm.

Sal walked over and spent several minutes examining the *Viking*.

"That's the *Viking 2*. Pretty cool, huh?" Mark asked.

"With all of these spacecraft entries, I'm guessing a lot of you were expecting Eric Sloane to be back judging this year's competition," Sal answered in a neutral tone.

"The thought never crossed my mind," Mark said, glancing over at Joshua.

Pam walked up behind Mark and put her arms around his waist. "Have you won yet?"

Mark's face lit up. "I didn't know you were coming."

"I wouldn't miss it for the world," she said.

Pam and Mark watched Sal walk around the Mars lander, jotting down notes on his clipboard. After peering through one of the lander's windows, Sal made some final notes and flipped the page on his clipboard. "Herbert?" he called out before walking away to judge the next entry.

"Did you bribe him?" Pam asked.

"Sal? Of course not," Mark said. "Why would I have to?"

"It might not have been a bad idea," Joshua said.

"O ye of little faith," Mark quipped.

"Do we have to wait around, or can we go on some rides?" Pam asked.

"Dennis said some of the lines are really long because the equipment keeps breaking," Mark answered, keeping his eye on Sal. "Also, I don't want to miss picking up my first-place trophy. How about we do the rides tomorrow after the log-carving competition?"

Pam turned to Joshua. "I thought you were going to talk him out of that."

Joshua shrugged his shoulders. "He's got his own reasons for participating. Just chalk it up to loyal friendship."

Mark tilted his head. "Why is Mackenzie pouring water into that duct tape toilet?"

"I couldn't guess," Joshua said.

They all watched as their friend Mackenzie "Mac" McGuire untied a bandanna from around Hank's neck and handed it to Tom Candor, who dropped it in the commode and then flushed. Even Mark admitted that it was an amazing demonstration of technical ingenuity. Hank, on the other hand, was appalled that his attire would be used in such a fashion.

Fifteen minutes later, Sal stood in the approximate center of all the entries. "The results of the Chatham County Fair Duct Tape Engineering Competition are as follows," he called out. "In sixth place, Jonathan Tucker and his Hubble telescope. In fifth place, the Great Barrier Reef, submitted by Hank."

Hank, who was standing close to his entry, blinked twice. To win fifth prize was a flagrant affront, and he chastised himself for bribing the judge with only five dollars.

Sal continued. "In fourth place, with his impressive replica of the Last Supper, is Jeremiah Abrams. In third place, the *Viking 2*, submitted by Mark Walker and Joshua Turner. In second place, the skeleton of a *Tyrannosaurus rex*, by Adam Massey and Katie Banks. And this year, the grand prize goes to the team of Terry McGuire,

Mackenzie McGuire and Tom Candor for a very impressive, fully operational commode. You may pick up your trophies at the awards table."

Mark high-fived Joshua. "We did good," he said, before dashing over to claim his ribbon and trophy cup, which to no one's surprise were both made of duct tape.

THIRTY-THREE

# Plans

Early that evening, Vince Shaw and Joan Stokes sat at a back table in The Green Chile, loose papers spread out before them. "So McNear wasn't pleased with my offer?" Shaw asked.

Joan frowned. "That would be the understatement of my professional career." She put down her pen. "If you want this property, you'll need to up the ante. I guarantee that he's not going to give his land away regardless of how impatient he seemed this morning."

"That's disappointing. I was expecting him to jump at a cash deal."

"He was certainly interested in the word. But the amount made him as angry as one of his dogs. He also balked at the four-month closing. He wants to wrap the deal up a lot sooner."

"But we haven't even done a feasibility study," Shaw griped. "Doesn't he know that I'm already taking a hundred-thousand-dollar risk by making him an offer today?"

"That's not his concern," Joan said.

"Well, it is if I pull out of the deal."

Joan began to organize the papers into two piles. "As you said this morning, there will be other developers knocking on his door within the week, and he knows it."

Shaw leaned back and put his hands behind his head. "So it's chess time."

"Chess?"

"We need to look at the board and see each piece—know exactly where we stand."

"That's one of the reasons why we're having dinner with two other men tonight." She glanced at her watch. "They should be arriving any minute." She carefully slipped the papers into a leather-bound folder. "Jimmy Daniels is the town mayor and is a good sounding board for how the community will react to your proposal. Regardless of zoning laws, in a town this small, you'll need the backing of most of the residents. If not, they can put up so many barriers that you'll still be looking at blueprints ten years from now. The sooner everyone gets on board, the better."

Gabrielle Beezer, the restaurant's owner, came up to their table. "Do you want menus, Joan?"

"Please, Gabrielle."

"Any drinks to start with?"

"Water for me," Joan said, and turned to Shaw.

"Nothing," he said dismissively.

After Gabrielle left, Joan continued. "Dennis Beezer will also be joining us. He owns the Chatham Press, The Bindery and the town's bookstore. He publishes the only local paper, which is read by ninety-four percent of our residents. He's very good friends with Jimmy, although they don't always see eye to eye, so he will be another good sounding board. By the way," she added, pointing discreetly at Gabrielle, "Dennis is the owner's husband."

"Got it," Shaw said, just as the bell above the front door chimed.

"Jimmy," Joan said, standing up to greet her guests, "thanks for joining us on such short notice. Gentlemen, this is Vince Shaw. Vince, Jimmy Daniels, the mayor of Lumby, and Dennis Beezer, owner of the Chatham Press."

"Nice to meet both of you," Shaw said, shaking their hands.

"Joan, you never told us what this meeting is about," Jimmy said as he sat down.

"I thought it best that Vince speak for himself," Joan said, "but perhaps we should order first. It's never good to talk business on an empty stomach."

After Gabrielle took their orders, Shaw pulled out two brochures and placed them in front of Dennis and Jimmy. Dennis picked up his copy and immediately began to skim the pages. Jimmy left his on the table.

Shaw began, "As you're aware, Joan recently listed a large parcel of land just west of town."

"Mike McNear's farm," Joan added.

"Through mutual friends in New York, I heard about it yesterday and flew in this morning to look at it myself."

Jimmy chuckled. "I didn't know there was such urgency to buy a bunch of dirty old cows."

"I assure you, it's not the cows I'm interested in," Shaw said. "I—"

"You're *the* Vince Shaw?" Dennis asked as he looked up from the front page of the pamphlet that included a large photograph of him. "Bradley, Wyoming, was *your* project?"

Shaw inhaled and said proudly, "It was."

Dennis shook his head. "Not here."

Shaw was expecting the man's reproach and would replay his standard response. "If you would give me two minutes to explain."

Dennis shot him a cold glance. "It's not going to happen in Lumby."

Jimmy's gaze moved from Shaw to Dennis and then back to Shaw. "What are you two talking about?"

Dennis continued to stare at Shaw. "Fine. You have your two minutes."

Addressing Jimmy, Shaw began to replay a script that he had told at least a hundred times in his career. "I'm offering an extraordinary opportunity for this town. You have all of the natural resources to make it one of the most sought-after vacation destinations in the country."

"How?" Jimmy asked.

"By offering Joe Public an escape to paradise at any time of year," Shaw answered.

Jimmy hadn't yet connected the dots. "To Woodrow Lake?"

Dennis jumped in. "Jimmy, he wants to build a hotel on McNear's mountain."

"Actually, more than a hotel," Shaw quickly corrected him. "I think the property could accommodate a full resort that would include chalets, vacation homes, and townhomes along with a proportionally sized lodge."

Jimmy's face glazed over with shock.

"How do you define 'proportionately sized'?" Dennis asked.

Shaw leaned back and crossed his legs. "At least four hundred rooms."

"That's insane," Dennis said. "That's more than the village population."

"We have repeatedly shown that the size of the host is irrelevant," Shaw said drily.

"You make it sound like this is a tick on a dog," Dennis said.

Shaw ignored the comment and pressed on. "Any additional town services that would be needed, from restaurants to medical care, would be built at the same time."

Dennis looked at Joan. "You're not going along with this scheme, are you?"

"This is a real estate transaction, Dennis," she reminded him. "It's not my role to tell Mike McNear who to sell his land to or to tell the buyer how to use it."

Jimmy sat in his chair, speechless.

"I think we should back up and take this more slowly," Shaw said, and then paused for emotions to calm. "In the last five years, my company has launched three major developments, the last being, as you said, Bradley, Wyoming. It was a podunk, run-down town four years ago."

As Shaw continued to speak, Joan was sure that the words he used were, verbatim, those he had used in her office. How many times has he repeated them? she wondered. And to whom?

"Your drinks," Gabrielle said, placing a pitcher of margaritas on the table along with three plates of assorted appetizers. She could feel the tension between her husband and Joan's guest. "Your dinner will be out shortly." Gabrielle walked away from the table knowing that something was very wrong.

Shaw leaned forward and lowered his voice as he spoke to Dennis. "Joan told me who could help make this project happen, and I would request that you consider this project objectively and from the standpoint of the town."

Jimmy finally spoke. "That is always our perspective."

Shaw nodded. "Then you must agree that an influx of resources and a tremendous amount of money would benefit the residents here."

"They could cost us more in other ways," Dennis interjected. "Such a project would change the unique character of our town and perhaps destroy our true quality of life."

"Says who? You?" Shaw asked. "Are you so sure that the owner of Dickenson's Grocery Store would say the same? Just driving by the building, anyone can see he needs a new roof. Or even your wife, who could have more customers in four days than she does now in a month? And your own business—would you not benefit from a newspaper circulation rate that's ten or twenty times more than it is now?"

Joan glanced over at Shaw. He was a clever businessman for making it personal, making it real to someone who was arguing against his plan.

"There will be strong opposition," Dennis warned.

"But less so if the project has both of your endorsements," Shaw said. "People will follow your lead."

Jimmy laughed. "You so underestimate the residents of Lumby. They never follow my lead. They're more likely to do what Hank tells them to do."

Shaw turned to Joan. "Who's Hank?"

"I'll explain later," she said.

"People care about what they are told to care about," Shaw said. "Dennis, you should know that better than anyone. You and your employees make the news; the news doesn't make the paper." He paused and collected his thoughts before continuing. "They want what you tell them to want. Without thinking, they'll follow whoever is in front. And that would be the two of you. Either you step forward and seize the opportunity that's being given to the town or—" Shaw stopped before making a threat. "I think it would be irresponsible of each of you to blow this chance for the residents of Lumby."

"It's not our decision," Jimmy said.

"I think it is," Shaw said. "I would guess that both of you have more influence in this town than you're aware of. All I'm asking is that you use that influence objectively and for the good of the populace."

Quite the talker, Joan thought. When your back is to the wall, play on their egos.

THIRTY-FOUR

# *Tequila*

The high-pitched jingle of the front doorbell rang out in the small restaurant as Pam walked into The Green Chile, followed by Mark and several of his relatives.

"The Walker clan, I presume," Gabrielle said, putting her arms around Pam and Mark. "I have a table ready for eleven right over here."

"This is perfect," Mark said, sitting with his back to the window so the others could look out on Main Street. Within the next few minutes, the remaining members of their family had joined the party.

"Gabrielle, I don't know if you've met everyone," Pam said, and proceeded to go around the table making introductions.

"It's been ages since we've had Mexican food," Kay said. "The last time was in the spring when Robert and I went to Tijuana for a long weekend—a delightful trip but someone kept on trying to sell us illegal peyote mushrooms."

Robert laughed at the memory. "That was funny." He turned to Pam. "Your mother tried to negotiate with the dealer just to see how low he would go."

"Way to go, Grams!" Jessica said from the opposite end of the table.

"Mother!" Pam said.

"Like mother, like daughter," Mark said. "If Pam was there, she would have asked what the profit margin was for one ounce and then would want to see his business plan so she could reduce his operating expenses."

Pam lovingly tapped her hand on Mark's cheek. "You're exaggerating. I would never ask for a full business plan, just a profit-and-loss statement."

Everyone at the table laughed.

Mark kissed her. "Is she a keeper or what?"

"How many for margaritas?" Gabrielle asked as she started to fill the glasses. When she got to Jessica, she skipped over her glass.

"You can fill mine up," Jessica told her.

Gabrielle studied the girl's face. "My guess is you're underage."

"Mom," the teenager whined across the table.

"No, Jess. You know how we feel about teenage drinking," Patrick answered.

"But Mom, this is a special celebration," she argued. "Just half a glass."

"After all, Patrick, it's a party." And then Elaine did what Elaine had become accustomed to doing over the last year: she caved to her daughter's wishes to avoid a scene. "I'm her mother," she said to Gabrielle. "Just pour her a small amount, please."

Gabrielle continued filling the glasses in front of the adults. "I'm sorry. You might approve, but unfortunately, I could lose my license. Is there something else you would like instead?"

"Yeah, a margarita," Jessica said obstinately.

Pam quickly intervened. "Elaine, have Jessica choose something else. Gabrielle's a good friend of ours, and I don't want her feeling pressured."

"But she's our daughter," Elaine said.

"Which doesn't override state law," Carter chimed in. "Just get her a Coke and while you're at it, bring a bottle of your best tequila and plenty of shot glasses."

"I'll take a Coke as well, please," Corey said to Gabrielle.

Knowing that she had lost the battle, Jessica slouched down and began texting messages on her BlackBerry. "Do you do that all the time?" Corey whispered.

"Texting? Yeah, when there's nothing better to do," she answered.

"What are you typing?"

"You wouldn't understand," she said, handing him the device. He looked at the screen and saw nothing but unintelligible words.

"What's 'sih' mean?"

"Still in hell," she said glibly.

Corey continued reading from the small screen. "What are all these numbers?"

Jessica glanced over. "404 means I don't know. 420 is let's get high . . . you know, weed."

Corey looked shocked. "Really?"

"You are such a geek. Oh, you'll like this one: lh6 means let's have sex," she said provocatively.

"Your entire conversation is in abbreviations?"

"JA," she said, but then saw Corey frown. "Just about."

"What is cuthurnte?"

"See you Thursday night," she answered.

Corey frowned. "Who did you send that to?"

"Marley3823 in Wheatley."

"You know someone in Wheatley?" he asked.

"I will Thursday night. I've been invited to a blowout party down there," she said in a whisper. "And we so need to talk about that." She took back her PDA and started feverishly hitting the keys.

Before she could explain the next set of abbreviations to Corey, her mother said, "Jessica, why don't you put that away during dinner?"

Jessica just rolled her eyes and continued texting.

Pam was amazed at how the teenager ignored her mother. “Doesn’t that bother you?” she asked Elaine.

Elaine was unsure what Pam meant. “What? That Jessica is always on her BlackBerry?”

“No. Jessica disregarding what you just asked her to do,” Pam said.

Elaine considered her daughter’s behavior for just a moment. “She needs to make her own decisions. The last thing we want to be are helicopter parents.”

“Helicopter parents?” Pam asked.

“You know, parents who constantly hover over their child. The results are just tragic,” Elaine said, shaking her head.

Pam frowned as she watched Jessica separate from the rest of the party as she became more engrossed in her texting. “Who’s on the other end?” Pam asked.

Elaine blinked. “I’m sorry?”

“Who is Jessica conversing with?”

The question threw Elaine totally off balance because she had never thought about it before. “I’m sure it’s one of her girlfriends back home,” she said, before turning to talk with Patrick.

When Gabrielle returned with a bottle of Corazon Reposado tequila, wedges of lemon and salt, Robert filled the shot glasses and offered one to Kay. She sprinkled salt on the back of her hand, licked it, downed the shot and then bit into the lemon.

“You go, Grams!” Jessica called out.

“Just like Mexico!” Kay said, placing the empty glass on the table. “Very smooth. Another, please.”

“My pleasure,” Robert said.

“It’s very good tequila,” Kay said to Gabrielle, who was placing baskets of tortilla chips around the table. “We need to buy some of this and take it home with us.”

“Mom, I don’t think you need to buy anything,” Pam said.

“Darling, try some—it’s very smooth,” Kay replied.

By the time dinner was brought out, the bottle was half empty, having been sampled by everyone except Jessica and Corey.

"So much delicious-looking food," Nancy commented as Gabrielle served one plate after another.

"Gabrielle is an amazing chef," Pam said, winking at her friend. "Her husband is sitting right over there."

Carter turned to look and, for the first time, noticed who else was there. "That's Vince Shaw," he whispered just loud enough for everyone at the table to hear.

"Who's that?" Patrick asked.

"One of the largest real estate magnates in the country," Carter answered, using a hushed voice that was very uncharacteristic of him. "He chums around with Donald Trump ever since they built a hotel together out in Las Vegas ten years ago."

"Do you know him?" Patrick asked.

"He's called into the show a few times," Carter boasted. "We always red-line him."

Pam interrupted. "What does that mean?"

"The call immediately goes to the front of the queue so he only has to wait a few seconds until he's put on the air," Carter explained. He glanced over at the other table again. "This is such an odd place to see Vince Shaw. I wonder what's up."

"Must something always be up?" Pam asked.

"For a guy like Shaw to be in a town like Lumby, I guarantee something is going on," Carter replied.

Just then, everyone at Joan's table got up to leave.

"Don't make a scene," Nancy whispered, pulling on her husband's sleeve. "This is Pam's party. Now's not the time to introduce yourself."

"He'll recognize me anyway," Carter said.

Passing by the Walker table, Shaw looked directly at Carter but gave no indication that he recognized the radio host. After staring at him for several moments, Shaw looked away and continued talking to Dennis as they walked out.

"Thank you," Nancy said to her husband.

"Whatever," Carter replied, feeling slighted by Vince Shaw.

When Gabrielle returned to clear the plates, Pam pulled her to the side. "What was Joan doing here?" she asked.

Gabrielle looked out the window and saw that her husband was still talking to the stranger. "It seems someone's in town looking to turn Mike McNear's farm into a ski resort."

Carter looked up. "Four words: I told you so."

"Pfft. It's never going to happen," Mark said. "Not in Lumby."

"There are a lot of folks who are really worried it might," Gabrielle explained. "Word about McNear's property has just spread through town like a wildfire. Several folks who live on that side of town are planning to rally tomorrow morning in front of Dickenson's to drum up signatures to force the town council to act before it's too late."

"But they never do anything," Pam said.

"And that's exactly why we all might be selling lift tickets and sitting in mile-long traffic jams in three years," Gabrielle lamented.

# THIRTY-FIVE
# *Eruption*

**Tuesday**

*"Good morning, America! Welcome back to* The Carter Reed Show *and the July seventeenth edition of Lumby on the Air, where we impartially pit ideology against ideology, idiocy against idiocy. Today is our second day of broadcasting from the magnificent Montis Inn, which I'll tell you about later in the program. But first, let's get to the Sheriff's Report in the local paper and see what type of violent crimes besiege the streets of Lumby.*

The Lumby Lines

# Sheriff's Complaints

BY SHERIFF SIMON DIXON July 17

**6:12 a.m.** Moose vs. Harley Davidson at MM15 west of Priests Pass. Antler broken and motorcycle mangled, so let's call it a tie.

**6:22 a.m.** Carnival vendor called from cell phone requesting assistance in extricating himself from Dumbo's nose on Cart #4 on coaster ride.

**6:34 a.m.** Caller reported wallet snatched by eagle while eating at the picnic table behind Moby Dick's Fish Fry.

**7:01 a.m.** Resident living at 108 Mineral Street reported that his stolen hose has been returned but it's six inches shorter than what it was.

**7:03 a.m.** Nadine Ralston reported that all of her husband's socks were removed from the laundry lines sometime during the night. Although they have a dryer, Burton prefers air drying.

**7:13 a.m.** Parks Department requested immediate assistance for trapped employee who had been attempting to attach commode to new Porta Potty shell. Arm lodged in drain hole. LFD dispatched.

**7:18 a.m.** Riding lawn mower that was reported stolen last night was found behind deck at Wayside

Tavern. Owner will be requested to move vehicle or proprietor will have it towed.

**7:33 a.m.** Deer vs. Kubota tractor on Farm to Market. No injuries but tractor off the road in ditch.

**8:19 a.m.** Call from Chatham Press that someone placed a live duck in the newspaper vending machine.

**9:46 a.m.** Parks Department reported that water from Goose Creek is flooding behind fairground parking lot. Beavers that had been relocated from Fork River in April have constructed an effective dam that has now blocked water flow. Jimmy D notified.

**3:59 p.m.** Caller reported wallet snatched by eagle while he was eating at Moby Dick's Fish Fry.

**6:06 p.m.** Uncontained barbecue fire reported at 102 Logger Road. Fourth one this summer.

**10:51 p.m.** Domestic dispute reported at 64 South Grant Ave.

**10:56 p.m.** Resident at 64 South Grant Ave. requested assistance in retrieving wedding ring after it was flushed down the toilet.

**11:18 p.m.** Three teenage boys arrested for underage drinking. Currently sobering up in town jail awaiting parents' arrival.

*"Let's run with that. I'm sure all of us can agree that unruly offspring are a burden to our education system as well as our social fiber.*

*But what can we actually do about the irresponsible offspring that are running around unparented and undersupervised? The lines are now open. Line one, Toby from Hamilton, ideo at will."*

*"I think it's wrong that today's younger generation has no concept of responsibility. They feel like they are entitled to anything and everything as long as they don't have to work for it. And most of them are pissing away their lives. I can't find one teenager who will rake the yard for less than fifteen bucks an hour. Can you believe that? Not one of them will rake the leaves or shovel the snow, so Martha and I have to go out there and do it ourselves."*

*"All right, if anyone's looking for a yard job, call Toby. In fact, I'll send my son Corey over. He's a good kid who never does wrong. Next we have Jill in Hudson Falls on line two. Jill, ideo at will."*

*"Thank you, Carter. It's such an honor to be on your show. I've tried calling in about a dozen times, but I've never made it this far. It's just such a privilege to be speaking with you. I'm totally tongue-tied."*

*"Just take a deep breath and tell us what's on your mind."*

*"All right. I want to defend all those parents who are blamed for their kids' wrongdoing. It's not always their fault. I have a twenty-year-old who was brought up in a strict, God-fearing home, and after he dropped out of college, he was arrested for selling some drugs, and now he's living with his girlfriend somewhere in New Mexico. But I know I raised him to be a good boy."*

*"Obviously, you didn't pull in those reins tight enough, Jill. Line three, Dale from Reston. Ideo at will."*

*"Carter Reed, this is Dale. I've listened to you for years and have called in a few times. I've always respected you until today."*

*"What did I do now?"*

*"I wouldn't call you a hypocrite to your face, but you're mighty close to crossing that line. To call yourself an exemplary father and say your son is a good kid is a joke. We've all seen exactly what your son thinks of you."*

*"I don't know what you're talking about, Dale."*

*"Corey's video on YouTube. It shows how out of control he really is."*

*"You have the wrong kid, Dale. Someone who must look like Corey, but my son would never do anything like that."*

*"That's what they all say."*

Kano, who was looking at a computer screen, motioned for Carter to kill the segment.

*"Okay, we're running long, so we're going to take a break. We'll be back in two minutes."*

"You're off the air," Kano said.

Carter ripped off the headphones. "What the hell was that about?" he said, storming over to look at Kano's computer screen.

"I just brought it up, boss. It seems Corey set up a Facebook page and uploaded some kind of video," Kano explained as he clicked the video link.

Suddenly, an image of Corey filled the screen and he began talking about Carter with frequently slurred words. Carter's face turned red with fury. When he couldn't bear to watch any more, he slammed the laptop closed. "COREY! GET DOWN HERE NOW!" he hollered. Not hearing a response from upstairs, he grabbed Worm by the back of his T-shirt and pulled him out of the chair. "Get my son! Drag his ass out of bed if you have to!" he yelled.

"Thirty seconds," Kano said. Carter spun around and shot a crazed look at his technician. "You need to go back on," Kano told his boss.

"Don't you think I know that?" he hissed. "It's my damn show." He looked upstairs. "Where the hell is he? Corey, get down here!" he screamed.

"Twenty seconds."

Carter paced around the table several times before taking his seat.

"Ten seconds."

Just then, Corey walked down the stairs, rubbing sleep from his eyes. "Sit down!" his father yelled. "You are so dead."

"Five, four, three, two, one."

Kano pointed at him. Carter took a deep breath and pulled the microphone close to his face. He had to force calm into his voice.

*"You're back with Carter Reed, live from Lumby. During break, I was reading more of the local paper and I can tell you firsthand that this country living is odder than any of you can imagine. The county fair is in town, and there are singles who are looking for a date. Now, folks, when I say fair, don't think Kansas State Fair. This is where a one-pig livestock show meets the church flea market. And when I say date, consider the word in its loosest definition. Reading directly from* The Lumby Lines.

The Lumby Lines

# Lumby Personals

July 17

---

Man with unresolved foot fetish seeks woman fascinated by nostril hairs. Must wear size five shoes. Box 37.

---

38-24-36: Pounds gained since the holidays, number of chin hairs plucked today, formula number for the hair color I use. If still interested, call 925-0728.

---

On Sunday mornings, do you like to do the *New York Times* crossword puzzle in bed? Don't reply—I'm so not interested. Male 29. Box 56.

---

---

Seeking woman who owns her own sporting goods store with brewery attached. Planned inheritance from a grandmother about to pass a huge plus. Box 49.

---

Indifferent SWF may be interested in meeting man or other, short or tall, rich or poor. Whatever. Box 83.

---

Realtor knowing the real meaning of "location, location, location" seeks man who knows the same. 925-9292.

---

If you're looking for your own Superman, I like to wear tights. Reply to Box nine.

---

SM seeks financially independent better three-quarters. Send photo of house and car. Call Eric 925-9178.

---

Woman who suffers from cataphasia. Woman who suffers from cataphasia. Woman who suffers from cataphasia. Box #44. Box #44.

---

Unabashed nude baton twirler, 76, looking for uninhibited hula hooper any age. Box #33

---

Did you notice the two typos in the newspaper yesterday? Anal-retentive woman with alphabetized spice rack. Box no. 127.

---

Attractive, intelligent, sensitive 60 year old with small ego and large prostate seeks patient woman who has bathroom on first floor. Send floorplan to Box 105.

---

If you look better than my cow and are a floozy by nature, I could be your dream come true. 925-7746.

---

Pharmaceutical rep for Viagra. I'm ready and able. Need I say more? F- 42. Box no 61.

---

Woman not into conversation who wants her own remote control seeks man who reads epic historical novels while sitting on the john. 925-0336.

---

38 SF contortionist who knows how to skin a deer and has a buxom twin sister that's game. Too many inquiries to reply to all, so give it your best shot. Brandy. Box 54, 55 and/or 56.

---

Exhibitionist fascinated with dog poops seeks partner for walks in the park. Reply Box 82.

*"Now let's rejoin reality. For our next segment, I want to go where no one has the guts to go: health care. But first, to set the stage, we're going to replay an eight-minute press conference with the Secretary of Health and Human Services, held in Washington earlier this morning."*

Kano hit three switches simultaneously, and over the speakers came the voice of a CNN reporter who introduced the press conference. "You're off the air," he said.

Carter stared at his son, who was sitting on the sofa across the room. Seeing his father's fury, Corey asked, "Now what?"

"How dare you make a public mockery of me!" Carter yelled.

Corey looked totally bewildered. "I have no idea what you're talking about."

"Your Facebook page," Carter spat out.

Corey thought back to the night he and Jessica had spent together.

"Oh, right. Jessica set up an account and profile for me. I don't remember it exactly, but it was no big deal."

"Why wouldn't you remember?"

"We were having a few beers," he admitted.

"Drinking with a minor is the least of your problems."

"I didn't know I had any problems," Corey said.

"You think a seven-minute video of insults and slander isn't a problem?"

"Who did that?"

Carter got up and stomped over to Kano's laptop. "Get over here," he yelled at his son before telling Kano to play it again.

One click later, Corey was on the screen. "Let me tell you about Carter Reed . . ." his inebriated monologue began.

When Corey heard his own voice, he leaped to his feet and ran over to look at the monitor.

". . . an explosive temper when I screw up, which I seem to do all the time . . ."

Carter grabbed the terminal off the table, ripping the cords out of their sockets, and raised it over his head, about to throw it against the wall.

"Don't!" Kano yelled out. "That's all our programming files."

Carter was shaking with rage, but he controlled himself enough to slam the computer back down on the table instead of hurling it through the window. "How could you do that to me?" he shouted.

"I don't remember it that clearly," Corey yelled back. "You can see for yourself that I was pretty wasted."

"Do you know the harm you've done to my career?"

Corey shook his head in disbelief. "Dad, you're just amazing. You're more concerned about your radio show than what I was actually saying about you."

"I don't give a damn about that."

Corey laughed bitterly. "Obviously."

"If I lose one point in the ratings because of this, you and I are going to butt heads."

"You are just unbelievable," Corey said angrily. "Why anyone listens to you is beyond me."

"How dare you say that," Carter yelled.

"Now you care about what I say?" Corey asked mockingly.

"Get the hell out of here! And delete that video NOW!"

Storming out of the room, Corey literally ran into Pam in the lobby, knocking her with his shoulder. "Sorry, Aunt Pam," he said. "I wouldn't go in there if I were you."

"Are you all right?"

"Much more disappointed in him than he is in me, that's for sure," he said softly.

"If you want to talk later, come by," she offered before he strode out the door.

Pam took Corey's advice and left the coffee and pastries at the registration desk and snuck out without saying a word.

## THIRTY-SIX
# *Secrets*

From the lobby, Pam made a beeline to her bedroom, where she booted up her computer. She had no interest in watching Corey's video, but overhearing Jessica's name come up in Carter's blowout with his son made her warning flags go up.

When the main menu appeared, she clicked to Jessica's blog using the web address Mark had saved in Favorite Places a few nights before. A favorite place—how ironic is that? Pam thought.

As Pam expected, Jessica's last entry had been made early that morning.

> the end of day 4 in lumby land. just kill me now. in total misery at reunion that just won't end. inn is 100 year old monastery--doubt anyone has ever had sex here. relatives are older than dinosaurs and total bore. can u believe--good times playing badminton. cardiac arrest. get me out of here. met marley3823 in chatroom and he's saved me--will be partying in a couple days. g2g.

Fuming, Pam then scrolled back to the preceding entries posted at four twenty-six a.m. and twelve nineteen a.m.

Doesn't this girl ever sleep? she asked herself as she printed off Jessica's posting.

Pam clicked off the computer and sat for a moment, trying to calm her nerves and think through different options. Speaking to Elaine would get her nowhere, and Patrick probably would be the same, although Pam had noticed his growing frustration with the situation. Going to Mark wouldn't work either—he would consider this typical teenage behavior and would want to ignore it.

Pam looked at the clock—six thirty-eight a.m. No time like the present, she thought, grabbing the papers from the printer before heading over to the guest annex. She tapped on Jessica's bedroom door. To Pam's surprise, Jessica immediately replied, "Enter."

When Pam turned the doorknob, she found the door locked. "Jessica?" she said, tapping again.

The door opened. Jessica was already dressed in a pair of jeans that was stylishly cut at the knees and thighs and an off-the-shoulder sweatshirt imprinted with a large DKNY. "Parent control," she said, referring to the locked door.

"Do you have a minute?" Pam asked.

"Sure," she replied, removing her iPod earbuds as she flopped down on the chair in front of her computers.

Pam looked around the room, and was shocked to see that none of the furniture was in its original place. "Wow. You've really changed the room around."

"I could use a couple more extension cords," Jessica said.

"You know, Jessica," Pam said in a calm but firm voice, "I would have appreciated it if you had talked to us before rearranging the furniture."

"It's no big deal. I'll put everything back before I leave."

"You're right, it's not that big a deal," Pam said, sitting down on the edge of the bed, "but there is such a thing as good manners."

Jessica began typing on her keyboard. "I'll put everything back," she repeated in an irritated tone.

Pam looked at her niece in disbelief. "Jessica, we're having a conversation. Please stop typing."

The teenager huffed loudly to show her displeasure, hit a few more keys on her keyboard and then turned to face her aunt. "Yes?"

"I want to talk with you about your blog."

"What about it?"

Pam handed her the printouts. "Jessica, what you wrote is really disparaging to our inn."

"Aunt Pam, it's just crap that no one reads."

"No one reads your blog?"

"No, I mean, I get a ton of hits each day, but no one that you would know comes to my site."

Pam curled her lips. "I wouldn't think so. Regardless of who reads it, why would you write something that is so insulting to us and to your family?"

"Everyone does it," she said.

"That's not a valid answer, and you know it," Pam said.

"Well, like, everyone gets that blogs are just bull."

"Probably your friends do," Pam said. "But don't you understand that anyone can go to your page and read what you've written? If they don't know you, or know us, then it's possible they might believe what they read."

Jessica laughed. "Then they're totally lame, and it's their problem."

"No, it's not," Pam said, struggling not to raise her voice. "It's *our* problem. If someone Googles our inn and pulls up your page, we could lose business."

Jessica shrugged. "No one would take what I write that seriously."

"How do you know that? How can you be so certain?"

"Because, like, *I* don't take myself seriously," she said. "You really need to lighten up, Aunt Pam."

"How can I make you see that what you're doing affects all of us?"

"You sound like my dad."

"Because he's right, Jess," Pam said. "You can't go through life thinking only about yourself."

Jessica rolled her eyes. "It's just for fun. We're just joking around."

"If you won't stop doing this on your own, I need to insist."

Jessica narrowed her eyes. "You can't tell me what to do."

Pam remained calm but firm with their gazes locked. "When you're living in my home, I can."

"But all the cool kids know I'm posting. They even get up in the middle of the night to see what I've written."

"Not anymore. Not about our reunion, not about Montis and not about Lumby," Pam said. "Consider yourself shut down."

"You can't do that. That's censorship," Jessica argued.

"Call it what you want, but I'm not going to let you write so disparagingly about any of us or about something we've work so hard to build."

"Go talk to my mom about it," Jessica lashed out.

"I don't have to," Pam said. "I'm talking to you about it."

"Well, Mom lets me write whatever I want."

"Not here and not now, Jessica. *This is not negotiable.*"

Jessica's expression hardened. "Fine. Is there anything else I can't do?" she asked sarcastically.

"No, but I do wish you would try to enjoy yourself a little more while you're here." Pam's voice softened.

"Coming here wasn't my idea."

"So I gathered. But Jess, there are times when it's not about you, and this is one of those times. This is really for your dad and Mark to spend some time together," she explained. "I'm sorry you don't see that."

"Yeah, whatever," Jessica said as she ran her finger along the edge of the chair.

"Why don't you come to the fair with us today?"

"Sounds like loads of fun," she said acerbically.

Pam nodded and forced a smile. "It is what you make of it."

Jessica swung around in the chair so her back was facing Pam. "I'll just hang out in some of the chat rooms."

Pam frowned. "How many chat rooms?"

"A few. You just hang out and talk to each other."

She grimaced. "But you don't know who they are."

"And they don't know me," Jessica replied. "That's what's cool about it, but it's not as cool as Second Life."

"What's Second Life?" Pam asked.

"It's, like, a virtual world where you create who you are. You pick an avatar of how you want to look, and a digital identity . . . you know, who you are. Like you can be a Japanese sumo wrestler or an artist who lives in New Zealand. I guess some people create a Second Life character that's close to their real lives, but most everyone wants an alternative persona that's not at all like who they are in the real world. You're just faking out everyone else."

"Why would you want to be anything other than who you are?"

"You just don't get it, Aunt Pam. You do it because everyone else is doing it, and because life is boring."

"I'm really sorry you think that, Jess."

"It's not just me," the girl whined. "There are millions of people who live on Second Life being someone they're not."

"I just hope you're careful, especially in those chat rooms. Remember, you never know who is on the other end."

"You don't have to worry about that. Everyone is real cool."

"Including all the predators out there?"

Jessica looked up in exasperation. "That, like, almost never happens. You hear about stuff like that because it's what's in the news. Everyone in the chat rooms I go to is cool."

"I wish you weren't making yourself so vulnerable," Pam lamented.

"That was your generation, Aunt Pam—this is mine."

*"Welcome back to the second hour of* The Carter Reed Show, *live from Lumby. It's Tuesday, July seventeenth. Before taking more calls, I want to spend a few minutes talking about my big day and night in Lumby. And yes, Kano and Worm are here to confirm everything I'm about to say. Yesterday, the three of us drove up Farm to Market Road—obviously the idea of numbering streets never here. We first walked the four—yes ideos, I said four—blocks in town. Their one traffic light on Main Street doesn't even work—it randomly blinks different colors. Whoever saw a traffic light turn blue? I'm sure there would be constant two-car collisions if two cars ever came to the intersection at the same time. So there you have my positive comment about Lumby: no traffic jams.*

*"From there, it's all downhill. There's this microscopic clothing store named Wools—couldn't find a white, long-sleeve shirt if my life depended on it. The bookstore had sold out of the two copies of John Grisham's latest bestseller. So Worm suggested we go to the library across the street.*

*"Now this is a gem: they have self checkout. Really, folks, I'm dead serious. Even though there's a librarian to help you locate a book, which can't be too trying since the library is smaller than a postage stamp, when you take out a book, you just write your name, the date and the title on a pad of paper. And it seems most folks around here only know how to spell their first name because I didn't see a lot of last names on the list. Have any of you ever heard anything so preposterous? I pretty much guarantee that the shelves in Seattle would be empty if they didn't have a copy of your credit card, which is how it should be.*

*"We then went up the road to the county fair, and I think we were transported back to 1940. Let me add, though, that the fair doesn't officially open until today. But twelve rides don't turn into a hundred and twelve overnight. And that was it, ideos: twelve rides. But I'll be objective, as I always am, and wait until after the fair officially opens before I give my commentary tomorrow.*

*"I can certainly tell you about dinner. It seems the only restaurant open past seven o'clock is a place called The Green Chile, where we ate last night. I've got to admit, they served up the best margaritas I have ever had. But other than that? Just get me back to Seattle. The menu was handwritten with only six or seven selections—can you imagine that? And our group took up most of the seats. The one waitress was also the cook. I'm telling you because it's hard to believe—Mayberry, USA.*

*"However, there was something of interest. Vince Shaw—you've all seen him on the cover of* Entrepreneur *magazine—was in town. In fact, he was eating at the same restaurant. What are the odds that a nowhere town like Lumby had both Vince Shaw and* moi *visiting at the same time?*

*"Turns out, Shaw has his eye on a large chunk of land west of town for his next ski resort. If he's still in town, I'm going to track him down today and try to buy a stake in his project. Anything that man touches turns to gold. So hopefully, he'll force the town to claim eminent domain, tear down the stores on Main Street and build what's really needed: a Starbucks next to a Barnes and Noble.*

*"So that leads us to our next topic for you to ideo at will: eminent domain. Just to set the stage, we're defining that—Kano just handed me this definition off of Wikipedia—as 'the inherent power of the government—local, state or national—to seize a citizen's private property, expropriate property, or seize a citizen's rights in property with due monetary compensation but without the owner's consent. The property is taken either for government use or by delegation to third parties who will devote it to public or civic use or, in some cases, economic development.' So what do you think? When can someone just walk in and seize your property? We'll take a news break and then get into it."*

Kano hit the feed switch. "And you're off the air."

"The calls?" Carter asked.

"Lines are flooded, boss. You hit a nerve."

Suddenly, Mark stormed into the room. "HOW DARE YOU SAY THAT!" he screamed.

Carter pushed back against the chair. "Good thing we're off the air, Marko."

"That's right, you're off the air! I can't believe you said that about Lumby!" Mark yelled. "I want you out of here by this afternoon!"

THIRTY-SEVEN

# *Snubbed*

At noon, just as the Presbyterian church bells began to chime, Jimmy D officially opened the Chatham County Fair by firing off the town's 1892 cannon. Although the trajectory of the cannonball went wildly astray during that ceremonial discharge, it would always be remembered that no one got hurt, that Tent 4 was in need of a new canvas anyway, and that the loss of Porta Potty No. 7, which had just been assembled from parts flown in the day before, was unfortunate but had little impact on the overall success of the fair that week.

By one o'clock, the walkways were filled with visitors. Some children were eating cotton candy, and others were watching rabbits that were being displayed for judging. Several owners of harnessed oxen were already in the main stadium in anticipation of a pulling event. Shouts of glee from the carnival rides, announcements over the loudspeakers and the voices of concession stand owners calling out their wares all blended into an amazing symphony.

"There's nothing like the sound of the fair," Brooke said, putting her arm through Joshua's.

"Or the smell," Pam added, inhaling deeply. "It's a combination of barbecue, syrup, popcorn and fresh straw."

Brooke looked down at the black-and-white duckling that Pam safely cupped in her hands. "What are you going to call her?"

"Lilly," Pam said without hesitation, holding the chick up to eye level. "Don't you think she looks like a Lilly?"

Mark pulled on the lead ropes of two unwilling sheep walking behind him. "Come on," he said impatiently.

"You seem a little distracted," Joshua said to him.

"He had a bad morning," Pam explained.

"Worse than bad," Mark said. "I kicked my brother-in-law out."

"Out of where?" Brooke asked.

"Out of Montis," he replied.

Pam looked alarmed. "You didn't tell me that! Did you really?"

Mark groaned. "I told him to go back to Seattle and that I never wanted to see him again."

"That sounds ugly," Brooke said. "What happened?"

"Mark said that Carter slammed both Lumby and Gabrielle's restaurant on the air this morning," Pam explained.

"Pam, you're not that upset because you didn't hear him," Mark said. "If any of our friends were listening to his show, I doubt they'll ever talk to us again."

"It couldn't have been that bad," Joshua said.

"Let's see," Mark said, yanking on the ropes. "In short, he called our town dumpy Lumby, he criticized The Green Chile by name, and he made fun of most of the town merchants but especially ridiculed Wools. He even took jabs at our library."

"So is he gone?" Brooke asked.

"No," Mark admitted. "I screamed at him for five minutes, kicked him out, but then Nancy walked in pulling him by the sleeve. I couldn't tell my own sister to leave as well, so I backed down. Nancy insisted Carter apologize, but he just blew the whole thing off."

Pam held the duckling in one hand and put the other on Mark's arm. "Don't let him ruin your day. Can I take you on the Ferris wheel?"

Mark looked up in the sky and watched the wheel circle lazily overhead.

"They call the ride The Air, and it's supposedly the largest Ferris wheel in the state," she said, hoping to entice him.

"Yeah, maybe," Mark said, a tinge of excitement returning to his voice. "They assigned us stall number four in building two. Since the shearing contest isn't until three o'clock, let's put these guys in their pen so we can look around."

"Lead the way," Joshua said, tapping the backs of the stubborn animals with his knee.

"You brought the shavers, right?" Mark asked.

Joshua nodded. "All four of them."

"Good, you never know when you'll need a backup."

"Or a backup to the backup," Pam teased.

Ten minutes later, Pam and Mark were in a Ferris wheel basket fifty feet in the air, looking across Mill Valley. "Our orchard looks so expansive from up here," Pam said, snuggling closer to her husband.

"Montis looks great, doesn't it?" he said. "Look! You can see both the barns, and there's Peanuts grazing in the lower pasture."

"Who's that standing next to Peanuts?"

Mark squinted. "All I see is short strawberry-blond hair. Is that Jessica?"

Pam studied the distant image. "Boy, that's a surprise. I would never have guessed her to be interested in horses."

Upon seeing their home and hearing the love in his wife's voice, Mark felt his mood brighten. "We are so fortunate," he said.

Pam sighed. "That we are."

Mark turned to look at the basket behind them. "Is this great or what?" he called.

Brooke and Joshua laughed. "Great!" Brooke shouted back to him.

"You guys decide where we should have lunch after the ride is over," Mark said. "I'm starved."

Suddenly, the wheel stopped, making the buckets swing back and forth. Pam grabbed onto the bar. "I hate this part."

"They're just letting some folks off, honey," Mark assured her.

Pam checked on the duckling, asleep in her lap. "Lilly was a nice surprise. Thank you."

Mark tightened his arm around her shoulders. "It's my way of telling you how much I appreciate everything you're doing for my family this week," he said, kissing her.

"You thank me with a duck?" she asked.

"I knew she would mean more to you than a diamond ring."

"That she does," Pam said, stroking the duckling's feathers. "Having our relatives here isn't easy sometimes, is it?"

"I don't think family ever is easy," he said, thinking back to the confrontation he had had that morning.

"Are you going to be okay with Carter for the rest of the week?"

Mark exhaled. "Yeah, for my sister's sake if nothing else." He looked at the growing crowd below them. "Speak of the devil."

Pam looked down and spotted Carter and Nancy in the throng. They were wearing matching bright pink Oxford shirts and navy khakis. "If I ever suggest we dress alike, just shoot me," she said.

The Ferris wheel turned for another few seconds and then stopped again.

"There's Joan Stokes," Mark said, pointing, "and the guy who was with her at dinner."

"Vince Shaw," Pam said. "And they're walking straight toward Carter. Oh, I wish I was a fly on that wall."

Forty feet below, Nancy put her arm around Carter's. "Don't worry about Mark," she said as they passed in front of a concession stand.

"Me? Worry? Don't be ridiculous," Carter said, waving the idea away. "Marko knows what I said wasn't far off target. He's just huffing over nothing."

"Maybe you can temper your comments about Lumby for the next few days, just to keep peace in the family," she suggested.

"I promise you that nine million listeners don't want me to *temper* anything."

"Well, *one* does, and he's very important to me," Nancy said.

Carter glanced over at his wife, surprised that she would continue pressing the issue. "It's a dead horse, Nancy. Let it rest." He looked down at the fairground map that he'd been handed at the entrance gate. "This fair is so small, it's almost unbelievable."

"I think it's quaint."

"Moby Dick's Fish Fry? Be real," he said.

Carter looked out into the crowd. Young boys were riding on their fathers' shoulders, mothers pushed baby carriages festooned with colorful balloons, and teens dragged unwilling cows to and from the 4-H building. American flags waved in the breeze.

"The greatness of our country lies in the work done by the masses who live in the city. That's where the pulse of the nation beats," he said.

"Even if you are right, it's still charming out here," Nancy said as she watched a young girl chase after an escaped chicken.

"It's not real, Nancy. It's an illusion. People don't really live like this."

Suddenly, Carter caught sight of Vince Shaw walking directly toward them. Shaw was between two folks whom Carter recognized but had not been introduced to the evening before: Joan Stokes and Jimmy D.

If Shaw saw or recognized Carter Reed, he showed no indication of it.

"There's Vince Shaw," Carter whispered to his wife. Before Nancy could respond, he called out, "Vince!"

Shaw looked at him but then dropped his gaze and returned to his conversation with Joan. Carter crossed to the other side of the aisle to guarantee that the two men would run into each other. "Vince Shaw," Carter said, walking up to him and extending his hand. Although Carter was significantly shorter and rounder than Shaw, he expanded his chest with self-importance.

Shaw narrowed his eyes and feigned ignorance.

"Carter Reed," Carter said.

"Of course," Shaw said, shaking the man's hand. "I listen to your show on occasion."

The two men stared at each other as if they were competitors in a game kept secret from the others, as inevitably happens when the very rich meet the very rich. "This is Joan Stokes and Jimmy Daniels," Shaw said politely.

Jimmy shook Carter's hand. "Mark told us his family was coming to town this week. It must be a packed house down at Montis Inn."

Carter ignored Jimmy altogether. "You're a long way from New York City," he said to Shaw. "In truth, I'm surprised to see you in this—"

"Town," Nancy said before Carter could use a more derogatory noun.

"Certainly not the word I would have chosen," Carter said, laughing. No one joined in.

Shaw turned to Nancy. "And you are?"

"Oh, right," Carter said. "This is Nancy, my wife.

"A pleasure meeting you," Shaw said. "Are you enjoying the fair?"

Nancy was taken aback by the question. Seldom did anyone solicit her opinion when she was with her husband. She looked around and couldn't help but smile. The sound of laughter filled the air.

"Actually, I am," she replied.

"A gift," Shaw said, placing a thick stack of tickets in her palm and closing her fingers around them. "I hope you enjoy all the rides."

Nancy's face flushed. "Thank you," she said. When she realized he was still holding her hand, she pulled it gently away.

Carter sniffed haughtily. "You're here on business?"

"Just relaxing for a few days," Shaw said, looking down at him.

Carter laughed. "You actually think I'm going to believe you're vacationing in *Lumby*?"

"It's the heart of our country," Shaw said, smiling at Joan.

"No, that would be New York and Chicago and Seattle. Most everywhere *but* Lumby," Carter said lightheartedly.

"As you made clear on your show this morning," Joan chimed in.

Carter raised both palms in self-defense. "Don't kill the messenger."

Shaw furrowed his brows. "It would be best if you curtailed any more negative comments about the town."

Carter grinned like the Cheshire cat. "So you do have something in the works here? Tell me—I might be interested."

"I don't think so," Shaw said.

"My company has handled a number of real estate deals," Carter said defensively.

Shaw turned a cold eye on him. "This is out of your league."

Carter visibly recoiled. No one had ever told him that anything, let alone a two-bit development project, was out of his league.

"Just be sure you lay off Lumby when you're on the air," Shaw added before walking away.

THIRTY-EIGHT

# Thrills

Across the path from the Agricultural Barn and directly next to the antique tractor pull arena, a long line of adults formed at the KF1 racing course. Similar in appearance to a revved up go-kart, the KF1 was the cart used in Formula One races and could obtain speeds of eighty-five miles an hour. However, the carnival owners had adapted the karts to max out at fifty miles an hour, which was fast enough when one was only inches from the road with only a metal frame for support.

"Wow," Mark exhaled in awe as he watched the two karts fly around the far end of the course. "Oh, honey, we've got to do that. Remember how great it was last year?"

Pam raised her hand to block the sun from her eyes. "Yeah, you plowed into the straw barrels at forty-eight miles an hour," she said. "I don't know. Those things are flying. It's pretty dangerous." She looked at the admittance sign: NO ONE UNDER 21—NO EXCEPTIONS! She then noticed that most of the people in line were in their twenties. "I don't know," she repeated.

"I promise I won't run into you or the hay bales this time," Mark said.

She kept her eyes on the two race karts. Although she couldn't see the faces of the drivers underneath their motorcycle-type helmets, the karts were obviously being handled by foolhardy kids who were only a day over the minimum age. Both drivers had their pedals to the floor when they came out of the curve and went into the final straightaway.

Onlookers cheered them on as they sped, nose-to-nose, to the finish line. The karts flew past them before skidding to a stop.

"I don't think so," Pam mumbled.

One driver, a tall man, stepped out of the kart and quickly helped the other, who was much smaller. They removed their helmets.

"Mother!" Pam screeched.

Mark started to laugh and clap his hands. "They were great!"

"Mom, over here!" Pam called to Kay once they'd turned in their helmets.

"Hi, darling," Kay said as Robert held up the guard rope for her to slip under. As she bent over, she moaned. "Are you as sore as I am?" she whispered to Robert.

"A little," he confessed with a wink. "We'll need to buy more Bengay."

Pam saw how stiffly her mother was moving. "Are you all right?" she asked.

"Nothing that a new twenty-year-old body wouldn't cure," Kay replied with a giggle. "It was quite a climb up this morning, but rappelling down was the experience of a lifetime." She patted her hair, straightened her scarf and turned to Robert. "Want to go again? We can make it best two out of three."

He raised his hands in defeat. "I'm exhausted," he said. "Mark, would you like to take her out?"

"In a heartbeat," he said, beaming.

"We need to get back in line," Kay explained. "Pam, come stand in the queue with us."

"Absolutely not," she said. "You could kill yourself out there. Why do you think they have you sign a disclaimer?"

"But it's the most exhilarating feeling," Kay said. "You're missing a tremendous thrill."

Before Pam could argue further, Kay and Mark were off to the end of the line. Kay was pointing to the course, apparently telling Mark about some of the subtleties of each hairpin curve.

Pam shook her head. "I just don't know what to do with her."

Robert placed his hand gently on her shoulder. "Just let her live her life and be happy for her."

The next two riders were strapped in, and within seconds, they were off.

"I owe you an apology," Pam said, finally pulling her gaze off the karts and looking at Robert.

"I'm sure none of this is easy for you," he said kindly.

"You're letting me off the hook."

"I know we've thrown you a lot in a very short time."

Pam grimaced. "You could say that. But you certainly didn't deserve my reaction in the kitchen last night."

"It seemed quite natural and honest to me," Robert said.

Pam crunched up her nose in embarrassment at her behavior. "I just wasn't at all prepared to hear that you wanted to marry my mom."

Robert smiled as he watched Kay standing in line. "Are you now? Because not much has changed in the last twelve hours—I still want to marry her."

Pam followed his stare. Mark had both arms wrapped around Kay and was lovingly rocking her back and forth. "And I'm sure she would want to marry you." She paused for a long moment. "After Dad died, she settled into a quiet life in Connecticut, occasionally coming down to visit us in Virginia. I was always comforted by the idea that she was safe and sound, emotionally and physically, and I thought Mark and I, along with a handful of friends, could watch out for her. So there I am thinking that she's playing bridge with Noreen Buckman, and I come to find out that, instead, she's in Mexico downing tequila shots and buying psychedelic mushrooms." Pam laughed under her breath before continuing with an admission she had shared with Mark only the night before. "I feel as though she's slipped away from me."

"But she hasn't," Robert said.

"I know, but that's how I feel," Pam said. "And my first instinct was to take her back, to want to put her in the life she had before she met you." She watched her mother and Mark laugh together about something. "But now I see how selfish that is and how unfair that would be to Mom." She turned to Robert. "And I don't think I could find a more perfect man for her if I looked the rest of my life. You two seem so right for each other."

"We are," he assured her.

"I think it's a wonderful idea that the two of you get married. You can make an honest woman out of her."

"She can make an honest man out of me," he replied with a grin.

"You most certainly have my blessing," Pam said, standing on her toes to kiss his cheek. "I know you two will be very happy together."

"Thank you," he said.

Pam's eyes twinkled in anticipation. "When are you going to ask her?"

"I'm not sure," he said, and then leaned closer to share a secret. "I had a ring made for her a while ago, but I'm waiting for the right moment."

Pam whispered, "Tell me if you need any help making it the most special day of her life."

"The most special day of Kay's life was the day you were born," he said, squeezing her hand. "I could never beat that."

ঌ

A short way down the path, Chuck Bryson handed out another brochure at the Green Nature Conservancy booth. On the table in front of him were various pamphlets and product samples. In between the piles of literature was a large glass bowl for donations.

"Thank you for your contribution," he said to one customer. "Please give us a call if you need help installing the solar panels."

Unobserved, Lynn stood to one side of a nearby concession stand, watching Chuck greet strangers and answer their questions. His warm smile and openness attracted many people walking by. When there was a lull in the activity, and just as Chuck leaned over to refill his pamphlet pile, Lynn sauntered over carrying two bags of popcorn and two cold beers.

"It looks like you could use a break," she said.

He looked up and smiled from ear to ear. "I'm so glad you came by."

"Popcorn and a beer?" she offered. "It's not gourmet, but I was told it's the best in town."

"If you bought it down by the dairy barn, you're right," Chuck said, pulling up two chairs. "Sit, please. You can help me."

"I didn't know you worked for Green Nature," she said.

"I volunteer whenever possible," he said. He took a sip of beer. "This is perfect, thank you."

An old man wearing a pair of large sunglasses approached the table. Tied to the belt loop of his pants was a rope that led to an even older horse walking behind him.

"Mr. Jeremiah Abrams, I haven't seen you in months. How are you?" Chuck said, carefully enunciating each word.

"Doing well, Chuck," Jeremiah replied. "But Isabella might think differently. She's getting awful arthritis."

Chuck looked at Lynn and winked. "What can I do for you?"

Jeremiah's hand shook as he reached inside his shirt pocket and withdrew a five-dollar bill. "I want to make a contribution to your cause," he said, as he reached out for Chuck to take the money.

"Jeremiah, that's awfully nice of you, but we've collected a lot of money today and our bowl is full. So please put your money away."

Jeremiah felt around the table until he found the donation bowl. He put his fist into it and grinned. "If you consider this full, then you'll be out of business before the end of the day." Jeremiah stuffed the bill into the bowl.

"Thank you," Chuck said, touching his friend on the arm. "How are your eyes doing?"

"Better than Isabella's but mostly gone," he said. "They've seen a lot in all of these years, and I think they've just grown tired of looking."

"Be sure you keep going to Dr. Madison," Chuck reminded him.

"Always do," the old man said with a wave as he walked off ahead of his mare.

"Is he blind?" Lynn asked.

Chuck nodded. "We think he might still be able to see some vague colors and blurred shapes, but that's about it."

"Then how does he get around?"

Chuck watched Jeremiah weave down the walkway. "He's lived here his whole life. He knows every inch of the town and the road to his home, and everyone knows Jeremiah. When he gets into trouble, Isabella helps him out."

Lynn laughed, thinking that Chuck must be pulling her leg. "No, really."

"Really," he said. "It's a unique partnership—they've been dependent on each other for the better part of a quarter century."

"You make the horse sound like more than just a horse," she said.

"Isn't Coco more than just a cat?" he asked. "The relationships we have with animals are no less valuable or significant or enlightening than those we have with people . . . occasionally even more so. Sometimes, our animals seem to be able to heal us more than we can heal each other."

"I think you're the first person I've met who really understands and believes that," she said. "May I make a contribution?"

"You already have," he said, lifting the popcorn and beer he was holding. "But perhaps you will join me for a ride on the Ferris wheel as soon as my shift is over."

Lynn looked up in the sky and saw The Air rotating gently overhead. "I would like that."

THIRTY-NINE

# *Shaved*

Mark pulled on the lead rope attached to the larger of the two sheep. "I weigh more than he does—why isn't he moving?" he asked Joshua, who was standing outside the fairground stall, keeping the second sheep well under control.

"He knows you don't really mean business."

"I mean business—the shearing competition is in twenty minutes. I know I'm not going to win, but I have no intention of looking like a total idiot either," Mark said.

"Maybe he knows *he'll* look totally ridiculous afterward," Pam joked.

"Would that be the sheep or Mark?" Brooke asked.

"I heard that," Mark called from inside the stall.

Brooke petted the sheep that was tethered to her husband. "Why do you need two sheep?" she asked.

"The contest is for the best combined time for two shearings," Joshua explained.

Suddenly, the sheep that Mark was working on went flying out of the stall at a full gallop. Knocking over the water bucket and sideswiping several other contestants, the animal ran down the center aisle with Mark sprinting full out on the other end of his lead line.

"Chops!" Mark yelled out, trying to dig his heels into the sawdust.

Pam looked at Joshua. "Chops?"

He shrugged. "We had to give them names when we registered for the event."

She cringed. "I'd run too if I had that name."

The start of the shearing event was announced over the loudspeaker. "We need to get to the judging tent," Joshua said, leading his sheep out of the barn. "I'm sure Mark and Chops will find their way over in a minute."

"The eternal optimist," Pam said, close on his heels.

When they approached the tent, Brooke noticed it was filled with young teenagers trying their best to halter rambunctious lambs. "Well, if that's Mark's only competition, he might have a shot at a ribbon."

"No, this is junior showmanship. *That's* his competition," Joshua said, pointing to an adjacent tent that was used as the waiting stage for the next event on the program.

Brooke and Pam looked over and started laughing. "You can't be serious," Pam stammered.

Seated on the bleachers were no less than thirty men who all looked like they'd just been plucked from a sheep farm in the Australian outback. Tall and barrel-chested, they wore the sleeves of their white T-shirts rolled up over bulging biceps and triceps. All wore cowboy boots and tight jeans, and some had leather chaps strapped to their legs.

Brooke ogled the shearers. "This is so much better than *The Thorn Birds*."

Pam grabbed her arm. "Wasn't that a great book?"

"That one on the top row looks like one of the brothers from the Cleary farm."

"Very handsome." Pam sighed. A well-built farmer who was the spitting image of Robert Redford walked into the tent. "Let me correct myself: very, *very* handsome," Pam added.

Standing next to a sheep, the man bent at the knees and wrapped his arms around the animal's body. With a loud huff, he lifted the sheep up to his chest and then did four deep squats.

"Must be warming up," Brooke said.

"That ram has got to weigh well over two hundred pounds," Joshua said in awe.

"Mark is so hosed," Pam said.

Just then, a sheep bolted into the tent with Mark clinging to the end of the line. Wearing khaki shorts, a short-sleeve yellow shirt and very white New Balance sneakers, he was a startling contrast to the other contestants. When Mark's animal saw the other sheep standing in a herd, quietly eating hay, it stopped dead in its tracks.

"How we doing so far, Mark?" Joshua asked.

"Fantastic," he said, catching his breath while rubbing his blistered hands.

"Are you sure you want to do this?"

"Yeah, why?" Mark said, looking into the arena. "Wow, those kids are pretty young to be shearing. And I was worried I didn't have a chance in the world of winning a ribbon."

"Did you notice those guys over there?" Joshua pointed to the bleachers.

Mark glanced over and then did a double take. "Man, those are big fellows. What are they doing here?"

Pam patted her husband's back. "They're waiting for your event to start, darling."

"No way," Mark said in disbelief. "Where did *they* come from? They didn't compete last year."

"Word must be getting around about our fair," Joshua said.

Several of the entrants stood up to collect their sheep. "Are those shavers in their pants?" Brooke asked.

"That would be a disappointment," Pam joked.

Mark pretended to sneer at his competition. "Not a problem. I'm much more limber than those guys."

The loudspeaker crackled. "Event 104, Sheep Shearing. Contestants to ring four, please."

"That's me," Mark said. "Joshua, I'll start with Mutton, and then we'll switch when he's shaved. Now, it's got to be smooth when you pass me Chops because I don't want to lose my momentum. Every second will count—I think this competition is going to be really close."

Pam leaned into Brooke. "I so envy his ability to ignore reality when it's staring him in the face."

When all was said and done, and well after the wool had landed, Mark had broken a fair record for sheep shearing; he took eight minutes and thirty-six seconds to shear his first sheep—a time that was easily bettered by the other contestants for shearing both their animals. The record notwithstanding, Mark was then disqualified from the overall competition on two different grounds. The judges determined that at least twenty percent of Mutton's wool remained on his hide (a violation). Plus, Mark never really began shearing Chops; after he shaved one wide strip down the center of the sheep's back, Chops took off for greener pastures and had not been seen since (another violation).

Behind the 4-H building, Chops and Hank hid together in silence, each licking the other's wounds of embarrassment. Still mortified that his Great Barrier Reef duct tape sculpture had lost to a commode—a common *toilet,* of all things—Hank found some solace in sitting next to the stupidest-looking sheep he had ever seen.

# FORTY
# *Confronting*

"A noble effort," Pam said as they walked back to the fairground parking lot to unload the car for that evening's picnic.

"It almost looked like you designed a special kind of haircut for Mutton," Joshua said.

Brooke laughed. "I thought he looked like one of those major highway intersections with ramps and loops going everywhere."

"Now that I know the level of the competition, I'm sure we'll have a good shot at it next year," Mark said. "One of the guys said he'll come over to Montis next week and give me a few pointers, which is mighty nice of him, given that I'm one of the competition and all." He glanced around the fairgrounds. "You think Chops can find his way back to the trailer?"

"He's a homing pigeon when it comes to getting his oats. He'll be back," Joshua assured him.

"What's next?" Brooke asked.

"We're all meeting by the oak tree in front of the stage at six o'clock. Did you guys bring some blankets?" Pam asked.

"We've got three in the car," Brooke said.

"Great. I have five, so there'll be plenty for everyone to sit on.

Mark and Joshua will set up two barbecue grills, and I have all the food in the coolers."

"When do the bands start playing?" Mark asked.

"I think around eight, and then there's supposed to be fireworks afterward."

"I really hope Chops shows up before then," Mark said. "If he's still free when the fireworks go off, he'll head for the mountains."

"Don't worry, someone will spot him," Pam said. "If he doesn't turn up soon, we'll ask Sal to make an announcement about a lost sheep that has a runway shaved down his back."

Twenty minutes later, Pam and Brooke had staked out a large area under an oak tree not far from the stage. Various colored quilts and blankets had been spread out on the grass and folding chairs opened. The food and condiments were unpacked on the picnic tables that Mark and Joshua had moved closer to the tree.

"Perfect spot, honey," Mark said to Pam, pouring charcoal briquettes into the grill pans. "How many are we cooking for?"

"Plan for about twenty: all of us, and then I asked Mackenzie and Tom to drop by as well as Gabrielle and Dennis. And we'll probably see Jimmy and Hannah at some point."

Mark looked at the large mound of charcoal already in the grill and thought more was needed, so he emptied the entire bag into the basin. He did the same with another bag in the other grill and then squirted a conservative amount of lighter fluid on each mound. Mark put a match to the briquettes, and they instantly ignited into a low flare.

From the bag of supplies that Pam had brought, Mark withdrew an immense spatula and a pair of barbecue tongs, then held them up in the air. "You guys want to see something?" he asked, clanging the stainless steel tips together to get their attention.

Joshua, who was lying on the blanket next to his wife, took his gaze off the Ferris wheel. "No," he said, glancing over at Mark.

"Really, guys, this is so cool. I've been practicing for weeks."

Pam and Brooke, lying side by side, leaned up and rested on their elbows.

"Go for it, honey," Pam said as all eyes turned to Mark.

Within a flash, Mark began twirling the utensils above his head as if he were a Ginsu chef. The steel caught the rays of the late afternoon sun in a dazzling display of culinary juggling. He tossed the tongs in the air and then caught them while still spinning the spatula. And then he flung the spatula high in the air and caught that.

Everyone clapped.

"Now watch this—I'm going to catch this spatula with the tongs," he said as he pitched the spatula straight up over his head. Unfortunately, in Mark's zeal, the utensil went much higher than he had planned. Ten feet above him, it looked more like a stiletto than a harmless spatula when it began its descent. "Watch out!" he called out.

As the spatula fell, Mark wildly snapped the tongs closed several times, trying to snatch the spatula out of midair, but he missed completely. The utensil landed in the middle of the burning coals, which immediately singed the wooden handle. Mark took the tongs and flung the spatula out of the grill and onto the corner of Pam's quilt, where it smoldered for several seconds before Mark threw a cup of water on it.

"That was great, Uncle Mark," Corey said, picking up the still smoldering spatula and examining the charred handle.

Mark kicked at the burn mark on the blanket. "Thank you," he said, looking over at his wife and friends, who were no longer watching. "It seems my crew has lost some interest. How would you like to be my copilot?"

"I was hoping you would ask. What can I do?" Corey asked.

"You can be the bartender. You need to put the white wine on ice and uncork the red. As soon as the coals are white, we'll throw on the chicken and pork."

Corey immediately got to work.

"You're a great help, Corey," Mark said. "Your father must be delighted to have you around."

Corey laughed, thinking back on their clash that morning. "I wouldn't necessarily say that."

Mark looked at the young man as he retrieved the corkscrew from the bag. “Are you and your dad okay?”

Corey was never one to dodge a bullet, but he didn’t look up at his uncle when he answered. “Not at present, but I’m sure that will change in time.”

“Everything does,” Mark concurred.

Corey and Mark were the first two people Elaine spotted when she and Patrick walked from behind the riding arena. Then, she saw Pam and two others lying on a quilt, but no one else.

“I thought Jessica was with Corey,” she said to her husband.

“She is,” Patrick replied.

“No, she’s not,” Elaine said, shaking her head. “Corey’s over there helping Mark.” When they reached an intersection of pathways, they stood to one side and scanned the crowd. “She said she would stay with Corey,” Elaine said.

“Since when has anything that Jessica said really meant something?” Patrick asked, visibly irritated.

Elaine looked at him. “It sounds like you’re angry with *me*.”

“I’m angry with her, but yes, I’m frustrated with us and how we coddle her.”

She winced. “I don’t *coddle* Jessica.”

“Elaine, *we* absolutely do.”

“This isn’t the time to talk about it,” she said, beginning to walk away.

Patrick grabbed her arm. “When is it, Elaine? Every time I try to talk with you, you shut down.”

Hearing his voice rise, Elaine pulled Patrick further off the path, away from the pedestrians.

“Not here,” she whispered. “Not in public.”

“I don’t care what these strangers think of me,” he said.

“Well, I do,” she said, turning her face away from the crowd.

“Elaine, whether you want to admit it or not, Jessica is acting like a spoiled brat, just begging for attention from these new friends of hers, and she doesn’t want anything to do with either of us. We haven't seen her for more than a couple hours on this trip. And when she *is* around, she's totally preoccupied with texting on her BlackBerry."

"So it's my fault I bought it for her?"

"No," he said. "It is *our* fault for not setting clear boundaries, for not saying enough is enough. Come on, Elaine," he said with exasperation, "who lets their sixteen-year-old daughter stay up until four in the morning?" Elaine dropped her head and looked down at the ground. "We're doing her such a disservice. We're not teaching her the lessons she needs to learn to become a responsible adult, to make decisions on her own and to feel good about who she is."

"If you push those lessons on her too hard, she'll—"

"What? Fight back? Run away?" Patrick asked. "We can deal with that. I have faith that, deep inside, our daughter is still there. She's just so lost in worrying about everyone else's perception of her that she's forgotten what really matters."

Elaine's face had turned ashen. "She's fine."

Patrick grabbed Elaine by the arm. "*Look at her,*" he said forcefully. "She's not fine. Do you really think she's happy? Do you think that allowing her to continue down this road is somehow fairer than taking a risk and disciplining her?"

Elaine wanted to run away and hide. She and Patrick had reached this same breaking point several times before, and she had always been able to convince her husband to give Jessica free rein . . . until now. Perhaps it was the urgency in his tone that led to Elaine's resignation.

She finally spoke so softly it was as if the words barely passed her lips. "What do you want to do?"

He sighed and put his arms around her. "Let's get her back on track."

"How?"

"We both know what needs to be done. We just need to agree to do it together, to be one voice," he said, holding her tightly. "We'll start with the basics. All computers except for her laptop need to go, and that she can only use for a few hours each day."

"What will she do with her time?"

"I'm sure she'll ask us the same thing. Hopefully, she'll read, spend time with us, even learn something new," he said. "And we need to take away her BlackBerry until we see some progress—until she starts to make good decisions on her own."

"All right," Elaine said, resting her head on his chest. "So I suppose the first thing to do is find our daughter."

"Then have a long talk with her and try to enjoy the rest of the evening," he said, taking her hand.

FORTY-ONE

# BlackBerry

After scouring the fair in an unsuccessful search for Jessica, Patrick and Elaine finally made their way over to the Walkers' picnic area. Pam and Mark were tending to the grills while others sat around enjoying cheese and wine.

"We thought we lost you two," Mark said to his brother.

"We've been looking for Jessica all this time," Patrick admitted.

"I thought she said she wasn't planning to come to the fair today," Pam commented.

"She must have changed her mind, because she's over there hanging out with a drummer," Mark said, as he pointed a spatula towards the makeshift stage where the bands would be playing later that evening.

They all looked toward the platform. On the side steps of the stage, Jessica sat next to a teenager who was using his drumstick to beat out a rhythm on her thigh. When he was done, he draped an arm loosely around her bare shoulder. He pulled out a pack of cigarettes and offered her one.

"Excuse me," Patrick said to the others. "I'll be right back."

Pam saw Elaine flinch as he stormed away. "Jessica is quite something," Pam said, opening the door for a conversation.

Elaine couldn't stop staring at her daughter. Sometimes, when Jessica turned a certain way, Elaine didn't even recognize her. "You can say that."

"I wanted to let you know that I talked with her earlier today about what she was writing on her blog." Pam spoke softly so that only her sister-in-law would hear.

Elaine looked confused. "I don't understand."

"She put some pretty derogatory comments up on the Internet about our town and our inn. In fact, she was less than flattering about all of us," Pam explained.

"Where did you see this?" Elaine asked.

Pam used the tongs to turn over a piece of chicken. "On her MySpace page."

"But she told us that was private."

"Nope," Pam quickly corrected her. "By choice, she made it very public and available to be read by anyone and everyone. We just can't afford to be slammed that way."

Elaine's face flushed with embarrassment. "I don't know what to say."

Pam shrugged. "Just please tell her to stop it."

Elaine's jaw quivered. "We'll talk to her," she said. "I could really use a drink."

"Corey?" Pam called out. "You have a customer."

Corey had been watching Anaïs play Frisbee with her father. He waved. "Aunt Elaine, what can I get you?"

"Something stronger than wine?"

"I'm afraid not," he said. "But you have your choice of white or red."

"White, please." Watching Corey pour her drink, she said to him, "I thought you and Jessica were going to spend the afternoon together."

"I certainly tried," he said. "I offered to go anywhere she chose, but it was pretty obvious that she wanted to ditch me as quickly as possible."

Elaine sighed with disappointment. "I hope she was at least polite about it."

Corey laughed out loud. "Jessica is a lot of things, but I'm afraid polite isn't one of them. She took off when I was looking through the Agriculture Barn."

Elaine lifted the glass she had just been handed. "Well, thank you for trying." She looked toward the stage and was surprised to see that Patrick was alone with Jessica, who was still slouched on the top riser. He was leaning over her and had a hand on her shoulder, perhaps to ensure she didn't bolt. Elaine could tell from both of their expressions that they were having a low-volume fight.

Suddenly, Jessica threw her BlackBerry into her father's chest. Unfortunately, he wasn't quick enough to catch it before it smashed on the ground.

"Dad!" she yelled out.

Everyone looked over in her direction as he picked up the device.

"A technical malfunction," Patrick called out with a wave of the hand. He took Jessica's arm and escorted her over to the party.

Elaine guzzled her wine and gave the empty glass to Corey. "Fill her up, please," she said.

Jessica pulled away from her father. "Did you see that?" she asked, running up to her mother. "Dad broke my BlackBerry. And do you know what he just told me?"

A lump formed in Elaine's throat, making it impossible to answer.

"Do you?" Jessica spit out.

Elaine swallowed hard. "Yes," she said, straining to speak. "Your father and I agree that there need to be a few changes."

"Like no computers?" Jessica asked dramatically.

Elaine looked at Patrick to say something, which he did. "I told you that you can use your laptop a few hours each day."

"But what good is it if I can't post when I need to? And who ever heard of anyone going to bed at eleven?"

"I used to when I was your age," Corey chimed in.

Elaine and Patrick looked up and realized that everyone at the Walker party had been watching their family drama play out. Their daughter's recalcitrant behavior and blatant disrespect had been seen by all—their dirty laundry was no longer hidden in the closet. Elaine could have died of embarrassment, so she did what felt comfortable; she took another glass of wine from Corey and guzzled it.

"Let's go over to the table and sit down," Patrick said, putting a hand on his daughter's back and leading her to a more private area.

Since Jessica no longer had a functional BlackBerry, her parents had her undivided attention. There, the three of them sat off to the side and talked until dinner was served. By the time they rejoined the party, Jessica was acting far more respectful to the adults around her.

After everyone had filled their plates and settled down for a nice meal, Pam looked around and smiled. This was one of the moments that she would cherish. Kay and Robert were talking with Mark, Gabrielle and Dennis about their plans to go white-water rafting the following day. Corey was trying his best to chat with Anaïs, and Jimmy D was talking to André about his tavern's menu. Brooke and Joshua, seated on a large quilt, were laughing with Chuck and Lynn.

Pam inhaled the clean night air and the sense of family. In fact, she was in such good spirits that, after serving herself, she sat down next to Carter. "You seem awfully quiet tonight," she commented.

"A long day, that's all," he said.

Nancy leaned forward as if to share a secret. "He had a run-in with Vince Shaw today."

A similar conversation was going on at the table next to theirs.

"The man was the most arrogant, obnoxious, self-serving person I've ever seen," Jimmy D said.

"See," Carter said, assuming Jimmy was talking about Shaw. "That's exactly what I thought of him as well."

Jimmy continued. "Shaw didn't know what to make of him."

Suddenly, Carter realized that Jimmy wasn't talking about Vince Shaw. Jimmy was talking about him—Carter Reed!

"Wait one minute," Carter said loudly to Jimmy D. "I was a nice guy today. Shaw pretended not to know me. Me, of all people! I've been on the cover of *Time* magazine . . . *twice*. He was conceited, pompous and presumptuous, and his need for power was leaking out of every pore."

Suddenly, everyone broke into laughter, seeing the obvious parallels between the two men.

"Laughing at my expense, I assume?" Carter said, angrily dropping his chicken leg on his plate. "You folks just don't get it, do you? It's people like me and Vince Shaw who control your little world of Lumby. We could make it and break it with just one signature. We're the ones who decide where you vacation, what you buy and who you listen to."

Everyone sat in stunned silence.

"Little people, little minds," he said, throwing his napkin on the table. "I'm going back to the inn. Unlike the rest of you, I have to be at work at five tomorrow morning. Nancy, we're leaving." He took a final gulp of wine from his paper cup and crushed it in his hand before throwing it into the trash can. "Pick up my plate," he told his wife before walking away.

Nancy was clearly embarrassed by her husband's abrupt departure and quickly cleared his mess from the table. "We'll see you tomorrow," she said weakly before chasing after him.

"You don't have to leave," Pam called out, but they were already too far away to hear her. She looked at her watch—peace and calm had lasted exactly three minutes.

Just then, the floodlights turned on and the stage was lit. All those who were scattered across the picnic grounds, as well as many who were still at the fair, hurried to the front of the stage to get the best seats for the show.

Caroline Ross-Talin, who had been standing offstage with her husband, Kai, stepped into the spotlight. As the granddaughter of Charlotte Ross, one of the deceased town matriarchs, she had taken over the helm of the Ross Foundation several years before, and under her skillful leadership, more frequent cultural events of high quality were being offered to the small town

She held up the microphone. "I would like to welcome all of you to the first annual Concert at the Fair, sponsored by the Ross Foundation."

Scattered applause broke out across the crowd.

"We have selected a wide variety of sounds—from baroque to jazz to rock and even an a cappella quartet—from the talented musicians who play and study at the Lumby Arts and Music Center, which we opened just last year in the restored roundhouse."

Louder applause and whistles came from the audience.

Pam moved closer to Mark. "I'm sorry Carter didn't stick around to see our definition of a cultural event in our little corner of the world."

Caroline continued. "Our first band tonight is Nebula, and they will be followed by Wafer Thin and C-Sharp."

The broader lights dimmed as stronger spotlights shone on the musicians. As always, Caroline was true to her word; the evening was filled with an eclectic but cleverly organized program of music, with each unique style complementing the next.

Unknown to Pam and Mark, Carter and Nancy were, in fact, still at the fair, hiding deep in the crowds far behind where the family picnic was being held. Although Carter was too embarrassed to stay at the picnic, he would never miss out on an opportunity to gather fodder for his show.

"What a waste," Carter complained. "This concert is just as boring as the ones we go to in Seattle."

Back at the picnic table, Corey took a seat next to Jessica. "Kind of rough with your folks, huh?"

"That's a huge understatement. And now I'm out one BlackBerry," she complained.

"How about some dessert?" he asked, offering her a slice of cheesecake.

"Great. Just what I need—more food," she said sarcastically. "Like Missy and the others don't already razz me for being the fattest and tallest girl in our group."

"They don't really do that, do they?"

"Well, *yes*," she said, drawing out the word so it sounded like the answer should be obvious.

Corey pushed the whipped cream off his dessert. "Then I'm confused. Why exactly are they your friends?"

"Because, Corey, they're *cool*," she said, looking down her nose. "You just don't get it because you're a geek."

Corey leaned in toward his cousin. "You can cut the I'm-better-than-you-are act, Jess," he said in a low voice. "I've known you since you were playing in the sandbox, and you've always been your own person. Since when did you become a little pawn in a high school clique?"

She swallowed hard and bit back tears. "You don't know what you're talking about," she said.

Corey shook his head. "I know exactly what it feels like to be taunted by classmates. You just need to rise above it. Just let them say what they want."

"But I'm not teased if I'm one of the cool kids, get it? No one's going to humiliate me again." She spoke vehemently though she kept her voice to a whisper.

"What do they tease you about?"

"Everything," she said angrily. "My height, my weight, my clothes, my hair, who I party with, my grades—"

"But you're straight A's."

"Not anymore, I can promise you that," she said. "And now, I can crap on all the other kids."

"And how does that make you feel?"

Although her lips trembled, she lifted her chin, refusing to let any hint of uncertainty or weakness show through her icy demeanor. "Just fine," she answered.

## FORTY-TWO
# *Cemetery*

**Wednesday**

*"Good morning, America! Welcome back to* The Carter Reed Show, *the only on-air forum that impartially pits ideology against ideology, idiocy against idiocy. Today is July eighteenth, and we continue our live broadcast of Lumby on the Air. Before we go to the phones, I need to spend a few minutes updating all listening ideos as to the latest events that have been unfolding in our favorite little town. First, the news from Main Street as presented by the Pulitzer-winning journalists of* The Lumby Lines. *Hold on to you seats—Kano just corrected me—that should have been the Putzer-winning journalists.*

The Lumby Lines

# What's News Around Town

BY SCOTT STEVENS July 18

A busy week for our quiet town of Lumby.

With hundreds of eager spectators standing by, the Chatham County Fair was deemed officially open yesterday with the firing of Lumby's very own one-hundred-year-old cannon. Unfortunately, just as Mayor Jimmy Daniels lit the eight-second fuse, the right wheel dropped off, radically changing the direction of the eight-foot-long barrel. The new trajectory took the cannonball through the side wall of judging tent #4 before hitting dead center on one of the town's new Porta Potties, shattering it to smithereens. Thankfully, no one was relieving themselves at the time.

Continuing with fair news, the only reported thefts have been committed by a bald eagle that seems determined to try this year's fish and chips. Thus far, from the Moby Dick picnic table he has stolen two cell phones, two wallets, one set of keys and a fried chicken thigh. Unfortunately, the bird seems to be suffering from severe arthritis in his claws, causing him to let loose the heavier items in flight. After the eagle dropped a trout, smashing the windshield of Dennis Beezer's Honda, reports of similar pummelings were reported around town, the latest of which was a fried half chicken going through the awning at The Green Chile. Dr. Tom Candor has been contacted for advice.

Two hundred and seven pairs of men's socks were

found in the Goodwill donation box yesterday morning, making it the largest single-item contribution of the year. As there have been reports of missing socks from clotheslines throughout the town, this reporter is assuming that they are one and the same. Does Lumby now have its very own Robin Hood, stealing from the socked and giving to the sockless?

One of the boat docks at Woodrow Lake detached from its mooring and floated away from shore late yesterday afternoon. Although Hank was sunbathing on the dock at the time, no injuries were reported. The dock will be towed to dry land this afternoon, returning Woodrow Lake to its pristine state. It has been called the most beautiful lake in the Northwest.

*"Now, let's take that rose-colored fiction they call hard news and add a harsh dose of reality. I have been down to Woodrow Lake. In fact, I walked the beach right after the broadcast yesterday. Believe me, it is not, repeat not, the most enchanting lake in this or any other state. All right, I admit that it has some natural charm: the backdrop of the Rockies is marginally acceptable, as is the continuous forest of aspens that lines the west bank. But there's not one house in sight. If it were my land, I'd surround the lake with town houses and some upper-end lakefront homes. Trees don't pay taxes and strengthen the economy—people do, so move 'em in.*

*"Ideos, the lake is only twelve miles long and a couple wide—at best thirty square miles. These folks act like it's another Lake Superior, which is—Kano, keep me honest here—about thirty-two thousand square miles. Which is a perfect segue to my next update.*

*"Ideos listening in yesterday heard that Vince Shaw—or should I say his eminence Vince Shaw—is in town. With plans for turning Lumby into the next Telluride, he's strutting around with his checks in one hand and his attorneys in the other.*

*"I had the opportunity to meet America's most infamous real estate developer yesterday in the modest setting of the county fair, and if the truth be known, I should have gone to the swine weigh-off instead—it would have been less offensive.*

*"The man was downright rude, to* moi *of all people! Let's face it, we are each kings in our own industries. If it's a ski resort he wants, be my guest. This town certainly could use an influx of money, culture, brains and sophistication, and if it comes in a package called Vince Shaw Enterprises, so be it. But you don't burn bridges you haven't even crossed, especially when you're staring at a gorge a half-mile wide.*

*"So, ideos, our question for today: Is it acceptable for the more rich, more famous, more intelligent to snub the world?*

*"All right, we already have four callers waiting. On line one, there's Cindy from—I'll be—none other than Lumby. Cindy, ideo at will."*

*"I've never listened to your show, Mr. Reed, but they had it on at S&T's. I just wanted to say welcome to our town and to tell you that you didn't miss much at the swine weigh-off. Jeremy Dakin won it this year with Jasmine, who weighed five hundred and forty-four pounds. He's having a spare rib sale through Saturday at his body shop. Thanks. Bye."*

*"Okay, Cindy, good to know. On line two, we have—well, look at this—Scott Stevens, one of Lumby's very own street reporters. Ideo at will, Scott."*

*"Hello, Carter. Ideos from all of us at* The Lumby Lines, *the finest local newspaper in the country."*

*"Tell me, Scott, how's everything in the thriving Lumby metropolis this morning?"*

*"Well, my desk at the Chatham Press looks down on the corner of Main Street and Farm to Market Road. And just between you and me, things are mighty slow in town this particular morning. One sidebar regarding Jeremy Dakin's blue ribbon that Cindy announced earlier: two protests have been submitted to the fair commissioner, so the contest is most definitely not resolved, regardless of Jasmine's recent demise. It is now pending investigation."*

*"And that's why you called in today, Scott?"*

*"Definitely not, Carter. I just wanted to give you and your listeners a Vince Shaw update. There appears to have been an emergency closed-door session involving some of the town council before daybreak this morning. I first spotted a few councilmen going into Town Hall at ten to five, and then Joan, Jimmy and a couple of attorneys were hovering around the entrance a few minutes later, apparently waiting for Vince Shaw to show up. At precisely five a.m., a limo drove up, Shaw got out, and they all disappeared inside."*

*"You're up might early."*

*"I cover the night desk every fourth week."*

*"So are they still in there?"*

*"No, the meeting lasted for twenty minutes, at which time Shaw walked out alone, got into his stretch and left. Joan and Jimmy didn't come out for another ten minutes, and to the best of my knowledge, the town council is still inside. I'll be heading over there as soon as I hang up."*

*"Spoken like a true investigative reporter. Anything else, Scott?"*

*"Not right now."*

*"Moving on. Kano says that we're being flooded with local calls, so we'll see what some residents have to say. On line three, we have Jeremy. Ideo at will."*

*"Hello? Am I on the radio now?"*

*"Yes, Jeremy, America's listening."*

*"Well, first I want to say that the swine weigh-off was fair and square. Jasmine, rest her soul, did an admirable job in porking up, and contrary to some opinions, it is possible for a pig to gain two hundred and seventy-two pounds since last year's competition. Now, about the Vince Shaw deal, most small businesses in our town could use a good shot in the arm, so I say bring in the bulldozers and cement trucks."*

*"I take it then that's an affirmative vote. Kano just said that we have one voice of opposition on line two. Rachael from Lumby, ideo at will."*

*"Mr. Reed?"*

*"Yes, Rachael, you're on the air."*

*"What Mr. Shaw is doing . . . I'm sorry for crying—it's just so upsetting. I don't think anyone knows how something like that touches our personal lives. My family owns . . . one minute, I need to blow my nose . . ."*

Carter hit his mute button. "Get these local yokels off the air, Kano! No more calls from Lumby. This show's starting to sound like a dysfunctional romper room with a bunch of whiners."

*"My family owns a small piece of land that borders Mr. McNear's farm just as you turn onto Killdrop Road. There are seven generations laid to rest in our little cemetery underneath the large oak tree just beyond the stone wall . . . I'm sorry I'm crying so much . . . but what will happen to them? It just breaks my heart . . . to think that someone might build a highway there. And then you go on your radio station and defend the developer."*

*"I need to interrupt you, Rachael. I never said that I specifically support what Vince Shaw is doing. I am, and always will be, neutral."*

*"But if you don't oppose his plan, you're giving your consent to destroy the land and ruin the lives of so many in town."*

*"I'm sorry, Rachael, but to clarify for the second time, what I said is that this is a free country, and if a man isn't breaking any laws, then he should be allowed to do what he pleases."*

*"But we have moral responsibilities to one another that go beyond the letter of the law. The least you can do is come out and look at what will be . . . I'm sorry, this is so hard . . . at what will be destroyed because of one man's greed."*

*"Unfortunately, time has run out for this segment, and we need to take a news break. Stay tuned for our next segment to begin in exactly six minutes."*

Kano swirled his finger in the air. "And you're off the air."

"What a flipping disaster that was," Carter said, throwing his headset down on the table.

Worm was frantically trying to juggle a spike of call-ins as well as read the instant messages that were flooding into their e-mail. “We’re getting a huge national response,” he said without taking his eyes off the computer. “People are getting wrapped up in this. Nine out of ten want you to go out and look at the property.”

“Like I don’t have anything better to do,” Carter said as he leaned his bulk against the back of the chair and ran his stubby fingers through his hair. “Vince Shaw is a prick, and the last thing I want is to give that man any of my airtime.”

Worm shook his head. “Your listeners are hooked on this,” he said as he read more messages. “They know you’re here for another couple of days, and I don’t think they’re going to drop it. You need to respond.”

“Fine,” Carter barked. “Pass me the phone.”

Carter pulled a business card from his wallet and dialed the number on it.

“Joan Stokes? Yes, this is Carter Reed. . . . Yes, thank you. Would it be possible to see the McNear property this afternoon? . . . No, I assure you I’m definitely not interested, but we’re getting a huge response from callers who suggest I look at the property, and I was hoping you could oblige. . . . I appreciate that. . . . Two o’clock at S&T’s. Thank you.”

He threw the phone back to Kano. “Whatever you do, keep Lumby *off* the air,” Carter insisted. “If it even smells like a local caller or a comment about Shaw, hang up.”

And that’s exactly what Kano did for the next two and a half hours until a call came in just six minutes before the show was over.

“Vince Shaw on three,” Kano said into Carter’s headset. “Do you want him on?”

Carter’s mind raced, weighing the pros and cons of talking to Vince Shaw, unscripted and live, before nine million listeners. A jump in ratings would be guaranteed.

Carter nodded.

*“All right, we’ll return to the subject of legalizing marijuana next*

*week, but right now we need to break for an unexpected caller. This man needs no introduction: Vince Shaw on line three. Welcome back to my show."*

*"Thanks for letting me break in."*

*"There's been a lot of talk about town, and your name has been front and center. Are you calling from Lumby?"*

*"No, I flew out this morning. I'm about fifteen thousand feet over South Dakota right now on my way back to New York City for a few days."*

*"The air is yours."*

*"It's obvious from your comments as well as those made by your ill-informed callers this morning that there are simply too many rumors and unsubstantiated hearsay about my plans for Lumby. So I thought everyone would benefit from the facts. There is no question that Shaw Enterprises will be acquiring four thousand acres on Killdrop Road as the first step in bringing prosperity to the area. The papers will be signed and the deal closed on Saturday. In the broadest terms, this project will support our corporate mission to make America stronger through carefully chosen investments across our marvelous country. It will make Bradley, Wyoming, look like a warm-up."*

Carter hit his mute button. "What a bunch of crap. I bet you fifty he's making all this up," he said to Kano before speaking into the microphone.

*"You make this real estate development project sound—"*

*"That's where you're wrong once again, Carter. This is not a building project, as you so ineptly label it. It is a community and economic transformation."*

*"Mincing words, but moving ahead. You make this 'transformation' sound philanthropic, for the benefit of the country, but the article in* Entrepreneur *magazine states that your profit from Bradley alone well exceeded four hundred million dollars. Isn't that the bottom line?"*

*"Carter, Shaw Enterprises is a privately held company, so those numbers are supposition at best. The bottom line is doing what's right*

*for America and what's best for a small town that desperately needs direction and help coming into the twenty-first century. The proof lies in what was said at the closed-door meeting I had this morning with Lumby's town council. They pathetically pleaded that we move forward with our plans.*

*"In fact, to enable a smooth transition, each council member offered his resignation so that the vacant seats could be filled by executives from Shaw Enterprises. Unbeknownst to you and your callers, it was confidentially told to me that Lumby is close to bankruptcy and is in dire need of strong, competent leadership."*

*"I must admit, I'm a bit surprised by your assessment. The town certainly is small, but I wouldn't call it impoverished."*

*"Well then, you're either wearing tinted glasses, or your mind is just as small as most of the residents' there. Give me a year, and I'll give them eighty million dollars and turn Lumby into the Las Vegas of the Rockies. After we're done with it, there won't be anything left of the dumpy little place we see now."*

*"And you think everyone will be pleased with that?"*

*"It doesn't matter. Those who support us will benefit and those who don't—well, we can make their lives pretty miserable. The people in Lumby need to wake up. Every resident should feel privileged and appreciative that Shaw Enterprises has the vision to work around the town's shortcomings and create a model community to make America great."*

## FORTY-THREE
# *Ghosts*

At ten minutes before two, Carter walked into S&T's and discreetly took a seat at the back booth, facing away from the door. Neither Jimmy D nor Dennis Beezer, who were huddled together in the adjacent booth deep in conversation, noticed Carter walk by.

"The council meeting with Vince Shaw this morning was a total fiasco," Jimmy told Dennis. "Most of us were still half asleep except for Shaw, who spoke circles around us, arguing against every concern we raised. I think the only person who came out unscathed was Joan Stokes because she didn't say a word."

Dennis raised his brows. "But she's not a council member. Why was she there?"

"Shaw insisted that she attend," Jimmy explained. "I really wish you could have been there as well."

"Me too," Dennis said. "Why did the council have it so early in the morning?"

"Shaw had to fly back to New York first thing."

"And why on earth did they agree to a closed-door session?"

"I don't know, but it was a mistake," Jimmy confessed. "The residents are going to go nuts thinking that this meeting was deliberately held behind their backs."

Dennis was peeved. "Well, wasn't it?"

"Russell Harris suggested it. It was out of my control."

"Since when does our town attorney get involved with town council issues at such an early stage?"

Jimmy glanced around to see if anyone could hear him. "When we're threatened with a lawsuit."

Dennis was shocked. "What!?"

"Vince Shaw made it clear to the town council that he would take every legal action to ensure that nothing stands in the way of getting this project completed as soon as possible."

"But he has a year's worth of approvals to go through," Dennis argued, "starting with an environmental impact study."

Jimmy rubbed his eyes. "He told us to waive that requirement."

Dennis felt his face flush with anger. "The state won't let him do that!"

"He said he had enough state politicians in his pocket that he was guaranteed a rubber stamp."

Dennis couldn't believe what he was hearing. "But the town council won't go along with such nonsense."

"That's exactly what Jonathan Tucker said before Shaw threatened to sue each council member personally," Jimmy said. "Jonathan walked out of the meeting, and then it turned into a major shouting match between Shaw and four other council members."

"What did Russell Harris do?" Dennis asked.

Jimmy shrugged. "Apparently nothing. I talked to him after Shaw left, and he said we would need to take it one step at a time. Russell said we can't do anything until Shaw makes the first move, which will be Saturday when he comes back to close the deal."

Dennis struggled to control his anger. "It's not going to happen," he insisted, trying to convince himself as much as Jimmy. "The residents would never agree to let a person like Shaw take over the town."

"And that's exactly what he wants—to take over," Jimmy said. "He even advised me to keep an eye out for another job."

Dennis sighed deeply. His voice changed, the hard edge replaced by sadness. "I just feel so sorry for this town. These folks aren't prepared to be ramrodded by someone like Shaw. The reality is that he's an international player who can buy and sell a town like ours in his sleep. People around here have no idea how much power someone like that has and what his money can buy if he puts his mind to it. They're good people—they don't deserve what he's about to dish out."

"You make it sound like it's a lost cause," Jimmy said.

"It might be. You know we would do anything to protect Lumby—I'll certainly put the paper behind the cause—but I've known a few men like Vince Shaw. Going up against him will end in a proverbial bloodbath."

Jimmy looked at his watch. "I need to get back to the fair. Do me a favor—keep this confidential until we think of something that might offer some hope to this dismal situation."

As both men stood up to leave, they began talking about the fair. Neither man noticed Carter Reed sitting just a few feet away. Shortly after Jimmy and Dennis departed, Joan Stokes walked into the restaurant.

"Mr. Reed?" she said, extending her hand. "It's nice to see you again."

"You can call me Carter," he said.

Joan slipped into the booth. "In truth, I was a little perplexed by your call. You said that you're not interested in buying the property but want to see it anyway?"

Carter nodded. "Did you listen to my show this morning?"

"No, I didn't," Joan said. "I had to attend a town council meeting."

"At Vince Shaw's request."

"Why, yes," she said in surprise.

Carter explained. "Shaw called in from his plane and used my show to announce his plans for your town."

"And he mentioned the town council meeting?" she asked.

"He did indeed," Carter answered. "He said it went swimmingly, adding that the members offered to relinquish their council seats to some of his executives who will be overseeing the . . . what does he call it?"

"Transformation?" Joan asked.

"That's the word," Carter said, slapping his hand on the table.

Joan walked a fine line between maintaining client confidentiality and correcting flagrant lies. "Although that may have been Mr. Shaw's perspective, I wouldn't say that the meeting was as congenial as he may have seen it."

"But he got what he wanted," Carter said.

Joan tapped a pen on the table. "That's to be seen. The town council explained that it would take at least a year to obtain the necessary zoning, environmental and building approvals before breaking ground," she explained in a flat, unemotional voice. "Mr. Shaw assured the council that he could have the papers stamped within two months. When the council pushed back, Mr. Shaw said that this project would hang over the town and burn through its legal resources until they decided to move into the twenty-first century."

"I got the sense that he may have threatened the councilmen," Carter suggested.

Joan raised an eyebrow. "I'm quite sure that Mr. Shaw could make some lives miserable if he doesn't get what he wants. But that's not my business. My job is to bring McNear a buyer."

"For which you'll receive a handsome commission," Carter said.

"Mr. Reed, are you insinuating that I'm selling out the town?"

Although that was exactly what Carter had implied, he softened his position. "Not at all," he said more congenially. "My only point is that you'll directly benefit from the deal."

She looked deep into his eyes. "You've never lived in a small town, have you?"

"I've been fortunate enough not to have had to."

"*Not to have had to?*" Joan said in exasperation. "Most people feel blessed to live here. This is a sanctuary from the harsher realities of the world. At the heart of our town is the decency of its residents. It is family looking out for family, neighbor being accountable to neighbor. I know you may have that in cities as well, but you can't escape from it here. The town may look like a throwback from yesteryear, as Mr. Shaw so quickly points out, but that's because we're a strong community—authentic and forthright." She exhaled and then paused. "And for your own curiosity, every dollar of my commission will be donated to the town to fight the development plan."

Carter looked down at the table, feeling like a boy who had been duly scolded by his teacher.

"So," Joan said, straightening her blouse, "putting that behind us, I think we should start again."

Carter straightened his back. "I was goaded into looking at the property by a caller from Lumby this morning. And with nine million listeners on the other end of the airwaves, I have to follow through."

"Then you have no personal interest in the land?"

Carter crossed his arms over his big chest. "I certainly didn't when I called you."

"Well, your timing is good," she said, taking her car keys out of her purse. "After Mr. Shaw executes the contract on Saturday, the property will officially be off the market and no one will be allowed in."

"So it's a done deal just as he claimed?" Carter gave a start of surprise. "I didn't think Shaw was being totally honest when he said that the land was already his."

Joan tapped her pen more quickly on the table. "Yes and no. He wants the land and has all the means in the world to pay for it, so it's just a matter of fine tuning. Mr. Shaw made a lowball offer after first seeing the property, but that was rejected by the seller. He headed back to New York after the council meeting this morning, before we had time to amend the contract. He'll be calling me Friday to finalize the terms of a counteroffer, which I'm sure will be for full asking price, and then Russell will draw up the papers. Mr. Shaw plans to fly in Saturday morning to close the deal."

~

As Joan drove over the bridge, she told Carter, "This is Goose Creek. It begins as runoff from the mountains all the way up in Canada and then flows south to Woodrow Lake, which you can see from Montis Inn."

She put her foot on the brake and turned off West Main Street. "Is this Killdrop Road?" Carter asked.

"Yes," she answered. "Mr. McNear's property begins two hundred yards further on."

Carter tried to lean forward to peer through the windshield and immediately spotted the immense oak tree just as it had been described to him by the caller earlier that day. "You can stop here," he said.

When Joan pulled her Audi off the road, Carter got out. "I'll be right back," he said.

As soon as he stepped over the stone wall, he saw the small cemetery. A cluster of two dozen very old tombstones, some broken and many slanted, was enclosed by a short, weather-washed picket fence whose gate had long since fallen off.

Although the family plot initially looked abandoned because of the uncut grass, upon closer inspection Carter saw small, tightly bound bouquets of fresh flowers at each grave site. It was obvious from the daisies that someone cared very deeply about the people who were laid to rest there, but it was equally obvious that whoever owned the cemetery was physically unable to keep up with its demanding maintenance.

Carter took several deep breaths as he walked slowly through the private graveyard, reading the etched words carved into the granite stones: Della Royce 1804–1861; Isaac Royce 1801–1853; Beatrice Jennings 1832–1897; Zachery Jennings 1852–1853 Beloved Infant of God; Gregory Jennings, 1828–1897; Alec Royce 1918–1943; Ruth Royce 1924–1978. The names and dates rolled off the tip of Carter's tongue. It was a progression of generations, a history of one family he had never known.

His fingers trembled as he stepped between the graves and touched the old stones. His heart ached so deeply that he was unable to push aside the pain, as he always did when guilt or sadness crept unexpectedly through his steel exterior.

It had been ten years since he had last visited his parents' graves in Seattle. On that blistery and wet January morning, exactly two years to the day after he had buried his mother next to his father, he'd brought flowers to their graves. The cemetery, though, was littered with trash; rusted beer cans and empty wine bottles were entangled in the weeds, tombstones were covered with obscene graffiti, and many had been knocked over to lie cracked on the ground. A marble crypt had been vandalized.

The vases that he had placed in front of his parents' gravestones were long since broken, shards of glass spread across their graves. Carter looked around in pained disbelief. The flowers that he had been holding slipped from his grasp and lay scattered by his feet.

He then did what he had always done when confronted with emotions he didn't want to feel or a situation he couldn't control; he walked away. Pulling up the collar of his overcoat, he buried his chin deep into his chest, turned on his heels and left the cemetery, knowing he would never return again.

He heard a rustle that jolted him back to the present. He glanced back toward the car to see if Joan was joining him, but he was still alone in the small cemetery, facing reawakened demons. "I'm so sorry," he whispered to his parents as he looked up to the heavens. He brought his fist up to his chest, wanting the pain to subside, wishing the memory would fade.

"Excuse me," a female voice called out.

Carter was startled back into the present. Walking toward him was a woman he guessed to be in her forties. Her ash-brown hair was swept up into a barrette at the top of her head. Her arms and face were deeply tanned. In her hand, she held a small cluster of daisies.

"May I help you?" she asked in a tone that was filled with genuine caring.

From the few words she spoke, he recognized her voice. "Are you Rachael?"

Her eyes grew wide. "Yes. Who are you?"

"Carter Reed. You called my show this morning."

She stared at him for a moment. "And you came here to see me?" she asked in disbelief.

"To see your cemetery," he admitted, "and to look at the land Vince Shaw is buying."

She walked across the cemetery, knelt down and replaced the wilted flowers on one of the graves: Hilary Royce 1982–1985.

"My daughter," she said, kissing her index finger and then touching it against the cold granite. "She died of pneumonia when she was three and a half."

Carter looked around the tombstones, following an invisible chain from person to person that finally led him to Hilary. "I'm sorry," he said.

Rachael then pointed to the tombstone to the right of where she was standing. "My mother and her mother before her." She looked solemnly around her. "How could you defend a man who would take this away from us?"

FORTY-FOUR

# Waiting

In her bedroom at Montis Inn, Jessica looked at the clock and realized that her parents would be knocking on the door any minute. At the fair the night before, she had promised them that her computer equipment would be packed up by noon, and that was several hours ago.

abt2party: is Marley3823 online?

She typed as quickly as she could. Hurry up, she whispered to herself.

flyman1964: hey abt2party. good 2 have you back

abt2party: hey fly

amhikt: you still in lumby?

abt2party: fraid so. has anyone heard from marley today?

amhikt: haven't

flyman1964: he was here a few minutes ago

roacher: he was online looking for you this morning

abt2party: getting heat from my folks. i want to get out of here and have some fun b4 I go nuts

2bshades: omg that was same w me. i finally left home last year couldn't deal with any of it

roacher: been thinking about leaving home. folks are a real drag. easier just to go.

flyman1964: been there, done that...its a stupid idea...stay home

abt2party: tell Marley

marley3823: i'm here

abt2party: yeah, i'm about to go offline. folks are unplugging everything

marley3823: after you told me about the fight last night, i knew that was going to happen. you still on for 2morow night?

abt2party: i'm hitching down

marley3823: beer coming in at 6

Six? Jessica thought. Who starts partying at six?

abt2party: seems early but I'm game. i'd go crazy if it wasn't for your rave

marley3823: its not really a rave

abt2party: ok a blowout

marley3823: you have the address? 17 west city road wheatley

abt2party: got it

Jessica hit the power button just as she heard the door start to open. She whirled around in her seat.

"Now you can just come into my room whenever you want?" she asked.

"You didn't answer when we knocked," her father said as he walked in. Elaine was directly behind him, her hand on his back.

Her father glanced around the room with a scowl. "You were supposed to have packed all of this up by noon."

"We didn't get back from the fair until late," Jessica complained.

Her dad lowered his brows. "For someone who is used to going to bed at four in the morning . . ." he said.

"Well, I was really tired," Jessica said. "I just got up, and I'm going to start working on it now."

He marched over to Jessica's makeshift desk, bent down and pulled out every electrical cord from the tangled web of wires. "Well, that was easy enough," he said. "We'll start with the keyboards." He placed one on her lap. "Wrap the cord around it and put it in that cardboard box."

For ten minutes, Jessica and her father worked in silence as her desktop computer was dismantled component by component. All the while, her mother sat quietly on a corner of the bed as Jessica felt her anger escalating until she could barely contain it.

When the desk was cleared, her father looked around. “Where’s your laptop?”

“You said I could keep that!” Jessica cried out.

“No,” he said firmly. “We said you could use it a few hours each day, but we’re going to monitor the amount of time you spend online by keeping the laptop in our room.”

“That’s not fair!” she shouted. “You’re going to *ruin* everything. I won’t have any friends when I get back!”

“I’m sure you will. As you get more on track, we’ll be more flexible about when and how you use your laptop,” he explained.

Jessica turned to her mother. “Mother?”

An expression of helplessness crossed her face, and she struggled for words but finally managed to say, “Your father is right.”

Consumed with fury, Jessica picked up the last remaining mouse pad from the desk and threw it across the room. “This is a bunch of crap!” she yelled.

“Jessica!” her dad said. “Keep up the tantrum and you’re grounded.”

“Like that really means something,” she hissed.

He held out his hands. “The laptop.”

“Here,” she said, pushing it at him. “And don’t look at my files.”

He placed the laptop in the only cardboard box that wasn’t already filled with equipment and then he stood. “Help me move this furniture back to where it was.”

Jessica didn’t budge.

“Jessica, get up,” he said.

“No!” She crossed her arms in protest. “Since this is your bright idea, you do it.”

Her father apparently knew that arm wrestling with a belligerent sixteen-year-old would do more harm than good, so he took a seat next to her mother. “Then we’ll talk,” he said.

“I thought that’s what we did last night,” Jessica said, the words dripping acid.

“Oh, no,” he said. “That was just the beginning.”

Jessica gawked as she began to realize that the worst with her parents was yet to come. "What now?"

"Jess, things aren't going well for any of us," he began.

Jessica stared at the floor, refusing to look at her father while he spoke. Patrick continued in a tender but firm voice. "We think you're headed down the wrong path with your new friends."

"How can you say that!? They're the most popular kids in school! Everyone wants to be in with Missy and Emily and Taylor."

"They're in a tight little clique, and you're jumping through hoops to change everything about yourself just to fit in."

Jessica's face was flushed. "What's wrong with fitting in?"

"Jess, we know you've deliberately dropped your grades to be cool, and we've stood by and watched you turn into someone we don't even recognize. Both of us have done you a disservice by going along with all of this, by never setting any limits on your behavior. So it may be a little late, but things have got to change. You're only a few years away from being a legal adult, and there's still so much you need to learn."

Jessica sat motionless, refusing to show any emotion, refusing to cry.

"So," he said, taking a deep breath, "the first thing you're going to do is put the furniture back to where you found it. If you don't know where something goes, ask Aunt Pam. Then pick your clothes up off the floor, make your bed and straighten the bathroom. I want you to apologize to Pam for not respecting *her* possessions and offer to have her inspect your room when you're done. You'll be responsible for keeping your own room clean, here and when we get home. A new rule of the house is that if we find any clothes on the floor or lumped onto a chair, they'll be donated to the Salvation Army—no arguments and no second chances. And you won't be given a credit card and sent off to the mall to buy new clothes. Any questions?"

Jessica was clasping the seat chair so tightly that her knuckles were turning white, but she didn't look up.

"All right then," he said calmly. "For the remainder of the summer, your curfew is nine o'clock on weekdays and ten on Saturday nights. You'll be in your room with lights out by eleven, and to make it easier for you, we'll be removing your bedroom phone and television for a while."

Finally Jessica lifted her head, her lips curled in anger. "That's not fair!" she screamed.

"You're a minor. It's our house and our TV, so it *is* fair."

"Then I'll leave," she threatened, staring directly at her mother.

Her mother swallowed with what seemed to be some effort. "We hope you don't," she finally said. "We love you, but Jessica, we can't step aside and have you do whatever you want out of fear that you'll leave."

Her dad laid his hand on his wife's leg and patted it gently. "Jessica, no more emotional blackmail. No more playing us against each other."

Tears were now rolling down Jessica's face. "You're ruining my life," she bawled. "You've taken away my laptop and my television. What am I suppose to *do*?"

"Read a book," her father offered.

"Geeks read," she spat.

"Find a new interest, a new hobby," her mother said.

Jessica was smart enough to realize that any further argument would not only be a waste of time but might also tighten the constraints that her parents were putting around her. "Fine, I'll take up knitting." Each word dripped with sarcasm.

"It's beautiful weather outside," her father said in a lighter tone. "Once you clean this place up, we'll be spending the day together. Unless you have a special request, we thought about going down to Woodrow Lake for some swimming and sailing."

Jessica glared. "Don't count on it."

FORTY-FIVE

# *Juxtapositions*

The approach to Chuck Bryson's house was almost undetectable. Six miles northwest of Wheatley, Gibbons Road changed from a publicly maintained paved street that meandered along the edge of Woodrow Lake to a privately owned dirt lane that turned westward and gained altitude while climbing into the foothills.

After a bumpy two miles in Chuck's SUV, Lynn asked, "How many people live off this road?"

Chuck grinned. "One."

Lynn raised her brows. "You live out here all alone?"

"Certainly not alone. I have several animals."

Just as the trees began to close in on both sides, the car crossed a stone bridge above a clear mountain stream. Directly ahead was a cluster of brightly hued cottages and outhouses, each painted a different color, all randomly placed on four acres of native wild grass.

"That's the main house," he said, pointing to a single-story stone dwelling with large windows on the east and south sides.

Getting out of the car, Lynn turned slowly, taking in the panoramic beauty of Chuck's homestead. She gasped at the beauty of Woodrow Lake stretching north and south. Behind it, on the opposite side of the lake, she could just make out the tree line that followed Farm to Market Road up to Lumby. In the distance, Montis Inn sat on a knoll. And beyond it, flat plains continued east as far as the eye allowed.

"This is breathtaking," she said, gazing out at the vista spread before her.

"It's just as beautiful in the winter," he said, also staring out over the landscape.

She looked up at the jagged mountains behind her and then toward the open plains to the east. "It's quite a juxtaposition," she said.

"That's one of the reasons I fell in love with this spot," he explained. "It's where the cliffs end and the flats begin—the dense forest to the west and the open plains to the east."

"You must have harsh winters up here. Do you ever get snowed in?"

"Not often. We're protected by the mountain range," he explained. "The west slope may get ten feet of snow, but the precipitation stops at the peaks. Even Franklin, where you visited St. Cross Abbey, is sheltered from the worst weather."

"But you do get *some* snow?" she asked.

Chuck laughed. "Enough to keep it interesting during the cold months."

She turned in a full circle. "This is enchanting. Your flower garden is spectacular."

"Thank you—it's one of my delights. Now, as for the buildings: the barn," he said, pointing at a bright red building with crosshatched doors, "is where the animals bed down. The yellow barn is used for beekeeping and gardening."

"And the blue cabin?" she asked.

"A studio for pottery and candlemaking. And finally, the guest cottage is over there," he said, pointing to the most secluded building, which was painted forest-green with beige trim. "Why don't we make some candles?" he suggested as he pulled some equipment and buckets from the back of the car and handed Lynn the lighter of the packages.

As they crossed the compound, two rabbits scurried in front of them. "Barn residents," Chuck said as he held the studio door open for Lynn.

She took a tentative step inside and was immediately struck by a complex fusion of scents. She inhaled deeply trying to identify them.

"Clay, glaze and wax," Chuck said, reaching behind her to flip on the switch and flood the space with fluorescent light.

"This is amazing," she said.

The studio consisted of two large rooms with a half wall separating them. Long white Formica worktables ran around all the walls. At the far end, a ten-foot counter with two deep sinks serviced both work areas.

Just glancing at the equipment in each room, Lynn could see how Chuck had allocated the space; the area to her right was for pottery with two electric kilns. Glaze buckets were stored neatly below the worktables, and a potter's wheel had been set up by the window.

The room to her left was for candlemaking. She walked slowly past the countertop, touching some of the candles hanging from a latticework of wooden rods above the worktable. Pails of different-sized wicks lined a long bench, and above that, various molds were stacked in an orderly fashion for ease of identification.

A furnace turned on, filling the room with a low hum.

"A humidifier that runs a few minutes every day," Chuck explained. "The single biggest challenge I had when building the studio a few years ago was controlling the inside environment. Some would disagree, but in my opinion, the hardest trick in both pottery and candlemaking is getting the right balance between temperature and humidity. Too warm and dry, and the clay loses water too quickly. Too cool and damp, and the wax of the candles doesn't set correctly. It was a real challenge."

Lynn was speechless as she picked up and examined the various vials of scents and dyes that were used in candlemaking. "It's not what I was expecting."

Chuck looked at her and smiled. "Why is that?"

"I thought it would be . . . messy, with wax residue everywhere."

"One of the unfortunate realities of these kinds of hobbies is that you usually spend as much time cleaning up as you do enjoying the creative process. I've certainly made it more of a challenge by using clay and wax in the same room. They're natural opposites—on a piece of bisque pottery, wax will repel glaze—so I really have no choice but to keep the space as clean as possible."

Lynn pulled a stool closer to the table and sat down. "Is this all right?"

"To sit and watch?" he asked. "No, you'll be making the candles today."

"But I just came to watch you."

"Do you always stand on the sidelines, watching?" he asked.

His casual observation made Lynn flinch. "Is that how you see me?"

He tilted his head. "I have noticed that you tend to watch before committing yourself. It involves less risk than jumping in with two feet."

Lynn raised one brow in a questioning slant. "And you're always a reckless jumper?"

Chuck smiled roguishly. "Definitely not. But I don't observe life from a safe distance either." He took her arm and led her off the stool. "And you aren't either—not today, at least. This will be loads of fun."

Lynn exhaled. "All right," she said, rolling up her sleeves. "Let's jump."

"Very good," he said. "You can turn on the wax burner right over there, and when you begin to feel some heat, place several pieces of beeswax in it."

Lynn did as instructed as Chuck began teaching her the fine art of candlemaking.

"Temperature," he said, "is so important. Not just the temperature of the room, as I said, but also the temperature of the wax as it melts and when it is poured—"

"Isn't the temperature the same for both?" Lynn interrupted.

"Contrary to what you might expect, it's seldom the same," Chuck answered. "The pour temperature for an identical wax may be different based on the room temperature. Most waxes will have a melting point of about one hundred and twenty to one hundred and sixty degrees. The pour temperature is totally dependent on what additives you combine with what kind of wax."

"I didn't know there were different types of wax," she said, keeping an eye on the burner.

"The industry has changed so much over the last few years. Companies now offer more varieties than most hobbyists could ever use. Not long ago, most candles were made of either paraffin wax or natural wax, such as beeswax or a soy derivative. At that time, manufacturers began offering blends and hybrids, either paraffin waxes with additives already infused or a proprietary mixture of different ingredients. Then there are gel waxes. But I would say that yellow beeswax and either straight paraffin or a paraffin blend continue to be the most popular waxes used by home candlemakers. Beeswax, in particular, is easy to handle and is very consistent and highly predictable, but blends are convenient because they are ready to use—no other additives are needed except for, optionally, scent and color."

"But you use beeswax," she said.

"Always," Chuck replied as he began to open the first jar in a long row arranged on the worktable. "In addition to temperature, the process is important. You will be measuring several different ingredients into your formulation, and you will be dipping or pouring scalding-hot wax, so how everything is organized should facilitate how you move from one stage to the next."

New aromas filled the room as he began to prepare the scents.

Chuck continued talking as he worked. "The final key factor is choosing the correct wick for the candle. How the candle performs—the burn rate, the amount of smoke and soot produced, the scent thrown and so on—is highly dependent on the wick, and unfortunately, there is no one wick that would work well for all candles.

"It's an interesting relationship; the candle's performance is highly dependent on the wick, and the effectiveness of the wick is dependent on the candle—the type of wax used, its melting point, additives such as scent and color, desired burn time, even the type and shape of the candle."

He held up a long string for Lynn to see. "This is a zinc core wick—a very popular wick that's used for votive and container candles. It offers good rigidity while pouring, but it tends to leave carbon deposits. What you're looking for is a wick that can be handled during the pour that will give you a consistent, well-shaped flame and one that creates a nice wax pool with little to no dripping."

Lynn rolled the wick between her fingers. "Despite all the candles I've lit, I've never thought about the wick or the shape of the flame."

"And you wouldn't, until a candle smokes uncontrollably, or the flame flickers constantly, or the candle drips a significant amount of wax."

"Yes, exactly!" Lynn said.

"There you have it," Chuck said, grinning. "You've seen what happens when the wrong wick is chosen—you just didn't put the two together."

"That seems to be the story of my life."

"What's that?" he asked.

"Not recognizing the cause and effect of things . . . of relationships." Lynn bridled as she thought about Dan. "My husband was having an affair for more than two years, and I didn't see it. In retrospect . . . aren't those comforting words—in retrospect . . . I'm sure he showed me every sign in the book, but . . ." She paused as she wrapped the wick around her finger. "I didn't see it. And I totally missed all of his lies, including the fact that he stole a quarter of a million dollars from Mark, from my own brother. And I defended Dan through all of his deceit."

"I'm sure Mark accepted your apology," Chuck said.

"*My* apology?" Lynn looked startled. "It was Dan who stole the money."

"Yes, but you must have been involved to some degree—siding against Mark. That's all I meant," he said as he continued to prepare the additives for the wax.

*My apology?* Lynn's own words echoed in her mind. Why would I apologize for my husband's wrongdoing? she wanted to ask Chuck, in order to reaffirm her blamelessness. But even with those few words spoken, the conversation was beginning to sound similar to the one she'd had with Pam while walking to the barn. *Why does everyone think I need to apologize?* Lynn thought.

"Is everything all right?" Chuck asked.

Lynn shook off her preoccupation. "Yes, I was just thinking," she said as she slowly dropped chunks of wax into the burner. "It's funny how life turns out," she said, almost to herself. "One minute, I have two feet on the ground walking a familiar road with someone I know. And then, the rug is pulled out and I become angry at the world, digging in my heels and refusing to take another step."

"Is that what happened?" he asked.

"Given that the closest emotional connection I have now is with a promiscuous cat, I'd say things aren't looking all that favorable for me in the world of relationships."

"But everything changes," Chuck said. "In fact, that is the only constant in life—change. The chunk of wax you just put in the burner becomes a liquid and soon it will be a solid again, taking on a different form for a different purpose. The opportunities for each of us to change are endless—it's just a matter of deciding how and when."

"I can see why Pam and Mark think so highly of you," she said. "You're very wise . . . for a physics professor."

For an instant, Chuck blushed. "You'd be surprised how much

intuition and physics have in common." He moved in front of her to reach another jar.

Standing close to him, suddenly, Lynn stood on her toes and kissed his mouth with a desire that belied her outward calm.

Chuck was surprised—delighted but very, very surprised.

She pulled away. "I . . ." she stuttered. "I don't know why I did that."

"Oh, I certainly hope you do," Chuck whispered before putting his hand behind her neck and drawing her close. His kiss was slow and tender.

## FORTY-SIX
# *Iced*

Standing by the sink in their home, Pam heard a car drive up Farm to Market Road and quickly pulled the curtain aside to glance out the window. When the car passed, she sighed. She looked at the clock. It was eight thirty at night.

"Where is everyone?" she asked aloud.

Mark walked through the door carrying empty serving platters from dinner. "Another outstanding meal, honey," he said.

"I'm getting worried," she said. "They should have been here hours ago."

"Robert and Kay or Lynn and Chuck?"

"All the above," she said in exasperation.

Elaine and Patrick tapped on their door. "More dirty dishes," Elaine said.

"Come in." Pam waved. "We're just stacking them in the sink."

As she took the used silverware from Patrick, she couldn't help but ask again, "Do you think they're all right?"

Patrick didn't know what else to say other than what he had already told her. "When we left the lake just before six o'clock, Kay and Robert looked like they were having a wonderful time. They were out on one of those small two-man sailboats. She was in front, dragging her feet in the water, and he was in back, steering and adjusting the sail. We tried to call out to them, but they were too far from shore to hear us."

"Was it windy?" Pam asked.

"More than what I had expected," Patrick said. "Elaine, Jessica and I took a sailing lesson, and as soon as we got fifty yards from the dock, the wind really gusted across the surface of the water."

"Were they headed in any one direction?"

"They were tacking toward the south, away from the dock."

Pam felt a stab of anxiety. "Maybe you should go find them," she said to Mark.

"Honey, I'm sure they're fine. Let's wait a little while longer. If they're not back in thirty minutes, Patrick and I will drive down to the dock and look around."

Suddenly, the phone rang and Pam jumped. She grabbed the receiver. "Hello?" she said urgently. She looked at Mark and shook her head. "Hold on." She covered the mouthpiece as she passed the phone to Mark. "It's Joshua."

"Hey, Joshua, what's up?" he said. "Yeah, I'm just doing the chainsaw competition tomorrow to help Jeremiah out. I could really use your help in holding the log. . . . No, would you assure Brooke that you will not be in harm's way. . . . You'll be balancing it at the bottom. . . . Okay, have a good night and we'll see you at the fairgrounds at two."

Pam frowned. "Don't tell me—Brooke is a little worried about you whirling a chainsaw in close proximity to her husband? Smart woman."

Pam heard a car drive up Farm to Market Road. This time, the car slowed and pulled into the parking lot. When she saw Robert step out from behind the wheel, she headed for the door, but Mark caught her arm.

"They're not children who just missed curfew," he said.

Their eyes met, and as soon as he released her, she flew out the kitchen and ran across the courtyard with Mark on her heels.

"Where have you been?" she asked, just as Robert was opening Kay's door.

Kay carefully swung her right foot out of the car. Her ankle was packed in ice and wrapped in a bright yellow beach towel. Robert pulled her up from the seat and put his arm around her.

Pam looked alarmed. "What on earth happened to you?" she said. "I knew you were doing too many dangerous activities. You should never have gone sailing by yourself."

"Pam," Robert said calmly, "this happened at the Farmer's Daughter ice cream stand. Kay stepped off the deck and twisted her ankle."

Pam looked confused. "But that deck is only six inches off the ground."

Kay shrugged. "What can I say? Call me a klutz."

"But we met a charming couple—about your age—who live just south of the lake. They gave us ice from their cooler and lent us this towel."

Kay raised a finger to remind him. "Which we must remember to return when we see them Thursday evening."

Mark was impressed. "Here only a few days, and you two already have a double date."

"Samantha and Greg simply invited us over to their home in Wheatley for a small get-together," Robert explained.

"We're going to churn homemade ice cream," Kay continued.

"Speaking of food, have you two eaten dinner?" Pam asked.

"We had some delicious crab cakes at the south end of the lake."

Pam tried to conceal her disapproving look. "So you did sail all the way down?"

"And back," Kay said proudly. "But dear, maybe we can talk about it later. My ankle is throbbing a bit."

"I'm sorry, Mom. Of course, let's get you to bed. Mark will help carry you in."

Kay put her arms around Robert's shoulders on one side and Mark's on the other. "Two strapping men—how lucky can one woman be?"

Pam watched her hobble off to the guest annex. "I'll be right over with an ice pack."

A few minutes later, Mark walked into the kitchen just as Pam was carrying a tray out for her mother. "You made her tea?" he asked. "My guess is that she would prefer a couple shots of tequila." He grabbed a bottle from their liquor cabinet and added it to the tray. "Just in case."

When Pam tapped on their bedroom door, it gently swung open. Kay was already lying on the bed, and Robert was sitting by her side, kissing her. Pam cleared her throat.

"Come in, dear," Kay said. "We're just smooching—it's very therapeutic."

Robert grinned and then winked at Pam. "I'll be back shortly. Is there anything I can get you?" he asked Kay.

"Some tequila for the inflammation," she teased.

"Got it right here," Pam said, holding up the bottle. "Robert, there are plenty of leftovers if you're still hungry."

"See you soon." He blew Kay a kiss before shutting the door.

Pam fluffed Kay's pillows behind her head. "Are you really all right? Do you need to see a doctor?"

"Pam, all I did was twist my ankle. I'll be fine tomorrow."

"I don't want you doing anything for a few days," Pam said. "You scared the life out of me when you didn't return for dinner."

"Darling, you're going to die before I do if you don't stop worrying so much."

Pam gently brushed the hair off her mother's forehead. "I just don't want anything to happen to you."

"I know you try so hard, but you can't control everything that happens in this world," she said.

Pam winced when she heard her mother use the same words that

Mark often said to her. “It’s not a matter of control,” she replied softly.

Kay chuckled. “That’s exactly what it is, sweetheart. If you control it, there won’t be anything left for chance . . . there won’t be change or any unexpected accidents.”

“And what’s so wrong with that?”

Kay touched her daughter’s cheek. “It’s not a very fun life,” she whispered. She looked deep into Pam’s eyes. “What did we do to make you so afraid?”

Pam’s face twisted with pain. “I just don’t want anything awful to happen to the people I love.”

“But bad things happen, dear—they always will,” Kay said gently. “Life is hard. The older you get, the messier life becomes, and that’s something you can never change.” She took her daughter’s hand in her own. “But in between those few bad days are the hundred sunny days that should be filled with courage and passion.”

“I have those,” Pam said.

“I know you do. You just need to let go a little.”

Pam sighed heavily. “All right, I promise I will try.”

“And you’ll be so much happier, I’m sure of it,” Kay said. “Now, you can help me.”

Pam looked puzzled. “Do what?”

“Plan my wedding.” Kay’s face beamed brighter than Pam had ever remembered.

She hugged her mother. “I knew he was going to ask you!” Pam spoke a mile a minute. “He told me the other day, and I told him it was a wonderful idea.” She laughed. “Well, after I got over the shock, I thought it was perfect. When did he ask you? Today?”

“He literally swept me off my feet,” Kay said. “He took me up in the Ferris wheel earlier this afternoon. Oh, it was so beautiful and romantic.”

“Let me see your ring.”

Kay held out the engagement ring that Robert had placed on her finger just hours before. “It’s stunning, isn’t it?” she asked. “Robert designed it himself.”

“It’s beautiful.” Pam kissed her mother’s hand. “What kind of wedding do you want?”

“I have an idea,” Kay whispered, pulling her daughter close so no one else could hear her secret.

They schemed for an hour before Kay fell into a deep, peaceful sleep.

FORTY-SEVEN

# *Qwerty*

In the backyard, Elaine and Patrick were playing a game of Scrabble against Corey and Carter. Jessica stood behind her parents.

"You can play 'fogdog' or 'fogbow,'" Jessica said to her mother.

Elaine looked up at her. "Really?"

Jessica scanned the board, calculating the points in her head. "Put down 'fogbow.'"

"You are *so* lucky that I've actually heard of that word," Carter quipped.

"One of you needs to play the word 'quizzically,'" Pam said to the group as she walked past the table. "I hear it has the most points."

Jessica corrected her right away. "I think that's 'quizzicality,' Aunt Pam," she said. When everyone looked up at her in surprise, she reverted back to her teenage ways. "Well, like, I don't know."

Not far from the Scrabble game, Mark swung lazily on a two-man hammock. "Slide over," Pam said, crawling in next to him.

"Is Kay all right?" he asked.

"She's just perfect. And she said thanks for the tequila."

"She really had some?"

"Two shots," Pam said, laughing. "I swear, that woman could drink a sailor under the table."

Mark pulled Pam closer, trying to rock their bodies together so the hammock would swing higher. "Right, left, right, left," he said, synchronizing their movements. "By the way, Lynn called about fifteen minutes ago."

"The other lost sheep," Pam said. "Where is your sister tonight?"

He grinned. "At Chuck's."

"Really?"

"Really," he said. "And she said not to wait up for her."

Pam laughed so loudly that the others looked over at her. "Mom said to let things go, and that's what I'm doing," she explained.

"Is that really a word, Jess?" Patrick's voice rang out.

Jessica rolled her eyes. "Yeah, Dad."

Patrick laid out the letters, covering an empty triple letter box.

Carter's voice suddenly boomed across the backyard. "What the hell is 'qwerty'?"

Patrick looked at his daughter for the answer. "It's the layout of a computer keyboard," she said.

"That's insane," Carter argued.

"I think she's right, Dad," Corey said. "Just write down the points."

"I'm not going to roll over and give them points they don't deserve. I use words for a living. If I've never heard of it, it doesn't exist," Carter bellowed.

Jessica jumped out of her seat. "But it is a word!"

"Oh, oh," Pam whispered. "Should we intervene?"

"Marko, where's your dictionary?" Carter demanded.

He lifted his head from the hammock. "On the top of the bookshelf by the living room sofa."

Before Mark finished the sentence, Jessica bolted out of the backyard and into their house. She returned to the table within seconds. "It's a word!" she yelled as she threw the book at Carter, hitting him square in the chest.

"Jessica!" Patrick said. "Mind your manners."

"You're defending *him*?" she argued. "I'm right, and I'm your daughter. You should be ticked off at Uncle Carter, not me."

"I'm not ticked off at anyone," Patrick said in a calmer voice.

"I'm so out of here," she said, running toward the guest annex.

Pam and Mark sank as low as possible in the hammock and lay motionless, waiting for the storm to pass.

Carter tore open the book, ripping several pages in the process. Turning to the last page of *Q*, he followed the alphabet as he read aloud. "Quran, Qtub, q.v., qwerty. Well, I'll be, here it is. 'Qwerty: of or pertaining to the configuration of a set of keys on a typewriter or computer keyboard.'" Carter looked up, totally unabashed. "Fine," he said. "You get the points."

Patrick stood up. "You know, it's getting late. I think we're going to call it a night."

Elaine followed his lead. "It is late," she said. "Pam, thank you for a delicious dinner. Mark, have a good night, and we'll see you all tomorrow."

Carter looked indignantly down his nose as he watched them walk away. "Poor sports," he groaned to his son.

Corey looked at his father in utter disbelief. "You just don't get it, do you, Dad?" he said as he jumped up, also intent on leaving.

"Don't you dare say something like that and walk away from me!" Carter said.

"Okay, you want me to stay and tell you what's on my mind? You just bullied a sixteen-year-old! And you're absolutely furious that she was right." Corey took a deep breath. "Do you know, I really felt sorry for you when everyone was saying that you and Vince Shaw were one of a kind. But the truth is, you are. You hate those qualities in him that you see in yourself—the arrogance, the need for control, the self-importance. You relish conflict, and you take delight in other people's hatred and prejudices. You even treat Mom like one of your employees. For the life of me, Dad, I don't know how you can live with yourself."

Corey was as stunned as his father that, after so many years, he had finally found the courage to stand up to the man who had pushed him down ever since he was a young boy. Corey took in a deep breath and exhaled loudly. Speaking his mind felt great.

He looked over toward the trees. "Thanks again for such a nice dinner, Aunt Pam, Uncle Mark. Goodnight, guys," he said to them.

From the hammock, two arms waved in the air.

❧

Two hours later, Carter walked into their room on the second floor of the inn. Nancy was already in bed, engrossed in her latest romance novel. She looked up briefly from the page. "Where did you take off to so quickly?" she asked.

"I took a long walk through the orchard," Carter said, kicking off his shoes. "I needed some time to think."

"About tomorrow's show?" she asked, her nose still in her book. She knew her husband liked to talk about the show the night before, so she always found a way to open the door for him to do so.

"About a lot of things," he said before disappearing into the bathroom. A minute later, he came out brushing his teeth. "Am I that bad?"

Nancy looked up from her book. "What?"

He took the toothbrush out of this mouth. "Do you agree with what Corey said this evening?"

She was visibly stunned by the question, amazed that Carter had heard what Corey had said and amazed that Carter was asking her for her opinion. "I don't know."

"You must have some idea." His voice was harsh, impatient.

Nancy set her novel down on the nightstand. "I do, but you probably don't want to hear it."

"So you think Corey was right? You think Shaw and I are alike."

"I can't answer that. I don't know Shaw," she said softly. "I can only say what effect you have on me and our son."

"And that would be what, exactly?"

Years of regret and sadness came flooding to the surface. "You're a hard man to live with, Carter," she said as tears welled up in her eyes.

"Why are *you* crying? I'm the one being attacked."

"Because . . ." Her voice quavered. "I still love you enough not to want to see you get hurt. I don't want to add to your pain."

"*What pain?*" he huffed. "I'm the happiest man I know."

Feeling a chill run through her, Nancy pulled the quilt higher on her shoulders. "No, Carter, you're not. And everyone knows it but you." To her surprise, he didn't interrupt her. "You're one of the most creative, hardworking, stoic men I have ever met, and I know that underneath all the layers of pretense and conceit and defensiveness is a really good heart. But it's as if you live every moment of your life just to prove that you're better and richer and smarter than everyone else. But you're not—we're not." She paused for a long moment. "Did you ever wonder why we don't have any close friends?"

"How can you say that? We entertain every weekend," Carter argued.

"But those people aren't friends. They're work associates or politicians or strangers who are willing to put up with your antagonism because they want something from you." Instead of feeling exhilarated by finally sharing the truth with her husband, Nancy felt a profound and exhausting sadness. "Carter, who would you call if tragedy struck our lives? If you really needed someone to be by your side unconditionally."

He thought for a long moment. "You," he said softly, dropping his shoulders. "Only you."

"Doesn't that say enough to make you wonder?"

"But that has nothing to do with the quality of our lives."

She quickly replied, "It has *everything* to do with it. The richness of a man's life is determined by those who love him, not by the balance in a bank account . . . or by how many millions of people listen to him on the radio. Obviously, they don't mind the arrogance or your need to control, but . . ."

"You do," he said, finishing her sentence.

"I'm the least of your problems. You have a son out there who has wanted to look up to you his entire life."

"And I've never given him a reason, is that what you're saying?"

"You've never made it easy for him," she confessed, and then more softly added, "You never make it easy for anyone to care for you."

After the lights went out, Carter lay silently in bed, wondering how he had come to this juncture in his life and what road he would choose next.

FORTY-EIGHT

# Darkness

**Thursday**

It was around two in the morning when Carter finally fell asleep, but it was a light sleep, easily interrupted by the faintest of sounds. An hour later, several simultaneous soft-pitched beeps woke him. Turning in bed, he looked at the clock that he had glanced at numerous times earlier that night, but there were no digital blue numbers glowing from the timepiece. He grabbed his watch: three thirty-eight a.m. The night-light was off in the bathroom, and then he noticed that there was no secondary light coming in through the window from the porch lamps below.

Blackout.

"Wake up, Nancy," he said, shaking his wife's shoulder. "Wake up—we have a problem."

Nancy opened her eyes to pitch-blackness. "Carter?" she mumbled.

"I think the power went out," he said, sitting up in bed.

"Go back to sleep. It will come on in a few minutes."

Carter began fumbling in the dark, feeling his way to the chair on which he had left his shirt and pants the night before. "My show is on in a few hours. I need to tell Mark so he can start the generator."

"Assuming they have one," Nancy said in a more alert voice.

Carter got down on his hands and knees, patting the floor in search of his shoes. He felt as if time was flying by as he groped for his clothes in slow motion. "I've got to tell Mark," he repeated as he continued to play hide-and-seek with his right shoe.

When he was finally dressed and heading out the door into a black hallway, Nancy said, "Watch the stairs. I'll join you in a minute."

"Dad, is that you?" Corey's voice came from the direction of the third-floor landing.

"It's a blackout," Carter said. "Watch your step coming down, son."

Suddenly, a beam of light slashed through the darkness downstairs, but then it was gone. A few seconds later, another streak of light entered through the front door, illuminating the staircase just enough to help Carter see his way down the steps.

The front door opened slowly, and Mark peered in.

"Mark?" Carter called out.

"Yeah, it's me. Are all you guys awake?" Mark asked, entering the lobby.

"Nancy is, but I think the others might still be asleep."

"Our crazy clock beeps every time the power goes out," Mark said, rubbing his eyes.

"Do you have a generator?"

"We have two online twelve-kilowatt generators downstairs, but they should have tripped on within thirty seconds of the blackout." Mark grabbed a flashlight from behind the front desk and handed it to Carter. "I'll be back in a minute," he said before disappearing back outside.

Carter shone the light up the staircase. "Can you see all right?" he asked Corey, who had already made his way down to the second floor.

"Yeah, fine." He followed the flashlight's narrow beam down to the lobby. "I came down to see what I can do to help—your show goes on in a few hours."

As Carter stared at this young man, profound guilt washed over him. Here was his son, whom he had treated so badly for so long, standing before him offering to lend a hand. "I don't deserve to have you as a son," Carter confessed.

"That's okay, Dad," Corey said.

He noticed Corey was barefoot. "Why don't you take the flashlight and run upstairs and put a pair of sneakers on? I think we're going to have to go outside. And you can see if your mother is dressed—maybe escort her down."

"You bet," Corey said as he bounded up the staircase with the flashlight in hand.

When the lobby was pitch-black again, Carter crumpled over and sat down in the chair next to him. His head dropped into his hands, and he began to sob so deeply that he thought he would never stop. His heart was breaking from the realization of just how badly he had treated the people he loved, the few people who loved him back despite all of his flaws. He pushed his fist into his chest, wishing the pain would go away.

A few minutes later, a streak of light shot through the front windows and then disappeared. Carter wiped his eyes and jumped to his feet. Another beam crossed the living room from the outside. Carter heard someone on the front porch.

Mark walked into the lobby, keeping the flashlight aimed to the floor, which Carter was thankful for.

"We have a problem," Mark said, expecting Carter to go off the handle at any second.

"No generators?"

"Neither is on, and I can't figure out why," he explained. "Blackouts usually don't last for long—especially in fair weather—but I know you must be concerned about your show." Here it comes, Mark thought, bracing for Carter's attack.

But to his surprise, Carter's voice remained calm. "Do you have any ideas?"

Mark was astonished by Carter's civility in the face of a crisis. "This is when we call in the cavalry." Mark pulled his cell phone out and dialed a phone number that he knew by heart. "Hey, sorry to wake you. . . . You too? Do you know what the problem is?" Suddenly, the sounds of two fire trucks could be heard in the distance, approaching quickly. "Hold on." Within seconds, the trucks were passing in front of Montis Inn with sirens blasting. Mark peered out the window and then said, "They're heading south on Farm to Market Road. Probably someone hit the transformer box. . . . Could be a long wait. . . . Would you spread the word that *we need help?* Carter's show is on in a few hours. . . . That would be great."

Mark hung up and slipped the phone back in his pocket.

"So?" Carter asked. He recoiled, hearing the demanding, accusatory tone in his own voice.

"It's taken care of," Mark said, sitting down in the dark living room.

Carter stopped his impulse to jump all over Mark for not being better prepared and held his tongue. In fact, he went so far as to silently acknowledge that the situation was probably out of Mark's control.

Corey and Nancy, led by a beam of light, entered the living room and saw both men sitting on the sofa. "Aren't we going to do something?" Corey asked.

Mark shone the light at his watch. "In about three and a half minutes."

"So they're restoring the power?" Nancy concluded.

Mark dismissed that possibility with a wave of his hand. "Definitely not. If someone hit the transformer box down by Fork River, we might not have power all day."

"So what is Dad going to do?"

"Allow himself to be saved," Mark said, mystifying the other three.

A few minutes later, Pam opened the front door. “Everyone okay in there?” she asked.

“We’re fine, honey,” Mark said, sounding amazingly chipper given the situation.

“Jessica’s in with Patrick and Nancy,” she said. “A car’s coming—it’s slowing down.”

“I think that’s for us,” Mark said, leading the others to the porch. “Let’s go see how we’re going to get Carter some power.”

Just then, the headlights of a car strafed the inn as it pulled into thc parking lot. “We’re over here,” Pam called out to the driver, waving the flashlight.

Before Joshua and Brooke could get out of the car, a van pulled up beside them. And then, immediately after that, a pickup truck drove in and parked adjacent to the front porch, not far from where Pam was standing.

“What’s all this?” Carter asked.

“The cavalry to the rescue,” Mark replied with a grin.

Carter watched as another car pulled into the lot. “What are they going to do?”

Mark lifted his shoulders. “I have absolutely no idea.”

Joshua smiled as he jumped up on the porch. “We’ve got to stop meeting like this.”

Mark watched as another car turned off Farm to Market into the Montis parking lot. “How is it in town?” he asked Joshua and Brooke.

“Pitch-black,” Brooke replied.

“So what do you think?” Mark asked Joshua.

He shrugged. “I have absolutely no idea.”

“Hey, that’s exactly what I said!” Mark laughed.

Dennis opened up the back tailgate of his station wagon. “Gabrielle will be here in a few minutes. She insisted on bringing enough food to feed everyone.”

“Doesn’t anyone—” Carter began, but then he stopped midsentence. Here was his opportunity to prove that he could go past the judgment and the criticism that came so quickly to mind. "Does anyone need a hand?" he offered.

"I could use a few," a woman's voice called out in the dark.

"Mackenzie!" Pam said, clapping loudly.

Mackenzie McGuire stepped into the glow of several flashlights. She wore dark work overalls, and her wild red hair was tied up in a large barrette that sat high on her head. "You really need to pick a better time for these get-togethers," she said to Mark as she waved to her other friends.

"Everyone, this is Mac, our general contractor—she restored every inch of this inn," Mark said.

"And she's the best electrician in the state," Pam added. "Thanks for coming."

"When Joshua called and told me that Lumby on the Air couldn't go on the air without some help, I figured it was the least I could do," Mac said.

"So you're a fan?" Carter asked.

"No, sir, I can't say I am," Mac said as she tightened the shoulder strap of her overalls. "Actually, I don't think I've ever heard your show."

Carter looked puzzled. "Then why are you here?"

"To help out our friends, of course," she said as she opened the back of the van. "So, Mark, what on earth did you do to those generators I installed for you?" she teased.

"Why do you always assume I was involved?" he asked, asserting his innocence. "They just seemed to crap out."

"Ah," she said slowly. "They just *crapped out*. Would that be before or after you had the propane tank filled when Dakin serviced them after the big storm last month?"

Mark moaned, scratching his head.

"Mark?" Pam asked.

"Well, honey," he said, looking as boyishly angelic as possible, "Dakin came out and . . . ohhh," he said, drawing out the word as he remembered what had happened the month before. "Dakin needed a part, and I was supposed to have called him with a credit card number."

"Which, I'm guessing, you forgot to do?" Mac asked.

"Maybe yes," he mumbled.

"Mar—" Carter began, but again he paused. Take the other road, he reminded himself. "I've done the exact same thing, Mark." Carter's reaction was so contrary to his character that for a moment, all eyes focused on the shock jock. "Well, I have," he said.

Jimmy D was standing next to Dennis by his truck. "What do we do, Mac?" he asked.

She thought through her options. "How much time do we have?"

Corey was the first to answer. "About two hours."

"Okay, then," Mac said. "We shouldn't waste any time trying to bring up the online generators. I have two five-thousand-watt Briggs and Stratons in the back of the van that I just picked up for repair. They'll have to be jury-rigged, but we should be able to get something running before then. I suppose you wouldn't have any LP in your reserve tank either, Mark?"

"Probably not," he said sheepishly.

She put her arm around Mark's neck. "Boy, I've missed working with you. It's always so . . . unpredictable at Montis."

Mark perked up. "Yeah, but isn't that the fun part?"

"Dennis," Mac said, "would you get Fred on the line and tell him we'll need a twenty-gallon LP tank?"

"Will do," Dennis said as he started dialing his cell phone.

"Also call Brad and let him know what we're doing down here. He may have to open up the hardware store if we don't have everything we need."

Carter watched in stunned amazement as the troops rallied together to help him. No, not to help *him,* he corrected himself, but to help Pam and Mark. He was just the fortunate recipient of everyone's goodwill.

"Come on, guys," Jimmy said, waving to the men on the porch. "We have some lifting to do."

Twenty minutes later, the group at Montis had grown to well over thirty Lumby friends and residents who had heard that Pam and Mark were in need of help. Gabrielle had already delivered two dozen breakfast burritos and three large urns of coffee before heading back to her restaurant for replenishments.

Mac lay on the porch with her hands deep inside the electrical panel of one of the generators. Mark was on the ground next to her, holding a flashlight on the work area. Several others stood overhead shining more light on the panel.

"Would someone grab another spool of sixteen-gauge copper wire out of my van?" Mac said.

"I'll get it," Pam volunteered.

"How does it look?" Mark asked.

"About the same as it did when you asked me two minutes ago," Mac said.

"By the way, thanks for coming," Mark said to Mac. "This is really important to Carter."

"If it's important to one of your friends, then it's important to all of us. But it would go much faster if you stopped shaking your flashlight." She laughed.

Carter, who normally would have been pacing as close as possible to the center of the action, sat in a dark corner of the porch. Corey noticed how uncharacteristically quiet his father was being.

"I wouldn't worry, Dad," he said, taking a seat on the railing next to him. "I think they'll get it going,"

"I'm sure they will," he said as he watched three other men begin to work on the second generator.

"Mac, how many lines will you need running from the house?" an older fellow asked.

"As many as you can round up," she answered. "At least a half dozen, and make them all heavy-duty exterior grade."

"There are two extension cords in the basement," Mark called out.

"I've got one in the truck," Dennis added.

Another two cars pulled up just as one was leaving. The level of community commitment was like nothing Carter had ever seen.

“So why aren’t you—” Corey balked.

“Going berserk?” Carter offered.

Corey wanted a second chance to ask the question. “Why are you so quiet?”

Carter looked at his son, who had become a man without his noticing. “I’m just remembering a few lessons I had forgotten along the way, son.”

Within an hour, both generators were humming, and with numerous extension cords donated by the townsfolk, Carter’s equipment was up and running well before airtime.

FORTY-NINE

# *Introduction*

*"Good morning, America! Welcome back to* The Carter Reed Show, *the only on-air forum that impartially pits ideology against ideology, idiocy against . . ."*

Suddenly, Carter stopped midway through the introduction that he had used every weekday for the last four years. Kano and Worm, who had both slept through the events of the preceding hours, looked up at their boss. The famous radio shock jock appeared exhausted.

Kano waved his hand in a circular motion. "We're on the air," he said into Carter's headset. Carter rubbed his face and pressed his fingers against his forehead. "Dead air," Kano reminded him again. "Cut to a news feed?"

Carter glanced at Kano and shook his head. Leaning across the table, he pulled the microphone closer to his mouth.

*"Good morning, America. Welcome back to* The Carter Reed Show.*"*

A different tone resonated over the airwaves. It was so unlike Carter's normal bombastic voice that many of his listeners didn't recognize him at first.

*"Today is July nineteenth, and thanks to many generous folks from around the area, we continue to broadcast live from Lumby. Before*

*another word is spoken, I would like to extend my deepest and most sincere appreciation to all the people who came to our rescue early this morning. When faced with an unexpected power outage that would have canceled this show, the residents of Lumby collectively stepped forward in a fashion that I have never experienced firsthand. It was one of the most affirming efforts I have ever seen. Thank you, one and all. So, to say the least, it's been an unexpected week, and it just keeps getting more interesting as the hours pass. But first, let's once again turn to the most recent issue of* The Lumby Lines *and see what the town citizens write in their open forum.*

The Lumby Lines

# Lumby Forum

July 19

---

For trade: Goat that just won sixth place in open youth judging, for any dairy cow who won anything better than fourth place. Call Michelle 925-4468.

---

SWM looking for lady to take on Ferris wheel ride. Pockets are bulging with unused tickets. Let me be your co-pilot. Phil 925-3928

---

Looking for female to breed with my Holland Lops rabbit. Has outstanding bloodlines from Wardlow and Naragon and just took Best of Show at the fair. 925-9113. Charlie or talk to my mom if I'm not home.

---

Price Correction: Dickenson's fresh lobster has been reduced from $1200 a pound as advertised in their circular to $12 a pound.

---

All 4-H members are requested to be at the judge's tent at 2:00 tomorrow for a club photograph. Please wear clean clothes.

---

I have been blessed with an abundant garden this summer and have more vegetables than I can possibly eat. Please come by and help yourself to carrots, radishes, cucs and any and all berries. Can deliver if need be. Rachael Royce at 1 Killdrop Road.

*"I'd like to step back for a minute and share a story with all of you faithful ideos. As some of you will remember, Rachael of Lumby called the show yesterday morning and was . . . distressed by the news that the real estate magnate, Vince Shaw, had earmarked property adjacent to her own for a major commercial development—a ski resort, planned community and transformed town that, I have since learned, would be named Shaw Ridge.*

*"Although I have taken no position on Vince Shaw or his development plans—other than to say that if no law is broken, he should be free to do as he pleases—several of our callers postulated that in the absence of condemnation, by default I was supporting Shaw's activities.*

*"That, in itself, is an interesting premise which we'll be returning to in a few minutes. But I took Rachael up on her suggestion and made the necessary arrangements to see the property firsthand. At Rachael's family cemetery, she and I unexpectedly crossed paths. In fact, we talked for more than an hour, or, more accurately, she spoke and I listened.*

*"And then I got it, or part of it. What I initially saw as significant differences between us—Rachael has never been to the big city, and I rarely step out of one—became irrelevant when I realized that she and I wrestled with the same problems and embraced the same joys in life. So, from that encounter, I need to correct a few misconceptions*

*I spoke on the air and say that, from what I've recently seen, a small town can, in fact, uniquely define the lives of its residents. There does seem to be greater personal accountability because there's no chance for the anonymity that is available in the city.*

*"This effectively segues to another philosophy that we have held near and dear to our heart on this show: the benefit of arguing polarized extremes. Perhaps it's time we reevaluate that as well. We've run with the premise that conflict and debate uncover truth, and that dissonance strengthens one's beliefs. But to what extent should this antagonism be taken? I have always said, give me two disparate opinions and I'll moderate the battle to the bitter end."*

Worm and Kano looked at each other in disbelief. Had their boss gone over the deep end?

*"But very recently, someone whom I respect a great deal has challenged not only the value of such discourse but also my role in it. So this morning's opening segment will be just that—a solicitation of opinions, in agreement or disagreement, as to the worth of seeking discord.*

*"Our lines are now open, and Kano is on task to accept your opinions. But first, a news break."*

"You're off," Kano said. "A little crazy this morning, but definitely off."

"Just an experiment, gentlemen," Carter assured his engineers, trying to disguise his own vacillation. "This might give us a nice bump in the ratings."

"You're not for real?" Worm asked.

Carter glanced over at Worm and pushed his glasses up on his nose. "Am I ever for real?" he asked rhetorically before burying his head in the paper until the news break was over.

*"You're back with Carter Reed and Lumby on the Air. We have Laura from Atlanta on line one. Laura, welcome and ideo at will."*

*"Thanks for taking my call, Carter. Hi, Kano. Hi, Worm. This is the first time I've called because I never felt inclined to jump in the water with your sharks. But this morning you seemed to open a door to peo-*

*ple like me. Sorry I'm rambling. I'm really nervous. I don't know what the right answer is because you're partly right: hearing dissenting views keeps our minds open and challenges us. That's why I've been listening to you for the last three years. But you allow facts to be thrown out the window and arguments to turn malicious. This shouldn't be about the person but about the idea. Does that make sense?"*

*"It certainly does, Laura. All right then, moving to Adele from Wichita on line one. Ideo at will."*

There were several seconds of dead air.

*"Ideo at will, Adele."*

*"Am I on?"*

*"Yes, you are."*

*"Oh, okay. I'm also a first-time caller."*

There were several more seconds of dead air.

*"We need to move along, Adele."*

*"Oh, okay. Sorry. I know you're not at all religious, but I'm sure God is looking down upon you and smiling. It is said in Matthew five nine, 'Blessed are the peacemakers for they shall be called the children of God.' And you, Mr. Reed, are a beloved and blessed child of God. Listen to your heart and you will follow His word and delight in His way."*

*"Interesting, Adele. Thanks for the call. Stay tuned for more of* The Carter Reed Show. *We'll be back in two minutes."*

"And . . . you're off the air," Kano said, and then he caught Carter's steely stare. "*What?* You told me not to screen the calls."

"So now we're going to be flooded by every religious zealot out there."

Worm, raised his hand. "Wait a minute," he said.

"What is it?" Carter asked.

Worm scanned his computer screen, reading the real-time rating numbers as quickly as they were coming up. "They love it."

"Really?" Carter asked.

"Your numbers just jumped. Looks like your show has gone viral in the last six minutes."

"But that's just a knee-jerk reaction. More people want to hear unscreened callers—they're waiting for that train wreck," Kano said.

Carter leaned back in his chair. "At least they're still on the other end listening."

*"Welcome back to the Carter Reed edition of Lumby on the Air. For those who are just joining us, we are examining the value of verbal opposition. Several ideos quickly voiced their opinion that consensus and accord are stronger than dissent. So we'd certainly like to hear from the other side. Frank, from my hometown of Seattle, is on line one to start us out. Ideo at will, Frank."*

*"You're a very clever man, Carter. The questions you pose are basically unanswerable without argument. Instead of asking, Do you beat your wife, you ask, Have you stopped beating your wife yet? You began this morning with a seemingly noble desire to move away from dispute, yet you stepped back into the septic tank by polarizing that very topic: Should we be polarized in our opinion? Yes or no, duke it out. I'm disappointed, to say the least."*

"Do you want me to kill the call?" Kano asked through Carter's headset.

Carter held up his hand and shook his head.

*"So you're saying it's an oxymoron in some sense? Let's have a debate about debates without debating? It could be a no-win or a solution to all of our problems."*

*"Like everything else, it's all in how you look at the world, isn't it?"*

*"I suppose it is."*

Carter glanced over at Kano who, after all their years of working together, knew what Carter wanted.

"We're cutting to news in three, two, one . . . and you're off."

Carter laid down his headset and ran his fingers through his hair.

"You okay, boss?" Worm asked.

"I'm exhausted," he said, "I'm just exhausted."

FIFTY

# *Rung*

Brother Matthew turned the monastery's van into the parking lot at Montis Inn just as the car's clock read eight thirty. He stepped out from behind the wheel and stretched. The buzz of a chainsaw could be heard in the background.

"This should take just a few minutes," he told Sister Claire, who was getting out of the passenger seat.

"Do you want me to come with you?" she asked.

"Most definitely," he said. "Pam and Mark will be delighted to see you."

Pam, who had been waiting for them, leaned out the front door and waved to them. "Mark and Joshua are down at the barn. Would you please ring the bell?"

Matthew waved as he headed across the main porch. Other than having a new rope, the old, iron-cast bell hadn't changed since the monks had used it during the eighty years they'd lived at Montis Abbey. Matthew pulled the rope three times, and a resonating ring sounded out across the property.

Within seconds, Carter Reed stormed out the front door. "What are you doing!?" he barked before seeing the monk.

Brother Matthew froze with the rope still in his hand. "I'm very sorry," he said.

"Oh." Carter cringed in embarrassment. "Sorry about that, but we're broadcasting live inside," he said, stumbling over his words. "I thought it was one of the kids, but obviously you're not."

Matthew looked down at his long black robe. "No, just at heart," he said with a smile. "We met last Sunday. I'm Brother Matthew."

"Carter Reed," he said, shaking the monk's hand.

"Yes, I remember. Thank you for your substantial donation."

Carter always had an arrogant, if not condescending response at the ready for such an occasion, but this time he stopped before the words were said. "You're welcome. It was an honor. Would you like to come in? We have another two minutes of news, and then we're back on the air."

"Is yours a religious show?" Matthew asked.

Carter laughed. "No, I wouldn't quite call it that."

"Unfortunately, we need to meet with Pam and Mark. Perhaps we'll listen tomorrow," Matthew offered.

"I hope you do," Carter said politely before disappearing inside.

Pam was holding the kitchen door open for Matthew. "Thanks for taking time out of your busy schedule to come by and talk about the ceremony," she said.

Matthew laughed. "Just between us, our *busy* schedule has us at the fair today. We had to see a parishioner in Wheatley, so this was a very convenient stop," he said.

"Please sit down," she said, placing several mugs on the table. "Mark and Joshua should be up in a minute. They're practicing for this afternoon."

"Should I ask?" Matthew asked cautiously.

Pam rolled her eyes. "Chainsaw sculpting."

Matthew laughed loudly. "Really? And he'll be in one piece for Saturday's ceremony?"

"Between that and the bull competition tomorrow, I seriously wonder," she said.

Mark hurried through the door, scattering sawdust all over. "The groom has arrived," he joked, holding out his arms.

"Looking filthier than ever," Pam observed. "Would you please go outside and brush off your clothes?"

Mark disappeared, then reappeared a minute later, grinning in excitement, Joshua close behind him. "Are you going up to the fair?"

"We're on our way there," Claire said.

"Okay, if you're available, you might want to go to tent six at two-thirty," he suggested. "I'll be sawing a bald eagle out of a huge piece of oak."

"Believe me, I wouldn't miss it for the world," Matthew said, chuckling.

Pam spread a diagram on the table. "We don't want to take up too much of your time, just long enough to finalize our plans for renewing our vows," she said. "We're expecting about sixty guests, and this is how we thought we would arrange the chairs."

Matthew and Claire studied the sketch of the backyard. "That looks charming," Claire said.

"Is there anything else we need to do?" Pam asked.

"You mentioned that you want to recite your own vows?" Matthew said.

Pam and Mark looked at each other and, in unexpected unison, said, "We do."

"We're each going to write our own," Mark said proudly.

Matthew nodded. "Very good. At the beginning of the ceremony, I'll request that the two of you come forward."

"We were hoping Joshua and Brooke would stand with us as best man and woman," Pam said, winking at Joshua.

Matthew smiled. "That would be fine."

"We're going to have a wind and string quintet there, and were hoping they would play during the procession. Is that all right?" Mark asked.

"Most definitely. Keep in mind that this is your celebration of marriage, so there are no hard-and-fast rules that you need to follow. I'll then speak for a few minutes about the two of you, the strength of your love, the commitment of your faith and the life you have built here."

"You have to mention Montis," Mark said.

"I will," Matthew assured him. "You'll then recite your vows. When you're done, I will bless the marriage and then introduce you to your guests."

"And then we party." Mark beamed. "This will be great, honey."

"Thank you so much," Pam said to Matthew and Sister Claire. "We hope everyone in your community joins us. I think most will be arriving at about seven."

"We're looking forward to it," Claire said, getting up from her seat. "Joshua, if you have a minute, could we talk about the berries?"

Joshua looked surprised. "Is something wrong? I thought I had another few days to find a solution."

Claire put her arm through his as they walked out the front door. "We have a proposal."

"Mark," Pam said, "I need to talk with Brother Matthew . . . alone."

Mark raised his brows. "What about?"

"It doesn't involve you, so why don't you go out and help Joshua," she said, pushing him toward the door.

"I thought you said everything we do involves each other?" Mark said.

"It does, except for this. Now go," she insisted.

When Mark was out of earshot, Pam turned to Matthew. "I need your help, but you must promise not to tell anyone."

Outside, Mark joined Claire and Joshua in the courtyard. "I think my wife just kicked me out of the house."

"She finally wised up," Joshua teased.

Mark grabbed Joshua around the neck and pretended to strangle him. "And you're supposed to be my best man."

"I need to talk with Sister Claire . . . alone," Joshua said. "Why don't you go back to the barn and keep Lynn company."

"What are you guys talking about?" Mark asked.

"Will you just leave?" Joshua said, nudging his shoulder.

"I can't believe this," Mark said, sounding insulted. "Now I'm being kicked out of my own courtyard."

"I'll be down in a few minutes," Joshua said before turning to Claire. "What can I do for you?"

"In truth, you've put us in a difficult position."

"*I* have?"

Claire grinned. "All right, perhaps not you. But you did show us that we may have a larger responsibility regarding the berries."

Joshua nodded. "I think you do."

"Several of the sisters agree with you," Claire explained. "In fact, to bury the berries or not to bury the berries has been the topic of heated discussion during our meals for the last several days."

"And is there a consensus?"

"Unfortunately, no. In fact, the more we debate the issue, the more . . . polarized and opinionated everyone is becoming."

"So much for 'The meek will inherit the land and enjoy great peace,'" Joshua said.

Claire smiled. "Psalm thirty-seven, verse eleven." She patted Joshua's arm. "Matthew told me many times that you would have made a good monk."

"Don't believe everything he says." Joshua winked at her.

"Certainly not!" she teased. "But yes, the berries have become our bushes of contention, you might say. As you can imagine, Sister Kristina and the others who are planting the vineyard want to bulldoze this afternoon."

"And Megan wants to wait?"

"She knows that any delay by more than a week or so will impact our schedule, but she presented a strong case for pursuing what many see as the environmentally responsible course of action."

"Taking the greener high road?" Joshua asked.

"After hearing the difference of opinions for several days, I became concerned that the disagreement was beginning to take on a life of its own. Those who initially cared very little about the decision began to take sides. Anyway, if these berries—"

"And ants," he reminded her.

"—and ants"—she nodded—"are the last of their kind and just happen to be on our property, then we do have an obligation to do what's right."

"I agree," he said.

"However, we can wait only so long before our production plans are seriously impacted. We have agreed to postpone the shipment of the remaining vines from Oregon until mid-September. That will give you eight weeks to figure out who wants them and where they will go."

"I guarantee they will be transplanted before then," Joshua promised. But even as he spoke, he had no idea how he would keep that promise.

FIFTY-ONE

# Lemonade

When the bells of the Presbyterian Church rang at noon, Carter had already been at the Chatham County Fair for an hour, sitting on the top row of the bleachers, silently watching and reevaluating some of his long-standing assumptions about life.

It wasn't the antique tractor pull that had compelled him to come alone to the fair after his show went off the air that morning. Nor was it the dairy goat class of the 4-H youth show or even the pig races, although Mark had repeatedly suggested that Carter not miss that specific highlight of the day's events.

"Mr. Reed," a lady called up from directly in front of the bleachers.

Carter squinted at the woman for a moment and then politely waved back. "Hello," he said, not wanting to start a conversation.

She stepped up on the bottom row. "Rachael Royce," she offered, assuming that he had forgotten her name from when they'd met at the cemetery the day before.

"Yes, Rachael, hello," he said, remaining seated.

"May I buy you a glass of lemonade?" she asked.

Carter noticed those who were sitting in close proximity were looking between the two of them. No anonymity, he thought. He struggled to find a polite way out of a insignificant social invitation, feeling the spectators' gazes settle on him as they all waited for an answer.

"Brigit's lemonade is delicious," commented a woman seated close to him.

Carter knew he was being dragged into something he wasn't ready for. "But be sure you add a touch of sugar," the woman's male companion, probably her husband, added. "She keeps it tart for Harvey."

Not getting a reply, Rachael stepped off the bleachers. "Perhaps another time," she said graciously.

"No," Carter said, feeling some pressure. "Lemonade would be very nice."

"Watch out for that third step," said another man sitting next to the hand railing. "The bolt needs tightening, and Jimmy lost the screwdriver that Hannah bought him at Brad's Hardware last month."

"Did Brad have those during his Fourth of July sale?" his companion asked.

"He shared a shipment with Sam's Feed Store but marked them down eighty percent," the woman replied.

By the time the screwdriver discussion was over, Carter was standing next to Rachael.

"It's good to see you again, Mr. Reed," she said, shaking his hand.

"Please call me Carter," he said. "So where is the lemonade stand?"

"Next to the fire department's stand. This way." She led him away from the tractor arena. "So what do you think about our small fair?"

Carter searched for the right word. "Educational."

She nodded in understanding. "Isn't that true. You can't learn too much about milking a cow or plucking a chicken, can you?"

Carter couldn't help but smile. "No, I suppose you can't."

As they crossed the first walkway, a man in his thirties caught Rachael by the arm. "We'll be coming by tomorrow morning at seven," he said.

Rachael stepped back, evidently surprised. "For breakfast?"

"No." The man laughed. "We're going to work on your cemetery. Those tombstones are too heavy for you to lift, and Brad said your lawnmower has just about seen its last days. And it's got to be too heavy for you to push anyway."

Rachael gazed at the man as if he were a saint. "I couldn't impose like that, especially with everyone so busy with the fair."

"How can it be an imposition when it was our idea? We've been talking about it at the station for weeks. We just feel bad that it's taken us most of the summer to get over to your place," he said kindly.

"Are you sure?" she asked.

"Absolutely. We've been turning folks away who want to help."

She lovingly brushed some dirt off the man's chin. "What would I do without all of you?" she asked rhetorically. "All right, I'll have fresh coffee waiting."

"No need to. Gabrielle wants to serve a full breakfast while we work," he said as he walked away. "See you tomorrow."

Carter noticed tears in her eyes. "Thank you so much," she whispered.

"Your son?" Carter asked.

"Oh, no. Dale works in our police department. He's just a neighbor."

"I see," Carter said. "He lives on Killdrop Road."

She continued watching Dale as he greeted another friend. "No, he lives on the other side of town, about five miles away," she explained. "When my husband died in a mill accident two years ago, the men in town took me under their wing. They feel they can never do enough, and I think they do too much. That's always the way, isn't it?"

Very seldom if ever, Carter thought to himself.

There was no line at the lemonade booth. "Two small lemonades, Brigit," Rachael said, taking out a small coin purse.

"Let me pay for that," Carter said.

"I wouldn't hear of it," she said, placing several quarters and dimes on the countertop. Rachael caught the eye of a young girl with long blond braids sitting on a stool behind her mother. It was obvious that the girl had been crying. "Hi, Annie."

"Hi, Mrs. Royce," the girl said in a soft soprano voice.

"Is she feeling better?" Rachael whispered to Brigit.

Brigit studied her daughter. "Not yet, but she will. She was just really disappointed."

"Annie?" Rachael said. "I thought your rabbit looked terrific. In fact, if I had been the judge, I would have given you a blue ribbon."

The girl's expression perked up. "Really?"

"Really."

"I have a rooster to show this afternoon at three," Annie said.

"And I'll be there cheering for you," Rachael said. "Just do the best you can." She handed Carter his lemonade. "You may want to add a bit of sugar."

"So I heard."

---

The loudspeaker crackled. "The chainsaw sculpting competition will begin in ten minutes."

"Okay, that's us," Mark said, heaving his equipment from the back of th Jeep. "Jeez, I had forgotten how heavy this thing is."

"You should have used it during your practice runs," Joshua said.

Pam looked perplexed. "What have you been using for the last week?"

"The little electric one down in the barn," Mark replied.

Pam laughed. "But that weighs two pounds, and this one has got to weigh fifteen."

"Twenty-one," Joshua corrected her.

"I wanted to get the feel of the wood," Mark explained. "Did you find out how many people signed up for the event?"

"Two—you and Jeremiah," Joshua answered.

"Okay, that's good," Mark said. "That will give me more space to help him."

A realization came to Pam. "Is that why you signed up for this insane event?" she asked.

"Yeah," Mark said, "but don't tell anyone. It's probably Jeremiah's last year, and his sight is pretty bad."

"That's sweet of you, honey," she said, kissing his cheek. "Just be careful."

As they approached the tent, they saw Hank leaning against the back bumper of the ambulance, talking with the other EMS volunteers. He wore blue disposable surgical garb, and a mask was draped around his neck that could be pulled over his beak and tied in an instant.

Jeremiah led his mare to the ring. "Mark Walker, is that you?" he asked, looking in the general direction of the voices he heard.

"It is—ready, willing and able," Mark said, jogging up to Jeremiah and patting his friend on the back. "Are you ready?"

"As ready as I'll ever be at my age," he said, handing Isabella's reins to Mark before removing his chainsaw from a satchel tied to his horse's saddle. "Good girl," the old man whispered, patting his mare's mane.

"I have your number," Mark said, slipping the numbered armband up the old man's sleeve.

"Are we the only entries this year?"

"That's it—numbers 608 and 609," he answered. "So it's a pretty good bet we'll each get a ribbon."

Jeremiah laughed warmheartedly. "You're a fine man, Mark Walker, but it would be a good bet that Isabella would get a medal if it were just you and she in the ring."

Mark scoffed. "You just wait, my friend. I've been practicing exactly like you told me to."

"Contestants only into the ring," Sal Gentile called out. "All others must stand behind the ropes and are not allowed into the sawing area at any time during the competition."

"Okay, let's go," Mark said, hoisting the chainsaw onto his shoulder. "Ow," he cried out when the blade hit his skin.

On the other side of the ring, Brother Matthew walked up to Pam. "Should we pray?" he asked jokingly.

She watched her husband with great pride. "You can, but I really think Mark's going to be okay in there."

"Number 608, Jeremiah Abrams. Number 609, Mark Walker," Sal said, and then began to read from the book of regulations. "You are each given a block of solid oak that measures no less than three feet in height, width and depth; that is secured to an equivalent-size block; and that is at least three feet off the ground. You will have eight minutes to carve an object of your choice using only one chainsaw of your choice. The sculptures will be judged on the following criteria: use of negative space, use of positive space, use of the wood grain, representation of sculpting skill, originality and creativity, likeness to subject matter, and amount of detail."

"The details," Mark whispered to Jeremiah. "That's where I did great in the barn."

The old man laughed. "I'm sure you got one of those eagle feathers down pat."

Sal continued. "The first-place cash award is sponsored this year by Lumby Sporting Goods. Are there any questions?" Sal paused. "Contestants, are you ready?"

Mark helped Jeremiah don his gloves and goggles and then positioned him two feet in front of the cutting area.

"Can you see that?" Mark asked.

"If it's a big block of wood, then I'm good to go."

Mark scrambled to put on his own gloves and goggles. He then nodded at Sal.

"Start your motors."

Mark pulled the ignition rope of his chainsaw several times, but nothing happened. He turned to Joshua and shrugged. "Turn off the safety," Jeremiah whispered to him. Mark looked at his machine and did as he was told. The chainsaw started up instantly.

Sal looked at the stopwatch. "If you gentlemen are ready." He paused before counting down. "Three, two, one, start."

Mark revved up the engine, lifted it over his head and brought the chainsaw down in the middle of the block. Unfortunately, the blade hit a large vein in the wood and broke off the top half of the left side in one solid chunk.

Mark looked at it in disbelief. "That was where the eagle's head was supposed to be," he called to Joshua, trying to be heard over the roar of the motors.

"Do something easier, like a bear," Joshua called back.

Mark glanced over at Jeremiah. Through the wood shavings that were flying everywhere, Mark could tell, even at this early stage, that Jeremiah was sculpting a moose.

"How on earth can he do that? He's as blind as a bat," he said in awe.

"Time's ticking," Joshua reminded him.

"Okay, I'll do a ferocious bear, just like my slippers. Grrr," he growled as he put the chainsaw blade to the wood.

Eight minutes later, Sal blew the bullhorn and Mark turned off his motor. Jeremiah, who had finished a minute earlier, had already put away his chainsaw and was standing next to his statue.

Mark ripped off his goggles and gawked in disbelief at Jeremiah's entry. It was, bar none, the most extraordinary wood carving of a moose he had ever seen. The animal was perfectly proportioned and had a full set of enormous antlers projecting out from either side of the moose's flawlessly sculpted head. One could see that the moose was grazing in a marsh because Jeremiah had even carved several cattails next to the animal's hindquarters.

Sal shook his head as he inspected the sculpture. "Astounding" was all he said before moving over to Mark's carving. Sal narrowed his eyes and tilted his head, trying to determine what the curved mound of wood was supposed to be. "A turtle?" he asked.

Mark slung the chainsaw onto his shoulder. "Not just any turtle—a *snapping* turtle," he replied with complete conviction.

"Where is its head?"

Mark looked down at his feet where the turtle's head had fallen when he'd accidently cut it off. "Inside his shell," he said.

Sal stood back and reexamined both pieces. "A close competition, but this year, first place goes once again to Jeremiah Abrams, with an honorable mention for Mark Walker."

"*Honorable mention?*" Mark looked crushed. "Don't I get a second-place ribbon?"

"When there are three contestants or fewer, this event only awards first placc," Sal explained, giving a long blue ribbon with a large rosette to Jeremiah.

"Honorable mention?" Mark repeated in dismay.

"You certainly deserve more than that, Mark," Jeremiah said.

"Can you see my turtle?"

"I'm not talking about your carving. I'm talking about your friendship," Jeremiah said, holding the blue ribbon up to Mark's chest. "Take this as my thank-you."

"Wow," he said, turning to his wife. "Look, honey."

"A fine effort," Matthew said, shaking his hand.

Joshua took the chainsaw away from Mark before he hurt himself. "And you still have a shot at another blue ribbon," he reminded his friend.

"What's that?" Matthew asked.

Mark's face lit up. "Old Jesse and the obstacle course."

∽

A half hour later, Mark and Pam were forty feet above the town of Lumby, swinging gently in a basket on the Ferris wheel. "I was very proud of you today," Pam said, nestling closer to her husband.

"Don't tell anyone this," he said, "but I'm glad Jeremiah won. I didn't throw the competition or anything, but I made sure that he would get first prize. He can really use the money."

Pam chuckled. "That was very noble of you."

Mark wrapped his arm tightly around her. "It's nice to finally be alone together. It's been pretty nuts the last couple days."

Pam smiled. "That it has, in more ways than you could guess."

"Have you enjoyed any of it?"

Pam thought before answering. "More than I thought I would . . . primarily because you're right in the middle of all the craziness," she said. "I love you for being so nice to my mom and Robert."

"And I love you for tolerating my crazy relatives," he said, kissing her lightly.

"Speaking of your crazy relatives, what's Carter doing down there?"

Mark followed Pam's gaze. "He's talking to Joan Stokes. Wow, every time we come up here, we see them."

Pam thought about Carter for a moment. "Do you think there's something wrong with him?" she asked.

Mark watched the two from high above the fairground. "All I noticed is that he didn't go bonkers about the power outage. Is that what you mean?"

"That and how he sounded on the air today."

Mark shrugged. "We were all up at three this morning. Maybe he's just exhausted."

FIFTY-TWO

# Marley

After spending ten minutes rifling through her parent's room in search of her laptop, Jessica gave up in frustration and switched to her alternate plan. As she ran across the courtyard to Pam and Mark's house, she wasn't afraid of being seen since she knew all of the adults would be at the fair for several more hours.

She feigned knocking on the front door before turning the knob and breathing a sigh of relief to find it unlocked. She stuck her head in and called out, "Anyone here?"

When she was sure the coast was clear, Jessica slid into the room and quickly shut the door behind her. It took her only another minute to find Pam's computer, which she booted up.

Jumping into the chat room, she let her fingers dance over the keyboard.

flyman1964: hey abt2party

abt2party: hey everyone

marley3823: didn't think you were going to be online

abt2party: had to use my aunt's computer

marley3823: you coming 2night?

abt2party: yeah. when?

marley3823: six or seven

abt2party: isn't that 2 early?

marley3823: the sooner we start . . .

abt2party: the sooner we party. i'll be hitching down so i don't know how long it will take me

marley3823: watch out for howard along farm2m road. nasty temper with horns

abt2party: howard? is he a truck driver or something?

marley3823: he's a moose

abt2party: sounds like my last boyfriend but he was more of a neanderthal

marley3823: howard is a moose

abt2party: got it...a real neanderthal weirdo, huh?

marley3823: no a MOOSE

abt2party: ok I won't let him drive me anywhere. g2g cu soon

Jessica closed out all the windows and then ran a program to erase her "footprint" from Pam's computer. She carefully slid the chair back under the table just as it had been when she walked in.

The idea of leaving Lumby and finding the party on her own was unnerving, but this was exactly what cool kids did, and it would give her great material for her next blog post. As she walked through the Walkers' kitchen, she opened the door of the refrigerator and pilfered four bottles of Heineken to fill in any courage she lacked.

When Jessica reemerged from her bedroom in the guest annex at six thirty, she was dressed with the intention of getting a free ride down to Wheatley and turning the head of Marley and any other guys she might meet at the blowout. Wearing more dramatic makeup than usual and a short black stretch dress with black leggings, Jessica looked more like twenty-six than sixteen.

Walking toward Farm to Market Road, she stopped to check her lipstick in a small compact she had in her purse. "Wow," someone said from the front porch.

Jessica jumped.

Corey, who had been sitting on a bench, bounded down the stairs two at a time.

"You scared the crap out of me!" Jessica wailed. "Why aren't you at the fair?"

"I was too tired from being up all night, and I just wanted to decompress and catch up on some reading."

"You're quite the partier, Corey Reed," she said sarcastically.

"You don't even look like you," Corey said, staring her up and down.

"Is that supposed to be a compliment?"

"Not really," he said. "You look older than I do."

She rolled her eyes. "No offense, but that's not that hard. You're a geek."

"Should I assume you're not going to the orchard to pick apples?"

Jessica nodded. "I'm finally getting out of here and having some fun."

“In Lumby?” he asked.

“No way,” she said, fluffing up her short hair. “I’m meeting a friend in Wheatley.”

Corey’s brows scrunched together, and he looked at her suspiciously. “Since when do you know someone down there?”

“You ask too many questions,” she said. She looked over and saw several cars parked at the inn. “Can you give me a lift?”

“Sorry, my dad took his car,” Corey said.

Jessica shot him a sinister look. “You can use my parents’ Volvo—they drove into Lumby with Pam and Mark.”

“Absolutely not,” he said.

She shrugged one bare shoulder. “Fine, but if I get hurt hitching a ride, it will be your fault,” she taunted him. “I’ve heard there’s a pervert named Howard who drives in between Lumby and Wheatley. Maybe he’ll pick me up.”

“You’re not serious,” he said. “You’re really thumbing a ride?”

“You bet,” she said, hiking up her dress and walking toward the street.

Corey shook his head. “Okay, okay. I’ll drive you,” he conceded.

Jessica ran back and gave him a wet kiss on the cheek. “I knew you would. I’ll get my dad’s keys.”

Driving along East City Road in Wheatley, Corey rolled down his window. “This is a really nice neighborhood, Jess,” he said, admiring the large estates set back on well-manicured lawns.

“It should be coming up on the right—there’s number fifteen,” she said, pointing to a mailbox. A Jaguar convertible was parked in the driveway. “This is going to be so cool.”

The next house, though, had the number nineteen scripted above the garage doors.

“We must have missed it,” Jessica said, looking in the rearview mirror.

“I don’t think so,” he said. “Check the address again.”

Jessica pulled out a slip of paper from her purse. “Seventeen West City Road,” she read.

"We're on *East* City Road," Corey said, stopping the car next to a man who was walking his dog. "Excuse me, could you tell us where West City Road is?"

"Just keep going straight for about four miles."

Corey waved out the window. "Thanks."

"Set the odometer," Jessica suggested.

After driving a dozen blocks, the estates had become large houses on more land. By the time they reached two miles, the homes turned modest and the land more vast. Soon they were passing substantial farms.

"We're back in the boonies!" Jessica cried.

Just past three miles, a road sign said "West City Road."

"I think this is it," Corey said, slowing in front of mailbox that read "17." Turning into the driveway, they passed by a large sign: "SUFFOLK SHEEP FARM."

"The blowout party is at a *sheep* farm?" Jessica said, mouth agape.

The farmhouse was situated some distance from the road and had several cars parked in front. Halfway down the driveway, Jessica put up her hand. "You can drop me off here and then back up," she said, opening the door as soon as Corey slowed down.

"Let me at least drive you to the door."

"Corey, you're a nice guy, but arriving in a Volvo driven by my cousin isn't exactly making a cool entrance."

Corey applied the brakes. "I can hang out for a while and then give you a lift back if you want."

Jessica shot him an angry glare. "No way, that wasn't the deal. I'll get a ride home later."

"Have you ever met this guy?"

"Lighten up," Jessica said, stepping out of the car.

Corey was getting angry. "Well, have you?"

"Look around, Corey," Jessica spat. "We're in the middle of freakin' nowhere. Are you worried I'm gonna be attacked by a bunch of horny sheep?"

Corey grabbed her arm. “Going in there alone is pretty stupid.”

Jessica pulled away from Corey’s grasp. “Leave me alone,” she said. “You did your good deed. Now, just leave.”

Corey was exasperated but knew that trying to talk with Jessica would be a losing battle. “Don’t hitchhike back. Just call me when you want a ride.”

“And have everyone hear you drive out of Montis? No way. I don’t want my parents finding out,” she said. “I’ll get a ride home on my own.” She slammed the door. “Later,” she said, straightening her dress and charging off in search of the rave.

Corey watched until Jessica reached the front porch. She was about to knock when the door swung open. A young man peered down the drive, and then, within a second, Jessica disappeared inside.

“About to party?” he asked, referring to her online username.

“It’s Jessica,” she said, nervously wrapping the hem of her dress round her index finger. She was several inches taller than he.

He closed the door behind her.

“Hi, I’m Marley,” he said, using his index finger to push up the pair of thick black glasses that were far too wide for his narrow face.

Jessica stared at the teen, who she guessed was at least eighteen. He wore a wrinkled mint-green shirt and striped knit vest through which she could see stretch suspenders that were holding up a pair of loose jeans. Oh, he’s a *nerd*! Jessica thought. She heard voices coming from another room.

“You look exactly like your photo on your webpage.” He was a little nervous. “Glad you joined us.”

“This your folks’ place?” she asked, peeking into the living room from the foyer.

“It really belongs to my grandfolks, who also live here,” he explained.

“Cozy,” Jessica said sarcastically.

“Follow me, we’re hanging out in the kitchen,” he said, heading down the hall.

The large country kitchen was filled with a dozen teenagers who all looked a few years older than Jessica. Both boys and girls glanced at her when she walked into the room.

"Everyone, this is Jessica." Various greetings wafted her way. "And these are some of my friends from our chess club. Oh, except Rodney and Laura, who are in our school's astronomy society."

"Fascinating," she said as she glanced around, looking at nerd after nerd. Everyone was wearing the same style clothing, 1980s geek, and Jessica in her short black DKNY dress stuck out like the sorest of thumbs.

"Wanna beer?"

"That's why I'm here," she said, forcing a smile.

Marley opened a can and passed it to her. "O'Douls?!" she said. "But there's no alcohol in this. You've got to be kidding!"

"That's what we have when we party," Marley said, taking another for himself.

I am *so* out of here, Jessica thought, and began planning her escape.

FIFTY-THREE

# *Duesenberg*

With the room getting noticeably warmer, Marley opened the windows above the kitchen sink. Suddenly, the kitchen aroma changed from freshly baked pastries to . . . manure?

Jessica turned up her nose. "What is that *smell*?"

"Sheep," a bass voice said from behind her. Jessica swung around and instantly caught sight of an irresistibly devastating grin. "I'm Chad," he said, "Marley's older brother."

Staring blankly with her mouth open, she could only shake her head. The muscles rippling under his thin shirt quickened her pulse. The very way he stood let her know that it was going to be a night she would never forget. She felt his eyes rake boldly over her body.

"I'm . . ." For a second, she forgot what she was saying. She was fighting a losing battle of seductive attraction. He was as close to an Adonis as she had ever seen, with a perfect physique, very tall and well built. He had hair the color of field oats, compelling green eyes and a firm mouth curled upward as if on the verge of a broad smile. She shook her head to clear her thoughts. "I'm Jessica."

"Marley says you're from Lumby," he said.

"Virginia," she blurted, hypnotized by his raw magnetism. The other people in the room, as well as their voices, became a blur.

"Let me show you around the place," Chad offered, opening the back screen door.

When she passed him, he placed his hand on the small of her back. She smelled his aftershave, and her head spun.

"Are you guys coming back?" Marley asked.

"Not anytime soon—don't wait up," Chad said over his shoulder.

Instead of escorting Jessica around the barnyard, as she had expected, Chad led her directly to a large barn situated well behind the main house. The interior was dimly lit by small bulbs affixed to the ceiling, but through the dimness Jessica could see that both floors were stacked high with bales of hay.

She pointed up at the loft. "So that's where you take all your girlfriends?" she teased.

"Not when they're wearing a black dress like yours," he said. "Take my hand." His fingers were warm and strong as they wrapped around hers.

"No lights?" she asked, noticing the row of halogens that ran along the ceiling of the barn.

His grin was sensuous. "Not unless you wanted to look at the barn cats upstairs. But I was hoping you'd be interested in other things."

In the center of the barn sat a 1932 Duesenberg roadster convertible with its roof folded down into the trunk. He opened the door to the backseat and bowed slightly. "My lady," he said, offering his hand as she stepped inside. The smell of leather was as intoxicating as his cologne.

Jessica slid gracefully into the deep seat. "This is so cool," she said, touching the velvet door panel beside her. With the top down, she could look straight up into the loft.

"It's from another era," he said, stepping in and closing the door behind him. As he settled next to her, he stretched his arm across the back of the seat.

The electricity between them was overwhelming, and Jessica's body ached to be touched. She shuddered when he dropped his hand on her bare shoulder. His finger traced a line up to her neck, which he gently cupped in his hand and pulled toward him.

"I'm so glad you came tonight," he whispered

A smile trembled on her lips, and her body quivered as he gazed into her eyes. His finger traced her jaw and curved under her chin, following the invisible line downward. Her pulse pounded and she leaned her head back.

As if he couldn't wait any longer, he pulled her close, burying his face in her throat. His tongue sent shivers through her, and she lowered her shoulders to allow her blouse to drop even farther.

Suddenly, lights flooded the barn. Both bolted upright, and for a moment, they were blinded by the jarring brilliance.

"Jessica!" a woman said.

Jessica was startled. "*Grams!?*" she exclaimed. "What are you doing here?"

"That's a question I should be asking you," Kay said. Beside her stood Robert and two other adults Jessica didn't recognize.

Chad jumped up out of the car before Jessica had time to straighten her clothes. "These are my grandparents," he said as a quick introduction.

Kay stared at Jessica as she lifted her blouse high enough to cover her shoulders. "Do your parents know you're here?"

"They're at the fair," Jessica replied as she stepped out of the car and pulled down her dress.

"That doesn't answer the question," Robert said.

Jessica dramatically rolled her eyes. "What does it matter to you?"

Kay stomped over to Jessica and took her by the arm. "We're going home."

"You have no right," Jessica protested.

"Your parents don't know you're here, and you're underage," Kay said.

"*Underage?*" Chad asked.

Jessica was mortified with embarrassment.

Robert turned to their new friends. "Samantha, Greg, it was a delight to visit. And we can't thank you enough for helping Kay when she sprained her ankle—your ice and towel saved the day."

"Don't mention it," the older gentleman said before turning to his grandson. "Chad, we need to talk."

After they pulled out of the farm's driveway, Robert looked at Jessica in the rearview mirror. "Are you all right?" he asked.

"No. I'm totally humiliated," she said angrily.

"You should be for doing what you were doing," Kay said.

Jessica slid lower in the seat. "That's not what I meant."

"I know exactly what you meant," Kay replied. "What were you doing down here?"

"Just having some fun," she said, crossing her arms.

Both Robert and Kay had a million questions to ask, but they knew that disciplining her was not their role. "So how did you meet Chad?" Robert asked, trying to sound as if they were having a casual conversation.

Kay didn't give Jessica time to reply. "And just out of curiosity, how did you get down to Wheatley?"

"You wouldn't understand."

"Try us," Kay offered. "We're not the old farts you might think we are."

It was a half hour drive to Montis, and Jessica knew she couldn't stall that long. "Okay, I was in a chat room, and Marley invited me to his party. It's that simple."

Both Kay and Robert remained silent.

"And Corey drove me down," Jessica added. "And that's where I met Chad." Her voice practically swooned as she said his name.

"Jessica, his tongue was down your throat. You did more than *meet* him," Kay said.

"*Grams!*" Jessica said in shock.

"Well, we were young once too, dear," she said.

"Fine," Jessica said. "Then you know it was totally harmless."

"Harmless?" Robert asked, trying not to raise his voice. "The kiss, perhaps, but do you have any idea what could have happened to you by walking into a stranger's house?"

Instead of responding, Jessica buried her chin in her chest and sulked in silence until they reached Farm to Market Road just outside of Wheatley. Finally, she broke her silence. "Are you going to tell my parents?"

"Of course we are," Kay said.

"That's not fair!"

"Don't raise your voice," Robert said.

"What you did was stupid, Jessica," Kay said. "How would you possibly know what you were getting into?"

"Everyone does it," Jessica said.

"I seriously doubt that," Robert contended.

"You don't understand." Jessica spat out the words.

Kay was becoming annoyed. "Oh, because we're a hundred years old?"

"You said it, not me."

"Jessica, we grew up just like you," Robert said.

Jessica's eyes filled with tears. "No, you didn't. You don't know what it's like."

"We know it isn't easy," Kay said.

"It's impossible," she admitted in a whisper. She pressed both hands over her eyes, trying to push back the stinging tears. "Do you know what it's like to try to be perfect so you can fit in for one more day? It's not cool to make good grades, so I don't, and then I get yelled at by my parents. And if I'm not wearing the right clothes or talking to the right guys, I get laughed at." She sounded miserable, her words half swallowed by deep sobs. "And there is no one I can talk to."

Kay's heart ached for the girl. "I do remember what it was like in high school," she said softly. "There were days I didn't know who I hated more—me, my friends or the kids who teased us."

During the long conversation back to Montis, perhaps a glimmer of understanding was built between Kay and Jessica. But when they arrived back at the inn, Jessica's well-being was turned over to Patrick and Elaine, who were sitting with Corey in the living room, hearing about their daughter's escapades.

It was a long night for Jessica, but in the early hours of the morning, a connection was finally made between parents and child that began a voluntary redirection of Jessica's life. Eventually that new path would lead to her growth into a self-confident, productive and happy young adult.

FIFTY-FOUR

# *Voices*

**Friday**

For very different reasons, just about everyone at Montis Inn was up before six o'clock on Friday morning. Mark had set the alarm for five o'clock in order to get an early start in preparing for Old Jesse's obstacle course event. Once Mark was out of the house, Pam found it impossible to fall back to sleep, her mind full of what would happen over the next two days, so she put the early hours to good use and had pulled freshly baked scones out of the oven long before Carter's show began.

An hour before, Patrick had left Jessica and Elaine sleeping in their beds and sat watching the sunrise from one of the benches in the courtyard, thankful that his daughter was unharmed and safe at home. When Carter passed by on his way to the kitchen, Patrick commended him on his son's behavior the night before. Patrick only wished his daughter would act half as responsibly as Corey had.

Lynn and Chuck Bryson were just pulling up to Montis after having spent the night at his home. Their evening of conversation had carried well into the early hours of the morning, and they had fallen asleep sharing a hammock under star-filled skies.

*"Good morning, America. Welcome back to* The Carter Reed Show. *Today is July twentieth and our last live broadcast from Lumby. To my surprise, this week, cards were dealt and hands were played that I wasn't at all expecting. In fact, I would go so far as to say that the last five days have been a real eye-opener for this city man.*

*"But first, let's begin Lumby on the Air with some final news from our favorite small town.*

The Lumby Lines

# Classified Ads

July 20

For Sale, Rent, Barter or Giveaway

---

Used socks. The Goodwill Store.

---

Moving sale at McNear Farm. Everything must go except for Bess, and even that's negotiable. Sunday after the fair. Killdrop Road.

---

For barter or sale: Sixth place goat at fair. Will trade for just about anything else or sell for $22.50. Call Michelle 925-4468.

---

In keeping with its hundred year old tradition of supporting the town when crisis strikes, Wools has reduced the price of all Hanes socks by 30%.

---

Free puppies. Half cute golden retriever, half sneaky neighborhood dog. 925-0227. Leave msg.

---

Pony for sale—looks a lot like a very small horse. $150.00 firm with little saddle included. See Stephanie at the fair's horse arena.

---

Jimmy D Bobbleheads now available; for sale $4.00 each or get one free with two pitchers of beer. Jimmy D's Main Street.

---

Lumby Monopoly Club would like to swap Scrabble boards for complete Monopoly games. Join us Tuesday nights.

---

Come try on many old dresses from Grandma in beautiful condition at the Presbyterian Church after Sunday's sermon.

*"Before going to the phones, I'd like to say good morning to several townsfolk who are, at this very moment, living the definition of what it is to be a good neighbor. For those ideos who were listening the other day, you may remember a call-in by, and my subsequent visit with, Rachael. Unbeknownst to her, a crew of good men and women who have no personal stake other than a desire to lend a hand are cleaning up the family cemetery she told us about. And why are they doing it? Simply because she needs help, and even though she didn't ask for it . . . simply because they feel responsible for others beyond themselves and their immediate families. Kudos to all of them.*

*"And speaking of people who are doing the right thing, I'd like to mention my son, Corey."*

Corey, who was listening to his father's show from the comfort of his bed on the third floor, propped himself up on his elbow. What did I do now? he thought in dismay.

*"It's come to my attention, although I should have noticed much earlier, that Corey has grown into an extraordinary young man, if one excuses a few brief hours of excess last Sunday night. He has shown more maturity, responsibility and decency than I certainly have during this family reunion. He is one of the few people I know who tries to walk the high road—and that may say something about my circle of friends. I'm embarrassed to admit this, but with Corey, the apple fell quite some distance from this tree."*

Corey flew down the staircase, taking the steps three at a time.

*"In fact, here he is now. Come in and join me, son. Kano, get Corey a set of headphones. While Corey gets wired in, I'd like to say a word about the county fair, which I admit to having belittled at the beginning of the week."*

Just as Corey took the chair next to his father, Kano pushed a large headset onto his head, snapping the rubber cups over his ears. Kano switched a dial at the main board. "Corey, can you hear me?"

Corey nodded as he adjusted the ear pads and the small microphone attached to the earpiece. It was the first time he'd ever been on *The Carter Reed Show*.

Kano looked at the young man. "You're on live with your dad in three, two, one," he said, swirling his index finger in the air.

Carter continued talking into the mic.

*"It's a fine gathering, although I still maintain my position that it just can't compare to the Washington State Fair—"*

Corey jumped in.

*"But keep in mind that Chatham County has a population one-tenth the size of Yakima's metropolitan area and probably one-hundredth the size of the surrounding counties. That would be like comparing* The Lumby Lines *to* The Washington Post.*"*

*"So Corey's mic does work. Good to have you here, son. Why don't you begin the next segment?"*

*"What would the topic be?"*

Pam and Mark walked into the room and quietly sat down on the sofa just as Carter was replying to Cory's question.

*"Today we're looking at a pretty basic question: How responsible are we for each other? How responsible are we for each other's well-being, for the decisions others make and for the consequences of those decisions? Another way of posing the question: How many degrees of separation are there for personal accountability?"*

Corey looked at his father out of the corner of his eye as his voice went over the airwaves.

*"And you want me to take a stand and wait for your callers to object?"*

*"No, not today, and I definitely don't want to put you up for slaughter, if you know what I mean. Until now, this show has been a national forum of verbal onslaught where we have deliberately pitted—as my introduction used to say—ideology against ideology and idiocy against idiocy. But we're going to change all that. So, ideos who are about to call in—and I'm addressing each of you ten million listeners out there—this is not a time for verbal sabotage. We are not raking anyone over the coals today. In fact, just the opposite—I want to develop a theory about personal responsibility to others that might work for many if not all of us."*

Corey grinned at his father.

*"That's quite a challenge given that the question you chose is something that's been considered by the greatest thinkers of our history. But sure, I'm game and I'll toss the first coin into the pond and see where the ripples may go. My dime's worth is that we are becoming a country of first-person-singular thinkers and that the sense of responsibility for our neighbor's well-being is not as strong as it used to be."*

Carter scribbled on his notepad and held it up to Kano: "# Callers?"

Kano made a big zero sign with this fingers and then checked the lines to confirm there were no technical problems. He looked at Carter and lifted his shoulders.

Pam, who had been watching the silent communication between Carter and his employee, stood up and left.

Carter interrupted.

*"The lines are now open for comments. While we're waiting for ideos to respond, do you have any other thoughts, Corey?"*

*"I do, but perhaps it's best to begin with a baseline that most people can agree upon."*

Carter saw one call-in light light up. Corey continued.

*"All right. On line one, we have Pam from . . . none other than Lumby. Ideo at will, Pam."*

*"Hi, Corey, it's nice to hear you on the radio."*

Pam, holding the phone tight to her ear, stuck her head out from behind the lobby wall and gave a quick wave. Corey couldn't help but laugh.

*"In fairness to our listening audience, I need to disclose that I have a personal relationship with this caller. She is my aunt. So, Pam, what are your thoughts on the issue?"*

*"I suppose I should begin by saying that I agree with you so far. It seems to me that we now live in a society in which people are very self-focused and first ask, 'What's in it for me?' instead of 'How can I help you?' So many people appear to be looking out for themselves and no one else. I have also observed that many people feel entitled to get and to have more than what they are willing to produce and to share with others. I don't know how we got to where we are, but I do know that the world is so much more complex than when I was growing up. Maybe it was easier for us to learn personal accountability and responsibility because we saw it and lived it every day."*

*"Thank you for your thoughts, Pam."*

During Pam's comment, Kano's call-in board had begun to warm up with a smattering of call-ins. Within another thirty minutes, and after three more callers, Carter's audience was responding with a fervor and excitement never before seen in the history of the show. Carter stepped in.

*"Kano just told me that we're being flooded with more calls than normal, so please be patient and try again during our next segment."*

Corey glanced at the digital readout on the control panel.

*"On line three, we have another call from Lumby. Rachael, what are your thoughts?"*

Carter felt a twinge of angst. How would his audience react when he did not personally introduce this caller, or say, "Ideo at will"? He looked at his son and smiled.

*"Mr. Reed?"*

Carter and Corey said "yes" simultaneously; then both chuckled. Carter winked at Corey and gestured for his son to take the call. Carter slipped off his headset and lay it gently on the table.

*"I want to thank you for coming to Lumby. You've touched many lives here in ways you can't imagine. I've never been to a big city like Seattle, and I've been thinking about it these last few days. I'm sure it's filled with the same type of good folks we have in our small town—neighbors taking care of neighbors, whether there are ten city blocks or ten acres of open pasture between them. Those basic kindnesses don't change just because of bigger buildings or more streetlights. Deep down, we all want the same things: to love and be loved, to share our lives with others without feeling alone, to help and be helped, to work so that we can provide for ourselves and give to others in need. I feel blessed to live in Lumby just like some other woman like me feels blessed to live in New York City."*

*"A valuable contribution that I'm sure the audience appreciates, Rachael. Next we have David from Cambridge on line two."*

When Corey wrapped up the show two hours later, the living room was filled with family and friends who burst into applause. Carter walked up and gave his son the strongest bear hug of his life.

"Well," Carter said, "either you just about killed my ratings and ended my career, or we're going to be welcoming another ten million listeners when the word spreads that you're now on the air. I know it's going to be the latter because you were tremendous, son."

FIFTY-FIVE

# Following

At eleven twenty Friday morning, the phone rang at the office of Main Street Realty. "This is Joan Stokes, how may I help you? . . . This is a surprise. Yes, sir, of course." Joan pulled a contract from her files. "I'm certain they would accept that offer," she replied. She listened to the caller's instructions for several minutes. "That can be arranged," she finally said. "And I agree, the townspeople will be surprised. . . . Yes, we can do that as well. . . . So I'll see you tomorrow, Saturday, as we planned."

As soon as she hung up, she slapped both hands on her desk in excitement. "Time to close the deal!" she said aloud.

By noon, Joan was standing on the front porch of the McNear farm, knocking on the door. "It's Joan Stokes," she called out.

"What a nice surprise," Bess said from the kitchen. "Come in."

As Joan reached for the knob, one of Mike's dogs charged past her, slamming into the door and ripping it from its hinges. Joan gasped and jumped back just as the door crashed to the ground.

Bess came running with a broom in one hand and a spatula in the other.

"Out!" she yelled at the dog, sweeping the broom toward the mongrel. "Are you all right?" she asked Joan.

Joan took Bess's hand as she navigated around the fallen door, which was now blocking most of the entrance.

"Mike!" Bess called out. "The door is off its hinges again."

Mike came from the direction of the living room, a huge smile on his face. "That damn door isn't my problem anymore, is it, Joan?" he asked, winking at her. "I haven't told Bess yet."

Bess glanced between them. "What haven't you told me?"

Mike took Bess by the arm and led her to the kitchen where he pulled out a chair for her. "You're scaring me," she said.

"Our dreams have come true," he said, sitting down next to her. "Joan called a little bit ago and said that we have been offered full asking price for the farm."

"By whom?"

"It doesn't matter who's buying it," Mike said, "or what they're going to do with the place. We got what we wanted in a cash deal with absolutely no contingencies. So, Bess, we're not asking any questions," he said firmly.

Joan withdrew the contract from her briefcase and placed it on the table along with a pen. "If the terms, as we discussed, are acceptable to you, all I need are your signatures," she said.

Bess looked up at Joan.

"I can assure you," Joan said softly, nodding, "you won't get a better offer."

When the documents were signed, Joan exhaled. "I'm going directly over to Russell Harris's office. He'll be acting as the attorney for this transaction. I spoke to him on the way over, and he said that we should deposit the down payment into his firm's escrow account, and since there are no contingencies of sale and no bank financing involved, he can have the deal wrapped up in a week."

Bess was startled, turning to Mike for answers. "But how can we move out in a week? Where will we go?"

Mike patted his wife's hand. "Let me take care of it, Bess."

ᔕ

In the barn at Montis Inn, Mark and Joshua continued to work on preparations for that day's fair competition, although they were making little progress.

"Ow!" Mark yelled when Old Jesse pinned him against the planked wall. "Pull him off! He's crushing me to death."

Joshua quickly refilled the bull's oat bucket and shook it loudly. Old Jesse stared Mark in the eyes for several seconds before turning around and following his nose to the sweet oats. That gave Mark the opportunity to slip out of the stall in which Jesse had had him cornered for the last ten minutes.

"That bull is crazy," Mark said, wiping its snot off his shirt.

Joshua sat down on the loft stairs. "I don't want to dampen your spirits, but if we can't control the bull in an enclosed ten-by-ten stall, how do you expect he'll do when he's in an open obstacle course with no halter and no oats?"

Mark looked puzzled. "Of course we'll have oats. How else would we stop him from killing both of us?"

"You haven't read the rules of the event, have you?"

"Why? We can't use any food?"

Joshua shook his head.

Mark slumped down in the corner of the barn. "Well, that's just nuts. What are we going to do?"

Joshua laughed. "That's the purpose of the competition."

"Okay," he said. "Before we get too depressed, let's think this through."

"I'll recap," Joshua offered. "You have an obstinate bull with a bad reputation for trying to gore whoever and whatever crosses his path. There's a half-acre open field in which he must walk through various cones and barriers with no human contact, while a hundred innocent and unarmed spectators watch within striking distance."

"Thanks, I needed that," Mark said sarcastically.

"And we can't even get the bull out of the stall because he has some perverted attraction to that cat."

Mark thought for a moment and his eyes lit up. "I've got it!" he yelled. "Stay right here. I'll be back in a minute."

Actually, it was closer to ten minutes later when Mark returned, dragging Lynn and Chuck with him. "Sorry for interrupting your lunch," he told them.

"Interrupting is one way of saying you grabbed the sandwich from my hands and threw it into the trash can," Lynn said.

Although few things Mark ever did surprised Chuck, he was actually confused by his friend's unusually erratic behavior. "Mark, you're acting very strange," Chuck said.

"Yeah," Mark countered, "because I have a plan."

"Which obviously doesn't include eating lunch," Lynn quipped.

"Okay, forget lunch, this is really important," Mark announced, walking over to Old Jesse's stall. "We have one last shot at winning a blue ribbon at the fair this year. In a couple of hours, we're supposed to compete in the bull obstacle course."

Lynn rolled her eyes and took Chuck's hand as she began to walk away. "That bull almost killed me—*twice*. I don't care what you're doing with it. I'm out of here."

"No, wait, Lynn," Mark pleaded. "I need your help."

She stopped in midstep. Over the prior week, she and Mark had come far in reestablishing their relationship, and she didn't want anything to jeopardize that. She stared at her brother. "What do you want?"

"Coco," he said.

Lynn gawked at him.

"Okay, maybe it's not obvious," he said, "but I know that there is one sure way to get Old Jesse around the obstacle course."

"We're going to shoot him and drag him around behind the tractor?" Joshua joked.

"You're not helping," Mark accused. "I'm absolutely sure that Jesse would go anywhere if . . ."

Lynn grew impatient, waiting for Mark to continue. "If what?" she asked.

"If Coco was in front of him."

The three stared at Mark as if he had elevated himself off the ground.

"Just think about it," he said, glancing first at Joshua and then at Chuck and Lynn. "Old Jesse would follow that cat to the ends of the earth. So all we need to do is use Coco as a—"

"Carrot," Chuck said.

Mark clapped his hands together. "Exactly!"

Joshua raised one brow. "You know," he said cautiously, "that's not a totally crazy idea."

Lynn had already turned white. "Of course it's a crazy idea!" she shrieked. "That's the stupidest suggestion I've ever heard!"

Chuck walked over to the stall and looked at the bull, which was standing over the litter of kittens with his muzzle inches away from Coco's face. "Actually, Mark may be on to something," he said.

She looked at Chuck as if he had betrayed her. "How can you say that?"

"For two reasons," Chuck explained. "First, we can assume that Jesse doesn't want to go anywhere without Coco, so the possibility of even getting him out of the stall alone is almost zero. Second, we know that he wouldn't do anything to harm Coco; in fact, just the opposite."

"That's it—you got it!" Mark said with excitement, and then turned to his sister. "And since Coco follows you, what we need is for you to lead Coco while she leads Jesse from the starting gate to the finish line."

"First, you drag my cat into this crazy scheme, and now, you want me to be involved too?" Lynn asked in disbelief.

"It would make the most sense," Chuck concurred.

Lynn shot him a scorching look. "Whose side are you on?"

Chuck considered the question for an instant. "I suppose I would have to say Mark's because I think he may be right." He took Lynn's hand in his. "You know Jesse won't let anything happen to Coco."

"I'd feel better if I heard the bull say that," she said.

"But that's exactly what he's been saying through his behavior during the entire week," Chuck said. "Animals are far more perceptive than we give them credit for, Lynn. You need to have a little trust in Coco and in Old Jesse."

"And in your brother," Mark added. "I really wouldn't be asking if I thought it would harm you or your cat."

Lynn glanced at the others and then squeezed Chuck's hand. "All right," she said with a sigh. "What exactly do you want me to do?"

That very day, at the county fair, the legend of Coco and Old Jesse was born. After most of the eighteen contestants had finished the course with varying degrees of success and failure, Mark's number was called. Lynn snapped a gem-studded leash onto her pet's diamond collar, placed the cat on the ground and called her name once. Then, side by side, Lynn and Coco stepped into the ring and walked slowly through the obstacle course, unhurriedly passing by dangerous-looking fences and calmly marching between construction cones and through corral gates. Not once in their procession did either break the pace or turn around to confirm that a two-thousand-pound bull was following no more than three feet behind them, never slowing and never balking at any of the barriers. To a cheering crowd, all three arrived at the finish line with a time several minutes faster than any of the other contestants.

After putting Coco and Old Jesse back into the trailer, Mark collected the blue ribbon and trophy, which he graciously offered his sister. Lynn declined, saying the experience itself was reward enough.

---

Ten minutes later, Chuck and Lynn were swinging softly in the highest bucket on The Air.

"You were amazing!" Chuck said, putting his arm around her shoulder.

From where they sat high up in the Ferris wheel, she looked out over Mill Valley. "Everything looks very different from up here, doesn't it?" she asked. "Everything seems smaller, less threatening."

Chuck smiled. "I suppose it does," he said. "Maybe the trick is to keep that same perspective when we're down on the ground."

"Easier said than done." She sighed. "Bulls are frightening . . . relationships are frightening."

"That's just because you're still feeling the pain of marriage . . ." His voice trailed off.

She lifted her shoulder. "So why did you want to go for another ride on the Ferris wheel?"

"To entrap you." He laughed. "The way I see it, I have four minutes of your undivided attention to try to convince you to stay around a little longer."

"You don't have to convince me," she said, to his surprise. "I've already thought of every reason not to return to Virginia. In fact, I've been thinking about little else. You've become such a close friend that it will be almost impossible to leave."

"That's wonderful!" Chuck's eyes danced with joy.

"Yes, and no," she said.

"Do I hear a 'but'?"

"A big one," she said. "I have a life back in Virginia that has too many open ends. Like you said, I need to put my divorce behind me, but the only way I can do that is to build a life for myself, independent of anyone else right now. My job at the American Horticultural Society is so fulfilling, and I'm actually looking forward to taking on more responsibility in my new position. Also, Joshua has asked me to work with the Horticultural Society regarding his five-hundred-year-old berry shrubs. And I have a new home that still has bare walls—I need to hang my own pictures and arrange my own furniture." She was sad but resolute as she spoke. "If I stayed, I would only be staying to be with you. I need to learn to be with myself first."

"I wish I could say that you're wrong." Chuck's voice was full of disappointment. "But I know you're not. Still, I can hold out hope that when you've tied up the loose ends and have defined your own life, you may find time to come back and visit?"

"Soon," she said, kissing him. "And I will never forget all that you've given me this week or how you helped me take that first step back to where I need to be."

## FIFTY-SIX

# *Letters*

**Saturday**

At six fifteen in the morning, Pam and Mark were still asleep when André walked into the inn's restaurant and began preparing one of the most memorable meals that would ever be served at Montis. At seven fifteen, Pam and Mark were most definitely awake, but still in bed, when the florist arrived with a van full of roses that would be used to decorate the platform and back arbor that had been erected the day before for the wedding ceremony.

There was a soft tap on the front door of Pam and Mark's home. "Don't answer it," Pam said, lying in her husband's arms.

"It may be about tonight, honey," he said, slipping out from under her. Pulling on his robe, he walked into the kitchen just as there was another knock.

Mark opened the door. "What are you doing up so early?" he asked Lynn.

Glancing at his fire engine–print pajama bottoms and grizzly bear slippers, she couldn't help but laugh. "You really haven't changed much, have you?"

"I'm a fashion statement through and through," Mark said. "Come on in."

"Are you sure?" she said hesitantly. "I can come back later."

Mark spotted the florist's van. "It's going to get pretty busy around here in no time, and I remember you saying that you have to leave right after dinner, so let's have a cup of coffee together."

Pam, who had slipped on a pair of jeans and a blouse, entered the room. "Great job yesterday with Coco and Old Jesse," she said to Lynn.

"That was pretty interesting," Lynn agreed.

"I really appreciated it," Mark said earnestly. "No one else could have done what you did."

Lynn took a deep, unsteady breath. "There have been a lot of things that only I could have done, and before saying goodbye, I wanted to tell you how sorry I am for hurting you the way I did during the lawsuit."

Mark kept his eyes on Lynn as he pulled out a chair from the table and sat down. "I don't know what to say."

Pam placed her hand on his shoulder. "Let her finish."

Lynn forced a weak smile. "I need to apologize for pulling our family apart by writing those critical letters after the trial. At that time, I really thought my husband was telling the truth and I was so angry that you would question his integrity. But still, that didn't give me the right to try and turn the family against you. And then, after he admitted to me that he had embezzled from your company, I continued to protect him by keeping that confession to myself. You didn't deserve that—you didn't deserve any of it." She withdrew an envelope she had been holding behind her back. "I'll never be able to repay the money that he stole from you, but I can correct my own wrongdoing. This morning I mailed a copy of this to everyone in our family who was involved." She removed a letter from the envelope and handed it to Mark.

Mark and Pam read the three pages in silence. Lynn's words were filled with revelations that, until then, had never been disclosed to the Walkers. The letter ended with expressions of deep remorse and an apology for her behavior.

Mark stood up and wrapped his arms around his sister. "You didn't have to do that," he said softly.

"Yes, I did," she said, fighting back tears. She placed her hand on his cheek. "I love you, and I'm so, so sorry."

"I know. I love you too," he said, hugging her again.

"Chops is back!" a voice called out from the courtyard.

Pam ran to the window and saw Joshua chasing Mark's favorite sheep behind the guest annex.

"I think you're being called," Lynn said, grinning as she wiped away another tear.

⁂

By midafternoon, the backyard of Montis Inn had been transformed into a floral wonderland. Sixty chairs covered in white silk had been arranged in five rows bisected by a center aisle covered with white rose petals. Tall lanterns placed at the ends of each row would be lit at sunset. At the far end of the aisle, an open semicircle was backed on three sides by arched, trellised arbors covered with white roses and purple clematis.

When Joan Stokes stepped out of her car, she immediately caught sight of Carter sitting on the inn's front porch. "A beautiful day for a wedding," she said, joining him.

He smiled. "I've been keeping an eye out for you."

Joan withdrew a thick envelope from her purse and handed it to him. "It's done," she said. "Congratulations, Mr. Reed."

"Thank you," he said, shaking her hand. He offered her a seat before reviewing the documents one final time. When he was sure that every *I* was dotted and *T* was crossed, he raised his arms as if he had won a race. "This is fantastic," he said. "Just what my son and I want."

"Have you told Pam and Mark yet?" she asked.

"That's next on the agenda." Out of the corner of his eye, Carter spotted Mark standing with Joshua and Pam. "Thank you again, but if you would excuse me. Mark!" he called out, rushing down the stairs.

"I thought you and Nancy were planning to spend one last day at the fair," Pam said to him.

"She and Corey went up for a while, but I had some business to attend to."

"It's your day off, Carter," Mark said. "Take it easy."

"This couldn't wait. I . . . *we* have a gift for the two of you," he said, handing Mark the envelope. "Happy anniversary."

Pam and Mark looked first at Carter and then at each other in surprise. "We said no gifts—you didn't have to do that," Mark said.

"Actually, this is more of a favor you're doing for me."

Mark opened the envelope and studied the first page. In bold type were the words "Corey Reed Land Trust of Lumby." Mark and Pam continued to scan the papers, looking more and more confused.

"I don't understand," Mark finally said. "You bought us McNear's farm?"

"Not exactly," Carter said. "I bought McNear's farm and his four thousand acres, which will be put in a land trust that you and Pam will steward."

"How?" Mark asked.

Even Pam was baffled. "What do we do with the land?"

"Anything you see fit. Corey and I had a long talk about it last night, and he's sure that there isn't anyone better to be the trustees."

"I'm not totally following this," Mark admitted.

"It's pretty simple, Mark," Carter said. "When I heard that Vince Shaw was going to take control of this town and everyone in it, I thought the residents of Lumby needed a little help. You two were right all along: there is something extraordinary about this place and everyone who lives here. All of you have taught me more than I ever thought possible, and in this one small way I hope to say thank you. So I made McNear an offer he couldn't refuse, and the land will now be deeded a nature conservancy to be overseen by the two of you."

Joshua, who had been standing behind Pam and Mark, laughed aloud as he slapped Mark on the back.

"What's so funny?" Mark asked.

"Not funny, just absolutely amazing—an answer to many prayers," he said. "Mark, how would you like to grow a berry—a very, very special berry—on a couple acres of McNear's hillside?"

"Oh, right . . . *the* berries," Pam said, immediately catching on to Joshua's idea. When Mark still looked confused, she explained, "The nuns' berries that need to be relocated from the monastery."

"Well, this would be perfect for them!" Mark said, thinking he'd just come up with the idea himself. "And there's four *thousand* acres—plenty of room for the shrubs to spread so there will be more berries for us to eat."

"You've got to love this man," Pam said, kissing his cheek.

## FIFTY-SEVEN

# *Vows*

When the sun set Saturday evening, it was as if an artist had brushed abstract swatches of pink and turquoise against clouds that hung over the mountain peaks to the west of Montis Inn. In the backyard, guests stood in small groups of friends and neighbors, talking softly. Off to the side, five musicians formed a circle around three music stands. Hank, smartly dressed in a tuxedo, sat in the middle with a cello between his legs. The quintet had begun playing soft classical music twenty minutes earlier when people first began to arrive.

In the front row sat Patrick and Elaine with their daughter between them. Although Jessica had spent much of the last day in her room, mostly talking with her parents, she appeared to be in good spirits. Attired quite different from the stylish and mildly provocative clothes she had been wearing during the week, she had on a pair of dark green slacks with a green-and-tan-striped shirt. Most of her jewelry had been removed, as had any trace of heavy makeup. She looked refreshed and, as Corey would later admit, genuinely cute.

She sat very still, apparently riveted by the music. "What's that song they're playing?" she asked her father.

"'Jesu, Joy of Man's Desiring.' It's by Johann Sebastian Bach," he said. "Do you like it?"

She listened for a moment longer to the cascading, repeated melody and nodded. "It's nice."

"Perhaps we can all go to an outdoor concert when we get home," he suggested. "Maybe even get you your own instrument."

Jessica looked at her father. "You don't have to try that hard, Dad."

He lowered his voice. "I'll try as hard as necessary to be there for you . . . for both of you."

Seated directly behind them were Chuck and Lynn, lost in their own conversation. "What time is your flight?" he asked.

"In a couple of hours—it's a red-eye to Dulles airport," she explained. "It departs at ten twenty."

"May I drive you, Coco and her litter to the airport?"

She kissed him on the cheek. "You're so sweet," she said, "but Mark and Pam have offered to take care of Coco and her kittens for a while. You were right—she likes the life of a barn cat, and the kittens are just too young to move. And unfortunately, I have a rental car that I need to return."

"Then I'll follow you to Rocky Mount," Chuck suggested. "We can have a final cup of coffee at the gate together."

She rested her hand on his knee. "It's going to be awfully hard saying goodbye to you."

"You know you don't have to," he said with a hopeful twinkle in his eye.

The music stopped and those who were standing took their seats. Among them were the monks and sisters of St. Cross Abbey and Pam and Mark's close friends from Lumby. Brother Matthew touched Joshua on the arm. "It's time," he said, escorting Joshua and Brooke to the front of the chairs.

Dressed in a long black robe, Brother Matthew faced the group and slowly raised his arms. "We are about to begin," he said softly, and a hush fell over the gathering.

Just as the band began playing Pachelbel's Canon in D Major, Pam and Mark appeared at the end of the aisle. Pam looked stunning in a full-length gown of lavender taffeta with a silk bodice. Mark took her hand, kissed it and held it between his own, and together, they walked down the aisle.

As the music faded, Matthew spoke. "Let us pray. Dear Heavenly Father, we have come together with joyful hearts as Pam and Mark Walker reaffirm their faith and love for each other and renew the vows that they made before you twenty-five years ago. We celebrate one of life's most treasured ceremonies and give recognition to the worth and beauty of committed love. Grant that Pam and Mark will be forever true and loving, and that they will find strength in the honesty of this union. Fill their wonderful home with warmth, and their hearts with kindness, patience and understanding, and keep them in the safety of your love. Amen.

"Pam and Mark will now share the vows they have written for each other."

Pam and Mark turned to face each other.

"I, Pam Eastman Walker, again choose you, Mark Allen Walker, to be my friend, my confidant, my partner and my husband. We have been blessed for twenty-five years with a love that is more rare and priceless than I ever thought possible. I vow to cherish, protect and nurture this love with generosity of heart and honesty of spirit. I vow to be your partner in sickness and in health, in wealth and in poverty, in good times and in bad until we are parted by death. Once again, I pledge myself to you in faith, hope and love."

Brother Matthew nodded to Mark.

"I, Mark Allen Walker, give to you, Pam Eastman Walker, a renewed promise and affirmation of love from the heart that has loved you for twenty-five years and will love you until my last breath. Together, we will continue this journey. I will laugh with you in joy and cry with you in sorrow and will always be by your side. Thank you for the love you have given me through the years, for the patience you have shown and for your enduring faith in us.

I will always stand next to you because you are and will be my only love."

Matthew stepped forward and laid his hands on theirs.

"Bless the marriage of Pam and Mark Walker. May you walk beside them throughout all the days of their lives. Amen."

Their embrace was heartfelt, their kiss passionate, while applause erupted from the crowd. Mark turned to escort Pam down the aisle, but unexpectedly, she pulled on his arm and shook her head. "Not yet," she whispered.

Confused, Mark looked to Brother Matthew, who raised his arms to quiet the crowd. Pam beamed as she addressed the guests. "I would like to present my mother, Kay Eastman, and her fiancé, Robert Day, on this, their wedding night."

As previously instructed, the band began to play the melodic Air on the G String by Bach. To everyone's delight, Kay and Robert processed down the center aisle. Kay was dressed in a champagne-colored evening gown, and Robert, like Mark, wore a tuxedo. Approaching Matthew, Kay handed Pam her bouquet of flowers. Mark stood behind Robert.

Matthew looked out over the audience. "Dearly beloved, we are gathered here . . ." And so began a wedding ceremony that was much more than Kay had ever dreamed it would be.

Twenty minutes later, Kay and Robert kissed for the first time as husband and wife.

Brother Matthew smiled and addressed the guests. "It is now my honor to present Kay and Robert Day and Pam and Mark Walker. May they go in peace and love."

The Lumby Lines

# What's News Around Town

BY SCOTT STEVENS August 18

Another normal week in our sleepy town of Lumby.

The cover story in the September issue of *Vintners International* magazine will feature the Sisters of St. Cross Abbey and how, through hard work and ample prayer, they successfully transplanted an entire vineyard of Merlot grapes from Troutdale, Oregon, to the monastic slopes just outside the town of Franklin. Although they will continue to distribute wine from purchased blends under their old label for another two years while the new vines take root, they have their eyes set on eventually introducing the St. Cross label.

*Ericaceae Vaccinium armandcrosstum*—a long name for a small berry that is as sweet as pure honey. It was reported in *Horticulture Today* that the very same Sisters of St. Cross Abbey, while clearing fields for their vineyard, discovered a new berry species on their property. Very similar to a shrub that became extinct five hundred years ago, it was identified as singularly unique and was registered by Joshua Turner for the sisters. Over the next few weeks, the shrubs will be transplanted to the rocky hills of the Corey Reed Land Trust of Lumby.

Also heading to the Corey Reed Land Trust may be our town's very own celebrity rooster, Mr. Clucks, who is being evicted from the Lumby Feed Store for antisocial behavior. Although many hoped he would show an improved attitude after rehabilitation, his old habits have returned.

From all indications, Hank has been finally cured of his coulrophobia—his abnormal fear of clowns. Although the fair vendors have long since closed up their concession stands, pulled up stakes, crated up their rides and driven out of town in an impressive 2 a.m. caravan, Hank continues to don his clown garb. It is rumored that although he was offered a full-time position as a carny, he's holding out for his own show under the big tent.

Godspeed to all.

Photograph by Claire Donley

**Gail Fraser** has written *The Lumby Lines, Stealing Lumby, Lumby's Bounty* and *The Promise of Lumby*. She and her husband, renowned folk artist Art Poulin, live with their beloved animals on Lazy Goose Farm in rural upstate New York. Gail and Art feel fortunate to live down the road from their close friends at New Skete Monastery, home to the authors of *How to Be Your Dog's Best Friend*. When not writing, Gail tends to her heirloom tomatoes, orchard and beehives. Or, she can be found in her pottery studio.

Prior to becoming a novelist, Gail Fraser had a successful corporate career, holding senior executive positions in several Fortune 500 and start-up corporations and traveling extensively throughout the world. She has a BA from Skidmore College and an MBA from the University of Connecticut, with graduate work done at Harvard University.

Please visit www.lumbybooks.com and join Lumby's Circle of Friends.

4-H
CLUB
HOUSE
HOTDOGS
HAMBURGERS
KETTLE KORN

OPEN
Tickets
Carnival Rides
Today's
EVENTS
TRACTOR PULLS
MAKING
AMERICA
GREAT
Pig Race
BACON BARN
KLUM

# The Lumby Reader

Spend more time with your favorite Lumby characters.
Discover new wonders of the Lumby lifestyle.
Share your Lumby experience with friends and family.

# Lumby Living: Tips from Home

Welcome to Lumby Living: Tips from Home, a capricious collection of recipes—in this edition, all appetizers and finger foods—plus yarns and personal thoughts for sharing a more bountiful and authentic life. In the next few pages, we turn to the good-natured townsfolk of Lumby and ask the simple question: *"What's in your . . . ?"* Pam tells us what's in the Montis Inn wine cellar, while Chuck Bryson looks into his potting shed for his favorite gardening tools. We discover what Gabrielle Beezer really grows in her raised beds—and it's not flowers! André Levesque shares what cookware he uses in his kitchen, and Mark lists his favorite places on the web. Their answers provide insight into personal preferences, best practices and some outstanding products you may want to try yourself.

As always, the townsfolk of Lumby are looking for personal favorite recipes and well-kept secrets, so if you would like to contribute your own tips from home, please visit www.lumbybooks.com and join the Lumby Circle of Friends. There, you may add your contributions, share your thoughts on a variety of subjects, and chat with others who have embraced Lumby.

Please visit www.lumbybooks.com.

## To Our Friends in Lumby, We Ask: What's in Your . . . ?

**Hank: What's in your safe deposit box?**

although i think that question a tad personal, i've once again been asked to lead the charge, to go where no fl-fl-flamingo has gone and open my wings to share my most personal secrets. and i, as a noble bald eagle, am on task and ready for the challenge. really, far be it from me to dampen your parade by saying that it's none of your business. here are the items in my safe deposit box that i'm willing to share:

a photograph of me and the lumby sporting goods' mannequin sharing a latte on a bench in front of the bookstore

a feather from my first girlfriend

seabiscuit's horseshoe

my expired passport with stamps from around the world

an autographed photograph of margaret thatcher on which she wrote a personal note

a small box of paper clips

a guitar pick given to me by james taylor

two ticket stubs to the opening of *les misérables* on broadway

tiger woods's right sock

a rock i found on my favorite secluded beach in hawaii

a hand towel from camp david

my first ipod

a photograph of me, my mother and my father at the parthenon in athens, greece

a matchbook from tavern on the green

my savings account passbook from childhood

a packet of heirloom tomato seeds

a piece of our family's scottish tartan

measuring spoons i used during my class at le cordon bleu with julia

an old toothbrush for good oral hygiene

a dried mushroom from mexico

my design for a cold fusion, low-energy nuclear reactor

a letter from katharine hepburn

a cd of patriotic songs sung by the u.s. army chorus

the flag i was waving from the stands while watching the *challenger* launch

a tooth from the *jaws* shark given to me by steven spielberg

a signed, first edition copy of d. h. lawrence's *women in love*

**Gabrielle Beezer: What's in your flower box?**

The flower boxes directly in front of The Green Chile are planted and maintained by town personnel, and they plant the favored regulars: petunias, geraniums and then mums in the fall.

At home, though, I have six large raised beds that Dennis built for me a few years ago. This year, every square inch of soil is used for bell pepper and chile pepper plants. I took what Charlotte Ross taught me about her heirloom tomatoes and applied it to peppers and haven't looked back since.

Peppers are definitely the single most important ingredient in my cooking at The Green Chile, so variety and freshness are both critical. Unfortunately, it's impossible to find peppers this far north that are fresh or unusual varieties unless, of course, you grow your own.

I purchase all my plants from Cross Country Nurseries in Rosemont, New Jersey—they offer at least four hundred varieties and probably many more than that. And when I need technical information, I turn to the Chile Pepper Institute out of New Mexico State University's College of Agriculture—a great resource.

So at home, I have three beds dedicated to various bell peppers. Beginning green and maturing to red are the California Wonder, Big Bertha, Bell Boy, and Fat 'N Sassy. For yellow bells, I plant Golden Calwonder, Sunbright and Early Sunsation, and for orange, definitely Ariane and Oriole.

Then, there's the world of chile peppers, which can be overwhelming. The confusion may come from a misperception that heat is the only important factor in classifying chile peppers, when in fact there are two ways of classifying the peppers: by shape and by heat. Within one shape, or pod type, you can find a full range of heat, which is generally measured on the Scoville scale.

On the sweet to milder scale, which is usually below 1,000 Scoville units, I have Peperoncini, Corno di Toro, Ancho San Luis (a delicious Poblano), Aji Rojo and Ortega. And then, stepping it up a notch to a medium heat of 1,000 to 8,000, I plant Ancho 211, Big Jim (a wonderful Anaheim), Jalapa Jalapeño and Cherry Bombs, which are great fun in cooking. For hot chile peppers, I grow Serrano, which is one of my favorites, and Cayenne Super. The only two very hot peppers I grow are the Habanero and a Thai Hot; I have to wear gloves to handle either of them.

**Mark Walker: What's in your "favorite places" file on your computer?**

www.amazon.com—for just about anything
www.wikipedia.org—for an explanation I can understand
www.howstuffworks.com—I go there every day
www.bing.com—can do just about anything but sing
www.stilltasty.com—can I eat that nine-day-old pizza?
www.instructables.com—one of my favorites
www.weather.com—rain or shine?
www.webmd.com—when it hurts
www.2020wines.com—would you like Merlot or Pomerol?

www.nytimes.com—to be reminded that Lumby is not the capital of the world

www.boingboing.net—quirky treasures

www.twitter.com—to tweet

www.gocomics.com—just for the yuks of it

www.mapquest.com—to appease Pam, since I never need directions

maps.google.com—there we are!

www.pogo.com—games for when I'm bored

www.etsy.com—for my one of a kind

www.nih.gov—do I have the swine flu?

www.wikihow.com—when I can't find what I'm looking for on howstuffworks.com

www.treehugger.com—to live greener

www.tripadvisor.com—this or that hotel?

www.moneycentral.com—MSN's financial center

www.nature.com—for the curious mind

www.cnn.com—it's all news

www.espn.com—it's a guy thing

www.kayak.com—find me the best deal

www.give.org—so we know how best to give to others

www.firstgov.gov—my government connection

www.hubblesite.org—is anyone out there?

www.loc.gov—library of congress when I have tons of time

news.bbc.co.uk—anything happening internationally

www.lumbybooks.com—enjoyment

www.download.com—freeware and software downloads

www.worldtravelguide.net—travel

www.lonelyplanet.com—more travel

www.rottentomatoes.com—how can one hundred movie critics be wrong?

www.fandango.com—movie schedules

www.bartleby.com—great lit

www.anywho.com—phone book

www.slate.com—good magazine to browse
www.yelp.com—is the sushi any good?
www.gardeners.com—gardening supplies
www.mayoclinic.com—for our health
www.gurneys.com—seed and nursery

**Pam Walker: What's in your wine cellar?**

We actually have two wine cellars at Montis Inn: the cellar below the dining room, which holds wines we offer our guests, and a small collection in our private home for our personal use. The types of wine and, as you can imagine, their cost are hugely different in the two cellars!

Our formal cellar is not very experimental since we don't have a lot of space—André has called it painfully conservative, which I suppose it is. It's filled predominantly with red Bordeaux and Burgundy from France. We were fortunate to fill that cellar with cases of very good vintages when the prices were still reasonable.

We have a limited number of Premier Grand Cru Classé including a few extraordinary bottles from 1982. Our Pomerols, which are my favorite, are from Pétrus, Vieux Château Certan and La Conseillante, and from St.-Émilion, we offer Ausone and Figeac. We might still have one or two bottles of Margaux and Lafite—both from the Médoc region—but their prices are astronomical.

Aside from the large chateaux, though, we have tried to concentrate on the petit château appellations that are just outside of Bordeaux; they offer wonderful reds at a more reasonable price. Lalande-de-Pomerol, which is our most popular wine, Côtes de Bourg, Premières Côtes de Blaye, and Côtes de Castillon are all reliable, and for St.-Émilion, we carry wines from Puisseguin-St.-Émilion, Lussac-St.-Émilion, and St.-Georges-St.-Émilion.

Most of our whites are from California. Our Chardonnays are from Grgich Hills, Far Niente, Jarvis and Newton in Napa; and from Chalk Hill and Kunde Reserve in Sonoma. And then, of course, we have a good selection from Simi.

For those who want an Australian wine, we have several outstanding bins from Penfold as well as from Peter Lehmann, who makes one of the finest Shirazes, in my opinion.

In Sauternes, we have both Château d'Yquem and Château Guiraud.

We have wines from one Italian vineyard in both our formal and personal cellars: Banfi. Perhaps we like it so much because we went there on our honeymoon, but they offer a wide spectrum of wines at several price points, and they're always good quality. We have Brunello di Montalcino, Summus and Excelsus for our guests, and then Mark and I have Centine as an everyday red.

Just recently, we stumbled upon a wine made from the Tempranillo grape in Spain. It was fantastic so we tried several other Tempranillos—all excellent and affordable! We now think it's one of the very best wines for the money right now. We buy young—2004 and 2005—cases of whatever Tempranillo or blend we can find. Venta la Ossa is a perfect example—it complements just about anything I make for dinner and is ideal for most recipes that call for a well-bodied red.

**Chuck Bryson: What's in your potting shed?**

Too many things! By the end of the season, I can barely find what I need, everything is in such disarray. So I used this question as an opportunity to take inventory, throw out what I didn't need and organize what I wanted to keep. Here goes:

Two pairs of Wellington boots, better known as Wellies—one pair with holes that I wear in dry weather and the other waterproof.

An L.L. Bean hammock that I forgot to put up in the spring.

Two pairs of Felco Secateur hand pruners although I only need one because they last for hundreds of years; it's a flawless product from a great company that believes in customer service.

Hanging from the walls, a dozen different birdhouses that will be sanded and repainted for next spring.

A screen (in need of repair) for the shed's window.

A knee-high terra-cotta pot that holds a ridiculous number of hats and deerskin gloves, both lined and unlined.

A colorful stack of Tubtrugs ranging in size from small to extra-large from Kinsman Company. These two-handled, multisized rubber baskets are indispensible.

One heated birdbath and at least a dozen feeders from Duncraft that I will use come fall and winter.

On the lower shelf, various bags of organic Espoma fertilizer and potting soil.

An eight-cubic-foot Jeep Wheelbarrow that's also indispensible.

A stack of old *Hobby Farm* magazines that I enjoy reading when I take a break from weeding.

A bale of hay that I bought several years ago.

A Green Steel yard cart with sides, which is perfect for hauling trees out to the orchard.

Hoses and more hoses hanging from the ceiling.

A Stihl chainsaw, Stihl weedwacker and Stihl bush hogger—all purchased during the Stihl sale at Sam's Feed Store.

And, of course, a full collection of gardening tools.

A ten-foot Werner ladder, because you always need a ladder.

More wooden stakes, balls of twine and bungee cords than I will ever know what to do with.

A double-wheel log cart that I use just about every day come cold weather.

A foldable director's chair for when I read *Hobby Farm*.

A small statue of St. Francis of Assisi with a broken arm that I keep intending to mend.

**André Levesque: What's in your kitchen?**

This is a fairly common question asked of any professional chef just because we have more opportunities to try different products. My choices, and what I use at Montis Inn, are as follows:

| | |
|---|---|
| Stainless Steel Cookware: | All-Clad (hands down for all skillets, sauté pans, saucepans, sauciers and roasting pans) |
| Roasting Rack: | All-Clad |
| Food Processor: | Cuisinart |
| Hand Blender: | KitchenAid |
| Mixer: | KitchenAid |
| Bakeware: | Pyrex |
| Dutch Oven: | La Cocotte (any size) |
| Cast-Iron Skillet: | Lodge (any size) |
| Nonstick Sauce Pan: | Calphalon |
| Cooking Sheet: | All-Clad |
| Gratin Dishes: | Emile Henry |
| Measuring Cups: | Pyrex and Cuisipro |
| Stainless Steel Measuring Cups: | All-Clad |
| Measuring Spoons: | Cuisipro |
| Chef's Knife: | Wüsthof Grand Prix |
| Bread Knife: | Wüsthof |
| Slicing Knife: | Wüsthof |
| Grill Top Cookware: | Williams-Sonoma Mesh Grill-Top Fry Pan |
| Cake Pan: | Calphalon Commercial Nonstick |
| Oven Mitt: | KatchAll Kool-Tek |
| Rolling Pin: | Fante's (tapered or handled, depending upon the need) |
| Pizza Cutter: | Oxo |
| Cooking Tongs: | Oxo |
| Salad Spinner: | Oxo |
| Food Scale: | Oxo |
| Mandoline: | de Buyer Professionnelle (not for the casual user) |
| Wok: | All-Clad |

And what we have as staples:

| | |
|---|---|
| Butters: | Land O'Lakes (salted and unsalted) |
| Cooking Olive Oil: | Colavita |
| Salad Olive Oil: | Banfi |
| Balsamic Vinegar: | Williams-Sonoma Olivier 25-Year Barrel-Aged |
| Chocolate for Baking: | Ghirardelli (either bittersweet or semisweet) |
| Cocoa Powder: | Hershey's European Style |

**Jimmy D: What is in your mailbox?**

I just opened a letter from Ellen Campbell. Let me read it to you:

Hi, everyone,

Not enough time to write to each of you, so I'm sending this in care of Jimmy, hoping he will pass on my message. I look at the calendar and see it's been almost a year since I left Lumby—how time flies! I miss all of you so very much, but my life is too full for any sadness!

My long-awaited vacation in Greece was everything I had dreamed of and more. Although I had planned to visit for only a month before moving to Colorado to be with my children, who now have children of their own, a serendipitous encounter with a man in a καφενείο (can you believe I'm actually learning Greek at my age?) changed everything. Stavros Papandreau—yes, the very same name as the olive oil you can buy at Dickenson's—literally swept me off my feet . . . but that's a long story. He owns the largest olive orchard on the Peloponnese, the enormous peninsula south of the mainland, and has four generations of his family working with him! So my own children in Colorado will have to wait a bit longer for me to join them. I'm having too much fun with Stavros, who seems to be a Greek version of my dearest friend, Chuck Bryson!

I've received all of your letters, and I'm so glad to hear that Tom Candor has more than filled my shoes as your veterinarian. Lumby is, indeed, a very special place. All of you are in my thoughts and prayers every day.

Love, Ellen

And here we have a stack of letters thanking us for hosting the county fair, and there's only one letter of complaint—from a Rocky Mount resident who was locked in Porta Potty No. 4 for thirty-five minutes. You know, those things happen; one minute you're forty feet off the ground in a Ferris wheel enjoying the sights of Mill Valley, and the next, you're looking at the bottomless pit in an outhouse.

**Brooke Turner: What's in your refrigerator?**

Other than several bags of "extinct" berries from the sisters' vineyard, which Joshua has been storing for the last week, the refrigerator drawers are filled with cheese! We're having a wine-and-cheese party tomorrow night, so we've bought samples of every imaginable American and French cheese we could find.

The whole cheese experience has actually been pretty interesting. I didn't know, for example, that France has ninety-six "departments" and twenty-two "regions" that administer cheese—I thought the cows and goats pretty much controlled that, but I was quickly corrected by the owner of Provence Gourmet in Wheatley.

Here is my French cheese assortment so far:

Bresse Bleu from Rhône-Alpes—a soft cheese with small patches of bleu

Bleu Du Quercy from Midi-Pyrénées—a mild, firmer bleu

Emmental Grand Cru from Bourgogne—a smooth and sweet cheese made using raw milk

Coulommiers from Île-de-France—a thick brie

Chevrotin des Aravis from Rhône-Alpes—a semisoft goat cheese

Explorateur from Île-de-France—a triple-crème soft pâté

And my American cheeses include:

Gold from the Grafton Village Cheese Company—a 30- to 36-month aged cheddar

- Soft Tilsit from Sonheim Fine Cheeses—an assertive, robust tilsit
- Sheep's Milk Cheese from Vermont Shepherd Cheese—outstanding in every way
- Fanny Mason Farmstead Baby Swiss from Boggy Meadow Farm—splendid
- Farmhouse Cheddar from Shelburne Farms—one of our personal favorites
- Traditional Jack from Sonoma Jack—perfectly tangy since the 1930s
- Chevre Spread from Haystack Mountain—goat cheese spread at its finest
- Humboldt Fog from Cypress Grove Chèvre—Joshua's favorite, bar none
- Farmstead Cheese from Wölffer—bought directly from their winery

We can't wait to try them all!

# From Montis Inn

## Cedar Grove Crab Cups

This recipe was brought to Montis Inn by André, who developed it while he was the chef at Cedar Grove Inn in Wheatley. A delicious finger food that's quick and easy to prepare.

- ¼ cup canola oil
- 1 package of wonton wrappers (24 wontons)
- 1 8-ounce package of cream cheese, softened
- 1 12-ounce can crabmeat
- 3 tablespoons minced green onions
- 1 tablespoon lemon juice
- 1 tablespoon Worcestershire sauce
- ¼ teaspoon dry mustard
- 1 dash garlic powder

Preheat oven to 350°F. Using a pastry brush or paper towel, lightly coat with canola oil the bottom and sides of each cup in a 24-cup minimuffin tray. Brush wonton wrappers with oil and press them into muffin cups, allowing sides to spill over—use one wrapper per cup. Bake for 8 minutes or until cups are very lightly browned.

---

In a large bowl, combine remaining ingredients until well mixed. Place one generous tablespoon of crab mixture into each wrapper. Return to oven and bake an additional 6 minutes or until filling is hot and the edges of the wrappers are a deep golden brown. Serve warm. Makes 24 appetizer-sized servings.

# *From The Green Chile*

## Queso Fundido Dip

Made from the fresh chile peppers that Gabrielle grows in her raised beds, this dip is standard fare at her popular Mexican eatery. Remember that when using chile peppers in any recipe, you're advised to wear plastic gloves so that no oils will come in contact with your skin or eyes.

| | |
|---|---|
| 6 Poblano peppers | ⅔ cup chopped onion |
| 2 large red or yellow sweet peppers | 1 teaspoon ground cumin |
| 6 cups shredded Monterey Jack cheese | 1½ cups half-and-half |
| 4 tablespoons all-purpose flour | Blue tortilla chips |
| 3 tablespoon butter | |

Preheat oven to 425°F. Cover a baking sheet with aluminum foil. Clean peppers and remove the stems. Quarter each pepper, removing the seeds and membranes. Place quartered peppers, skin side up, on the baking sheet. Bake 25–30 minutes or until skins are dark and blistered. Wrap peppers in foil from the baking sheet and allow them to sit for 15 minutes. Open foil pouch and use a paring knife to remove skins from peppers. Discard skins. Finely chop peppers and set aside.

---

In a large bowl, mix cheese and flour, and set aside.

In a medium saucepan, melt butter, add onions and cumin, and cook for 2 minutes over medium heat. Slowly stir in half-and-half. Gradually add cheese mixture in small amounts, stirring constantly until cheese has melted. Reduce heat. More cream may be added to thin the dip, if desired. Stir in roasted peppers. Serve warm with chips. Makes about 6 cups.

# *From Montis Inn*

## Prosciutto-Wrapped Asparagus with Garlic Mayonnaise

Elegantly simple, this classic combination is served at the finest restaurants in New York and is a perfect hors d'oeuvre to complement any wine-and-cheese party.

| | |
|---|---|
| 1½ cups mayonnaise | 24 asparagus spears, rinsed and trimmed to 6-inch lengths |
| 2 crushed garlic cloves | 12 wafer-thin slices of prosciutto |
| 2 tablespoons minced fresh parsley | ⅛ cup olive oil |

Preheat oven to 375°F. In a medium bowl, combine mayonnaise, garlic and parsley. Cover and refrigerate to chill.

If you prefer easy cleanup, line a baking sheet with aluminum foil. Wrap each length of asparagus with half a piece of prosciutto. Arrange wrapped asparagus on the baking sheet and drizzle with olive oil. Roast for 5–7 minutes, depending on the thickness of the asparagus. Do not overcook—the asparagus should be slightly crisp to the bite.

Transfer hot asparagus to plate and serve with garlic mayonnaise as a dipping sauce. Makes 24 spears.

## *From The Green Chile*

# Artichoke and Peperoncini Dip

For this favorite appetizer, Gabrielle again turns to the peppers she grows in her garden. Although one can substitute two jarred peperoncinis if fresh ones are not available, the taste is slightly compromised.

| | |
|---|---|
| 4 9-ounce packages of frozen artichoke hearts | 1 teaspoon extra virgin olive oil |
| 2 cups shredded Parmigiano-Reggiano cheese | 5 medium cloves garlic, crushed |
| 1½ cups mayonnaise | 1 teaspoon cumin |
| 1 large red sweet pepper (such as a Marconi), seeded and finely chopped | Salt and ground black pepper |
| 1 medium fresh peperoncini pepper, seeded and very finely chopped | Pita bread cut into small triangles |

Preheat oven to 400°F. Cook artichoke hearts following the package directions. Drain and coarsely chop. In a large bowl, combine artichokes, cheese, mayonnaise, sweet pepper, peperoncini pepper, olive oil, garlic and cumin. Add salt and pepper to taste. Transfer mixture into a 2-quart baking dish. Bake 30 minutes or until mixture is bubbling and golden brown on top. Serve with pita bread. Makes 6 generous cups.

## *From The Green Chile*

### Charielle's Bean Dip

This was the very first collaborative recipe that Charlotte Ross and Gabrielle developed shortly before The Green Chile opened its doors. Since then, this smooth, sultry bean mix has been a menu favorite. Gabrielle serves it with either grilled pita bread or tortilla chips.

- 3 fresh mild green chile peppers
- ¼ cup olive oil
- 3 garlic cloves, minced
- 1 large sweet onion, finely chopped
- 1 fresh sweet green chile pepper
- 2 teaspoons chili powder
- 1 14-ounce can light-colored kidney beans
- 1 14-ounce can dark-colored kidney beans
- 1½ cups grated cheddar cheese
- 2 tablespoons sour cream
- Grilled pita triangles or blue tortilla chips

Wash, pat dry and quarter the mild green chile peppers. Remove and discard the seeds and membrane; then finely chop. Set aside.

In a medium-sized sauté pan, heat the olive oil and then add the garlic, onion, sweet green chile pepper and chili powder. Cook over low heat for 8 minutes, stirring regularly until onions are about to turn brown. Reduce heat.

---

Drain the light-colored kidney beans, saving the juice. Drain the dark-colored kidney beans, saving the juice. In a food processor, puree all of the light kidney beans and half of the dark kidney beans. Add puree to the mixture in the sauté pan. Add juice from both cans of beans to the sauté pan. Stir thoroughly and cook 5 minutes over low heat. Slowly add grated cheddar cheese, allowing cheese to melt as you go. After cheese has melted, gently fold in remaining whole dark kidney beans. Transfer to a serving bowl and add two tablespoons of sour cream on top. Surround bowl with either grilled pita triangles or blue tortilla chips.

# *From Montis Inn*

## Baby Yukons with Blue Cheese

This is another simple but delectable recipe that André brought to Montis Inn. Preparation takes no more than a few minutes, which is very much appreciated when you're asked to make a second and third batch!

| | |
|---|---|
| 24 baby Yukon potatoes, washed and dried | 1 cup sour cream |
| ¼ cup olive oil | ½ cup crumbled blue cheese |
| Salt | 3 tablespoons fresh chives, minced |

Preheat oven to 350°F. In a large bowl, toss potatoes in olive oil and sprinkle with salt. Spread the potatoes on a baking sheet. It may be lined with foil for easy cleanup, if you prefer. Bake for 45 minutes or until potatoes are tender.

In a small bowl, combine sour cream and blue cheese.

Cut an *X* through the top of each potato. Gently squeeze the potato in the middle, allowing the top *X* to pop open. Into the opening, spoon a generous dollop of the cheese mixture. Garnish with chives and serve warm. Any additional cheese mixture may be placed in a small bowl so guests can help themselves. Makes 24 individual, bite-sized potatoes.

## Questions for Discussion

1. Family reunions are often an interesting blend of joy and stress, especially around the holidays. Do you have any secrets for having a successful family gathering? What have been your experiences?

2. One theme that runs through the book is that what we fear will happen is frequently much worse than what eventually *does* happen—we see this with Lynn as she enters into a new relationship and with Elaine as she struggles to discipline Jessica. Could fearing the worst be a self-fulfilling prophecy, or is it merely human nature to put up defenses when we are faced with uncertainty?

3. Pam voices her disapproval of Kay's activities out of fear of losing her mother. How can we, as Kay advises, simply "let go" of something that's very important to us? Does Pam ever do that successfully?

4. Raising a teenager in these times is tremendously challenging given the technology to which they have access. Discuss some of those challenges and how parents can use the technology to help a teenager grow into a responsible adult.

5. Elaine Walker appears to be trapped: she is too panicked to move forward because of what happened in the past. Have you

ever felt unable to do what you knew you needed to do? How did you eventually overcome your resistance or the barrier that was in your way?

6. What are some ways one might handle an abrasive, overly competitive personality like Carter Reed? Could Mark have done anything different to soften Carter's impact on the reunion?

7. When Pam and Lynn walk down to the barn together, Pam unexpectedly blurts out exactly what she thinks of her sister-in-law. Does she do the right thing in being so honest with Lynn, or should she keep her feelings to herself? How do you know when it's right to openly speak your mind about your feelings toward another person?

8. Lynn's cat Coco plays an important role in her life by offering her hope and companionship. Chuck suggests that sometimes an animal can provide more comfort than another human. Do you feel that's true? Discuss the relationships you've had with your pets.

9. Both Lynn and Chuck are aware that their relationship is going to be short-lived, but they are able to embrace the moment and simply appreciate each other's company for the time they have together. Do you have any fond memories of a brief encounter that helped you along in life?

10. The county fair is a community event that the residents of Lumby enthusiastically embrace. When was the last time you attended a fair? Are there other public events that bring your community together?

11. Hank may be the only one who is less than thrilled about the fair, but he puts aside his own feelings and becomes an ambassador for Lumby, greeting all those who enter the fairgrounds. What can we learn from his behavior?

12. Kay Eastman and Robert Day are healthy, vibrant senior citizens who make the most of each day. They also both feel tremendously blessed to have found love a second time. Have you ever found your soul mate? How many times have you found love?

LUMBY LUMBER
FIREWOOD
WOODSMITHE
COUNTRY FURNITURE
To THE BARNS
Lumby Lumber
WOODSMITHE

If you missed the previous book in the Lumby series,
you might want to take a peek at

*THE PROMISE OF LUMBY*

which starts with a flip of the page. . . .

## Fifteen Years Earlier

Dr. Jeffrey Thomas Candor's life was abruptly redirected the afternoon of February 3 by a series of related tragedies that would have exploded through the national press had the storm of the century, which crippled the East Coast under as much as four feet of snow, not stolen the headlines. Afterward, events of the day were successfully buried for nearly twenty years until the residents of a small town unearthed the veterinarian's dark secret. But on that winter morning, the possibilities of the accidents as well as the distant town of Lumby were the farthest thoughts from Jeffrey's focused concentration.

Standing at the kitchen sink of his Redding, California, town house, Jeffrey looked out at the frozen yard. The boughs of the pine trees bent unnaturally, weighed down by needles encased in heavy ice. Frost glistened in the rising sun.

"The roads will be bad in the mountains. You should postpone your trip," he advised his wife.

Laura sat at the dining room table, staring into her coffee mug. "My parents are expecting us," she repeated without looking up.

"I told you, I'm sorry but I have no choice. The surgery is scheduled for this morning. You'll just have to go alone."

"So you've said," she replied indifferently.

Jeffrey studied his wife for a long moment and wondered if there was one irreversible moment that had broken their marriage. He thought back on the eight years of their relationship, as he had been doing with increasing frequency during the past few months. Where in the path of their togetherness had their roads separated? He was growing weary of trying to diagnose their discord, of trying to cure them as he would a critically ill patient.

Sensing she was being stared at, Laura glanced up. "What is it?"

Jeffrey sighed. "Absolutely nothing," he said sadly and then looked at his watch. "I need to get going. You'll be home by dinner?"

Laura glanced out the window. "I may spend the night there," she replied.

He was no longer surprised by such a vague response and had long since stopped questioning Laura about her unplanned absences. "Whatever you want," he said as he pulled on his trench coat. "Just let me know when you're on the road."

She nodded, still looking away from him.

~

As Jeffrey expected, the roads were slippery, doubling his commute time. Thirty minutes later, he waved to the guard as he drove past the gate of the staff entrance to the American Zoological Park. The veterinary clinic was located on the north side of the complex, so Jeffrey followed the park's perimeter road as he had most every day since joining "The Park" seven years ago.

Although in acreage The Park was only the sixth-largest zoo in the country, for nearly eight decades, it had enjoyed a renowned reputation for its captive-breeding program for endangered species. By adding Dr. Candor, the nation's preeminent Ursidae or bear veterinarian, to its staff The Park had become a prime destination for endangered animals from around the world that would have otherwise been sent to large zoos.

Jeffrey lowered the window a few inches and inhaled crisp air heavy with the scents of pine and fresh straw, of which he would never tire. The feral sounds of the enclosed animals were usually also good for his soul, but on that cold and somber morning most of the animals were still inside, so an unusual quiet hung over the exhibitions.

Walking into the small clinic, Jeffrey went directly to his office and immediately read through a long fax written in broken English that had arrived from China a few hours earlier. He withdrew a medical textbook from his briefcase and opened it to the same page he had studied the night before, once again scrutinizing the illustrations.

Jeffrey scanned the bookshelf for yet another reference that might be of help, but couldn't find what he was looking for. Crammed between and in front of the books were stacks of research papers and back issues of veterinary journals. Tucked in the corner of the top shelf was his University of California Berkeley undergraduate diploma, covered with dust.

A young man, one of Jeffrey's two vet technicians, knocked gently on his open door. "Jan and I are ready for you," he said. "I'm about to scrub and our girl is on the table, drowsy and ready for you to prep her."

"Good. I'll be right there," Jeffrey said, and quickly reread the fax one final time before going down the hall.

In the pre-op room, Jeffrey pulled a pair of blue scrubs from a box marked "Candor" stored above his locker. It was generally assumed that Jeffrey was issued his own scrubs because he was the medical director of The Park, but the more accurate reason was that at six feet five inches tall, he didn't fit into standard-sized garb. On the one occasion he had had to resort to using staff-issued pants, the bottoms came halfway to his knees.

After snapping on his gloves and pulling up his surgical mask, Jeffrey walked through the swinging doors. The compact operating room was flooded with fluorescent light. On the closest wall, four X-rays hung on a view box for Jeffrey to reference during the resection.

He glanced over at the narrow observation window and saw three men and a woman behind the thick plate glass. Jeffrey nodded to the executive director of The Park. Standing to the director's left was the chairman of the board, whom Jeffrey distrusted, and to the chairman's right the senior curator. With them was a small Asian man, who appeared to be taking notes.

"All okay, Doc," the second tech said, carefully watching the animal.

Jeffrey looked at the X-ray viewer and then down at the patient. A beautiful two-hundred-fifty-pound giant panda that had been loaned to the zoo five years earlier lay motionless on the metal table with two sheets covering her body. Through a collaborative effort between the U.S. and Japanese governments, Ming had been successfully bred by artificial insemination in 1987. That year, she and her baby were more famous than many Hollywood movie stars.

The bold black-and-white markings on Ming's face made Jeffrey smile. She had always been a gentle animal, far more trusting of humans than was natural for her breed. During her stay at The Park, she had remained in good health—until recently, when she had suffered an alarming loss of weight. After monitoring her for several days, Jeffrey had run a battery of tests. An ultrasound had revealed a large mass in her upper intestine. In Jeffrey's opinion, all noninvasive efforts to correct the problem would be futile. He was about to perform the operation necessary to save her life.

Jeffrey glanced at the observation window and then at his staff, all of whom were wearing surgical masks. Tension gripped the operating room. "This is a simple operation, folks," he said. "Everyone take a deep breath and relax." He followed his own advice as he put the anesthesia mask over the panda's face. Only when he was sure that she was fully under did he pick up a scalpel.

During his career, Jeffrey had operated on most species of bears. In fact, the prior fall he had traveled to Washington, D.C., at the request of the National Zoo, to lead one of their more complicated surgeries on a pregnant polar bear. But he had never operated on a great panda or on an animal that was as critically endangered as this one. With only sixteen hundred pandas in the wild, and another one hundred eighty in captivity, the value of each fertile female was incalculable.

Jeffrey's hand was steady as he made a fourteen-inch incision in the animal's abdomen, cutting easily through the thick layer of fat. Once the blood was suctioned and the epidermal layer pulled back, Jeffrey changed scalpels and continued through the layers of dense muscle to reach the intestines. He glanced up at one of the techs, who, after studying the panda's vitals, nodded back.

Forty-five minutes later, the tumor was successfully removed and Jeffrey began cauterizing the numerous arteries and veins that had been severed. The surgery was going better than expected. Just as he picked up a suture needle to close the stomach wall, a woman rushed into the operating room. Not wearing any scrubs, she stayed near the door.

"Jeffrey, there's an emergency call for you," she said.

He looked up only for a second. "It can't wait?"

"He said no."

Jeffrey assumed it was the call he had put through to China about Ming's operation. "Put it on the speaker, please."

Suddenly, the quiet of the operating room was broken by a voice booming out of the speakers. "Dr. Candor?"

Jeffrey continued suturing. "Yes, this is Jeffrey Candor."

"This is Dr. Wilson at United Hospital. Your wife has been in a car accident and is in critical condition. She's on life support. It would be best if you could come immediately."

Jeffrey's heart began to race and nausea came over him. He shook his head to clear his thoughts and glanced up at the clock, trying to calculate the minutes. "I'll be there in less than an hour."

Jeffrey knew better than to look at his two technicians, to see the alarm in their eyes, or worse, to allow them to see the alarm in his. Then everything began to move in slow motion; each suture seemed to take an eternity to knot. Jeffrey's eyes blurred and he felt sweat beading on his forehead. He couldn't help but look at the clock again.

Thirty agonizing minutes later, the final suture was tied and sterile bandages were taped over the incision. Jeffrey quickly removed his mask.

"We need to give her some antibiotics, but you can start waking her up," Jeffrey said as he crossed the room and reached into the drug cabinet. He grabbed a vial of clear liquid from the shelf and a syringe from the drawer. The simple act of loading a syringe, something he had done thousands of times before, served to calm his shaken nerves. Returning to the operating table, he quickly injected Ming and, without thinking, put the empty vial into his scrub pants pocket.

Jeffrey headed for the door. "You can reach me on my cell phone," he said.

"Let us know how Laura is," his vet tech said.

Jeffrey didn't take the time to change out of his bloodied operating garb. Storming through his office, he grabbed only his car keys, forgetting both his wallet and cell phone. Once outside, he immediately noticed that much of the ice had melted, and within minutes he was traveling eighty miles an hour down the freeway. An overpowering blend of fear and regret washed over him as his thoughts darted from one memory to the next. He and Laura had been so distant during the last six months, but he still loved her. Perhaps there was a chance for them . . . if she survived.

~

Arriving at the emergency room forty minutes later, he looked frantically for help, for someone who could tell him where his wife was.

"Dr. Candor?" asked a nurse in a white lab coat.

"Yes. How is my wife?"

"We have her stabilized," the nurse explained. "Her hip is fractured in multiple places. The surgeon requested an MRI after seeing the X-rays."

"When will they operate?"

"She'll be taken into the OR directly from imaging. But I need to tell you . . ." The nurse paused. "I'm sorry. She lost the child."

Jeffrey's eyes blurred. "What child?"

"Your wife was about ten weeks pregnant."

Jeffrey hunched over, as if someone had struck him in the stomach. "I didn't know."

"There's a doctor's conference room at the end of the hall. Why don't you wait there? The surgeon will be down as soon as possible."

"Thank you," Jeffrey said, nodding weakly.

In the empty lounge he sank into a chair and rubbed his eyes. It's true that time passes at different speeds, Jeffrey thought. It slows down so we can remember each excruciating detail of horrendous events in our lives: the color of the walls, the coffee stain in the carpet, the noise of the water fountain, the betrayal of a wife.

Jeffrey wondered who Laura had turned to for the intimacy that had been missing from their relationship for quite some time. Who had made love to her and how would Laura look into that man's eyes and tell him that she had lost their child, a child conceived in an illicit affair?

Oddly, among all of the emotions that surged through Jeffrey, jealousy was not one of them. Nor was anger. What he felt was far worse: a dispassionate resignation, and chilled indifference that his marriage was over. At that moment, with this knowledge of his wife's unfaithfulness, all feelings he had for her were abruptly and permanently deadened.

He dug his left hand deep into his pocket and began playing absently with the small glass vial that had contained the antibiotics for the panda. Realizing what was in his hand, Jeffrey walked over to the trash can marked "Medical and Hazardous Waste." Just as he was about to throw the vial away, something on the label caught his eye: a small red line across the top of the text. He was confused; the label on the antibiotics vial had a green background, but this one was bright red—the color of warning. He read the label carefully: “Potassium Chloride.” And then he realized that he had done something that every veterinarian has done at least once: he had grabbed the wrong vial. The tragedy was that this one time, with that extraordinary panda, he hadn’t caught his error before injecting the drug into the animal.

In that instant, he knew Ming was dead. “Oh, God,” he moaned, “what have I done?”

**Present Day**

Just south of the small town of Lumby, in the richly scented kitchen of Montis Inn, Pam Walker wiped her forehead and retied her apron strings, then tucked the end of a kitchen towel at her right hip. Mark, her husband, was bent over the larger of two stainless-steel farm sinks with one of his arms elbow-deep in water. For most of the evening, he had been trying unsuccessfully to repair the garbage disposal.

“What in the world did you put down this thing?” Mark asked, feeling blindly around the disposal blades.

“Nothing. Just scraps from lunch,” Pam said.

With one arm still in the sink, Mark tried to reach for a screwdriver on the counter. The stronger he pulled away from the drain, the tighter the pressure seemed to increase around his wet wrist. “Honey, I think my hand is stuck.”

Expecting another of her husband’s ill-timed jokes, Pam didn’t even look up from the stove, where she was busy cooking. “Stop horsing around, Mark. The dining room is still half full of hungry guests.”

“No, seriously,” he said, with enough panic in his voice to catch his wife’s attention.

Pam looked at Mark trying to free himself from the sink and started to laugh. "You're kidding."

"Don't turn on the disposal!" he implored.

Pam walked over to their commercial refrigerator and searched for the lard.

"Here," she said, opening the small plastic bucket and scooping a cupful of grease into his palm. "Rub it on your other hand."

Mark did as instructed, and seconds later, his hand popped free, splashing water across the floor. He noticed Pam's reaction, and thought it best to head right for the mop closet.

"Don't worry," he said. "I'll wipe it up. It could have been worse—I could have lost an arm in there."

"Since you didn't, why don't you wash up and bring the desserts to table four? I still have one more entrée to go."

It was a night like most others at Montis Inn: controlled chaos among the understaffed and overextended.

Pam was so occupied with preparing the last dinner plate that she didn't notice Mark's return. He went over to the linen closet, which also served as the "wine cellar" for their small collection of grand cru wines, and pulled a bottle from the bottom row.

Returning to the kitchen door, Mark nudged it open with his toe while he uncorked the bottle, and peered out at the gentleman who was seated by himself at the table closest to the fireplace.

First and foremost, the man was distinguished-looking. Although small in stature and quite lean, he had a relaxed confidence about him. Most people who dined alone either kept their eyes glued to their plates or looked nervously around the room. In comparison, this man smiled after completing his appetizer of parsleyed escargot in simmered brandy. "Delicious," he said aloud, and then leaned back, crossing his legs and opening the newspaper.

His short gray hair and closely trimmed beard framed the intense blue eyes that Mark had first noticed when greeting him that evening. Before beginning to read, the man pulled a pair of silver-and-tortoiseshell glasses from the breast pocket of his crisply pressed striped shirt.

"You don't know who he is?" Mark asked Pam.

She wiped her hands on the kitchen towel. "Who?"

"The guest eating alone," Mark said. "He asked for a bottle of nineteen eighty-two Lafite."

Pam looked up in surprise. "Well, he certainly knows his wines—there's not much better than that," she said, beginning to stir the raspberry sauce that would be drizzled over the seared duck–and-vegetable confit. "Did you tell him we don't have that vintage?"

Mark let the door swing closed and walked over to the island. Carefully he popped the cork. "Indirectly. I suggested the nineteen eighty-two Château Palmer would better complement his dinner. That's the best bottle we have."

Pam felt a tinge of regret. "I thought we were saving that for our anniversary."

"Honey, it was on the wine list," he explained. "Sorry."

Pam pulled a hot serving platter from the range. "Do you really think it will go well with the duck?"

Mark shrugged as he removed a decanter from the shelf. "I have no idea. I've never tasted anything that cost this much." After pouring the wine into the crystal carafe, he sneaked another look into the dining room. "He looks familiar. Are you sure you don't remember his name?"

"I think his first name is Christian, but I'm not sure," she said as she began preparing the plate. "Two parties checked in at the same time, so I didn't have an opportunity to speak with him."

Across the dining room, a couple folded their napkins and pushed their chairs away from the table. "The Reynoldses are leaving," Mark reported.

"Would you clear their table after you serve the wine, please?"

Mark smelled the decanter. "I hope it's not bad."

"The meal or the wine?" Pam asked glibly.

"Your cooking is always outstanding. I've never seen anyone put more time and effort into a menu."

"My problem exactly," she said under her breath.

But Mark was already out the door. "Remember the bread!" she called out as loud as she dared, but he didn't hear.

Pam took a deep breath and rubbed her neck, rolling her head from side to side as she exhaled. For three years she had been cooking breakfasts and dinners for the inn's guests, and trying to keep up with her growing restaurant clientele, but each meal seemed progressively harder to put together.

"We need a change," she said aloud, although no one was there to agree.